THE
HOME FRONT

A NOVEL

ALAN J SUMMERS

Ordering Information:

Prime Seven Media
518 Landmann St.
Tomah City, WI 54660

Printed in the United States of America

Apart from the historical figures who feature,
hopefully in character, all the personnel in this story
are fictitious and any resemblance to real persons,
living or dead, is either coincidental or homage.

PROLOGUE

Britain declared war on Germany on the 3rd September 1939 in reaction to a treaty obligation with France, who also declared war as a consequence of Germany's invasion of Poland two days earlier. The year before, Prime Minister Neville Chamberlain had visited Chancellor Adolf Hitler and signed what he told the press on his return was 'peace in our time'. He did not believe that himself, of course, and Britain spent the next year preparing for the war to come. By mid-1939, Britain had completed the 'chain home' radar station network, issued gas masks and started conscripting young men into the armed forces. Hawker Hurricane and Supermarine Spitfire monoplane fighters had started reaching the squadrons; each aircraft armed with eight machine guns and equal to anything else in the world at the time.

As soon as war was declared, 'Operation Pied Piper' evacuated children from London and other cities to the supposed safety of more rural areas. The Land Army started recruiting women to work on farms, making up for the labour shortage caused by conscription and by the spring of 1940, village life had changed quite a lot. Young men were away in the forces, evacuee children placed great demand on the frail infrastructure of village schools and many jobs in teaching, farm work and forestry, public transport and utility services were being filled by women, who had to learn as they went.

Events moved quite quickly in 1940. The 'phoney war' period – during which the RAF were constantly in action - ended in the spring with the German invasion of Norway, Belgium and France, which pushed the British Expeditionary Force back to Dunkirk from which it was evacuated by an ad hoc assortment of ships, large and small. With the French ports for their submarines and coastal land on which to site airfields, the German assault on Britain began with attacks on shipping in the English Channel. Belatedly, local defence volunteers were recruited and subsequently renamed the Home Guard. Only six weeks passed between the call to arms and the first stand to for an invasion threat, but in that time one and a half million men had volunteered. They mostly had to arm themselves in the early days with rifle club weapons, war souvenirs and sporting guns, as the army had left so much equipment behind in France that some German units used British weapons and ammunition throughout the war.

The invasion never came; the Luftwaffe attacked the radar stations, south-of-England airfields and any RAF machines that scrambled to meet them. The RAF had lost half their fighter pilots in actions prior to the Battle of Britain starting in July, 1940. They found that Hurricanes were slower than the German fighters, so they were used to intercept bomber formations, while the faster Spitfires kept the German fighters busy. The battle raged all summer during the long hours of daylight; on the ground, people did what they could, carrying on as normally as possible, contributing to national security as necessary. The air war became known as the Battle of Britain; the ground became the Home Front, if only to distinguish it from the other fronts that developed.

The air battle ended with October as the days shortened. The Luftwaffe switched to night bombing, attacking London every night for more than two months before widening their attacks to other cities and ports. Nowhere in Britain was beyond the range of German aircraft at the time, so the Home Front was everywhere in the United Kingdom and nowhere was safe. All the stories assembled in this book are fiction, but are based on anecdotes and reminiscences of the people who were there; mostly too young to serve in the armed forces, they did what they could in support of the adult units before they grew up and entered national service during, or just after the war.

I am most grateful to all those who did their best in those dark years and especially to those who shared their experiences with me in the lighter years that followed. In preparing this book I am also grateful to Francis Berry in Glasgow and Peter Brookesmith in Pembrokeshire for reading my manuscript and for their helpful comments. More than eighty years have passed since the events that this book mentions took place and most of the participants are no longer with us, such is the march of time.

AJS
Pembrokeshire, 2022

CHAPTER 1

Neither holiday makers nor day trippers enjoyed the fresh air of the beaches and resorts of sunny southeast England that August; the reason was that in 1940 Britain was at war with Nazi Germany and the sky above southern England was where the Battle of Britain was fought out.

The Luftwaffe had tried to win the sky – attacking British airfields and coastal radar stations, but without the complete success they had hoped for. Most German daylight air raids into the United Kingdom's airspace were intercepted by British fighters. The summer battles wore both sides down, as is evidenced by the horrendous casualties and Britain was hanging on by its collective fingernails when Flight Lieutenant Mark Brabham flew a Spitfire out of Croydon as part of Eleven Group's desperate struggle to stop the Luftwaffe attackers.

Eleven Group put the Hurricane squadrons up to intercept the bombers while the faster Spitfires concentrated on keeping the German fighter escort busy. This technique had started to turn the tide in Britain's favour slowly, however; on the 31st August 1940, Mark had engaged the enemy over the Thames Estuary when something went wrong immediately after he fired a burst at a German fighter. He was comparatively inexperienced; sixty-four hours flying since joining his squadron on the 3rd July, one hundred and thirty two hours since he started keeping his pilot's log; more than many of those he flew with, but less than most of those whom he flew against.

The engine missed a beat, then the cockpit filled with smoke as the controls went soft. In a Spitfire, the pilot is sitting on his parachute, which serves as a cushion and his seat is the fuel tank. The slightest concern about fire thus makes a pilot keen to bail out; anything else and the pilot would more likely try to glide down to safety.

Mark realized that he was on fire so he held the stick over, turning the machine upside down as he slid the canopy back and released his seat harness. He smelled aviation spirit and sensed fire as he fell clear of the machine, which, next time he saw it, was headed downwards to the sea streaming black smoke and red flames. He delayed activating the parachute until he saw the 'plane hit water; then he pulled the ripcord.

The crew of a small fishing boat saw the aircraft crash and they steered for him. He was floating face up, supported by his 'Mae West' inflatable lifejacket. His head and face were badly burned and when they dragged him out of the briny water it was clear that he had also suffered burns elsewhere. Knowing nothing about treating burns, the fishermen did their best by making bandages from his silk parachute and keeping the dressings damp with the cold estuary water.

Mercifully unconscious, Mark felt nothing of the journey back to land. The crew had problems, however, and could not put into their usual birth on the Isle of Sheppey due to enemy air activity. They tried going up the River Medway, but there were German aircraft over Rochester, so they went down the river and landed at Seasalter, in Kent.

There was no hospital or medical service close at hand, so they manhandled the unconscious airman to the district nurse. She had no experience of large surface area burns, so she soaked stuck clothing off him with salty water; then she dressed the deeper wounds with honey and the milder ones with a poultice of lemon juice and vinegar, before telephoning for an ambulance.

The ambulance crew took him to hospital in Canterbury. Doctors there were aghast at the old wives' remedies applied to the young airman, but they were unable to scrape the honey off and replace it with shellac, so they made him comfortable in a sort of hammock that kept his worst injuries from direct contact with the mattress and reviewed his condition every few hours. Mark remained unconscious and oblivious to the efforts of his own body to fight the damage and the treatment, off and on, for weeks.

How to treat large burns was in its infancy in 1940: such injuries usually proving fatal. Medical interest in treatment had been stimulated by the Great War from which it was observed that navy casualties who had been in seawater seemed to heal better than army casualties, who had been in mud.

Mark had subjected himself to a seawater treatment by landing in the estuary and the fishermen had kept him wet with the salt water. The district nurse had used honey. These treatments were not in the first aid manual at the time, but the positive effects were observed.

Neither the fishermen nor the district nurse had been able to pay much attention to Mark's head and face, so it was the injuries to these sensitive areas that the medical profession directed its expertise. Relatives came visiting. Mark vaguely remembered some of them waiting with him in the darkened room. Sometimes he was lucid, at others sleepy or drugged, or just asleep. His body had developed the knack of shutting down functions that were unnecessary to the healing process, so his hair fell out and he was often simply not awake. A specialist burns doctor from Sussex came and looked at him and said he would like to get this flight lieutenant into East Grinstead for repairs if or when he was fit enough to travel.

Two months of slipping in and out of consciousness and being wheeled in and out of the operating theatre passed before the morning Mark awoke in the Royal Victoria Hospital, East Grinstead, knowing that this was the day on which the bandages from his head and face would be removed, giving the air a chance to take over the healing process of his facial injuries. He was mentally prepared for the shock of seeing what was left of his visage, but when he did, it was a shock that he realised he was not prepared for.

"Monster."

It was hard to speak, difficult to form just that one word, never mind a sentence. The doctor chatted on regardless.

"Not at all, you've had the bark knocked off, but that which won't heal of itself can be replaced by grafts. It's not rapid progress, but it is effective."

Mark struggled with the conversation. He had not used his voice much since the crash and now he wanted to it would not come; this being a by-product of the trauma he had been through. He planned what he wanted to say and then blurted it out.

"What will people think? I can't see my family like this."

"Of course you can; your eyes were protected by your goggles."

"Not what I meant." Making the words was getting easier; making sense wasn't.

"I know, but they want to see you. I've met most of them; your Mother, Uncle Tom and Aunt Hetty, Granddad Herbert and his charming wife. They've been giving me a hard time and now they should see what I have managed to achieve so far."

"No face, no hair, can't talk."

"If talking's difficult it's because you're not used to it. You haven't spoken for a while, not much anyway. Think of a beautiful woman walking into the room. She smiles at you and what happens? You can't make the words; you trip over your tongue and make foolish noises. Do you know why that is?"

"No."

"Me neither; but being struck dumb by a beautiful woman is only temporary. I think it's a safety mechanism God equipped them with. Their beauty silences us to give them time to take charge or to get away. It usually works and I think it's a brilliant theory; trouble is, nobody cares what I think on the matter, but your speech, the difficulty of making words, that's temporary too. Don't force yourself to talk if you don't want to, in case it causes a stammer. People who stutter as a side effect of their injuries take longer to get over it."

Mark nodded, so the doctor continued; "You're a hero; they all said so, Herbert in particular. He was keen that I understood just how much it mattered to him that you get well."

"I flew with him when I was small."

"And he flew in the last war. He's a charming man, looking forward to seeing you over Christmas. He talked to everyone in the ward, you know and then he sent in flowers and beer. Your uncle was decorated in the last war so going to his rectory you'll be recuperating in the company of aviation veterans."

Mark had been struggling with a thought, which he now articulated.

"No face. What will girls think?"

"That's not for me to say, Mark, but if I mention that I have more problems with my burn patients getting young ladies pregnant than I have with treating their burns, would you believe me?"

"No."

"Well then, I didn't mention it. Still, you need to get out and recover from your injuries; you need somewhere to stay that's not too inconvenient for visiting here, whilst you need to be with other people – real people - and not on a military base, which is why everyone wants you to go to your Uncle Tom in Lavering."

"I haven't seen him for ages."

"He was here two weeks ago."

"I don't remember."

"It has been difficult for you, sleeping so much, but a visit from the Reverend Tom Brabham is not to be forgotten in a hurry, not by me anyway. How far from civilisation is his parish?"

"East side of Essex."

"I shall speak to the Wing Commander; your car will be ready for you and you must telephone your uncle. I think you can drive short distances, but you must exercise your fingers doing something more than gripping a steering wheel. Remember that you sleep like Rip Van Winkle, so you want to be near to where you can rest. Don't worry about the hair; I can fix you up with a wig and as to speech, you've made giant steps forwards in the last two minutes. Do you have a girlfriend?"

"No."

"You soon will have, I'm sure."

Thus it was that Mark was released for a period of recuperative leave at his uncle's village parish near the Essex coast. An RAF car took him to Croydon, where he received a muted but heartfelt welcome from the few people there who remembered him. His squadron had been redeployed to Debden, although only four of the men now with it had been there when Mark was operational. Of the eighteen pilots in his squadron on the day he was shot down two months earlier, half were missing, or casualties like Mark, while others had been transferred to meet the needs of the depleted service.

Mark went to see the Station Commander, who seemed pleased to see him.

"Doctors think you'll be fit next year, so do take all the time you need to get better. Is there anything I can do to make your leave more comfortable?"

"Sir...if there is anything..."

"Yes, of course, just place a telephone call to me and if it is something that I can sort out, consider it done. I have put you in for the Distinguished Flying Cross; your record and general service practically guarantee it."

The Wing Commander looked at Mark's expression. "Doesn't such a decoration mean anything to you?"

"Didn't do much."

"Yes you did. You destroyed two enemy machines in the action in which you lost your aircraft, which you won't have to pay for, seven other German machines that are lost to them forever and you have the skill and courage to inspire others. You stand head and shoulders above some people who have served here and whilst I would not wish to belittle any of them, you do stand out. Get well soon; this war has years to run and you have a significant role to play in the Royal Air Force as things develop."

"Like last time; the DSO, nothing came of it."

"Yes it did, your DSO has been approved. The hospital should have told you. I'll make a telephone call; see what's happened to it. Air Vice Marshal Park wanted to decorate you with that himself."

Mark left the meeting feeling buoyed up, but also with the foreboding that a burden of responsibility awaited the moment when the medical experts thought him ready to take it.

His little car started with the first turn of the crank, but he was not well enough to drive it due to his hands having been burned, despite his protective gauntlets. The RAF spared two men to solve this problem; one would drive him to Lavering and the other would follow on a motorcycle to take the driver back afterwards.

II

The Lavering church tower can be seen by passing ships although it is two miles from the high tide mark. The beach is shingle to the south and sandy and with some inland dunes to the north. Mark had spent many school holidays there in his youth. His father's brother had held this incumbency for a dozen years or more and it had been a place of respite from boarding school each summer when his parents had been in the Middle East and he was thought too young to travel out to see them.

It was also the place to which they returned from overseas duties occasionally and where their reunions took place, so it was filled with the happy memories of family get-togethers, Christmases with all the trimmings and long summer holidays filled with bird-nesting and blackberrying, raft-building, pirate wars with local boys, fishing in both river and sea and long-netting for rabbits. That was, he worked out during the drive down, a long time ago. His last summer in Lavering had been when he was twelve and now he was turned nineteen. He spent that birthday unconscious in hospital so it was one to forget.

His own, rarely visited, home was in Cheshire; lovely place but a bit too far from the hospital and in any event, neither of his parents were there. He wanted see his Mum, but did not want her seeing a hairless multi-coloured monster who could just about dress himself, was in pain all the time and short-fused. He did not know then how often she had been to the hospital, nor how intimately aware she was of his condition.

His father had been in the army before his career took a more diplomatic path. Often abroad and usually in the Middle East, so bringing up Mark had been the responsibility of nannies and boarding schools. His dad was a remote figure. His uncle would be more understanding, he felt. Uncle Tom had served in the Great War as a Royal Flying Corps pilot. Now he was a clergyman with an interesting past, which included the Victoria Cross and the Mons Star for standing in a trench. He also had the Distinguished Flying Cross and had done in the last war what Mark seemed destined to have to do in this one if he lived long enough.

Flying was a family thing. Granddad Herbert had bought a Bleriot Eleven after the plane's manufacturer became the first aviator to cross the English Channel in 1909. In later years he had other aircraft – Mark had flown a war surplus Bristol aged four, sitting on his Granddad's lap. He soloed in it aged eleven – a misunderstanding; he thought he had been given permission, which granddad denied it afterwards. There had been many trips with granddad, who was well connected in aviation; a former racing pilot, he was now an investor and knew as much about aircraft as he did about soldiering and the family timber business.

Mark had to direct the driver as they got close to Lavering. Main roads were all right, but with all the signposts removed in hope of fooling enemy invaders, one had to know which road was which to get anywhere and mistakes in navigation were harsh on the limited fuel ration. When the rectory roof hove into view, Mark felt ten years old again and looking forwards to all the things that there were to do in this rural backwater. He fumbled for a handkerchief, telling the driver that the cold wind was getting to him.

He also had to find himself; throughout his life he had been bundled from one place to another, looked after by a succession of people, as though his parents had no time for him. He spent more school holidays with other relatives and his parents dropping in than they spent together. As he got older, he seemed to have become more acceptable to his father, as evidenced by the four wonderful summers he spent in Egypt – because his dad was working there. Now, here he was again, being bundled off to a relative to be looked after.

What he missed through staying in so many places was his friends; he needed to mix with and be accepted by people of his own age. What he really wanted was the comfort of his peers caring about him and he wanted a girlfriend, as the hospital had promised.

III

His uncle appeared at the front door, looking greyer than Mark remembered, but still fit and handsome.

"Mark, welcome; you look better than they led me to believe."

Once inside, Mark, with Uncle Tom, the RAF driver and the motorcyclist had tea and they told the story of Mark's last flight, feeling that a Victoria Cross holder could be privy to what happened.

"We think he collided with the ME109 he'd shot up. That 109 hit a Ju88 bomber on the way down so he was credited with two kills that day and has been put in for the DFC."

"Yes." Uncle Tom seemed to be thinking back to his own time in small and vulnerable aircraft, "I was luckier in my service that I never caught fire. We didn't have parachutes then, you know; what's it like, when the 'chute opens Mark?"

"Shock, like stopping suddenly."

Tom asked how Mark managed to get burns in so many places. The best guess was that he was sprayed by aircraft fuel before it ignited. The conversation drifted around general matters of interest before the driver and motorcyclist took their leave.

Once they were alone together, Tom started discussing his recuperation ideas.

"The village is changed from the place you remember – it's seven years since you were here, Mark. We will make you welcome, but it's not like when you were twelve."

"What's different? I know there's a war on."

"Well, for one thing a lot of the young men, your contemporaries, boys that were in the choir when you had holidays here – they're all gone now, into the forces. James is training for his wings. The older men regrouped as the Legion of Frontiersmen before rebadging as the LDV and then the Home Guard; the beaches are part mined and part wired to stop an invasion landing. There are pillboxes and trenches on the cliffs and in the dunes. There are a lot of newcomers. Children evacuated from London and some young families of servicemen stationed in the area. The school is fit to burst. We are short of teachers. This is a community with complex social problems, Mark. You will need to see what you can do to be helpful."

Mark planned what he had to say and then forced the sentence out.

"No face or hair and movement is painful. I look scary and I'm stiff; how am I meant to help?"

"You've been put in for the DFC. It means that no problem is too great for you to overcome. I have that medal too and I know what it means. Whatever the task, you will prevail."

"DSO coming as well; I will do my best."

Making conversation was getting easier.

"That's the spirit; what I have in mind is that you need to do something for the evacuees. They have quadrupled the school, not to mention the cubs and scouts and those units are leaderless. There's a land girl running the brownies with a couple of mothers. She's trying to manage the cubs as well, but she needs a man in there. The troop leader is running the scouts, but he'll be off to the war next year. They stand tall in this community for taking the scout boat to Dunkirk and you'll stand taller – Battle of Britain veteran - how far did you get in scouts?"

Mark was a king scout and had been invested as a rover scout before the Battle of Britain started. There had been a rover crew at Croydon and he had attended meetings, but being a scout and indeed a rover scout was a far cry from running a section.

"Have you any of the books – Scouting for Boys – that sort of thing?"

"Oh, yes, no problem with books."

"And what about my burned face?"

"They'll recognise a hero when they see one. Tell them straight. Let them have a good look, let them touch if you can stand it. Once they have had the chance to evaluate your injuries, they will accept you as you are."

"I wish I could."

"Given time, you will. The doctor told me that there are improvements he can make for you. You may never have the face you had before, but that was a kid's face. Now you've got a hero's visage and the medals to go with it."

"I wish the medals didn't matter so much."

"I know; they won't matter to you, maybe not now nor ever, but they matter to other people, Mark. I am no hero, but I survived three years in a war where the average life of a pilot was just eight days. I achieved recognition for my survival and I am grateful to God every day that I did. And I pray for the souls of those who died in my war every day also."

"How's Aunt Hetty? I suppose she's out doing something?"

Mrs Tom Brabham was always busy.

"She's at a meeting in Chelmsford at the moment, should be back for tea. We all seem to have three or four jobs at the moment, Mark; she's District Commissioner for guides as well as working in the WVS, not to mention things she does in this parish. We've got a new housekeeper called Martha; her husband's in the RAF, overseas at the moment. Her daughter Esther is in the brownies. One other thing; how much do you know about market gardening?"

"Bugger all."

"Me too, but we are enjoined to dig for victory, so I have given much of the garden over to vegetables. If you get the urge to play outdoors, do have a look and see if there is anything useful you can do to help with our victory garden."

IV

Settling in was easier than Mark had expected. Word of his presence got around and the first couple of days were a mixture of unpacking and meeting parish officials. It was therapeutic, being welcomed by so many people he knew, even though they could not recognise him in return either from his face or his voice.

He fitted borrowed badges to his RAF uniform – a pair of Rover epaulettes on a shirt and the green badge of a cubmaster on his forage cap – as preparation for meeting the boys.

Various movements were difficult, muscles and sinews having shrunk in the fire. Mark was concerned about his hands and took to playing scales on the drawing room piano, hoping that the exercise would help his fingers loosen up a bit. Aunt Hetty played a couple of duets with him but sensed that Mark would rather have the piano to himself and left him to it.

CHAPTER 2

IT WAS HIS THIRD day in Lavering before he ventured outdoors. A short walk to the Post Office would do him good, he thought, with the added benefits of being seen by locals and having a chance to look in on the Home Guard at the Village Hall. He wore his RAF uniform and greatcoat for the venture, slinging his civilian gas mask case over his shoulder.

The sharp autumn air stung his delicate face as he opened the front door. His eyes watered and he fumbled for his handkerchief and thus preoccupied, failed to notice the postman's arrival.

"Good Morning Flight; nice weather for the time of year."

"Yes, good morning, thank you." Mark got his handkerchief clear and his eyes wiped so that he could see the postman. Once he could, he found that his focus went to the medal ribbons on his uniform. Those military veterans of the Great War who went on into uniformed civilian employment usually wore their campaign ribbons and these were a familiar sight on railway porters, policemen, AA patrolmen, commissionaires – and those in the Home Guard. And as Mark would discover, they also appeared on Sunday best suits, along with silver lapel badges.

The postman waited for a moment while Mark read the ribbons.

"The Queen's South Africa medal, sir; got it in the Boer War. I got the trio in the Great War."

Mark looked at his face. Rather square, a stocky fellow with broad shoulders. He was pushing sixty – as he must be to have been in South Africa forty years ago and if that was so, he would have been in his higher thirties in the Great War.

"Volunteered in the last war, Postie?"

"Sort of; I joined the territorial army when it was formed in 1908 and then got mobilised in 1914. Spent the war as a driver, looking after machine guns and mules."

"You make it sound...not so hard."

"I was at the front at times, sir; we got shelled a lot behind the lines too – phosgene gas put me in hospital once. I can see you know what it's like. You've been there, you know what I mean."

"I do. I came out to go to the Post Office."

"Walk with you then, sir, if I may. I'll just put these through the box for the rector."

They walked out of the gate together. The postman skipped to get into step with him as they marched down the street, he a proud veteran of two past conflicts, while Mark was a casualty of the third, so he straightened up and made sure that he marched in step. The conversation continued about the postman's experiences until he reached his next delivery address.

"You know where the Post Office is, Flight, along the High Street."

"Yes, thanks."

Mark continued alone, turning into the High Street and marching towards the village Post Office, which was also a small shop and the source of all gossip in the neighbourhood.

A Lockheed Hudson flew overhead. Mark heard the twin-engines above him and as he looked up he saw both the Hudson and a vic formation of Spitfires. He felt crushed. They were on their way to wherever – death or victory – while he was walking along a narrow High Street fifteen thousand feet below them to expose his wounds to public gaze.

He paused, leaning against a fence. He felt unready for this, but on turning to retrace his steps he found his path blocked by the postman catching him up.

"It'll be alright Flight; took me a while after the last bash."

"What do you mean, Postie?"

"Going outdoors, sir. After the war, when it was safe to go out anytime I wanted I found it scary. There were days when I couldn't face crossing the road from my house to the pub, but I had to force myself – only way to walk the dog."

Mark thought about it for a moment. He had not been out, like this, walking along a street, since before...when? Before his escapade with a parachute, certainly; he had not walked out around Croydon – drove there when he wanted something – so before that? Hendon? School maybe?

"Flight Lieutenant?"

"Sorry. Postie, lost in thought for a moment. Was it like that for everybody?"

"Can't say, sir; I was in the open most of the time and my doctor said that a fear of open spaces was natural. Colonel Mallinson was the opposite – he'll doubtless tell you himself - after the war he bought that yacht so he could go out to sea and have the big sky instead of being indoors where he felt cooped up, like in the trenches. Doc said that I'd get over it eventually and so I did, by going fishing with the colonel."

"My war's not over yet," said Mark.

"Our war, sir," said the postman, "I'm in this one too."

"What are you doing this time?"

"Air Raid Patrol; I look out for people in the village who forget their blackout curtains, then if the Germans come over at night I'm looking out for any fires that they start."

Another aircraft passed overhead and they both looked up to see an Avro Anson.

"The air is where all the war to hit Lavering has come from so far," said the postie, "so looking up has become a habit."

They resumed the walk to the Post Office and the postman had determined to accompany Mark all the way there. He could double back and finish his round later. The young airman needed a chum right now and he was there, as his mukkhas had been for him in the old days, when he'd needed them.

The Post Office stood double-fronted in the High Street; a single door for entry between two windows that were intended for the display of goods for sale. But there was a war on, so the displays had been moved clear of the windows to make room for the blackout curtains. Tape criss-crossed the windows to prevent splinters if a bomb blew the glass in. This had not yet happened, although a few bombs had landed in the salt marshes and dunes, dumped by German aircrew abandoning their missions.

The narrow windows either side of the door still carried small adverts written on postcards, offering anything from a second-hand typewriter to a house for rent.

Within the Post Office Miss Everett stood behind the counter, as she had since leaving school, her life dedicated to the General Post Office. One man had come close to breaking her devotion to duty. She had been engaged to the son of the then rector in 1914, but he had answered Kitchener's call to arms and that had earned him immortality on the Menin Gate memorial at Ypres in Belgium. If they had married before he went, she would have been a widow at twenty-two; but he had not, so she'd remained a spinster, as had many of her contemporaries. Her clothing struck Mark as old-fashioned and with her hair in a tight grey bun, she reminded him of Queen Victoria on old pennies.

Miss Everett's sister Mrs Harvey staffed the shop part of the Post Office. Her husband had answered Kitchener's "your country needs you" poster campaign and lay in the cemetery Pozieres, near where he died on the first day of the Somme campaign in 1916. Older than her sister, Mrs Harvey looked younger and more contemporary.

"Ladies, Flight Lieutenant Mark Brabham is both our rector's nephew and houseguest whilst he recovers from his recent injuries."

The postman had the knack of public speaking and thus got Mark the immediate attention of Miss Everett and Mrs Harvey, as well as their several customers.

Mrs Harvey was the first to break the brief but uncomfortable silence that followed.

"Mark, so pleased to see you safe."

"Mostly safe, Mrs Harvey; I lost some skin and hair, but I am promised that it may grow back."

"Indeed, it looks so painful at the moment." Mrs Harvey advanced to see Mark clearly and he took his hat off.

"Yes, but the doctor tells me that's what healing feels like."

It was not going well. Mark was an ugly survivor and was being stared at by two middle-aged women whose men had not made it home. They had nothing to say that could be of any comfort to him, while his injuries were scratching at their memories; telegrams from the War Office acting as full stops to the letters they had to that point received from the front.

The postman took charge again. "It's not going to be easy for us to look at him, but we are all in this war together and his is the face of this war."

Mark said, "My uncle hopes that I will try to help with cubs and scouts whilst I'm here. He said that there are a lot of evacuees in the village."

"There are indeed," said Miss Everett, "and many of them less well-behaved than we like to think our own village children were before they grew up and went to war."

"Does that mean you remember me being well-behaved on my holiday visits here Miss Everett?"

"No, Mark; your returning here has reminded me of what it used to be like when you and the choirboys got going and the evacuee children we have here now are not all that bad; but we only allow them in the shop two at a time, nevertheless."

"Have you met Miss Fforest yet?" asked Mrs Harvey, "she's running the cubs at the moment and I help out when I can."

"No, not yet. I heard she's in the land army."

"Working on Home Farm," said the postman, "there's three of them there, but only Miss Fforest is helping in the village."

"Well, it's nice of her to help at all," said Mark, "I expect the others have their time occupied in other ways."

Miss Everett gave him what he would later learn was an old-fashioned look.

"I suppose visiting the boys on the searchlight battery is essential war-work," she said.

"Obviously," said Mark, "RAF stations are mixed bases and the presence of the Women makes men like me far more careful about our appearance. I bet the searchlight and ack-ack batteries are smart and ready for anything because they've got the land army watching them."

It still was not going well, despite his sense of achievement at getting such a long speech out; the postmistress, her sister and their three silent female customers were a tough audience for a naive young man, conscious as he was of them staring at him.

"Miss Everett, could I get four stamps for postcards, please; then I'll get on and see the Home Guard."

"Yes, of course." She served him his stamps.

II

They left the Post Office, Mark feeling five pairs of eyes on him as he donned his visor cap and turned right to walk along the road towards the village hall. He also felt quite a bit better. He had been able to speak well and he felt good about that. The hall had been built with money raised by public subscription to commemorate the coronation of the fifth King George in 1911 as a secular meeting point for the community.

In the last war it had been where the young men went to sign up; the place they marched away from and to which many of them never returned. The current war had not called for volunteers; this time conscription had been introduced in the spring of 1939, so when the war started in the September, the armed forces were swelling with trained young men. Ration books were printed and gas masks issued. Nevertheless, men did volunteer in droves and Mark would meet one such soon.

Mark had sat in his cockpit often enough during that hot summer of 1940, engine running, waiting for the order to intercept enemy aircraft. Their movements were monitored by the radar stations and a network of observers. Simple code words directed him and the men he flew with to find them.

The squadron leader would shout the code for 'enemy sighted', which was 'tally ho' and then it was every man for himself.

Man; before the crash he shaved twice a week, but because the Royal Air Force was a disciplined organisation, he had 'shaved' on the other days without putting a blade in the razor. He felt a twinge of self-pity. He missed the action and hated the pain he was in, but what was starting to gnaw at him was that he had missed the battle's climax. He realised with a jolt that the postman was talking; "...so if I were you sir, I'd take that extra bit of care with the Colonel."

"Sorry, Postie, miles away."

"No problem sir; Colonel Mallinson is the most bemedalled veteran in this village and he went to Dunkirk to help with the evacuation, so I suppose nobody wants to push him out in favour of somebody younger and possibly less able. And there he is now."

III

Colonel Mallinson was standing in front of the village hall, fiddling with his pipe. The hall was in the colonial style with four steps up to a full width covered walkway in front of its large windows and wide double doors. The Colonel was also large, but well dressed in his greatcoat and breeches. His kindly, if rather pink face framed by silver hair and decorated with a slim moustache.

"Good morning Colonel, this is the rector's...."

"I know who he is, Ron, Flight Lieutenant Mark Brabham, on sick leave, what?"

"Yes Colonel," said Mark, "I am expected to be useful whilst I am here..."

"Yes, there was talk of you looking after the scouts and such, but they only have single-shot rifles, won't be much use in a scrap, so you might want to meet the Home Guard."

"The scouts have rifles?"

"Oh yes, the evacuee scout troop brought their rifles with them, single shot .22 War Office pattern drill rifles. The local boys have scrounged up some repeaters, but .22 bullets don't have the range and ammunition is in short supply. If there's an invasion, which is looking less and less likely, it will be .303 that the Boche must face and the younger scouts can't handle the recoil."

Mark found that he did not get time to think, as the Colonel continued,

"The scouts parade on Tuesday evenings, the wolf cubs on Thursdays. The brownies are here on Wednesdays, but early and the Home Guard parade after them and again on Friday nights. The cubs and scouts man the observation posts during Home Guard parades and act as signallers and runners at other times."

"What about the girl guides?" Mark wanted time to take in the information bombardment.

"Mondays, before the Women's Institute or Mother's Union – not sure what they are. You'll be taking the cub and scout parades, frees the land girl up to concentrate on the female sections. Oh, my apologies; do come on in."

Mark shook hands with the postman, who finally introduced himself as Ron Wilkinson; he wanted to get back to work and Mark followed the Colonel into the hall. The portico had cloakrooms either side, and a spiral staircase to the left. The inside of the main hall would have been light and airy, but for the heavy blackout curtains that seemed to be permanently fitted to the higher windows. Blackouts on the lower windows were drawn back and tied. The hall had a stage at the back, which seemed to have rooms either side of it and a door below the stage leading to whatever void was beneath. There came from the stage wings the gentle hum of voices, which the Colonel said was the overflow class from the school using the rooms for lessons.

The walls between the tall windows were adorned with evidence of the various functions to which the building was being put. Mark noticed progress charts for the cubs and brownies, aircraft recognition posters and other stuff he associated with the Observer Corps. The Home Guard space included a skeletonised Lee Enfield rifle and various other bits of hardware.

"How many men in the Home Guard?"

"Twenty-one, including me; not many men left in the area as you might imagine, which is why the cubs and scouts are so useful."

"Are they supposed to be used for military purposes?"

"Well, any second-class scout is eligible for the civil defence badge; I may have stretched things a bit here, but we're on the coast and we must be vigilant. Even little girls can manage that. The brownies have been amazingly useful as signallers; the guides don't have so much time because they serve in turns in the cottage hospital."

"The Germans have dispersed their invasion barges away from the Channel ports," said Mark.

"I know, but there is nothing wrong with us maintaining a high state of alert, forges these disparate souls into something. You have local boys outnumbered by London boys; they like to be kept busy, and under a bit of stress they learn more and remember more of it. These children have consistently exceeded my expectations, praise where it is due, but there are further trials and tribulations to come and they must always be prepared."

Mark was beginning to warm to the Colonel.

"Do you attend the cub or scout parades, Colonel?"

"On occasions – when invited. The rector and I took it in turns until the land girl took over and now I put my face in when I'm welcome."

"How often is that?"

"About one week in three; I tell tales of India to the cubs, I'm not as good as Rudyard Kipling but I was there for quite a few years and know some stories. I've told yarns to the scouts – they prefer ghost and horror stories I think. The rector is better at organising games and we're both counting on you to get the boys' training moving."

IV

This being Wednesday, Mark decided to attend the Home Guard parade that evening. He told Colonel Mallinson that he would, asking him to make sure that the land girl knew he would be coming, that he might meet her.

The brownies met at 6pm for an hour and a half after which their parents or landladies collected them. The Home Guard started at 8pm with a kit inspection. The scouts covering positions during that time would go straight from their homes or billets in time for the men to get back to the hall.

It was dark when Mark left the comfort and comparative safety of the rectory for the eight-minute walk, accompanied by Martha, the housekeeper and the first black woman he had ever met.

From Jamaica we are, Mark," she said. "My husband joined the RAF in 1935 and we came to England, now he's off somewhere hot and left me and Esther here in the cold and rain."

"How did you come to Lavering?"

"He was stationed at Rochford and wanted us off the base before the German attacks started, so I answered your uncle's advert in the paper for a housekeeper. He took me and Esther; my husband was always welcome to visit, but he got transferred and thought we should stay here."

Due to the Colonel's Swiss-watch timing, the main street was quite busy throughout that walk. Women going to collect brownies in the dark, supplementing the gentle moonlight with torches or lanterns, as boys dashed about and the men of the Home Guard headed for their parade. No vehicles used the road during the time Mark and Martha walked along it. Although he had his car, the meagre three gallons a month fuel ration meant that he would not use it for short journeys at all and longer trips would have to wait until necessary.

The hall's blackout was effective, so Mark could see nothing until he stepped through the door. The Colonel was planted in the vestibule and waiting with him was the land army girl and Martha's daughter Esther in her brownie uniform. Mark focussed on the land girl; she was wearing the expected jodhpurs, jumper and slouch hat, but with a yellow scarf and a bone woggle to suggest affinity with the Brownies. She had her overcoat draped over her arm and had been listening intently to the Colonel until distracted by Mark coming in. She glanced in his direction and smiled, although it was more than just a smile; it seemed to involve her whole body; she lit up like an electric light bulb.

The Colonel made the introduction; "Flight Lieutenant Mark Brabham; Elizabeth Fforest, land army, attached to Home Farm."

"Two 'Fs in Fforest," she said. "Your wounds seem to be healing quite nicely, Flight Lieutenant Brabham; the Colonel has been preparing me for..."

"Your condition," interjected the Colonel, "can't have you scaring anybody can we?"

Nobody had prepared Mark for her thick Welsh accent or her beauty; raven black hair, held in a ponytail under her slouch hat. Pleasingly tanned skin, reflecting her outdoor lifestyle; she looked slim and fit, tough, wiry with petite features and taller than he expected. If she was in the market for an ugly boyfriend, he thought, he would like to get in the queue.

"But I think he's exaggerated a bit." She flushed, dropping her eyes as she did so.

Mark felt his words catch in his throat, as his doctor predicted; he gave himself time to prepare a sentence, but it disintegrated against her smile. He tried again, desperate to avoid stammering.

"I did catch a glimpse of myself in a mirror this morning and it scared me." He felt the need to speak slowly, hoping that she'd do the same.

"Don't be silly," said the Colonel, "what we see in your face is the reflection of the horror you have been through. The man beneath the repairs-in-progress is the same as ever."

Elizabeth moved her coat to the left arm and extended her left hand to shake Mark's in the style of the boy scout movement. He reached forwards and while their hands were in contact their eyes met. An inch or two shorter that he, at five feet six – unless her shoes had higher heels than his.

"Colonel Mallinson is quite right, you know," she said, holding his gaze, "the man beneath shines through the eyes."

"Good job I kept my goggles on then," stammered Mark.

"So now you've met him, Miss Fforest, what do you think the boys and girls will make of him?"

"The boys want to know how many Germans you shot down; they want to know what it's like to fly a Spitfire. They all heard Winston Churchill's praise of our fighter pilots in Parliament repeated on the wireless and they want to meet you."

"I hope I don't disappoint," said Mark, "how much do they know about my injuries?" He'd realised by now that not looking at Elizabeth as he spoke made getting the words out easier.

"I couldn't tell them much," said Elizabeth, "not having seen you for myself. We have told them that you suffered burn injuries in the crash and that your wounds are still healing. They will make sense of that when they see you. The oldest boys pulled a badly burned airman out of the sea near Dunkirk, but he didn't survive."

"Dunkirk?"

"The sea scouts took their motorised whaler over to help with the evacuation," said the Colonel, "with Miss Fforest here as navigator and they may have seen other burn casualties. There have been several such in the parish on sick leave."

"Every burn injury seems to be different," said Elizabeth, "the guides do voluntary work at the cottage hospital and they've seen some horrific wounds."

"I was disappointed," piped up Esther, "when I heard he was burned I thought he'd be black, like me."

Martha looked horrified at her daughter's remarks, but Mark accepted that small people tell it like it is.

"I'm more pink and red," said Mark, "bit of blue and yellow. The black has faded or fallen off. Anyway, you're brown – a real brownie."

"You're the rainbow warrior," said Esther, "you only scared me the first time I saw you."

"Boo."

Martha took Esther's hand and dragged her away. Esther, for her part, would happily have stayed in earshot of the conversation between her Brown Owl and the rainbow warrior.

"I must be going," said Elizabeth, "so we'll meet again tomorrow night for the cub meeting."

"How will you introduce me?"

"The Cubmaster is Akela, so I thought you would take that title."

"What do they call you?"

"I couldn't think of a jungle name for myself on the spur of the moment, never having read the book, so I took the name Tarka from the otter in Henry Williamson's book. Mrs. Harvey from the Post Office shop comes sometimes, and she uses the name Bagheera."

"Tarka; I like that, but if I'm Akela at the cub meeting, what does that make me at scouts?"

"They will expect to call you skipper."

"I see; two new identities in the same week."

"It will be fine, you'll be good for them and your wounds will heal quicker as you won't have time to dwell on them. I'm Miss Fforest, or Elizabeth, or Tarka; Brown Owl or Captain, depending on who's talking. On the farm I seem to be called Oy you."

She moved to put her coat on, Mark taking it to assist. Their goodbye moment was interrupted by men arriving for the Home Guard parade and the Colonel greeting them. Elizabeth slipped past them and said 'nos da' as she stepped into the outer darkness. Mark, facing the door as she left, was in position for greeting the men arriving. They were in uniform, wearing medal ribbons from the Great War. One carried a rifle and the other had a shotgun. They saluted Mark and the Colonel and then passed on into the hall.

"Your men keep their weapons at home?" Mark asked.

"There are some rifles here, five I think. There's a bit of an armoury under the stage. Spare scout rifles and some air guns in there as well. The rest are on issue to the men so that they can go straight from work to their lookout posts and so forth. I see the weapons to check them each week and to have an ammunition count."

"What about the shotgun?"

"Oh, that's his. The War Office issued us some shotgun cartridges before we got enough rifles and he's stuck to carrying it."

Other men had passed into the meeting hall, from whence a harsh voice could be heard calling the men to order.

"FALL IN BY SECTIONS; SECTION LEADERS REPORT TO ME."

Mark followed the Colonel into the room as the men sorted themselves out. It reminded Mark of the scouts he'd been in, as they fell in forming three sides of a square. This meant that the nearest men had their backs to the door, while the voice calling them to order emanated from a sergeant standing in front of the stage.

The Colonel marched round the formation and took his place front and centre. Mark followed him to the corner of the stage and waited there.

"Parade, at…. ten…SHUN." The sergeant called them to order.

"Thank you sergeant, stand at ease," the Colonel handled the parade almost as Mark's scoutmaster would have done, several counties away and, it felt, a lifetime ago. "Let me begin by introducing Flight Lieutenant Mark Brabham, on convalescent leave whilst recuperating from injuries sustained in the summer's air engagements."

Mark stepped forwards and saluted. The sergeant led the response;

"Three cheers for Flight Lieutenant Mark Brabham, Hip, Hip,"

The 'HOORAH' from the eighteen men present came as a shock to Mark, standing in front of them. They repeated it twice more in the customary style, making Mark feel pride swelling from the recognition. The Colonel started outlining the evening's activities and while he was doing so Mark looked around the men before him. At least a couple were in his age group, so either not called up yet, or reserved occupations or failed the medical.

Most were older; if he'd had to put figures on this it would have been thirties and forties. About half of them sported uniforms and Great War medal ribbons. They all had rifles of various types except for the shotgun artist. Those without uniforms wore armbands 'LDV' and everybody seemed to have a Brodie helmet. Mark's mind faded back into the meeting in time to hear the Colonel telling the men that his talk about the Battle of Britain would follow the mid evening tea break.

The weapons inspection started, during which the young man next in line leaned Mark's way; "I'm Lawrence Hilton, Troop Leader, look forwards to working with you at the scouts. Frank Ball, with white section, is a scout as well."

A bit taller than Mark and thin, he'd be easy to remember. Looking to Frank Ball, Mark noted that he was in school uniform, which made him look younger than his seventeen years; Hilton wore his sea scout uniform with an LDV armband.

"We'll break into sections; Flight Lieutenant Brabham with red, blue with Sergeant Pavitt and white on me. For the first exercise you will use what you have to improvise a stretcher that will carry an unconscious casualty the length of the hall, into the side room, up the stairs, across the stage, down the other side and back to where you started. Red section will not use Flight Lieutenant Brabham as their casualty."

The sergeant took over; "FALL OUT AND GET WEAVING."

"I'll be the casualty," said Hilton, "I'm the lightest."

Red section slipped off their webbing and set to work preparing a stretcher. As they worked, Mark and Lawrence Hilton could chat.

"People call me Laurie and at scouts I'm 'Flags'; don't know why and if I go to the cub meeting I'm Kaa."

"I don't remember Kaa in the Jungle Book," said Mark, "but then it's sometime since I read those stories."

"He was the rock python."

"Ah, yes, I remember now. Got filled in by Nag in a bathroom. Why that name?"

"No, Nag was another snake, got filled in by Riki Tiki Tavi in a bathroom. Kaa has always been used here for the Troop Leader when he's a Cub Instructor, so it was my turn to be he."

Mark asked, "Do you remember me from my holiday visits? The last time I was here would have been 1933?"

"Vaguely; I joined the choir in 1931, but you played with the older boys and they are all away in the forces now. It will be my turn next year."

"What branch of service do you have in mind? Are you going to volunteer for something?"

"I don't know yet; I'd like to finish King Scout and I am getting useful experience here in the Home Guard. Probably the navy."

"Do you still sing in the choir?"

"Yes, but it's a problem; you'll see on Sunday at church parade. Those of us with more than one...I don't know... position, have to choose what to do at church."

"Hilton, lie on the stretcher. That's your next position."

The exercise intervened; red section was first ready, blue a close second and it had turned into a bit of a race. Mark watched them run across the stage, grateful that the casualty was not he. The exercise over, Colonel Mallinson ordered the men to reassemble their kit and fall in.

Tea was served by a volunteer who must have been over eighty, following which Mark knew the spotlight was to fall on him and he had nothing prepared. He stood in front of the aircraft recognition posters and the men drew chairs up in a double semi-circle, ready to listen to him.

"I don't know how many of you remember me from my holiday visits here;" that generated a few hands, which he reckoned was about a quarter of them, "but I like to think that I have grown up since." Gentle applause. "I joined the Royal Air Force last year and learned to fly various aircraft before being assigned to fighter training." He picked up a swagger stick from the table and pointed to the aircraft silhouettes; "I have flown various machines including a Gladiator, a Hurricane and a Spitfire."

He stumbled on for a bit, trying to find a line between being informative without giving away secrets. The Colonel sensed that Mark did not have a structure for his talk, so he intervened and said that Flight Lieutenant Brabham would now take questions.

"Sir, if we see a parachutist descending towards our positions, is there a way of recognising friend from foe by looking at the 'chute?"

"Afraid not. British and German parachutes are white and much the same size. Different flying suits of course. One tip I heard from a military policeman is that German jack boots tend to come off when the parachute opens, but you can't guarantee that a man in stockinged feet will be an enemy."

"How do we recognise allied pilots, Poles and other foreigners?"

"They have all been taught to introduce themselves. They will give their name and say that they are Czech or Polish attached to the RAF. They will not tell you their squadron or the name of their commanding officer until they are sure who you are."

Colonel Mallinson intervened, "our orders are to escort such men to a police station for identification purposes."

"Good," said Mark, "at the police station they will give the name of their airfield. It occurs to me that there are differences in the personal kit that pilots have, I'll see if I can get mine here and maybe some German stuff so that you can see."

There were a few more questions, all focussed on the general need to recognise friend from foe. Nobody asked about Mark's injuries so he decided to deal with that himself.

"You can see that I was burned and you have been told that I am on convalescent leave. I can't discuss the operation that I was involved in, but I was engaging the enemy when my machine caught fire and I bailed out into the sea from which a fishing boat rescued me."

Mark's moment in the spotlight over, Sergeant Pavitt fell the men in for the closing ceremony and dismissal. Mark again felt that the Home Guard was being run pretty much as a grown-up scout troop, albeit with a training programme suited to their war service activities. He also felt quite comfortable being with the men at this meeting and thought that he would attend further parades if he had the strength.

Following dismissal he caught a quick word with Frank Ball, who said he was an evacuee; his Scout uniform was a bit tight, so he reserved it for Scout meetings. He hoped to have a Home Guard uniform before Christmas.

V

Mark walked home accompanied most of the way by Laurie Hilton, who said that he'd attend the cub meeting next evening.

"It's a bit tricky, as I get a lot of homework, but I can get my head down on that a bit once you've got your feet under the table as Akela."

"Who was Akela before me?"

"I never knew her proper name, but she had to move when her husband's job relocated more than a year ago, so Bagheera kept it together until Tarka came along. She's marvellous, but I have to do the shouting, like Sergeant Pavitt does at Home Guard parades."

Back indoors, Mark found his uncle in the study.

"Are you allowed alcohol Mark? I have this rather good port on the go."

"Just a small one then, who knows where you'll get another bottle after that one."

"From the cellar."

Which was quite well stocked, Mark discovered. Tom reckoned that with the amount of fortified wine he used for communion services and what he drank in the evenings, and assuming that he could buy no more, he would run out near the end of 1943.

"I don't think that will happen, though," he said, "Portugal is neutral and needs us as an export market. Spain's neutral too and is the only source of Seville oranges and I don't expect a shortage of marmalade or sherry anytime soon either. French wine is already hard to find but the Spanish reds are tolerable if a bit fruity."

CHAPTER 3

MARK AWOKE, FEELING SORE. Maybe the port had upset the balance of his medication. Whatever, he felt sandpapered and delicate and he would have to be Akela in 12 hours time. He set about trying to restore his body, but he did not fancy dressing so he put a dressing gown over his silk pyjamas and set off in search of breakfast.

There was nobody in the kitchen, but a large kettle boiled on the range so he made himself tea and then went through to the drawing room. The piano stood waiting for him so he sat at it, drinking his tea and leafing through the sheet music on top of the instrument. Nothing inspired him so he played a few scales; that made him feel better, so he struck a few chords as Tom came in.

"I am trying to work up the enthusiasm to be a hero to the cubs tonight."

"Just be yourself, it will be fine," said Tom, "remember that courage rises to meet danger, overcoming fear."

After breakfast and ablutions Mark hung around the front hall hoping to catch the postman, but it seemed that there was nothing for them. He decided to go out for a walk, perchance to run into the postman, so he donned his greatcoat and cap and went out into a pleasant autumn day.

He walked along the main street and had made up his mind to go as far as the hall when he spotted the butcher's shop, open fronted, somewhat like an indoor market stall. In front were displayed various bits and pieces, including some rabbits hanging, paunched but with their skins on. Mark ventured inside; no customers within, but the butcher was working at his block.

"Good morning Flight, what can I do for you?"

"Just out walking, thought I could pause here for a moment."

"And most welcome, sir, my name's Harold Roberts, as it says over the door although that was painted for my father. Friends call me Harry."

"Is your father still with the business?"

"No sir, retired, although he helps out. He's good with rabbits."

"Like those hanging up."

"Fresh this morning."

"Do you shoot them?"

"No, sir, we get them using a long net. Have you ever seen that done?"

"Yes. I used to come here for school holidays and I've been out with the men netting. Maybe I met him then."

The conversation drifted around to the butcher's shotgun that he took to the Home Guard parade.

"Let me show you."

Harry Roberts led Mark into the back room and opened a cupboard, handing Mark the gun.

One barrel was much smaller inside than the other, although they looked much the same when the gun was seen from the side.

"My father brought this back from South Africa, sir, the right barrel is an ordinary 12 bore, but the left is rifled .303 inch. Boers call it a Cape Rifle. It's got these leaf sights for ranges of up to 500 yards. This is the one I'll be carrying if we get into a fight on this coast."

Mark enjoyed the chat and the rabbit he was presented with. He set off home with his parcel of meat and was nearly back there when he ran into the postman.

"Am I early or are you late, Postie?"

"Bit of each, I'd say, Flight. How went the Home Guard parade?"

"Good, I felt welcome; who told you?"

"Everyone, that's why I'm a bit late; Cubs tonight then?"

"Yes."

"I'll look in if you don't mind; I usually start my blackout check at that end of the village."

II

After that, the day dragged. He spent the afternoon flicking through the various books that were supposed to be useful, but not taking anything much in. His uncle had gone to a meeting and his aunt was out visiting. As it started to get dark, Mark went round the house drawing blackout curtains, then dressed in his temporary Scout/RAF mixed uniform and let himself out to get to the hall early.

The cloak of darkness was descending, but not to the extent that a light was necessary. Mark hoped to meet Laurie Hilton on the way, but had no such luck. In fact, the street was quieter than the night before, leading Mark to paranoid thoughts about the Cubs boycotting the meeting. The walk up to the village hall door felt a lonely one.

The scene when he opened it, however, was almost the same as the night before; the Colonel talking to Miss Fforest, who hung on his every word and the background noise suggested that some boys were already in the hall.

"Good evening, Flight," said the Colonel, "took the liberty of inviting myself tonight; thought I'd keep in the background. I have a tale ready to tell, so any time you need a little respite, tell the boys the Colonel will tell them a story and then I'll take over with my slices of ham yarn."

"Noswech Dda Flight Lieutenant," Elizabeth Fforest saluted and Mark stared for what felt afterwards much too long before he returned her salute. "I have a programme prepared, following what is the usual routine here."

Mark had not thought for a moment about the sequence of events that evening. It had taken all his conscious effort just to get there.

Elizabeth continued, "grand howl to open, then a game; bulldog is favourite with Kaa in the middle to start with. Once that's done you should make your introductory speech, then another game - split them up for badge work and the Colonel's yarn at the end. What do you think?"

It was the sort of Cub meeting Mark remembered from his youth when he had a face.

"If you have a problem speaking to the boys after the first game, we'll just switch the Colonel into that slot and you talk at the end."

She made it all sound quite simple. Several boys had entered the hall while this conversation was taking place; all had stared at Mark for as long as they could.

Now it was time to enter the hall, where Kaa was already in position near the front.

"PACK, PACK, PACK," he shouted to bring the boys to order the moment he saw Mark. They fell in to their sixes, of which there were five. Nearly thirty boys on parade, set out as a loose horseshoe with the open end ready for the leaders to take their place. Mark marched into the space that awaited him, standing front and centre; Kaa to his left, Tarka to his right and the Colonel to her right. Bagheera took her place to Kaa's left.

"DRESS YOUR SIXES; EVEN UP THE CIRCLE, STAND EASY." Kaa even sounded a bit like Sergeant Pavitt.

Mark looked around the pack and they looked back at him. The local boys had green scarves, bordered white and most of the evacuees had plain grey scarves. Otherwise their uniforms looked much the same. Green caps with gold piping, green jumpers to which were sewn the badges each boy had earned, dark shorts and socks with green striped tops and green garter tabs showing. The economies of wartime and the boys' growth spurts were reflected by their shorts; some came a bit below the knee, as was proper and others were getting shorter as the boys themselves stretched.

"Grey Brother will lead the grand howl."

The Grey Brother is the senior sixer. In this pack it was Derrick Forder, London evacuee, who also sang in the church choir. Aged ten, he was a two star Cub who would move up to the Scouts in the spring. Following the opening ceremony and inspection, Mark handed over to Tarka and Kaa to take the game of bulldog. He went and stood with the Colonel and Bagheera.

"Excellent," said the Colonel, "They've all had a good look at you and nobody's been sick."

"Thanks."

"You OK for your speech?"

"Yes, I think so. I'll say much the same as I did at the Home Guard last night."

After the game, Mark took his place at the head of the horseshoe, ordered them to sit cross-legged and told them a little about his war, his injuries and that the bits of him that looked painful were sore and were sensitive to the touch.

"I am getting better and I hope to fly again next year," he said, "but until then I will be here full time and I will make every effort, with the other leaders, to get your badge work moving. I know that you have other duties, helping the Home Guard and the Air Raid Patrol, coast-watching, fire-watching and signals. This civil defence work is important to us all. As a pilot, I was at the sharp end. I met the German aircraft attacking our country, but I could not have done that without the support of all the personnel who kept us flying, or the people in the factories who are making 'planes, or those on the land growing our food, or the Observer Corps looking for the enemy and the people supporting them. We all have a contribution to make and the work you do here, now and in the future all adds to our nation's war effort."

"How many Germans did you get?" asked Andrew Taylor, red six.

"Counting the operation I was injured in, I have shot down nine German aircraft," said Mark, "but we count the machines, not the Nazis in them. I also got two Spitfires; the one I was wearing when I was injured and one I brought down near Boxhill in Surrey."

"Were you at Dunkirk?"

"No, I returned from France on a ferry out of a port further down the coast."

..Questions continued, as boys tried to fit Mark's experiences into what they knew about the war from others. It used up the training time.

Kaa got the next game going and Mark let it run until the Colonel signalled that he was ready to give his yarn.

"Lights down," said the Colonel, "and I will tell you of my experience in the last war in France. I was with three friends, returning from leave…"

Mark slipped out into the entrance hall, Elizabeth and Laurie following.

"So far, so good?" asked Mark.

"Yes," said Laurie, "you've taken charge and you have their attention. It feels good."

"They want to respect you," said Elizabeth, "It's going well."

The lights came back on.

"FALL IN".

The meeting concluded with a grand howl, which sounded to Mark a much better effort than the opening one.

Bagheera announced the church parade on Sunday and the Colonel listed the Saturday jobs for those who were available.

"I want you and the Scouts on a beach patrol, Saturday morning," he said, "it will be low tide about eleven hundred, which gives you the chance to patrol further from the dunes than usual and to report anything that you find."

Mark dismissed the boys, who drifted towards the doors where parents could be seen waiting to take them home.

"Did you like that?" asked Tarka.

"I'm exhausted," said Mark, "enjoyed it, but I feel wrung out."

"Take a few days off," said the Colonel, "your next duty, apart from the church parade on Sunday, is Scouts on Tuesday. I'll take care of Saturday."

"What will they be looking for?" asked Mark.

"All sorts," said the Colonel, "we've found a torpedo, an empty lifeboat, bits and pieces washing ashore. I've had tins of cigarettes off the beach, a wooden aircraft propeller and a small bronze one, maybe from a fishing boat. My men saw a German fighter ditch out there three weeks ago and since Saturday is a very low tide, we may be able to reach it."

"Where's the pilot?" asked Mark.

"Not sure; they never saw if he got out or not. If he did, he didn't land here, but with the tide ebbing at the time he could have been swept out to sea."

Elizabeth had her coat on and Mark had promised himself that he would try to walk with her part of the way without saying so. He just engineered it so that they left together. It was a short walk, as Home Farm was the opposite direction, so they parted company when they reached the street. Mark would have liked to escort her at least part of the way home, but he felt too tired to chance walking away from his destination.

"I'll say goodnight here," he said. She turned to look at him.

"Yes, goodnight, nos da, get plenty of rest. The Scout meeting is harder work."

III

Mark spent Friday getting over Thursday night. A bath, some piano playing, hot food and a log fire in the study; he started working his way through Uncle Tom's library. The scout books were already together in a heap next to the armchair, but he wanted something else.

Browsing other people's libraries is interesting. Most book collections are eclectic, compiled over a period of years reflecting the owner's youth, studies, leisure, quest for wisdom, widening horizons, specialised preferences and eventually, nostalgia. Uncle Tom had not reached the nostalgia stage, but he'd touched most of the other milestones. Mark hunted for anything from the Great War and found Uncle Tom's flight log.

He was still absorbed in it when its writer returned.

"Find that interesting?"

"Couldn't put it down. You flew eleven sorties in one day in 1916."

"Yes, it was a busy year."

"Busy week, busy day. What was that like?"

"Well, I can't remember without a glass of sherry."

Mark got up and poured.

"Thanks; well, it was wet. On the ground everything got damp from the snow or the rain or the river or the dew or in summer the sweat. In the air it's colder than on the ground, so wet clothing starts to freeze in the open cockpit, goggles mist over, my nose felt like it would fall off. We needed all sorts of things that we hadn't got. I couldn't hear anything but the engine, so the first I'd know about ground fire was Archies bursting and if the enemy 'planes got too close to us before we saw them it was curtains. My head was on a swivel, spinning all the time; it was quite helpful when Richthofen's circus painted their 'planes in bright colours."

Mark resumed flicking through the flight log intending to alight on something interesting that he could ask about.

Tom continued, "The problem with flight logs, Mark, is that we write things down so that we don't have to remember them. I went through that book about ten years ago – I was thinking of writing a war memoir – and I found that entry after entry did not help me remember the incidents. There are things that stick in my mind, for sure. In the early days, I remember shooting my revolver at an enemy pilot whilst he was shooting at me with his pistol; we flew side by side, almost in formation. After my six shots, I was struggling to reload but my hands were cold and the cartridges were in my trouser pocket; it was hopeless, I couldn't do it. I looked back to the German and he was holding his pistol up with the toggle stuck open; he couldn't reload either so we saluted and broke off. Now, I can't find that flight in my log. I have no idea which one it was, although it must have been in my first year."

"Do you still have your revolver?"

"No; I bought a Colt automatic pistol later in the war and I still have that. Do you want to carry it for Home Guard parades?"

Mark thought it might be useful. His own was missing. He was wearing it when he bailed out but it was not with his kit in the hospital. "I don't know how to work an automatic pistol," he told his uncle, "I had a revolver and we did a bit of drill with rifles, never fired either though."

"Well, if you prefer a revolver, I've got one that was given to me," Tom said, fumbling through his desk. He produced the weapon in a leather holster. Mark took a look at it; made by Colt, it was different to the British issue, but easy to understand.

"Uncle, why does a clerk in holy orders have two guns?"

"Believing in God means respecting his decisions, Mark. I didn't think much about it after the war, but I left the service with my pistol and a good stock of ammunition. That revolver was given to me quite recently, along with some ammunition. There must be a reason why and that is not for me to question. I don't expect to have to shoot anyone, but the fact that I have the means to must stand for something."

Mark thumbed back through the log to the first entries in 1915.

"Weren't you at the front in 1914? Is there an earlier log?"

"No; in 1914, I was with the Artists Rifles in the trenches."

"The Christmas truce?"

"Yes, I didn't see much though. I heard that there had been fraternisation in no man's land, but in our sector it was quiet and we stayed in the trenches. The Germans came out their side with stretchers to collect up some dead soldiers, so later on we did the same and then we had a burial service for them behind our lines, so for me, Christmas 1914 amounted to attending a large funeral without getting shot at. You dad wasn't so lucky; he was wounded on Christmas Day 1914."

Tom fell silent, dwelling on his experience that winter. There had been rumours of football matches and all sorts of things happening, letters in newspapers mentioned such events, but they were outside his personal experience. He was not in the trenches for long; his application to the Royal Flying Corps was accepted when it was realised that he was an experienced aviator and he went to the rear and then back to England to join the Corps.

That experience was courtesy of his Uncle Herbert who wanted to fly. He had to master the Bleriot in order to teach him. Later, Herbert was able to buy a two-seater so he could fly his wife Annie to interesting places; he even crossed the English Channel in 1915 to Le Touquet to meet Tom when he got a short leave from the brutal military camp at Etaples.

"There's a lot said about chivalry in the clouds," he continued out loud, "and some of it's true; but later in the war it got far bloodier – our new pilots would be butchered like pigeons over decoys on their first flights."

Mark thought back to his first operational sortie, "I was shepherded by my squadron leader into the first action. We were supposed to intercept bandits over Biggin Hill; never saw them, but we found some Stukas attacking the radar west of Hythe and hit them hard, as you said, pigeon shoot; we didn't dare give them a chance."

"Well, that's war, but there will come a time when you hear about acts of chivalry, or mercy. There will be a moment when you'll want to do the decent thing."

Mark thought about that for a while, but the image of dead WAAFs was etched on his mind. The women had taken cover in an air raid shelter at the airfield. Mark was caught in the open and lay down as the first bombs exploded. When he thought it was best to move, he ran to cover but when he scrambled in, he saw they were dead, without a mark on them. The percussion of the bomb had killed them outright in the confined space while he had survived in the open.

He told Uncle Tom about finding all those women.

"War," said Uncle Tom, "is a waste of people. Politicians and generals, as well as bereaved relatives, usually look for some reason to say that the dead did not die in vain, but most deaths are pointless and many are ridiculous. Few people actually die whilst engaged in direct combat with the enemy, such as when we fight them in the clouds. Most casualties die as the result of indirect fire; whoever killed those WAAFs with his bomb was after your kites on the ground. When the postman was hospitalised in the last bash by a gas shell, the artilleryman who fired it had no notion of our postman as his target. Most killers don't know that they've murdered somebody and those of us who have seen someone die don't usually know who killed them."

Mark pondered for a while, before saying, "we were ordered not to follow enemy aircraft down, so in the case of enemy 'planes I have shot at, I don't know what happened to the men inside."

"That may be best," said Tom, "in the last war we followed our enemies down to see what happened, so that we could log our victories as 'forced to land' or 'crashed' or 'crash landed'; we weren't interested in putting the man out of the fight so much as grounding his kite. A wounded man would break off action; even Von Richthofen, when he got shot up, managed to land his 'plane before succumbing to the bullet that killed him."

Mark's thoughts turned to the present; Tom continued talking, "and then there's accidents. I don't know how many pilots we lost in mishaps and prangs in the last war, but there's always death caused without the intervention of the enemy. Men drowned in flooded trenches, you know, and we lost so many pilots crashing during take-off or landing procedures. There are over three thousand eight hundred officers of the Royal Flying Corps currently serving with the Commonwealth War Graves Commission in graves or on monuments, as they will forever."

Mark knew about accidents. Starting and finishing were still the most dangerous elements of each sortie. In flight, stalling was a risk, as was running out of fuel. Being on the ground could be just as dangerous; Mark's squadron had lost one pilot killed and another badly injured in a car crash.

"What did you get the VC for?"

"Being there, Mark; such awards are political. They are meant to raise morale in the service and among the public. In the RFC, they were usually to highlight achievements, to remind everyone that we were in the war."

"Is that the same this time? Do my medals just encourage the others?"

"Yes and no, Mark; the boys who went to Dunkirk will tell you that the soldiers did not believe the RAF were in that fight until they found a dead pilot in the sea on their way home. In my war, the public just didn't know about the flying corps and what we did in France, as fighting in the air did not develop until later. We spent our time spotting for the artillery and taking photographs but when the Zeppelin bombers started coming over Britain Leefe Robinson brought one down in nineteen sixteen and got the VC for doing so. By the end of the war, just eighteen VCs had been awarded to airmen and that was the combined total for the corp, the Royal Naval Air Service and the RAF."

"But there were other medals as well?"

"Oh yes; but it's all politics and publicity. The big morale-boosting publicity splash came in nineteen seventeen when air to air combat was really hotting up and three VCs were announced at the same time. Albert Ball was killed before being gazetted. That was a game-changer as the VC's royal warrant did not recognize posthumous awards but they announced Billy Bishop and Frank McNamara at the same time to publicise just how widely drawn our pilots were: Frank being Australian and Billy coming from Canada. When Billy was invested at Buckingham Palace he got his VC, DSO and a military cross all at once."

"Wow, that's a hard act to follow."

"That's politics; are you going out with the Home Guard tomorrow?" Tom's question brought Mark's mind back to his current circumstances.

"I thought I might take a look. The Colonel said that there's a crashed German fighter in the sea and that they might be able to reach it with the low tide."

CHAPTER 4

SATURDAY LOOKED NICE WHEN Mark got up, so after his bath and breakfast he felt ready for a walk to the beach to see what was happening. He dressed in his RAF uniform and tried the revolver on, but it looked bulky in the mirror strapped over his greatcoat and like a strange bulge under his coat when he tried it over his tunic. In the end, he opted for putting the revolver in his greatcoat pocket and some cartridges in the opposite pocket. That made it invisible, but it banged on his leg when he walked, so he took to walking with his right hand in his pocket holding the grip.

It was two miles to the sea and he did not know where anyone would be, but almost as soon as he left the drive he ran into Laurie Hilton.

"Where's the action?" he asked.

Laurie said that he was waiting to hear. There were two Scouts on top of the church tower equipped with semaphore flags and a Morse lamp. They could see the main coastal pillbox and that position would send them a message about where to deploy.

"Won't that mean anyone at sea could also read the message?" asked Mark.

"That's why we have Morse and semaphore," said Laurie, "the beach signaller can use Morse if there's anything at sea and it's up to the lads on the tower to scan the horizon. We also have some codes from the Colonel. It's basic– there are twenty-six messages and either end can signal 'code' and a letter for the other end to look up that message."

"I'll need that again a bit more slowly," said Mark.

"OK, Code 'A' means read message 'A' from the codebook. Message 'A' is all units regroup at village hall. 'B' means that a runner is on his way with detailed orders and so on. Message 'Z' means that we deploy to our invasion stations. We've done that as a drill a couple of times and once for real last summer. If the coast is clear, we can exchange longer messages."

The Scout on the tower shouted down that a message was coming in from the beach. Laurie and Mark walked into the church where Derrick 'Grey Brother' Forder was seated at the bottom of the tower taking dictation from the boys on the roof reading the message. They shouted the letters down to him one at a time.

When it was finished, Derrick went through it drawing lines to separate the words; "it says – Home Farm cart to beach."

"Maybe they can see the 'plane," said Laurie, "last time we had that rig out it was for a torpedo. That must have weighed four hundred pounds, what does a Messerschmitt weigh?"

"No idea," said Mark, "but more than a big car, as it has a huge engine, guns and ammunition. A couple of tons, maybe two and a half?"

Laurie said that he'd use his bicycle to go to Home Farm, then on to the beach. Mark asked if he could do that job, since riding out to the farm and then on to the beach might be less strenuous than walking to the beach - and Elizabeth would be there.

"Sure," said Laurie, "I'll get on to the beach; Mister Murrell will be half expecting to be called out. He'll moan about it but he's willing enough. He doesn't like being taken for granted, so make sure you ask as a special favour."

Mark knew where the farm was, as he'd helped with long netting there in his youth on holidays. He remembered Farmer Murrell; the sort of person who undoubtedly got on well with the likes of his uncle and with Colonel Mallinson, but probably would not remember him.

He put his greatcoat on the luggage rack and set off on Laurie's bicycle. A bit wobbly at first before he got into the swing of it, riding down the High Street, past the Post Office and the butcher's shop, to the village hall. Then he stopped to put his gloves on, as the wind was chilling his hands and they felt quite poorly. He had a pair of white silk lining gloves and a pair of leather motor gauntlets to put on over them. Fiddling with the gloves took a couple of minutes, during which time Sergeant Pavitt appeared.

"Running an errand, Flight, or enjoying the autumn air?"

"I'm to Home Farm to turn out the horses and wagon that the Colonel wants on the beach," said Mark.

"Any message for us?" asked Pavitt.

"Not that I have; I left as soon as the message to get the cart was received. Laurie Hilton said he'd head straight to the beach and that's the last I know."

"OK," said Pavitt, "I'll get my detail down there."

II

Mark rode north for a bit over a mile, then turning east onto Home Farm's private road. The farm itself was half a mile up that drive and all the fields either side belonged to Farmer

Murrell. He did not own the coast, though. There were several small farms in between his land and the sea.

The brace of Suffolk Punch carthorses stood in the yard, harnessed to a stout haywain, like they were expecting him. Mark looked around and saw no people, so he headed for the farmhouse door when he was accosted from behind; "You'll be Tom's nephew, I take it."

Mark turned to see Farmer Murrell approaching him from the milking parlour opposite.

"Yes, sir, Mister Murrell, I have a message from Colonel Mallinson."

"Wanting the horses and wagon that you see waiting for you."

"Yes, sir, the Colonel…"

"I know what he's like, boy; he told me in church last Sunday that he had a chance of salvaging that 'plane today, so I have things ready. You can put your bicycle on the wagon and get going – you don't want to keep old Mallinson waiting."

Mark looked at the haywain. The horses looked at Mark, then back to Murrell.

"I don't think I can drive that rig," said Mark, "I can ride a bit, but I've never driven horses in harness like that, sir."

"I didn't think of that," said Murrell, "still, put your bike on the wagon."

He walked to the far side of the farmyard and bellowed "Oy, you!" into the distance and moments later, Elizabeth trotted into view.

"The Colonel has sent this officer to commandeer our wagon and horses," said Murrell, "and the Colonel won't like it if the officer turns up driving himself, so you take the rig down to the beach and follow the Colonel's instructions. You can catch up with your work when you get back. Oh, and take the accumulator with you; change it in the village."

Elizabeth put her bucket down and fetched her coat. Mark had been putting the bike onto the wagon, which he noticed had quite a few bits and pieces in it; ropes, blocks and tackle, pioneering poles. Farmer Murrell had intended the rig to go out prepared for what might be a difficult salvage effort.

Mark waited for Elizabeth.

"Which side do you sit to drive?" he asked.

"On the right," she said, "so that I can reach the handbrake."

They got up onto the broad seat and Elizabeth unwound the reins from the handbrake, loosed it and set the horses to trot by shaking the reins. Sitting on the seat was high up, Mark noticed as they progressed down the drive. The carthorses must be standing seven feet tall, he mused, and he had a clear view over their heads. On the way up he'd been riding a bike between two tall hedges, but on the way back he had panoramic views over them. The coast was visible behind them and he could see the church tower in the distance.

"So if you were looking out for a signal from the church, you could see it here?" he asked Elizabeth.

"Yes, but we'd need a telescope or something to read it," she said, "unless they use the Morse lamp; I can read that OK."

"What's the accumulator for?"

"It's a battery to power the wireless because there is no electricity on the farm. We change it Saturdays for a charged one at the ironmongers. You're lucky in town to have electricity. On the farm we have oil lamps."

Mark had not thought of that as the places he had lived in England had it, although two thirds of domestic houses did not.

Fields either side of the coast road gave way to salt marshes and dunes before the coast opened up before them. In peacetime the beach was used by fishermen and holidaymakers, but now it was off limits except to those with some responsibility for Britain's security. The pillbox was a concrete construction in the dunes and behind it stood a small watchtower. The tower was a Boy Scout affair, poles lashed together with cod line and the observation balcony accessed by an old ladder. It stood about twice the height of the pillbox, so from his vantage point on the haywain Mark was looking up to the Scouts on the tower and down at the pillbox roof. A clear line of trenches stretched away from the pillbox; dug in the sand and shuttered with corrugated iron, they looked neglected, perhaps reflecting Colonel Mallinson's opinion that there would be no invasion this year.

The Scouts looked at him before returning to their observations, one scanning the sea and the other keeping an eye on the church. Colonel Mallinson stood on the roof of the pillbox staring out to sea. His horse was parked next to the road and seemed to be leaning on the hedge.

"Good morning Colonel," said Mark, "we have some tackle in the wagon..."

"Excellent, good morning," said the Colonel, "if you climb the tower you can get a good view of the tail plane sticking out of the water. Low tide is about another five and twenty minutes and if we have any chance of salvaging the 'plane it's a half-hour slot before the tide starts racing in again."

On some parts of the Essex coast the tide can ebb four or five miles, but when it flows, it comes in fast. Mark descended from the haywain and climbed the tower, which felt sturdier than it looked. The two Sea Scouts manning the post broke off their observations to eye Mark close up. He took his hat off and they did the same.

"Skipper, I'm Peter Law, seagulls patrol leader and Frank Maynard here is second of the curlews." Peter was distinguished by his round spectacles and straight dark hair. At sixteen, he was third in age after Laurie and Frank Ball.

Frank Maynard, at fifteen, was one of six that age. His curly brown hair reminded Mark of a coconut, but only until Frank put his hat back on.

"Good morning each; I'm looking forward to meeting everyone on Tuesday."

"Are you going on church parade tomorrow?"

"I'll be in church without doubt, but with the Cubs, or the Scouts or the Home Guard? Three new identities in a week. I'll probably go as myself."

Mark took the binoculars and looked at the sea where Frank pointed. The tail plane was visible.

"It's not moving with the tide," said Frank, "I have been watching it for about half an hour and the 'plane is definitely stuck."

"The water can't be more than about six feet deep there," said Mark, "a bf109e stands taller than those carthorses when it's on its wheels, so on its belly quite a lot less."

"It might not be that deep," said Frank, "you can paddle out a long way without the water getting deep enough to swim in. We think the 'plane has settled in the sand, you know like a stone; the water sort of washes around it and it settles in. That's why it's not moving."

"Signal from the church." said Peter. Frank picked up the slate ready to take dictation. Mark looked at the tail plane again and then scanned the horizon.

"Colonel," called Frank Maynard, "message reads white section moving up."

Mark climbed down from the tower. Apart from the two Scouts, himself, the Colonel and Elizabeth, he had seen nobody else.

"Is white section Sergeant Pavitt?" he asked, "I saw him when I was on the way to Home Farm and he said he'd be coming down."

"Yes, no point him getting his section here too early; he knows the tides as well as anybody else."

The pillbox was empty, save for a Vickers machine gun tripod and a signal lamp. The front line of the Home Front was a retired Colonel and two Scouts.

"Is there a gun for that tripod? Mark asked.

"Yes," said Peter, "they've got a Vickers gun and a Lewis. They don't keep them here, but when we got the code for 'invasion imminent' last July, we came here with all the weapons."

"Orders;" said the Colonel, "fight them on the beaches, said the Prime Minister, and that's what we were ready to do. It doesn't take long to get the trenches sorted out, so we'll have time if we get the codeword again."

"What codeword?"

"Cromwell means that an invasion is about to happen. Then we come here to win or die; there's nowhere for us to fall back to, whilst the Germans can always retreat into the sea."

Mark scanned the horizon, but apart from the submerged air machine, there was nothing war-related to see.

"Boys are patrolling the shoreline," said Colonel Mallinson, "as the tide goes out looking for anything interesting and they'll signal the control tower here if they find something."

"Speaking of which," said Frank Maynard from above, "the curlews are signalling now."

Peter took the slate for dictation. "Send the Colonel."

Mallinson mounted his horse and trotted off to see what they'd found. Mark wandered back to the haywain where Elizabeth was standing, almost between the giant horses.

"They like me," she said, "and they'll do anything I want them to."

"How do they get on with Farmer Murrell?"

"They respect him, but they like me. I fell asleep in the stable once and when I woke up they'd put a blanket over me and were standing either side of where I was sleeping, like book-ends."

"Can they get that 'plane out of the sea?"

"They'll try. I assume we tie the ropes to it and pull."

"It probably weighed more than two tons," said Mark, "before it filled up with water."

"Well," said Elizabeth, "they weigh about two tons each themselves and I've seen them pulling an elm tree trunk that Mister Murrell reckoned weighed eight tons, so we should be OK."

Mark joined Frank and Peter in the tower. Frank gave him the binoculars and pointed to where the curlew patrol and the Colonel were, near the water's edge. Mark could not see what they'd found, but the Colonel was dismounted and bent down with the boys standing around him.

"Pavitt's here," said Peter, "nine of them altogether."

Mark descended the tower and told Pavitt that the Colonel was down the beach with the curlews, the tail plane was visible and the tide was still going out.

"Firm sand here, Flight," said Sergeant Pavitt, "so we'll all get in the wagon and Miss Fforest will drive it towards the tail plane. Colonel Mallinson will ride over to us when he's ready to."

So that's what they did.

"The horses seem to like the water," observed Mark as they progressed.

"They go swimming sometimes," said Elizabeth, "on the beach off Jade's Farm. The bull likes the sea as well."

They were about half way to the tail plane with the water up to the axles when Sergeant Pavitt told Elizabeth to aim to the left of it.

"We want to turn in a half circle and end up with the rear of the wagon pointed at the tail plane."

Elizabeth drove as directed. The water did not get much deeper, but with the wagon in it they could see the speed at which the tide was ebbing. Pavitt said that the water could at times make twenty miles an hour, on the ebb and the flow.

She turned the wagon and got it where she thought Sergeant Pavitt meant. The horses stood still, the sea water racing against their fetlocks.

"Another few minutes and you'll see the tide ease," said Pavitt, "then we have about half an hour of slack before it starts pushing in again."

"So if we have the 'plane harnessed to the wagon, the flow might help us draw it to shore," said Mark.

"Maybe," said Pavitt, "or it might just wash over us and the 'plane and we'll all be swimming for it."

The Colonel rode up as the tide settled. The fuselage was now exposed, the cockpit canopy was closed. Colonel Mallinson dismounted his horse, stepping onto the submerged wing. The water did not come to the top of his riding boots. He edged to the cockpit and peered in.

"Chap's still in there," he said to nobody in particular, "so we'll try to get the machine closer to shore and then see what's to be done."

"What did the Scouts find?" asked Mark.

"Human remains. Hilton is sorting that out."

Men from white section slipped into the water and started rigging the ropes to the 'plane, around the wings and tail. Sergeant Pavitt set up the pioneering poles, which were already lashed to form a tripod.

"The idea is this," he said, "the ropes from the 'plane pass over this tripod to the back of the wagon. When the horses pull, they will be lifting the 'plane as well as pulling it back. If it works right, the tripod will fold under the 'plane and serve as runners to help ease it along the sand."

It did not work quite as intended. When Elizabeth set the rig moving, the tripod collapsed, but the wagon followed the horses and the 'plane dutifully followed the wagon. Five minutes later, the 'plane was in less than six inches of water. Mark got down to look at the damage. The propeller must still have been turning when it hit the sea. The whole nose seemed bent and the engine had, as best as he could tell, shifted backwards. One wing was bent and twisted.

"Try the cover, Sergeant Pavitt, let's see if we can get this chap out," said the Colonel.

As Pavitt fiddled with the canopy, Mark got closer, imagining that he, with his experience of Spitfires he would somehow be better qualified than the Home Guard sergeant at opening the Messerschmitt, but as he approached, it gave way to Pavitt's bayonet.

Nothing to that moment had prepared Mark for the stench. He'd smelled his own flesh burning, smelled other men who had burned; he was familiar with blood, sweat, puss, blisters, gangrene and vomit, but none of these was much of a learning curve for the experience of smelling a dead man who'd been sitting in the confined space of his cockpit in sea water for three weeks.

"We'll take care of this, sir," said Pavitt, "see to Miss Fforest if you wouldn't mind."

Elizabeth was watching from the driving seat of the haywain and despite being more than forty feet away, the paleness of her face and its greenish tinge told Mark that the smell had reached her there. He walked through the shallow water to join her on the bench.

"He wasn't as lucky as me," he said, "I managed to get out."

"What killed him?"

"I don't know; I can't see any bullet damage to the aircraft, but we can only see the top and bullets might have hit it from underneath."

"I don't think so," said the Colonel, "we'll know once the doctor has seen him, but I rather think he drowned; brought his kite down OK and then couldn't get the cockpit open from inside. The whole frame's bent; he should have released the canopy before impact."

The men managed to get the German pilot out of his cockpit and onto the stretcher they'd brought with them. Colonel Mallinson stepped forwards and took a cloth from his pocket, which he unfolded and used to cover the upper part of the man's body. As the Home Guard carried the stretcher past, Mark saw that it was an old Imperial German flag shrouding his enemy.

"Souvenir of the last bash," he said, "found it in a bunker when those chaps left their positions on Armistice Day and headed for home. Interesting day; rich pickings for those of us with souvenirs in mind."

He told Elizabeth to resume pulling the 'plane, which continued to follow the will of the carthorses. Half an hour passed before the wreck was above the high water mark. The troops detached the ropes and stowed all Farmer Murrell's kit in the wagon, laying the stretcher on top.

Mark sneaked a look at the cadaver. His body was bloated, swollen and waterlogged and with the German flag covering his upper body, no skin was visible. Mark could see that his boots looked like leather Wellingtons. His gauntlets were like those a motorcyclist would wear.

"Miss Fforest, take four men of white section to handle the stretcher, drive them to the Doctor Hardmann's house and then you can go back to the farm. Flight Lieutenant Brabham,

I'd appreciate it if you could remain here, so take your bicycle down."

Thus deployed, Mark waved goodbye to Elizabeth, who then set to delivering her gruesome cargo to the unsuspecting doctor.

The two Scout patrols returned, intent on playing with the aircraft.

"Not yet," said the Colonel, "Your skipper and I must first make sure that the guns are safe. We can't have you lot popping off valuable ammunition."

It was a struggle. They did not know how to clear the guns from the wreck, but they did manage to find the way in through the armourers' hatches to remove the ammunition from the four machine guns the 'plane was equipped with.

"Not much of it left," said Mark, "one good burst maybe, He'd used most of it up before his flight ended."

"Well," said Colonel Mallinson, "as far as RAF recovery is concerned, he'd used all of it up and if Pavitt finds a way of ripping that wing off, we'll detach the gun from it at leisure and the RAF can have the rest."

Colonel Mallinson slipped Mark a damp brown paper bag, "souvenir of the day for you," he said, "might be useful."

Mark looked in the bag, which seemed to contain a wet greenish lump of something leather and sort of heart-shaped. He took it out of the bag and saw a buckle in the middle; undoing the buckle revealed the handle of a rusty Luger pistol.

"I borrowed it off that pilot," said the Colonel, "he didn't object. Your uncle will show you how to clean it. The ammunition may still be OK, but if not I've got some you can have."

Mark had a revolver with him but had not told anybody. So now he had a pistol as well and what he needed was somewhere discreet to try them both out. By then he was feeling quite used up and asked the Colonel if he could be excused.

"Yes, of course; tell the rector what's been happening. The doctor will give us a cause of death and report the casualty to the coroner. I expect that we'll bury that chap locally, so your uncle will need to plan. Can't have him above ground for long, smelling like that."

Laurie joined them with the human remains they'd found in a canvas sack. Mark returned his bicycle and then walked to the village, where he saw that his uncle was standing outside the butcher's shop holding his horse and talking to Harry Roberts.

"Well, Mark, you look worn out; I heard about the 'plane having the pilot in it, just on my way to see the doctor now."

"Good," said Mark, "saves me asking you to. The Colonel assumes he'll be buried here."

"Yes, once the coroner has been informed and we have a death certificate. Probably Tuesday. You headed home?"

"Yes, I need some rest."

"OK, can you take the meat I've just paid for up to Martha?"

Harry Roberts handed him the brown-wrapped parcel. Mark fumbled a bit to take that without it touching his damp brown-wrapped souvenir of the day.

"What's that?" Both Roberts and Uncle Tom asked him, almost in unison.

"Er, gift from Colonel Mallinson."

Uncle Tom took the package and peeked inside. Then, without fully unwrapping it, he turned the bag so that Harry Roberts could look in.

"Ah-hah."

"Uh-huh."

"The Colonel said you would show me how to clean it."

"Did he indeed, well be careful getting home with it. You've got a pistol you shouldn't have and some meat that exceeds our rations and the police station to get past between here and the rectory."

CHAPTER 5

MARK SCUTTLED PAST THE police station without anyone accosting him and made it home. He'd left both the meat and the pistol with Martha in the kitchen in his haste to get to a bath and she showed Tom the holstered gun when he came in.

"Hmm, what would be best to clean the leather up, do you think? It's quite smelly."

"Maybe soap and hot water first, then get lots of your saddle soap on it before it dries out and cracks."

"OK, you tackle the holster, I'll take care of the pistol."

Mark came down from his bath and they had a drink together before dinner.

"Did you see the pilot?" Mark asked his uncle.

"Yes; the doctor was looking for a cause of death when I got there."

"I haven't seen a dead body close up like that before; the smell..."

"It's a reminder that we are all mortal, Mark; he had his dinner jacket and medals on under his flight suit. The last morning he got dressed he'd planned on going straight from his sortie to a party."

Tom said he'd drowned, but he had also sustained injuries in the crash-landing as the airframe bent damaging his legs. They talked about Colonel Mallinson's attempts to keep the machine guns for the Home Guard. Tom said that they'd failed because word got round that the 'plane had been salvaged and too many people had been down to the beach and seen it with both wings.

"The policeman was also there asking why Colonel Mallinson hadn't reported the aircraft to him. Colonel said he had his own chain of command to report to, through which RAF recovery would be triggered. The bobby reckons he should take charge of military salvage, the finding of human remains and so forth so the Colonel gave him a pair of legs in a canvas sack to deal with."

II

Sunday morning dawned. Mark had seen many elements of the community, but this Sunday was the monthly church parade for all the uniformed organisations; cubs and scouts, brownies and guides, local military personnel, Home Guard and other civil defence volunteers would all parade. The convention that had built up since the start of the war was that on the church parade Sunday, veterans would wear their medals and servicemen would wear their uniforms. On this day, the Home Front paraded in an expression of their faith in God and their solidarity with one another in the common purpose of preserving England as a free country.

Mark had considered his options and decided to wear his RAF uniform, as befitted a serviceman on sick leave in the parish, but he'd attend the village hall in good time and then march up to the church with the youth groups. The day was crisp and bright when he set off and he was halfway to the village hall before he became aware of the revolver in his greatcoat pocket. Nothing to be done about it now, he decided; at least it was discreet, as opposed to being in a holster and visible to all. The only problem was he could not clutch the grip while marching.

There was quite a crowd outside the hall when he got there. Laurie Hilton was organising the scouts. Elizabeth Fforest arrived in her Land Army uniform, one of three riding in a small pony and trap. They came straight over to Mark and she introduced Alice Buick and Hilda Clark, who both looked very fit. Then she went off to sort out brownies and guides.

All Mark knew about these two ladies was the rumour from the Post Office that they preferred hanging around the searchlight battery crew to doing any community work.

"Do the searchlight crews parade to this service?" he asked, not being able to think of anything else to say.

"No," said Alice, "Eastminster is nearer for them and they have to march to the service."

"Pity," said Mark, "I haven't met any of them yet."

"We go over once a week in the trap," said Alice, "we're doing their laundry for them at Home Farm, so if you want to tour the positions, you could join us Tuesday morning."

"Mister Murrell lets you do that for them?"

"It was his idea; he got talking to their officer. The men have no facilities and they are living in tents. Mister Murrell wanted to do something for them and clean, dry clothes is what they wanted."

Alice had, Mark judged, a London accent. Enfield born and bred where her father worked in the rifle factory. Hilda said she was an army child. She'd been born in Belfast when her dad served there during the troubles in 1920 and she'd moved around with his postings.

Colonel Mallinson appeared on horseback riding next to Farmer Murrell; the two in deep conversation. Their wives rode behind, both side-saddle and engaged in a lively debate.

Scouts were knotting together and staring at Mark and as they were the one section that he had yet to officially meet he went over to Peter Law for introductions. He took his hat off and said hello to everyone, that he was looking forwards to the troop meeting on Tuesday and took the chance to look at the badges they had on. The locals were Sea Scouts, while the Londoners were a mixture. Mark saw London county badges on both land and Sea Scout uniforms. Some first class Scouts, some with second class. Several national service and civil defence badges, ambulance badges, a couple of marksmen. He noticed that the Honour Guard for the flags had .22 rimfire ammunition in their woggles.

"We carry five rounds that way," said Derek Pilley, patrol leader of the otters, "the ammunition is in cardboard boxes and they fall apart in pockets." Derek was the thickest set of the boys Mark had met; short and with curly blond hair that would not be managed by his hat.

Laurie Hilton took charge of the scouts;

"COLOUR PARTY, FALL IN."

Elizabeth returned from the hall, the cubs in a crocodile behind her. She told Mark that the cubs would fall in behind the scouts and then led them round into position. Mark called the cub flag party to fall in and then took a position next to them; Elizabeth went off to sort the brownies out.

Sergeant Pavitt fell the Home Guard in ready to march in front of the scouts. The Home Guard had no flag of their own, so they paraded the flag of St George that belonged to the Rover Crew, all of whom were absent from the parish on military duties.

Elizabeth sorted the brownies out to march behind the cubs. They had no flag party, just Esther carrying their small brown pennant. The guides sorted themselves out behind the brownies with Mrs Harvey taking charge. Behind them an assortment of adults took positions. The postman and two other men in their Air Raid Patrol uniforms: several land girls and a couple of nurses: Bob Murrell and seven other veterans. Colonel Mallinson had a word with Sergeant Pavitt, and then fell in with the veterans at the rear.

The column wound its way out of the village hall yard and into the street where PC Fidgeon stood in the road to stop traffic for the column, had there been any traffic to stop. When the column finished passing him, he stepped into the rear rank and marched to the church with the veterans.

The church tower stood at the west end of the building and entry to the church was through the door in the bottom of the tower. The front of the column reached the church door before the whole column was in the churchyard. Sergeant Pavitt fell his men out; his flag-bearer and guard waiting to one side while the other men took their caps off and went into church.

Laurie halted the Scout section and fell the colour party out.

"CUBS AND SCOUTS IN THE CHOIR, FALL OUT AND GET ROBED."

"That includes me," he said to Mark, "send the remaining cubs and scouts into church. Those who have relatives inside will go and sit with them, those who do not occupy the front three rows on the south side of the main aisle. Sergeant Pavitt will take care of the colour parties."

Mark dismissed the cubs so that the brownies and guides could move up. Elizabeth released the brownies and them followed them into church. Mark timed it so that they went in together; his plan was to sit with her, but due to the agility of the verger, he wound up with three books and sitting in the south aisle with his Aunt Hetty and Martha.

"We'll keep the seat nearest the aisle for Esther so that she can join us after the colour parade," said Hetty, "It's a good turnout."

This seat placed Mark next to the pews occupied by the unaccompanied cubs and scouts. Elizabeth was in the north aisle next to the brownies. The other two land girls had joined her; Mrs Harvey was in the pew behind them with her sister Miss Everett. Colonel Mallinson had joined his wife halfway back up the centre aisle with Farmer and Mrs Murrell sharing the same pew.

The tone of the organ changed from incidental music to what amounted to a fanfare, and then went silent for Tom to announce the hymn, the jingoistic 'once to every man and nation', serving Mark as another reminder of his country's expectations of him when he got better.

The choir moved into their stalls and the colour parties brought their flags to the altar. By the time the hymn was over, everybody was in place and the tune was fixed in Mark's mind as a powerful incentive to get better and to fight again; he looked forward to the moment to decide and he felt quite good about himself, in that church and surrounded by that congregation, despite every healing wound screaming for attention.

Tom read out the bans of marriage for three forthcoming weddings. He followed this with notices of events and meetings in the coming week and then announced that the German airman brought in from the sea would be buried in the churchyard during the week, "probably Tuesday, but I will put notice of the day and time in the usual places as soon as I can. I expect the coroner to release the body tomorrow."

The service proceeded through to communion, partaken by sixty-two people. The colour bearers collected their flags during the final hymn and processed west along the centre aisle, followed by the choir. Tom gave the benediction and grace and then waited by the door to greet people as they left. The march to the village hall was the reverse of the march up, except that the flags were raised into the leather buckets and flown and, led by Elizabeth, the cubs and brownies sang the Welsh lullaby 'Calon Lan' as they marched.

"She's taught the little ones several Welsh songs," said Derek Pilley in response to Mark's unasked question, "and if you look back, Colonel Mallinson is singing it as well."

Indeed he was; knowing the words from having commanded Welsh soldiers in the last war.

III

At the hall, the units were dismissed; some people drifted off or were met, while most stayed for tea. Mark perched himself in a position near the stage and soon found that he was popular, as lots of people wanted a word. He still felt uncomfortable, but he enjoyed the morning. People were getting used to him, he thought. Mrs Murrell introduced herself with an American accent.

"Heard quite a lot about you from Miss Fforest," she said, "although I thought you would have been more disfigured from the way she described you."

"Sorry to disappoint," said Mark, "although I still scare myself when I encounter a mirror."

"I didn't mean it like that," she said, "I suppose it's hard to describe your injuries to people unfamiliar with burns. My husband suffered a serious burn in the last war, so when she talked about you I tried to picture your injury the way Bob was hurt."

"What was he in?" asked Mark.

"Navy; H.M.S. Chester and he was wounded at Jutland. His legs were burned and his face was damaged."

"His face looks fine now."

"Yes, and I think it was as bad as yours. He got better in time, but he still finds strong sunlight a problem. He thinks the salt water did him some good."

"My doctor thinks that as well; I landed in the sea but my lifejacket kept my head out of the water."

Mark looked around for the land girls, but not seeing them he drifted to the door to look for the trap, which was gone. PC Fidgeon, standing across the yard, came over for a word. Taller than Mark, he had a round face, sandy hair and matching moustache.

"I hear you'll be running the cubs and scouts whilst you're here Mister Brabham," he said, "so we'll doubtless see quite a lot of each other."

"Flight Lieutenant Brabham and quite possibly," said Mark, "although I need to be careful as I am only slowly recovering from my injuries."

"Indeed," said PC Fidgeon, "but another pair of eyes and ears in the village. I heard you were at the beach when that German fighter pilot was recovered."

"Yes,"

"I'm looking for his pistol. Those Boche usually carry one but that pilot was unarmed when I saw him at the doctor's."

"Indeed. What was he wearing?"

"Sort of flight suit and boots, life jacket, gauntlets, leather helmet; had his dinner jacket and bow tie on underneath."

"Well, there's your answer. If he'd got home, he'd have left the flying kit in his cockpit and gone off to whatever function he was dressed up for. He wouldn't wear the pistol to a party and he wouldn't have left it in the 'plane either."

"I see; did you carry your pistol in flight?"

"That's straying into the confidential, Mister Fidgeon and on a need-to-know basis I'm sure you'll understand..."

"Police Constable Fidgeon and yes indeed sir, but we must be careful about guns where the public might have access to them. Those rifles the Scouts have; I want them handed in at the police station for safekeeping. They've no business keeping them in houses and billets and carrying them about in the street."

"Really? I thought there was a war on."

"There is and civilians shouldn't get mixed up in it. If the Germans come, they'll be in trouble, whereas if they stick to being schoolboys, they should be all right. Look at it from my point of view; if the Germans come, like they did in the Channel Islands, who do you think the Germans will expect to go around collecting the guns up? It will be me, like on Guernsey."

"So you want to disarm the county before the German invasion to make your job of policing it afterwards easier?"

"And safer for all, sir. Guns and people are a bad combination."

Mark had no answer so he pondered and in doing so he noticed that PC Fidgeon's chest was devoid of medal ribbons, as was his own.

Eventually he said, "I don't think the Germans will come. I did my bit to stop them in the recent air battle and next year I'll be ready to do it again, but if they do come in the meantime, the people here will make them sorry that they did."

"No good will come of children carrying guns about, Flight; it's only a matter of time before there's an accident, or worse."

Mark took his leave of the police constable and, having no reason to re-enter the hall he set off along the street, heading home. He'd reached the butcher's shop before Laurie Hilton caught him up.

"What was that copper after?"

"Your rifles; thinks that they should be kept at the police station instead of in homes and billets."

"and what did you say?"

"I didn't know what to say. It's none of his business, is it; the rifles belong to the London scouts, so they are responsible for them. What do you think?"

"I think you're right about the scouts who are responsible for them remaining in charge of their property. You'll see them all on Tuesday, maybe that's the time to take a view."

IV

Tom was already in his study with a cup of tea when he entered. Mark told him about the conversation with the policeman before edging to the subject of the weddings and that he didn't recognise any of the names.

"That's because of the way the population has shifted due to the war. There's a lot of people come to the area from London and not just evacuees. People who can find somewhere to live and maybe some work have left London too. The three happy couples are all notionally of this parish and live here at the moment, but that's because they got on trains and this is as far as the lines go from London."

"So, refugees, sort of."

"Yes; people were filtering into Britain from Europe for some years before the war. A lot had to get out of Spain after the civil war there and Chancellor Hitler's Nazi Party made life impossible for some people in Germany. They revoked the German citizenship of people of the Jewish faith, you know, so some of them came here, including our Doctor Hardmann."

After a bit of lunch, Mark walked across to the church. The scouts kept an observation position on the tower, logging aircraft movements and keeping in visual contact with the Home Guard observation point on the beach. The scout on tower watch saw Mark cross the churchyard and acknowledged him by raising his lemon-squeezer hat when he saw Mark look up.

Entering the church, Mark turned through the small door leading to the spiral staircase by which the tower could be ascended. On top, the roof was flat and surrounded by battlements, apart from the corner where the staircase opened onto the roof. The centre of the spiral staircase was also, for the last twelve feet or so, the base of the church's flagpole. Three flags lay furled on a shelf just inside the door; a Union flag and a Cross of St George were easy to identify, but the third?

"It's a church flag," said Frank Ball, "not sure what it does; they haven't wanted it flown since I got here."

Frank Ball was a London evacuee, dressed in a khaki shirt, covered by his overcoat, and navy corduroy shorts. They shook left-handed in the Scout style;

"Gently, Frank, that's my gammy hand, you see. You are in the Home Guard as well?"

"Yes, skipper. There's no rover crew for us to go up to when we are old enough, so the Colonel takes us into the Home Guard as the next step toward growing up, but we parade as scouts and take our turns as scouts on the observation duties. If there's an invasion, Laurie has a Home Guard rifle and I've got a twenty-two repeater; we'll find a way of stopping them."

Mark wanted to see the aircraft movement log, from which it was clear that enemy activity was much reduced in daylight.

"What do you reckon, skipper?" Frank was keen to hear a qualified interpretation of the detailed observations that had been kept from the tower all summer. Mark flicked back to 31st August, the day on which he fell from the sky - an event that passed this church tower unnoticed - and then forwards analysing the gradual shift in behaviour.

"My best guess is that the Germans are switching tactics to fit the changing seasons," said Mark, "they've been hitting military targets all summer; airfields, factories, the docks and now they seem to have switched to night raiding to take advantage of the longer hours of darkness."

Night flying was quite different to daylight sorties. The aircraft could not fly in formation, so they instead flew in a stream, following a compass bearing. They could not identify individual targets, so it was a case of bombing the area in which the target stood instead of aiming at it. Londoners were experiencing this night after night and the glow of the city burning could be seen in the night sky from the church tower.

It was a grim time for the evacuee cubs and scouts; they knew that they'd been moved out of London for their own safety, but they all had friends and relatives under that blitz. The RAF were limited in their ability to intercept such raiders at night; they flew Bristol Blenheims and tried to infiltrate the unescorted bomber streams to get individual aircraft either on their way to a target or on their way back, using a primitive and still secret radar system. The ground defences of London were searchlight and ack-ack batteries, barrage balloons and hope.

"We can't count their aircraft at night," said Frank.

The tower was equipped with a ship's binnacle and a good telescope on a tripod. The compass in the binnacle was what they used to try to get an alignment of any raider's course. The raiders themselves were using the last of the limited November daylight to take off and gain height; then they could align themselves with the Thames estuary and fly on instruments towards the target areas.

Mark wondered about the return flight; the log showed that the raiders followed a reverse bearing to get home at greater height, but they would have to land in the dark. So, were pilots radioing their bases? Were landing lights being turned on? Could RAF night operations use those lights to damage enemy airfields as they raiders landed?

"Sorry, Frank, lost in thought for a moment. Any signals from the coast?"

"Separate log, skipper," said Frank, handing him the book, "but nothing today. It's all quiet."

Mark used the telescope to see how well it showed the beach position. He could see where the German fighter was resting, now covered by a tarpaulin and awaiting RAF recovery.

Returning to ground level, he exchanged pleasantries with the lads in church, and then headed back to the rectory. It occurred to him that Monday was his day off; he was scheduled to be at scouts on Tuesday, then the Home Guard met on Wednesday, cubs on Thursday, and Home Guard Friday. He wondered whether he could ask Elizabeth out on Monday night, but dismissed the idea, as she'd be at the guides meeting. Friday night would be a better bet; he could avoid the Home Guard parade, not being an official member.

The next problem was where to go? Lavering was not a hotbed of nightlife. Tom said that Chelmsford had a cinema and that would be a possibility. Would she go out on a date though? He had two of the three necessities for attracting a young lady to take an interest in him – money and a motorcar. He no longer had the good looks that ran in the family, but in the circumstances, two out of three was better than nothing and there was no obvious competition in the land girl dating stakes in Lavering yet.

The next problem was one of discretion; Lavering was small enough for no secrets to hide in, so if she'd go on a date with him, everybody would know of it. Chances were, if she said no, that would become common knowledge, so how to approach this?

He kept his thoughts to himself, the better to wrestle with them at leisure and spent the remainder of Sunday using it as the day of rest God intended it to be.

CHAPTER 6

Monday's post brought Mark two letters, both in brown envelopes. The first advised him to attend an outpatient appointment at the hospital on Friday, so that blew his fantasies about taking Elizabeth on a date this week, and the other advised him that he had been gazetted for the Distinguished Flying Cross.

After breakfast, Mark headed for the beach on a borrowed bicycle, intending to be there when the RAF recovery crew turned up. As it happened, they had beaten him to it and the Home Guardsmen who had been waiting with the machine had gone on about their business. The military police were in a private motorcar and the RAF crew of six had a flatbed lorry and winch. Mark chatted with a military policeman while they watched the recovery in progress. The men knew how to unbolt the wings, which they did efficiently. The fuselage was winched onto the flatbed and the wings loaded either side.

"Local Home Guard will be sorry to see it go," said Mark, "they did so want a machine gun from it for the pillbox here."

"There's no ammunition left on that crate," said the military policeman, "and no easy way to mount one of those guns for hand operation anyway."

"I know it's not practical," said Mark, "it's a morale thing really; the Home Guard work so hard and are dedicated to what they are doing, but they lack equipment."

The recovery complete, the crew piled onto their lorry and started the drive to the airframe graveyard near Debden. The military policeman went to the boot of his car.

"Got this machine gun off a Ju88," he said, "you can present it to the Home Guard to keep them sweet. I haven't got any ammunition for it, but it takes the same belts as the guns on that fighter."

"Thank you," said Mark, "they'll be delighted with it."

The MP saluted Mark's rank and then went on his way escorting the lorry. Mark had a look at the weapon; long barrel and receiver with a large pistol grip. He could envisage it on a bomber, sticking out of the back of the cockpit canopy spitting bullets at passing RAF fighters. Then it dawned on him that he was by himself on the beach with a bicycle and a weighty machine gun. The weapon had no sling, since on the aircraft it would be spigot mounted. Mark looked to the church tower but could not see if it was manned.

He had a look in the pillbox, which had no door as such. He could see a pair of semaphore flags and the Aldis lamp, which he took outside and set it up to signal the church tower.

He signalled to see if the tower was occupied. The reply was immediate, but in semaphore and read 'S.E.C.O.N.D. O.T.T.E.R.'

So why was that scout not in school, Mark wondered. He hit the Morse key again to send 'W.H.E.R.E.I.S.C.O.L.M.A.L.L.I.'

Before he got to the end of his message the reply signal started and read;

'A.T.H.O.M.E.'

Mark sent 'O.K.B.E.A.C.H.E.M.P.T.Y.' He knew where the entrance to the Colonel's drive was and it was about two thirds of the way back to the village. He considered his options and then resolved to put the machine gun on one shoulder and push the bicycle in preference to trying to ride it. He figured he could get to the Colonel's house in about twenty minutes.

It took more like forty minutes; he had to change shoulders several times before he thought of putting the weapon on the bicycle. Then it was easy and he turned into Colonel Mallinson's drive feeling quite pleased with himself.

The drive itself was gravel and passed through some mixed woodland. After about fifty yards the vista opened out onto a lawn at the back of which stood the Colonel's large, rambling house. Mark continued up the drive; there were several ways into this property and while Mark was making up his mind which to head for, he saw the Colonel and his butler, one each end of a long crosscut saw, grinding away at a log perched on a saw horse.

"Flight Lieutenant Brabham bearing gifts, good morning," said the Colonel.

"Good morning sir," said Mark, "I..."

"You found that weapon and thought to deliver it to a good home."

"Sort of." Mark explained the morning's events and how he came to have the machine gun from the military policeman.

"Jolly decent of him," said the Colonel, "and it's the same belts as the guns on that fighter?"

"Yes," said Mark, "according to the MP."

Colonel Mallinson relieved Mark of the weight and they headed for the open French doors together.

"Do come in, Mark, but please leave the bicycle outside."

The doors led straight into the Colonel's study, which was the sort of room he would have imagined for the Colonel; large desk, several leather chairs, hundreds of books lining the walls, a few hunting trophies, a portrait of...an ancestor perhaps?

Colonel Mallinson laid the weapon on his desk, and then fiddled with the receiver until it flipped open.

"Definitely belt fed," he said to himself; "have a play later. We'll have tea, Eric, can we have tea please? Then we'll see if we can get this gun working. Do we have any of that German belted ammunition here?"

"Yes," said Eric, "I split it between here and the butcher's shop."

He went to make the tea.

Mark looked around the room and his eyes landed on a rifle rack in the corner. Glass-fronted and baize-lined, it held several weapons.

"I was in India for many years," said Colonel Mallinson, "and when I came back to England I brought my guns with me. Nothing special – a big game double rifle and a double shotgun, my old Martini Henry and a Howdah pistol. I picked up that Lee Metford in South Africa at the end of the Boer War and I finished the last war with a few more souvenirs, some of which are serving with the Home Guard, including my Fulton-regulated Short Lee Enfield and my target-sighted P14."

Mark knew that a Howdah was an elephant saddle, but otherwise all that jargon went over his head. What he did spot in the back of the cabinet was the Colonel's medals. It had not occurred to him before, but most people he'd met had been wearing their ribbons, so he could read their chests. Colonel Mallinson did not, so Mark saw the gongs for the first time.

"I had a letter today," said Mark, "I am gazetted for the Distinguished Flying Cross."

"Well, congratulations," said the Colonel, "you undoubtedly deserve it. Do you know when you'll be decorated?"

"Not yet," said Mark, "I thought you might have an idea, as you've been there a few times yourself."

"Oh yes, but that was all a long time ago," said the Colonel, "and all my medals are routine issues – the Coronation medal for Old George the fifth and the Delhi Durbar in 1911. They came in the post. I expect that the way things are done has changed. They'll probably slip it to you at the hospital, some old coffin-dodger like me will be handing them out and saying something gracious to each new hero. I'm quite jealous, you know, I'd give anything to have flown against the Germans in the summer battle."

"Can you fly?"

"No, never been off the ground, but to have eight machine guns to point at the enemy all at once...must have been terrific."

"Yes, terrific." Mark's mind flashed back to the horrors of burning alive in his crippled machine four miles above the earth.

The tea arrived. Mark and the Colonel discussed current German tactics for a while before Eric returned with some German ammunition in a belt. Mark's attention returned to the Colonel's medals; a Distinguished Service Order and Bar, Military Cross, Sudan medal, Queen's South Africa trio from the Boer War: Great War trio, Croix de Guerre, long service, Territorial Decoration and a couple Mark did not recognize. The Colonel had been around.

"DSO and bar and the MC weren't for attending parades, Colonel? How is it that you don't wear your ribbons to the Home Guard parades?"

"It's because I haven't got the ribbons," said the Colonel, "they were on the tunic I used to wear to territorial events and the like; gave all that up in '31. Then in 1936 Mrs Mallinson and I were invited to a garden party at Buckingham Palace, Edward the Eighth you know; so I got my tunic out and it didn't fit; must have shrunk in the wardrobe. Anyway, my good wife threw it out, ribbons and all. My best fountain pen in the pocket, my pipe…threw it out. So I haven't got the ribbons, nor have I got around to picking up some more yet; there's a war on, you know."

"I didn't realize that you'd carried on after the war."

"Well, I did and I didn't. I was surplus to government requirements when the fighting ended, so when we were shipped home, most of the men were demobilized and the rest of us went on leave. That's when the claustrophobia caught me, arriving at my own front door – I couldn't go in so I went for a walk. That took me to the creek and past the boathouse and that's when I realized that I wanted to be out in a boat and not indoors, so before setting foot in my house I went to see the scoutmaster and we made a date for the scouts to take me out in their cutter gig. Then I felt able to come home."

"So it was like a shock, after the danger was over?"

"Yes, just like that. Not a twinge of anything through all my military service and then -wham – after it was all over. I was comforted by the scouts rowing – I took the tiller to steer – but it wasn't enough. I went on every boat parade, learned to row, skull and sail. Then butcher Roberts got wind of the steam yacht being available to buy. Love drove a steam roller before the war and he reckoned he could get it going and Roberts knew the sea. We used to borrow scouts to crew it until it was mentioned to me that Wilkinson never went out. I visited him and discovered we had opposite problems, him not going out and me not liking being in so I persuaded him to come boating with me and he taught me to fish. We used to go out so often that Roberts called himself a butcher and fishmonger for a while."

Mark decided that this would be a good moment to take his leave of them, which he did with a minimum of fuss since both men clearly wanted to get on with playing with their new machine gun.

II

After lunch he asked his uncle about the scout being on the church tower instead of in school.

"It's complicated," said Tom, "but when the London children were evacuated last year they came with two teachers. One went back to London, couldn't stand it here, so there are too many children and not enough teachers or classrooms. They have been divided into four ability groups and each group gets half a day's schooling. There's only one classroom in the school so one lot go there and the others use the village hall."

"Why did the teacher go back to London; surely you need them here?"

"Not everybody appreciated being evacuated from London, or other cities come to that. Some of the kids have gone as well, run away home. It's hurting those who are still here, you know, as their mates are under the nightly bombing, along with their friends and relatives. We have been lucky, so far, that none of the civilians killed in London has been related to any of our evacuees."

"I hadn't thought of it like that; some of them seem to fit in quite well."

"They do; some love it here, but others struggle. Peter Law and his brother are camping in Home Farm's orchard. They couldn't stand their billet for some reason; never got to the bottom of that. They wanted to go home but their mother told them to stay put; she works in London and their Dad's away, so they've been camping out for most of this year. Others have fitted in better; they aren't all in school either. Harry Roberts the butcher has a delivery boy who is an evacuee and the two lads delivering the baker's bread are from London as well."

Settling into his leather chair Tom explained the culture-clash between town and country;

"Out here the pace and pattern of life is dictated by the changing seasons, while the London kids had no idea about the way the corners of the year are turned. All they know for sure is that summer is warmer than winter. They didn't understand the significance of spring, or the way country work builds up to the harvest. Some like it more than others. The land girls are all keen; given the choice I don't think they'd rush back to the cities, but many of the children, especially the younger ones, would rather be with their parents, whatever the risks and privations."

Mark did his best to absorb the information; beneath the apparently smooth way that village life was ordered were all sorts of pressures and problems. The village society was much changed by so many people having gone away to the war, and that war had, in turn, tipped many strangers into the village who did not fit in.

"I have been wondering," said Mark, "about asking Elizabeth Fforest to go out with me."

"Well, simple solution," said Tom, "is the monthly dance in the village hall; no need to invite her, all the local land girls turn up anyway, some RAF personnel from nearby facilities along with the few eligible bachelors still in the area."

"Are there many of them?"

"Eligible bachelors, no; the oldest scouts will attend, as will any servicemen on leave. Maybe a few from the coastal batteries, but girls outnumber boys at such dances these days."

"I meant land girls: I'm in with a chance?"

"I'm guessing, but a battle-scarred RAF man with a medal on his chest must be an attractive proposition for a working-class Welsh girl. You could do better, you know. There are plenty of other land girls, nurses, WAAFs and some young widows."

"With no face?"

"Mark, I don't know quite how to put this; when she's walking beside you, she can't see your face, same as when the lights are out."

"Why would the lights be out?"

"We are going to have to have a long chat sometime about what grown-ups do. There are things that you should know before embarking on such an adventure with one of the fairer sex, even a dark Welsh working-class one."

Mark fell in with what was being said; sitting in the dark saved money and reduced the risk of breaching blackout regulations.

"Oh, and whilst I think of it this parcel came for you."

III

This proved to be some bits and pieces of his scout uniform and a letter from his mother, which did not mention that she had been to the hospital more than once while he was asleep. She found herself in the conflict of her duties to national security and the needs of her son. She was now engaged in secret war work and returning home to Cheshire occasionally – but her letter made it clear that visiting him should have been her highest priority, especially after Prime Minister Churchill's kind words about so much being owed by so many to so few.

Two resolutions formed themselves in his mind as he fought his tears; one was to see his mother as soon as he could and the other was to fly again in combat. Colonel Mallinson was right to be jealous of him flying the fastest eight-gun monoplane fighter in the world into the packed ranks of the Nazi war machine. He would joyfully do it again; he would do it against the odds; in fact, if he were guaranteed that he could not survive a sortie he would still do it, paying the Germans back for the perpetual itching of his wounds and the reflection in his mirror. He would rather be one of the glorious dead than a living cripple.

He was just getting over that thought with the aid of a handkerchief when Aunt Hetty breezed in, towing Martha in her wake.

"Mark, are you unwell?"

"No, the Scout stuff is dusty, it got to me...."

"Does it need washing?" asked Martha, "I can do it now and dry it for tomorrow if you like."

"I think it will be alright, thanks," said Mark, "I can't wear the shorts or socks yet. I think what I'll do is wear the shirt with my RAF trousers and Scout belt."

"OK, I'll wash the other stuff so it's ready for when you are," said Martha, "and I'll put them in the wardrobe, so they are easy to find."

Aunt Hetty poured sherry; a large one for her and a small one for Mark.

"So, how goes it between you and Miss Fforest?"

"I need a bigger sherry than this to discuss such a delicate matter, Aunty."

She topped him up: he took a healthy mouthful and she topped him up again. The sherry was brownish and quite sweet, but it also packed a punch.

"How are you getting on with Miss Fforest, the land girl?"

"Very well, I think. I have been thinking of asking her out, maybe to the cinema, but my next chance was Friday and that's out now because I've got to go to the hospital."

"What's the matter with Saturday?"

"Nothing, really. I didn't know about the dance. Uncle Tom thinks she'll be there anyway, so there's no need to ask, but that doesn't seem quite right."

"I don't see why not," said Hetty, "before we married, Tom and I met all the time at functions without either of us inviting the other."

"Just turn up and see what happens?"

"Yes; you'll see if anyone else is interested in her and whether she's interested in anyone. The war makes a difference, you know; like last time – class distinctions become less important, less relevant."

Tom ambled in at this point.

"The funeral will be Wednesday. Can't have it tomorrow because the gravedigger can't get here until first thing Wednesday morning, but he says 11am would be good so that's what we will do."

"What's the form?"

"There isn't one. I will treat him as a stranger from the sea, rather than thinking of him as an enemy alien. I will write to the War Graves Commission – they keep an account of such matters and I will also place an entry in the Times newspaper. German spies read the Times and the Red Cross will pass details of his funeral to the German Embassy in Switzerland."

"What was his name? Do we know?"

"Yes, he was Adolf Heimsch. We don't know how old he was, but he'd been around: quite decorated. It is to be hoped that the Germans will let the Red Cross have a few details for his headstone."

CHAPTER 7

TUESDAY DAWNED; MARK WAS ready for it and to get to Home Farm to join the land girls on their tour of the guns and searchlight batteries he would use his car.

It started for him first twist of the crank handle and throbbed reassuringly, so he set off, driving cautiously. The main street was quiet and other than PC Fidgeon patrolling near the butcher's shop, Mark saw nobody he recognised until he got onto the road out of the village where he saw Elizabeth Fforest driving the small cart loaded with milk churns. They waived to each other as he passed her. The drive to Home Farm took him less time than the walk to the village hall. He parked the car where he hoped it was out of the way and wandered towards the main farmhouse, as Hilda emerged from one of the sheds;

"Good morning, ready for the battlefield tour?"

"Yes, sort of."

Alice was harnessing the carthorses in the next yard. Robert Murrell was in the milking parlour and Mrs Murrell in the kitchen. Everybody acknowledged him when they saw him, but each continued with the morning's chores.

"I saw Elizabeth with the small cart," said Mark.

"Taking milk to the station," said Alice, "we do that every day and she'll bring the empty churns back for cleaning."

Once the wagon was ready, Hilda and Alice climbed up onto the seat, squeezing together to make room for Mark. They took off at a steady pace out of Home Farm's drive, north towards Bradwell, then right towards the coast. The land was flat, apart from a few bomb craters. Alice pointed to one she said was new, then another and another. Between the girls they reckoned that six of the craters had appeared since last week.

"It's like having a really nasty mole, always making a mess," said Alice.

Mark was left wondering if all the bombs had gone off. He knew from airfield attacks how often they failed to explode and then had to be dug out and defused.

"Well here it won't matter," said Alice, "they can stay where they are."

The fields gave way to shallow dunes, marsh grass and then the first military camp; six brown tents, each fourteen feet square, stood with their doors and walls rolled up. There was no perimeter fence as such, but Mark saw sandbagged positions scattered about. A machine gun pit occupied one side of the road, with slit trenches nearby and beyond he could see the covered positions containing the guns and searchlights.

These were quite well spread out. Mark guessed that the six positions he could see were distributed along more than a quarter of a mile of coast. Their spacing was random, it seemed. They weren't in a straight line, nor were they evenly staggered.

"It's to do with the lie of the land," explained their officer, "when I surveyed the area I wanted the guns in natural depressions to make them easier to conceal and there was our track plan to consider also."

Mark took a tour of the positions, which consisted of four 3.7-inch guns and two 90-centimetre searchlights.

"We watch and listen at night," said the officer, "radar tells us if or when enemy aircraft are going to come in range of our position. When that happens, we try to illuminate them – that helps us gauge their height, then we try to shoot them down."

"Any success so far?"

"Hit one the other night on his way in. He dumped his bombs in the fields behind us and made a wide turn back out to sea. We don't know what happened after that, but we stopped him delivering the payload where he wanted to. That makes six whose missions we've interrupted, so far."

Mark looked around for the church tower but it was out of sight. The officer said that it was out of sight, too many trees in the way, but if he put a position forward on the beach, he could see the Home Guard's pillbox signals.

"We have field telephones to keep in touch with radar," he said, "we aren't integrated with the Home Guard – separate command structures and everything, although we keep in touch. Colonel Mallinson had me brief his men, so I could use them if necessary and he can call us out if he needs extra people in the village."

It felt isolated and desolate on this stretch of coast in November. The officer was cheerful enough, but his men – all from Ulster – were tired and homesick.

II

The laundry mission accomplished, Mark joined the land girls for the drive back to Home Farm, where Robert Murrell was idling in the yard when they got there.

"I've been thinking," he said to Mark, "ever shot a shotgun at birds?"

"No," said Mark, "the air gunners on the bombers used to get some shot gunning at artificial targets, but I think that was cut from the training programme to save time."

"Well, I think you should try. If you're trying to kill a bird you have no choice but to study the way he flies and if you are focussed on how certain birds fly, it might help you in the future. What do you think?"

"It's interesting; do you have something in mind?"

Murrell handed Mark a shotgun. Old, double-barrelled with outside hammers. The barrels were quite a bit shorter than the butcher's gun, but it felt nice and handy.

"Know what a magpie looks like?"

"Er, black and white?"

"Yes, like a penguin, white on the front, but they fly like nothing else in the sky. Here's six cartridges; what you do is try and get me a magpie. Once you've done that, do it again, then we'll pick a different species, different sort of flight; what do you think?"

"Yes, I'd like to try."

"Well, go on then."

Mark took a walk out of the farmyard. I am a fighter-interceptor, he thought, mission, to intercept and destroy magpies; no ground control, no radar plots, just patrol and engage targets as they appear.

By early afternoon, Mark had accumulated ten sightings of magpies, although they may all have been of the same bird, teasing him, as he had not fired a shot. Murrell was right, he thought, the magpie is an exceptional flier. He wandered back to the farm in hope of some lunch, unloading the gun as he entered the yard. At the kitchen door, Mrs Murrell gave him some farm-baked bread, cheese and fresh milk. He found a spot to sit and eat and while doing so, turned the gun over in his hand, looking at it.

The woodwork was quite worn, as though handled often. The blue of the metalwork had faded to grey and the maker's name was stamped on the rib and on the lock plates – 'Wells-Fargo'. Mark had heard of them, but thought they were a transport company. Elizabeth spotted him and came over. She'd heard about the task Murrell had set Mark.

"Those birds are quite paranoid," said Mark, "and they have such control in flight; they can practically hover, they glide over hedges following the contour of the bush, very tricky."

"They are vulnerable as the light goes," said Elizabeth, "they don't fly at night and they get more interested in getting into their favourite tree to roost than in anything else. If you can work out where his roosting tree is, you stand a good chance as he comes in on the dusk."

Mark decided to give it a go. Dusk would be early and he'd have time after that to get back for the scout meeting. Besides, being beaten by a bird was not an option. He walked back out to the edge of the copse and sat where the hedge dividing two fields met it. He had several distant sightings of magpies and changed position to the apex of the copse. Sure enough, as the light started to go, the magpie flew along the line of the copse straight towards him. He eased the gun round and the magpie turned on a sixpence and entered the copse, flying out of his sight.

Mark waited and within five minutes a magpie appeared on the same flight path as the last one. Mark already had the gun pointing roughly in the right direction, so all he had to do was shoulder the weapon and shoot. As he shouldered it, the magpie landed on a branch, less than thirty feet from his position. It seemed unsporting to shoot, but it was not his fault that the bird had stopped playing.

BANG

Mark did not remember aiming or firing; his next conscious thought after the noise of the gun going off was that the bird swung upside down on the branch and then fell like a stone. Mark waited, and in less time than it would have taken to smoke a cigarette, another magpie came in to land on the same branch. This time, Mark got his shot off while the bird was still in flight and saw it fold and drop.

He picked both birds up and strode back to the farmyard, confident in his victory.

Robert Murrell was leaning up against the gatepost waiting for him;

"Two shots, two kills. Nice work."

"I think I was lucky."

"They'd think they were unlucky, but skill, patience and determination all play their part."

Murrell took the gun and the remaining four cartridges and then he called to Elizabeth, who was coming out of the milking parlour.

"Oy, you!"

She trotted over. Murrell told her that Mark was ready to return to Lavering and that if she was intending to go to the scout meeting she should get ready now and then she could ride there in Mark's car. She went off to get her things and Mark asked about the gun.

"Wells-Fargo, yes, it's an old souvenir of mine. I've got a newer gun but this one is special; I've had it a long time."

"How long? I thought they were a transport company."

"You want my life story, young Mark Brabham?"

"If that's not an intrusion."

"Well, it is and it isn't. We'll chat about it sometime over a beer or two. It's a long story and I haven't told it for a while. I doubt if I've done anything or learned anything over the years that will help you, but I'll tell you my yarn, right enough."

Elizabeth scooted into view, ready to go. Mark opened the car door for her. The magpies featured in their conversation as soon as the car was out of the yard.

"How did you know that the magpies would be easier to get as the light failed?" Mark asked as he turned on the blinkered headlamps.

"Mister Murrell said that perseverance was the key; if you gave up too soon you'd fail. I know you can't shoot in the dark and they were evading you in daylight, so I assumed there was something special about night drawing in. There had to be some trick, some edge; I suppose that's the same when you fly against the Germans?"

"There are techniques that work, yes; we need to be higher than them and preferably with the sun behind us."

"What if the sun isn't shining?"

"The sun is always shining above the clouds, it's just that you can't see it from the ground. When I'm above the clouds I can see 'planes lower down hiding in them, but they can't see me; that's why gaining height is so important."

"So, shooting magpies and shooting Huns is the same; you just need to know the trick and have some luck?"

"In simple terms, yes."

"But your luck ran out?"

"Sort of; my 'plane caught fire. I thought I'd get out and walk home, but I didn't think that quickly enough and it brewed up with me still fiddling with the cockpit cover. I'd got spattered with fuel and that's what did the damage, mostly on the way down."

The car chugged into the High Street. Mark knew that he needed to go and change, not to mention eat, before the Scout meeting. Elizabeth said that she'd come and wait for him.

Tom opened the door as Mark parked his car.

"One extra for dinner, Martha."

"I know; Mrs Murrell told me this morning at the butchers."

The conversation at table ranged around Mark's visit to the shore batteries, what Tom and Hetty had been up to all day and Mister Murrell's test of Mark with the shotgun.

"Two magpies then with two shots."

"Yes, I thought I did quite well."

"You certainly did; Murrell will respect you for that and it takes a lot to earn his respect, I can tell you. Do you know how old he is?"

"I think he's a bit older than Colonel Mallinson."

"Yes, he is. Mallinson is over sixty, but Murrell, he's over eighty."

"Eighty? He was wearing Great War medals in church, so he'd have been in his fifties then. Is that possible?"

"Oh, yes. He's had a long and adventurous life."

"He's half promised to tell me his life story, but over some beer."

"It will be worth the beer; I only know bits of it, but the bits I have heard about were worth listening to."

Elizabeth said, "Well, give us a hint."

"No, let Murrell do his own talking. Suffice to say that he'd had a lot of experience at sea before joining the navy for the war. Before that, he worked in America for a while."

"The gun he lent me said Wells-Fargo on it," said Mark, "and Mrs Murrell has an American accent."

"He lent you that gun?" said Tom, "he must like you. That gun is special to him; so special that I have never seen him use it. It's always clean and ready, but he usually carries a hammerless Purdey to the pheasant shoots."

III

It was time to head off to the scout meeting. They stepped out into the darkness of that November night and headed for the village hall. Mark positioned himself nearest the road, so Elizabeth walked at his right side, slipping her arm through his. The road was, as usual, devoid of traffic. Some people were out walking, and some of them were scouts on their way to the meeting.

Entering the hall was different to other nights; for one thing, Elizabeth was at his side instead of standing there already listening to the Colonel. The Colonel, in his greatcoat and cap was standing in his usual position talking to the postman, who was dressed in his Air Raid Patrol uniform. In the hall beyond, it seemed that there was a riot in progress, if the general noise was anything to go by.

"They're a bit excited," said the Colonel, "but nothing to be alarmed about."

Mark looked at his watch, which said fall-in was in two minutes.

"I think I'll get started," he said, "is Laurie Hilton in there?"

"Flags, yes."

Mark unbuttoned his coat so that he could reach his Scout belt, then opened the door and stepped through. Most of the boys were running about, some sort of tag game. The older ones were grouped to one side with Laurie at their centre. Mark acknowledged him and then blew his whistle. At the end of that blast, all Mark could hear was its echo from the stage.

Everyone stopped what they were doing and turned to face him. Laurie gave directions from his position behind them.

"TROOP, FALL IN."

It took less than a minute for the boys to form up as three sides of a square, the same as the Home Guard had last week. Mark walked around to the open side where his back would be to the stage. He took his great coat off so that the badges on his shirt could be seen. Colonel Mallinson, Ron Wilkinson and Elizabeth filed in behind him and took their places. The meeting opened, as was customary, with the flag being raised; in this instance it turned out to be a red ensign, as flown by any British subject at sea.

"STAND AT EASE; STAND EASY."

Mark decided to address the boys right away.

"Good evening. I have met some of you already whilst you have been going about your duties and most of you will have seen me around the village or at church parade on Sunday. My name is Mark Brabham; I am the rector's nephew and I hold a short service commission as a flight lieutenant in the Royal Air Force, from which I am on convalescent leave following a slight flying accident. While in this parish, I have been asked to serve as your skipper – until somebody better happens along. I am also serving the cubs as Akela. That means I have a lot of you to remember names for, so please excuse me if I can't remember all of you at once."

"Looking around this troop, I see we are a mixture. I am wearing the dark blue scarf of my parent Scout group in Cheshire. I see the green and white scarves of the local troop; I camped with this troop in the summer of 1931; none of you will remember that."

"The war has brought us together and I know that is hard for you all, being in many cases a long way from home. It is hard for everybody, as you can see from my face. I can't wear my shorts yet; my legs got burned and whilst I am healing up quite nicely, the woollen socks were just too itchy to wear tonight."

"While we are together, we must make the best of things; you all have a good reputation in this village for the work you are doing for civil defence. It will be my task to make sure that you earn the badges that your service entitles you to and to do my best to see that you make good progress through your scout training. I do not imagine that this war will be over anytime soon; you know that conscription to the armed forces started eighteen months ago and that your turn will come. I trust that your experience in this scout group will stand you in good stead for your future service to our country."

Mark put his cap on. He had amazed himself with his speech. Speaking to a group was easier than trying to carry on a conversation. Flags – Laurie Hilton, took over and set the boys up for their first game, which was bulldog, same as at cubs. Mark stood back and let Laurie run the game. Colonel Mallinson and Ron closed in on him.

"Excellent speech," said the Colonel, "just what they needed to hear."

After the game, Mark worked with the younger boys on their Morse code. It's one thing to learn the Morse alphabet and quite another to read and send signals with the letters ordered to make words. After a hefty work session and another frantic game, it was time for the Colonel to tell a yarn. The boys settled, sitting in a loose horseshoe formation while the Colonel took the centre position and the lights were turned down. He told his yarn about an Indian magician's last spell. Once it was concluded, the lights were turned up and Flags set about the final game, "give them a chance to work off steam," he said.

"Let the Colonel run it," said Mark, "gather the patrol leaders and seconds to the upper room for a court of honour."

The upper room of the hall provided them with some insulation from the noise of the game below.

"Brief agenda," said Mark, "I didn't want to keep you behind after the meeting, not without notice; we'll have a full meeting later but for the moment I want to hear from you how it's going with the signalling and such for the Home Guard."

"It's hard work," said Frank Maynard.

"There's something to do all the time," said Frank Ball, "school, homework, signal stations; there's always something to do."

"Should we try to ease up? Make more time for school and scout work?"

"No," said Laurie, "the war determines the pace of what we do here. We are doing less with the short days now, so it's a respite."

"It may pick up in the spring," said Peter Law, "but we'll be ready for it when it happens."

"OK," said Mark, "so we can trust the Colonel to dictate the pace of our contribution to civil defence. Next item is the rifles; how many have we got, where do we keep them and who is responsible for them?"

"They are shared out," said George Ibbett, "we each have one and there is a third one in each patrol that the boys take it in turns to look after. That leaves four, which the cubs have got and some air guns under the stage."

"PC Fidgeon thinks that we should keep them in the police station instead of in billets," said Mark.

"Does anyone care what PC Fidgeon thinks?" asked Laurie.

Nobody moved.

"Is everyone, apart from Fidgeon, happy with the current arrangement?" asked Mark.

The meeting assented; the current arrangement was what they'd decided in the spring and it was working well enough.

"OK, I just wanted to know; third thing – the boats. What has the group got and where are they kept?"

"Top of the creek," said Frank Maynard, "in the old boathouse."

"We've got the motor lifeboat," said Laurie, "a whaler. There's a cutter gig and two canoes. One of the canoes belongs to Harold Roberts senior."

"Do you get much boating in?" asked Mark.

"Not really," said Laurie, "none of us is qualified to take charge of a motorised vessel in tidal waters; that's why Tarka - Miss Fforest - skippered the lifeboat to Dunkirk last May. Four of us crewed it; that was tough, but we lifted more than two hundred men off the beach and ferried them to bigger ships."

"We came home with twenty-five men in the boat," said Frank Maynard, "and cubs including Derrick and Andrew cleared the boat up afterwards; body parts and bloody bandages. Mister Roberts had the ammunition."

"That's the only time we'd seen a burned flier before," said Derek Pilley, "fished him out of the water; hardly anything left to bury."

"We're passive participants in this war," said Frank Ball, "for the moment. We've been bombed and shot at in Dunkirk. We get the odd bomb here. We are working towards - and training for - our turn at hitting back."

"We do what we can," said Laurie, "we've collected stuff for jumble sales; pots and pans for Spitfires. When the men came for the churchyard railings, we helped with that too. Our boat was damaged at Dunkirk and we've not had the time or the materials to do anything about it yet."

When the troop assembled for the final prayers and flag ceremony, Mark announced the German flier's funeral for the next day, should anyone wish to attend;

"I do not hate that flier or any German," he said, "they fight for their Nazi cause, an odious apparatus, which I do hate and we fight for ours, which I love dearly. He is, I think, entitled to our respect. After all, he will always be with us, here in this village."

CHAPTER 8

THUS ENDED MARK'S FIRST week of convalescent leave in Lavering-on-Sea. It occurred to him on Wednesday morning, as he dressed for the funeral, that each week would be the same round of meetings for as long as he was here on leave. That thought exhausted him and he said so to Martha at breakfast.

"But look at you; much better than when you got here. Brighter cheeks, more weight – ten days here and you can handle cubs, scouts, Home Guard, Miss Fforest and even Mister Murrell's shooting test. You couldn't have done that before I cooked for you."

"True. Do you think I've improved much in a week?"

"Sure you have, just look in the mirror, like you've been on holiday. I'm telling you, good food, plenty of it, salty baths, some rest and plenty of exercise, you'll be flying again in no time."

That gave Mark an idea, which he developed when Tom came in for breakfast.

"Uncle, does Granddad still have that Miles Falcon Six?"

"No, he gave it to the RAF last year. He knew they'd commandeer it once the war started and he wanted it to be him giving it rather than them taking it; why, might I ask?"

"I was just wondering; a chance to get a flight in – nothing hairy, just to get off the ground for a few minutes."

"Hmm. No, that's gone, but he's still got the Bristol."

"The biplane? Will it still fly?"

"I suppose so. He moved it to Stapleford to make room for the new 'plane at Southend. I don't know if he's ever used it from there, I haven't. We'd have to ask. It's not far from North Weald, won't your boys have been using it as a satellite airfield?"

"I don't know, it might be too close; too easy to spot if you're looking for North Weald you'd see Stapleford at the same time from twenty-thousand feet."

"I'll make a telephone call. If it's there and flyable, you should visit your Granddad and get his permission, you know. It's not far to Brentwood. I might come with you, I haven't flown since Le Touquet in '38."

II

The funeral was quite well attended; Colonel Mallinson and an LDV honour guard, some of the older scouts and guides and a few villagers. The undertakers brought the coffin in their horse-drawn hearse, PC Fidgeon accompanying them, marching in front of the horses and alongside the undertaker.

"You can say a few words, by way of eulogy," hissed Tom as they walked into church.

"No need," muttered Colonel Mallinson, "The RAF have sent a staffer to do that."

Mark looked and truly, the RAF had sent somebody; a large car was following the hearse into the churchyard. It stopped well back to give the funeral party room. The WAAF driver stepped out, straightened her skirt and opened the rear door, out of which unfolded the long frame of Air Vice Marshal Keith Park, MC and Bar, DFC, CdeG.

Tom walked back to greet the visitor, who saluted, as is proper for anyone in uniform meeting a Victoria Cross holder. Then they shook hands. A bit of conversation drifted Mark's way – "twenty years and the years have been kind to you..."

Tom returned to lead the cortege into church. Mark saluted Air Vice Marshal Park, who stopped for a word.

"Flight Lieutenant Mark Brabham, I presume?"

"Sir."

"Well, good; I wanted to see you. I have your DSO in my pocket and I'm just longing to pin it to you. Congratulations, my boy."

"Thank you, sir."

Park strode on into the church – Mark thought he might have to duck to get through the door - and joined Colonel Mallinson in his pew. The Colonel was wearing his decorations, so he and Park spent a moment reading each other's chests. Mark slipped into the pew behind them and the WAAF driver sat next to him.

In the church, the organ music died away and Tom started the funeral service from the prayer book,

"We brought nothing into this world and it is certain that we can take nothing out..."

Mark's mind wandered to the WAAF driver, who sat rigidly facing the front. She knew where his eyes were and didn't dare return his gaze.

Tom announced, "My old squadron leader will say a few words."

"Thank you, Reverend Brabham. We have come together to decently bury our vanquished enemy, giving his mortal remains to the earth from which we all came, giving his memory the dignity that may not seem appropriate now, with the heat of battle so fresh, but will, in the future, I am sure be respected by those who loved him and thus I trust that they will also respect us, this community, this nation, for the decent way in which we deal with our enemies, both living and dead. I did not know this young man, although I have known many like him; undoubtedly professional and a patriot to his country. I knew your rector when he was just such a young man and look what's happened to him since. This young man will not grow old as we have, the burden of years is not his to bear; he will now always be what he was when he died – a Nazi fighter pilot. He won't be a politician or a priest, a banker or hotelier. He has carved his niche in the history of the world and must ever after occupy it. The late battle has cost both nations a lot of young men like him and robbed others of parts of their bodies and changed their lives. It is with a sense of sadness that we commit him to our ground, as in doing we think of those young men of our nation similarly buried by our enemies in Norway, France and Belgium in plots that will be forever England – or New Zealand in my case. I would also ask you to spare a thought for those of our air force who flew off into the blue, never to return. I can't say that this young man is luckier than they, but I suppose his kin will eventually know where he is to be found and that is a kindness by our nation to his family."

The organ played as Tom led the procession to the open grave on the north side of the church.

"Man that is born of woman hath but a short time to live..."

Mark's mind wandered again. His Air Vice Marshal had been his uncle's squadron leader.

"...In the midst of life we are in death..."

How many of their mates were buried in France? How small would their squadron reunion be if one took place? How many of his own mates would be able to attend a squadron reunion in twenty years' time? His mind wandered back to the WAAF driver, who stood detached between the funeral party and the north wall of the church; pretty girl, nicer to look at than the funeral in progress.

Tom was dropping earth onto the coffin, now resting at the bottom of the grave. The Home Guard fired three volleys of blanks over it and the mourners filed past and regrouped outside the west door of the church. Mark contrived to get next to the WAAF as he walked back.

"Where are you from?"

"I'm Carol Davies and based at RAF Rochford."

"So Park flew in there and you drove him here?"

"That's it. You must have seen him before; he's always popping in."

"Yes, at Croydon, but never to speak to."

Tom and Keith Park crossed to the door in conversation; Mark heard "...and McNamara's in London, you know, based at Australia House..." before they faced the group. Colonel Mallinson said loudly, "Air Vice Marshal Park has a few words to say."

Park said, "I felt it important for me to be here today for three reasons. It is appropriate for a representative of the Royal Air Force to attend on such occasions, whether it is for one of our own airmen or an enemy flier being committed to where he will wait for the resurrection promised us by our Lord. Secondly, your rector, the Reverend Tom Brabham flew with me in the last war and I jumped at the chance to meet him again and lastly; most importantly, the Reverend Brabham's nephew, Flight Lieutenant Mark Brabham has been awarded the Distinguished Service Order for his actions in the sky over the Isle of Wight on eleventh of August last and it is my privilege to present him with that decoration."

Mark stepped forwards and saluted.

He took the cased medal from his pocket, slipped the medal out into his hand and passed the box to Colonel Mallinson. As he reached forwards to pin it on Mark's tunic, Mark realised that his chest had swelled up to meet the decoration. His throat contracted and he could feel tears behind his eyes. The eleventh of August had been a hard day for his squadron and for the relatives of the men who did not return. He hoped he did not have to say anything.

"Not having gained this decoration myself because Trenchard downgraded the recommendation to an MC bar," said Park, speaking to Mark as though he were the only person there, "I am also just a little jealous of you." Park continued, now addressing the small crowd; "Flight Lieutenant Brabham has also been gazetted for the Distinguished Flying Cross for his actions in the sky over the River Thames on the thirty-first of August. I don't know if I will get the chance to present him with that medal; I tried to get one for today, but the red tape; anyway, congratulations, Flight Lieutenant Brabham, for both decorations. If I can't pass this way again soon, I will make sure you get the other medal you so richly deserve without any delay."

"Sir, Colonel Mallinson could..."

"A privilege, if called upon to........."

"MESSAGE FROM THE BEACH" screeched a voice from the top of the tower. They looked up to see a Brownie hanging over the battlements. "READS: AIRMAN D.I.N.G.H.Y. LANDING. WHAT'S THE D-WORD MEAN?"

"It's a rubber boat," shouted Park, and then to Colonel Mallinson, "who is at the beach?"

"A couple of signallers," said the Colonel, "it's an observation position, not a fortification."

"OK, we'll use my car."

Carol Davies had already turned it round. Park returned to the vehicle, twisted the boot catch and pulled from within a webbing belt on which was his holstered revolver. He and Colonel Mallinson piled in; Mark followed, as he still had the Colt revolver in his pocket. The Colonel gave Carol directions and the car purred along the country lane towards the beach. Just as the sea came into view, so did the airman. He had one Brownie on his shoulders and was holding the other by her hand. The one riding had an RAF webbing belt and holster, worn like a bandoleer. The walker carried a rifle at the trail.

Mark got out first, hand on revolver, but with the weapon in his pocket. His overcoat was open, so the airman caught sight of the shiny new DSO on his chest. Mark should have asked him something, but the airman spoke first.

"Officer of Polish armed forces, sir, attached to Royal Air Force."

"What station?" Park had joined Mark and the airman now faced an Air Vice Marshal, fully bemedalled, not to mention armed.

"Sir, I...er..."

"Take your time, what is your rank?"

"Pilot Officer, Karol Dubiel, sir." He put the Brownie down so that he could slip out of his Mae West and show them his RAF tunic, on which he had a DFC ribbon. He was wet through, and chilled. A bit shorter than Mark, pleasant round face and a mop of dark hair that needed cutting.

The rifle-toting Brownie said, "he had a boat – he says it's a dinghy - and a paddle. We signalled him with the Morse lamp and he came to us. If the tide had been going the other way, he would have gone with it."

"We'll regroup at my house," said Colonel Mallinson, "that's nearest."

"We'll sort his dinghy out," said the other Brownie, "and signal the church that you're going to the White House." She took the belt off over her head and handed it to Park.

In the car, Park had some hard questions for Colonel Mallinson about Britain's coastal defences being manned by brownies who should have been in school. The Colonel handled them the way he usually did and Mark sensed the Air Vice Marshal warming to the Colonel the way he had. The Polish pilot officer listened intently; Mark could not be sure whether or not the man could follow the conversation.

At the Colonel's house, PC Fidgeon was waiting for them.

"Downed airmen are supposed to be taken to the police station," he said, "for proper identification."

"How interesting," said Park, breezing past.

PC Fidgeon tuned to the airman, "I'll take your gun."

The pilot officer looked at the policeman, "I surrendered already," he said, indicating that he had no gun. This was true; Park had it from the brownie and he'd walked on into the Colonel's house carrying it.

Colonel Mallinson told PC Fidgeon that in all probability Air Vice Marshal Park was perfectly capable of identifying the airman's unit and returning him to it. He was equally capable of shooting the man if he turned out to be an enemy. That left PC Fidgeon with nothing to do except worry about what might happen next.

In the Colonel's study, wearing a heavy bathrobe and clutching his second tot of the Colonel's whisky, Karol Dubiel waited while Park got through to Bentley Priory on the telephone. Once connected, Park asked for the Polish liaison officer, told him what was happening and handed the telephone receiver to the Pole.

Two Poles conducting a conversation always make it sound like an argument and being able to hear only one side of what is said makes it sound no more friendly than usual. The Pole handed the receiver back to Park, who listened for a few moments, said thank you and replaced it on its cradle.

"This chap's been missing since Monday. He was on a standing patrol in a Hurricane over the North Sea out of Northolt. His flight leader lost sight of him. This chap says he went low to investigate a small boat, which fired on him. He fired back and he says the boat was burning when he left it, but so was his 'plane. He ditched and paddled for the shore. Came in on the brownie's signal. How the hell am I going to mention brownies with a rifle and a signal lamp in my report?"

"There's a war on," said Mallinson, "and we're all in it. I'm running the war from here with the people I have available."

"I suppose; I'm not for the moment; I'm on leave and awaiting a new assignment."

"You're leaving Eleven Group?" Mark knew what that meant. The Pole stood up, listening.

"Yes, the battle we were engaged in is over for the winter and they'll be something else for me to do. I won the battle and lost the politics. I didn't say that and you didn't hear it."

"Sir."

"One other thing, Brabham; those brownies are still on the beach I suppose. Would you go and check on them? I don't like them being the front line."

"Sir."

Mark took his leave of the Colonel, the Air Vice Marshal and the pilot officer; Carol Davies left the room with him and they exchanged addresses in the drive. Mark gave her the rectory telephone number and said that he seemed to be in most mornings, at least up until about ten. As they completed this ritual, Uncle Tom arrived on his horse. He had the signal that the party was at the Colonel's, so his plan was to see his old chum for as long as the war allowed. Mark introduced Carol to his uncle, but his mind was on Keith Park.

"I didn't know you flew with him."

"Briefly; he came to the air service late, you know. He got a taste for flying when he saw what we could do for his artillery, then after he was invalided out of the army he joined us. Funny really, the army let him go because his wounds meant he couldn't ride a horse. He shot down more Germans than I did."

III

Mark borrowed the horse and set off for the beach. He had not ridden since before the war, but as luck would have it, the horse knew what to do.

At the beach he debriefed the Brownies, who had obviously enjoyed their part in the day's events. They showed Mark the pillbox logbook in which they'd recorded the Pole's arrival.

"He gave his name as Karol Dubiel," said the shorter one, "he had to spell that for me and 'dinghy'. We got him to sign the entry. He was ever so polite."

They asked Mark about the funeral, his medal and how the Pole was.

"He's quite well, given that he's thoroughly wet and cold; he's lost his 'plane, needs a haircut and he's got a girl's name," said Mark.

"It's not a girl's name with a 'K'," was the reply, "and anyway, if his mum called him that it must be a boy's name in Poland."

Mark was again struck by the Welsh accent on some words, which was obviously Elizabeth's influence. He checked what the Brownies were supposed to be doing next. They expected to be relieved so that they could have lunch before afternoon school, so Mark left them and rode back to the Colonel's House.

Park and his car were gone. Colonel Mallinson said that they'd dried Dubiel's clothes and Park was taking him to Rochford, from whence he would be flown to his own base at Northolt. Tom had enjoyed the surprise meeting with his old mukkha and was on a promise to meet up again in London soon. He had other duties to attend, so he relieved Mark of his horse and left. Mark went back into the Colonel's study, just as the latter realised that the Pole's gun belt was still on his desk.

"He surrendered it to the brownie and she gave it to Park."

"Yes," said the Colonel, "let's have a look."

He snapped the brass stud on the holster and slipped the pistol out.

"Hmm. Yes. Nine-millimetre. Made in Poland, no doubt. Nice heavy gun; doesn't look mechanically much different to the Colt models, so I should have no problem cleaning it up for him. He said he'd be back to visit."

CHAPTER 9

MARK'S HOSPITAL APPOINTMENT ON Friday the eighth of November concluded with the medical opinion that he should return in a further two weeks – Monday the twenty-fifth - and stay for four days to have his left eyelids sorted out. That meant repeating the cycle of cub, scout and Home Guard meetings twice more before more surgery.

Carol Davies telephoned him every other morning; she'd told the other WAAFs about meeting him and was pressing him to visit Rochford. He mentioned the Saturday dance to Carol on the telephone, but there were obvious difficulties for her and her friends getting from Rochford to Lavering, a journey of more than twenty miles.

Mark had asked Laurie Hilton about the dress code for the dance; Laurie said that those with uniforms wore them, so the land army turned up in their breeches rather than skirts and servicemen dressed to be recognised as such. Attendance, according to Laurie, was mostly those who were single. A few of the married couples whose unions were yet unblessed with children would be there, but in general it was a get-together for the young, free and single.

He felt odd walking to the dance with Laurie Hilton, refocused on the hope that Elizabeth Fforest would be there, despite his not having invited her. He need not have worried; as they entered the hall he saw some dozen or more land girls and a few nurses dancing together in a crocodile as the band played the suffragette hymn 'march of the women'. The various young men present stood to the sides and were few. The band consisted of a couple of Ulstermen from the coastal fortifications, armed with an accordion and a violin; the others were a pianist, a drummer and a cellist; weird assortment of instruments, but they made the hall throb.

Mark would have liked to join the wallflowers, but a quick look round gave him the impression that he was the senior officer present, which meant setting an example. The dance ended and the female crocodile disbanded. The 'orchestra' struck up a softer tune and Mark walked up to Elizabeth.

"Are you free for this dance?"

"If not free; at least reasonable or cheap."

"You charge for dances?"

"I won't charge you anyway, let's dance."

Mark was grateful for his education having included how to glide around a dance floor as he twirled Elizabeth about the hall. A few other couples joined in, filling the floor.

"I never realised that there were so many land girls around here," said Mark, "you seem to outnumber the men."

"Lot of men away," said Elizabeth, "and we are fighting in the fields, of which there are many here. We may be civilians, but we wear the King's Crown on our hats and no field is going to beat us. We dig for victory."

With the dance over, they moved to the side, where the Land Army surrounded Mark for Elizabeth to introduce them all. It was pleasant being the centre of attention and amongst young, enthusiastic girls, whose accents identified them as drawn from across the country and from all classes of society. Hard working and full of beans, they brought a real energy to the evening. The Home Farm three had been in the parish the longest, he discovered. The others had gradually drifted in as required. Land girls, although belonging to a uniformed organisation, were employed by the individual farms where they worked and getting positions had been quite hard, due to a mixture of official indifference and male farmer resistance. Robert Murrell had done a lot to make girls welcome and acceptable, but it was a slow process.

The nurses worked in the cottage hospital in rotation and otherwise served in the county hospital in Chelmsford. Local girl guides also worked as volunteers in the cottage Hospital. Mark did some counting and figured that there were twenty-eight available young ladies at the dance. Men and boys, barely a dozen, including the Ulstermen in the band, which meant Mark felt obligated to dance in turn with several girls and not just with Elizabeth. Doing so was uncomfortable, though, as her eyes were on him throughout, watching what he did with his hands.

II

The Remembrance Sunday service next day was a muted affair, as the parish's veterans all went to functions elsewhere in London, Chelmsford or Southend. Tom went through the motions of the service and the two minutes silence, confiding to Mark afterwards that his personal remembrance was on the first of July each year; a day when he tried to take the time to pray and meditate, thinking of the worst loss of British life in any military action before or since. It was a day on which he'd lost friends; school friends and army friends; a day that changed British military history forever.

In Lavering, being both cub and scout leader was becoming a routine. By the time he was due to go to hospital he decided that Martha was right; the air, the exercise, the work in the community and the good food she packed into him was all making a difference, as was his feeling of being welcome. He was becoming a part of the community.

The war was both near and far; they heard the German aircraft pass overhead on their way to their targets. The coastal batteries and searchlights were in action most nights, both those that Mark had visited and units more distant, around Southend, Rochford and Foulness. The glow from London could be seen reflecting off the low clouds and occasionally one could discern aircraft in trouble, losing altitude, trying to make it home. Apart from the night-time fireworks, though, the air war did not directly affect Tom's parish until after the huge air attack on Coventry overnight on the fourteenth tore some families apart and displaced others as bombed out families sought safety in the countryside.

Mark found that Coventry had sent him four new cubs and two scouts and their integration to the small Essex community was difficult. One of the Scouts was completely deaf; his friends said that he had been able to hear perfectly before the bombing, but it was as though he'd shut his ears to the noise and could not reopen them. The London boys were readily distinguishable from the Essex natives when they spoke, as were the new lads from Coventry. Both the Londoners and the Lavering boys made an issue of not being able to understand the Coventry twang, although at the heart of it, Mark thought, they were jealous. These boys had been through a major war action that had been national news; something the Lavering boys had not. Mark tried talking that through with his patrol leaders in a Court of Honour meeting.

"But skipper, you fought in the summer air battle; the biggest boys went to Dunkirk and saw the evacuation. We haven't done anything much yet."

"Getting bombed isn't a great experience," said Mark, "I was bombed on the ground at Croydon. I saw dead bodies after that and I wish I hadn't. If the war misses Lavering and we come through the blitz unscathed, that would be better."

"Well they talk it up like they are more important than us. Even cloth-ears has a lot to say about it."

"No, they talk about it to try to make sense of it; to come to terms with it in their own minds. It's hard facing up to such dangers. We all must come to terms with what happened and talking about it is better than bottling it up. And don't call him cloth-ears; if his hearing is damaged the doctors will fix it, like my face. If not, he needs our support. Anyway, as far as accents go, you all managed with Tarka."

"Yes, but she's pretty. So how about you, skipper? Do you want to talk about what happened to your face?" Frank Ball posed the question.

"At times, yes, but I had doctors and nurses to talk to as well as relatives. Do you think I should talk to you about it as well? And in reverse, I've heard mentions of the scout boat going to Dunkirk, but not the full account."

"That's in our log book," said Laurie, "Colonel Mallinson went in his boat too, which is just as well as he towed us back here after."

Frank again, "We've got you to talk to about our worries, but we don't know how and you don't talk about yours, so how were we supposed to know that the Coventry lot need to talk about their problems?"

Mark took a deep breath, "well, when I got here, I was sore all over. I found dressing difficult and speaking was hard. What you have done for me is let me get my voice back. I struggled at times to talk, but you let me take my time; you were patient with me and didn't take the mickey. That was helpful. As the weeks have gone on, I feel better in myself, small wounds are healing and I can dress more easily. I feel welcome here, among friends and I feel quite safe; now tell me what's on your mind."

"It's hard; there are so few grown-ups apart from you. Tarka, but she's only a girl; there's your uncle but he's busy. The Colonel, he's busy too. The schoolteachers...hmm, hard again, 'cos they're women. The choirmaster...he worries us, skipper; you should ask Derrick Forder about him, he has the most trouble with him."

"In what way?"

"We think he's weird; it's a worry."

"Alright, I'll see to that, but if you're sending me on a wild goose chase..."

"Not at all, skipper. We're trying to explain," said Laurie, "it's hard for the younger ones, no parents, no caring adults to talk to. I'm well connected here; family, scouts, Home Guard and choir, but I keep my distance from the choirmaster and I worry about him and the younger boys."

Frank Ball proposed a vote of thanks for Mark as skipper. "I never noticed you had trouble talking," he said, "Peter stammers a bit, but we're used to him."

"While on that subject," said Mark, "how come, Peter, that you and your brother are camping at Home Farm? What became of your billet?"

Peter sat for a moment, composing his thoughts. "We didn't get on. Wasn't really room for us. The tent was meant to be for the summer, our mum sent it down to make being here more fun, but then we got used to it and we can use the coach house loft on Home Farm as an alternative if we want to."

"Can you say what was wrong?"

"Not really; it's over anyway, we've got a place."

III

Mark told each group in that third week that he'd be away for the week after. He talked to Uncle Tom about the choirmaster. Tom's answer was not encouraging.

"Some people are attracted to same-sex relationships, Mark; it's a Greek thing I suppose. Alexander the Great seems to have had close male friends as well as a wife. Young boys in Greece are still mentored by older men, who behave 'inappropriately' in our terms. It also goes on in boarding schools, did you not see anything at Shrewsbury?"

"Maybe I didn't want to see anything; but boys messing about is not the same as an adult taking advantage, surely?"

"You're right, of course, but men who have that sort of preference are drawn to activities that give them responsibility for young boys; so using that logic, one might suspect everybody involved one way or another in the care of children, although only a few actually misbehave."

"And is the choirmaster one of them?"

"I don't know. Did Derrick say anything to make you think he might be?"

"No; not exactly. All he said was that he didn't like practicing his solo singing in church."

"Hmm. Alright, I'll see if I can get anywhere. I want to be sure that the boys are kept safe from all harm, and if that means a new choirmaster, I'll find one."

IV

Mark had arranged to see Farmer Murrell at the pub the night before he went back to hospital for a beer or two and a chat. Before the war the village had boasted four pubs; one near the church, two in the lower High Street and the coaching inn on the Eastminster road, which also served as a lodging house. The 'Coaching Inn' had closed and the building was in the process of becoming, according to local rumour, a hostel for working women. With the hotel gone, Farmer Murrell favoured the 'Lord Napier' near the bottom of the High Street. He said that he tried to have an evening of drinking every week, "to give the girls some privacy to use the bathtub in the kitchen, you know."

"Are you going to ask that land girl out on a proper date?" he continued, "and can you understand her when she speaks?"

"I was going to but it will have to be after I get my eyelids now. She's been busy and I'm run off my feet. I can follow what she says if she's talking slowly."

"It's good for you, being busy; like when I sent you out after magpies. Did that teach you anything?"

"I'd never studied the way any bird flies before that. I can't do what they do with a 'plane, but yes, I'm sure that I'll be in combat sometime in the future and remembering that magpie will help me."

"Good, I studied birds carefully to see what they do, and I think that has made me a better shot. In my youth I studied people, the better to anticipate what they would do next; now then, you asked about that gun. It's a long story. How old are you?"

"Nineteen."

"Nineteen; I was nineteen in 1878. I went through Dodge City that year, on my way down into New Mexico."

"So what drew you west?"

"I'd turned fifteen and I wanted to travel, so my dad let me. I went out west until the tracks ended, then took to horses. Got work driving cattle."

"So you were a real cowboy?" asked Mark.

"Sort of, exciting times. I fell in with men who'd driven cattle up from Texas and rode down there with them. I got on one cattle drive, might have been the last big one. We got attacked by Mexican bandits and by Indians, but made it through. Ten thousand beef animals on the hoof; it was a wonderful sight and I doubt if anybody will ever see such things again. Got to know people, got to be known as reliable. Got a reputation."

"I'd moved down into Arizona territory, because New Mexico had got a bit rough at the time – they called it a war afterwards - and I fetched up in a mining community called Tombstone. Virgil Earp was a lawman there by then with his folk and had a feud going on with the Clantons. I never knew what it was about or why Earp was making things difficult for the Clantons and I got caught in the middle."

"He and the Earps got in a gunfight. I say a gunfight, Ike didn't have a gun but the Earps did and Mister McLaury was killed by a deputy called John Holliday, using that shotgun. He borrowed it from the Fargo office on his way down to meet the Clantons, hid it under his duster coat. Anyway, there was a court case after that and then the gun was given back to Wells Fargo; except that they didn't want it because it had been used to kill somebody, so I traded them my thumbhole Purdey for it and I've had it ever since."

Murrell had been drinking steadily while talking, and Mark could see his eyes were glazed, partly the alcohol, but mostly the memories. He knew little of the American frontier beyond a few movies and he was ready to bet that the movies were nothing like real life. That meant he could not ask sensible questions, so he sat in silence waiting for Bob Murrell to continue.

When he did, it was with a question; "Do you think we'll see Americans in this war, like last time?"

"I expect so," said Mark, "there are a few with the RAF already and I suppose that they will be drawn into this war as a nation. That's what the Americans I met at Croydon think."

"Hmm; I met a few last time, but they were all city boys from places like New York and Chicago."

"Where is Mrs Murrell from?"

"San Francisco. Met her when I tried shipping cattle from there; she told me it was silly, better by rail to the Atlantic than taking them by sea around the Horn. She keeps in touch with people there, but we don't know anybody to write to in the old west."

"How is it here? Land girls on the farm and all?"

"We had land girls in the last war; I went off to the navy and Mrs Murrell ran the farm with women helpers. When the land army re-formed I was pleased to take them, knowing how good they were last time."

"So, what was the war in New Mexico?"

"They called it the Lincoln County range war. Fancy name for a few murders; more like a feud really. I rode with men trying to keep the peace. They called us the regulators and when that got too dangerous, I headed further south."

They drank on for a while before Mark took his leave to return to the rectory where Tom was in the study with some port on the go.

"Nightcap?"

"I'll try, but I had so much beer it might run out of my ears."

"How was Bob Murrell?"

"Talkative; I got his life story and quite a life he's had. I'd never imagined him being over eighty. He's so spry."

"Nor, I suppose, did you imagine the things he's packed into those eighty-odd years."

"I didn't; cattle drives, stock breeding, the wild west, Indians, Wyatt Earp – and then he went into the Great War in his fifties."

CHAPTER 10

THE FOLLOWING MORNING MARK was ready to return to hospital in Sussex. Tom got ready to accompany Mark to the station, but the postman met them at the door.

"The line is out; no passenger trains this morning. Railway staff are suggesting that if you get to South Woodham Ferrers there is a bus service running from there to Dagenham East where you can pick up the London trains. There might be trains from Ongar, but I haven't been able to check."

"OK", said Tom, "that means I can drive you in your car to South Woodham Ferrers to meet the bus."

"Or I could drive you to South Woodham Ferrers to meet the bus and you could bring the car back," said Mark.

"Family rule, Mark," said Tom, "if we go in a car together, I'm the driver. Anyway, I've got more medals than you."

So they set off in Mark's little car, Tom driving. The problem with this arrangement was that Tom treated the road as he would the air. The main mercy of this trip was it became a short ride when measured in time.

The single decker bus was comfortingly slow after his experience of Tom Brabham's driving. His fellow passengers were a mixed bunch; a few office types who needed to get to their desks in the City, if their desks had survived the night: then there were a handful of servicemen, like Mark, with places to go; a seaman with his kitbag and a large bunch of bananas, several soldiers and two nurses.

The main road was quite busy; sufficient cars and lorries for there to be a traffic jam near Romford. The bus had to queue for several minutes because there was a Spitfire partially blocking the road. He'd landed east to west and his starboard undercarriage had folded, the machine coming to rest half in the road and half in a front garden. Traffic was having to take turns to get by.

The bus had to take several detours as they entered London. The main road was closed due to a crashed German aircraft, so they were diverted past Hornchurch airfield up to the Romford Road and back down again to Dagenham East. Trains were running, so Mark was able to board a train for Liverpool Street and relax.

It did not last. He got as far as Aldgate before the train had to stop due to an unexploded bomb. Up at street level he found a taxi driver who would take him to London Bridge station. Throughout the ride the taxi driver kept up a constant bombardment of information about which roads were closed by which emergencies. At one point they drove past a docklands building that had a bomb sticking out of the wall.

"They don't know about that one yet, sir," said the taxi driver, "and when they do it'll make this journey next to impossible."

"Have you reported it?" asked Mark.

"No sir, not my job as it were;" said the taxi driver, "there's so many devices in London that haven't gone off. In the last war, sir, about a third of all the German shells never went off and they are still sitting in the mud around our positions.

They didn't do their job then and they don't matter now, same as these buggers."

London Bridge station was a mine of disinformation but eventually Mark found out which train would take him to his Sussex destination. Ensconced in a first class carriage, he started writing a letter to Elizabeth. He'd got as far as heading it with the hospital address before the train started moving. What he'd got stuck on was whether to write "Dear Elizabeth," or "Dear Miss Fforest"; he was stuck on what would be proper in the circumstances.

His pencil wandered back to the paper and he wrote "Dear Tarka," and that seemed to do it for now. The letter had rambled on to three whole paragraphs before the train made an unscheduled stop in a railway tunnel just after Oxted. He hastily signed the letter off in the dark and enveloped it ready for posting on his way to the hospital.

He assumed that the train was hiding in the tunnel for an air raid alert; soon enough it set off again and made progress into East Grinstead station where he spotted a post box outside the station at the same time as an RAF driver spotted him.

"Guinea Pig Club this way sir."

"What?"

"Sorry sir; the lads being treated by Doctor McIndoe call themselves guinea pigs, so we refer to all his patients unofficially as the Guinea Pig Club."

"Well, that really fills me with confidence."

"You'll be fine, sir, honest; I've seen his results, but don't let me fool you. I am sure it's painful, but it's part of getting better. Could I take your name please sir?"

"Brabham, M, flight lieutenant."

"Thank you Flight. Congratulations on your DFC sir, the adjutant has one for you at the hospital."

"Thank you."

On the way to the hospital the driver asked Mark if he'd picked up the DSO in hospital, which he had not so Mark told him about the Luftwaffe officer's funeral.

"Hard act for the Adjutant to follow then, sir," said the driver, "but we have had all sorts of brass and politicians visit the burns unit so you may get it from somebody important, we'll see."

Arriving at hospital necessitated a flurry of form filling, after which Mark was escorted to the ward. Twelve beds, of which eight were occupied and two appeared recently slept in. The smell hit him like a brick as he walked in; like overcooked breakfast, mingled with decay and antiseptic and sweat mixed with bad breath, puss and carbolic. There was also a hint of stale beer and cigarette smoke; like a pub when it first opened.

"Walking wounded then," piped up a voice, "not privileged enough to be wheeled in eh?"

"My brain got more of a frying than my legs," said Mark, "how about you?"

"Face and hands mostly," came the reply, "cockpit canopy wouldn't slide back when I wanted it to."

A nurse showed Mark which bed to use.

"Another DSO on the ward, Fred, you're not as important as you used to be."

"Fornicate elsewhere, there's a good fellow," said Fred, "the quality of the company here just improved."

As Mark took his tunic off everybody saw that he still had his Rover Scout epaulettes and shoulder flash on the shirt. That set the conversation off again and Mark had to explain what he'd been doing with his time while not in hospital. Taking his vest off was tricky, because of the huge scab on his back and that set off more conversation amongst men who were becoming quasi experts when it came to looking at each other's burns and how they were – or were not - healing.

"Haven't seen one like that before," said Fred, "the scabbing usually sticks to the shellac and peels off with it leaving a nice mess of gangrene and goo."

"What happened to you?" asked Mark.

"Got burned crash landing somewhere near the Belgian border with France back in May," said Fred, "the hospital used shellac to keep the air from my wounds and it was a comfort for a while; then you get the itching underneath and when they take it of...oh boy, what a sight, what a smell."

"Is it getting better?"

"Some of it is; they couldn't save my left leg but what's left of me seems to be repairing. This time next year I may be helping you with the cubs, who knows?"

The doctor assessed Mark's left eye for lid-repairs, made a few comments about the left ear, mostly to himself and then had a look at Mark's back and legs.

"Quite a scab you have there," he said, prodding Mark's back none too carefully, "it's tempting to slice that off and graft straight away, but on the other hand, it might well heal up beneath. Heck of a scab though. I'll think about that one."

Mark's legs were still tender in places. The full thickness burns had scabbed like his back and where the smaller scabs had come off around his left knee, the flesh was extremely tender.

"The subcutaneous fat has burned off and not been replaced," said the doctor, "and the membrane that has grown over the wound under your scabs is not yet sufficient to repair the wound properly, although your body is doing its best in the circumstances. Lavering is doing you good; you've filled out a bit, but the scabs aren't stretching as the rest of your body does. Looking at your knee I can now envisage what's happening under the scab on your back, so I'll think about how to deal with it."

"You make it sound...I don't know...strange?"

"Not at all. The way you were treated was done with the best of intentions. It is the case that people we've had who have been in the sea seem to heal faster and better than those who haven't; poor Fred there, evacuated through Dunkirk without getting wet at all and his repairs are less advanced than yours although he was wounded three months before you. The honey...interesting...I suppose it worked quite well; better than shellac, anyway, so I think that the treatments you have had so far have not impeded your progress. Meanwhile, you're obviously ready for the left eyelids, so I'll schedule that and I will improve that left ear at the same time."

Once the doctor had left, Mark dressed and went to sit on Fred's bed to compare wounds, scars, DSOs and the healing process. Fred's leg had been amputated, Mark discovered, not so much because of the burns, but because of the mess he'd made of it on landing. He'd been trapped in his cockpit by the crash and had been pulled out by Belgian farm workers.

"Wish they'd worked quicker, though; it would have been nice to have been out of that kite before she blew."

II

Mark's stay in hospital stretched to ten days, during which they worked on his eyelids, ear and a couple of grafts on small areas of his leg to see what would happen. Outside of ward rounds, he was free to mingle with the other patients. There were some facilities in the hospital for socialising – a piano and a beer keg.

"Burn victims are usually in shock," was the explanation, "and the doctor thinks that taking airmen off beer and flying duties during treatment could prove fatal. He can't let us fly, but he does let us drink."

Mark felt rotten after the last round of surgery and stirred from the anaesthetic to find a small crowd of his fellow patients surrounding him.

"You've got four letters," said Fred, "waiting to be opened, and since you're bandaged up we've used the official ward pack of cards to determine who will read them to you."

"They could just wait until I can see again," said Mark.

"Nonsense," said Fred, "you might need to dictate replies. We take it in turns to be each other's secretaries at times like this."

Four letters. "What are the postmarks?" asked Mark.

"Chelmsford, Chelmsford, War Office and Buckingham."

"Start with the War Office, then, in case they want me on duty this afternoon or something."

The War Office letter was a timid enquiry as to whether he had received his DSO safely.

"There's probably a form Keith Park should have sent them after he issued it," said a voice, "so that's easy to answer since we all know the story from your own burned and blistered lips."

"Buckingham will probably be my Mum," said Mark, "so let's have that next. I wonder why she was there?"

The gist of it was that Mum intended visiting him at the hospital before he was released, probably on day nine of his incarceration, which would be Tuesday the third of December.

"We'll write an acknowledgement postcard and hold it under your hand for you to sign."

The two from Chelmsford could be Uncle Tom and – maybe - Elizabeth? Tricky; did he want the ward sharing her letter? While he thought about that they'd opened them anyway.

"This one's from 'Tarka', whoever he is. Wait a minute, he's a she."

"Just read it out then."

Elizabeth had started it off 'Dear Mark', so she was either better informed of etiquette than he, or completely ignorant of such things. Either way, it was a nice letter, praising the improvement in the boys due to his influence, their kind regards and everyone looking forwards to him returning to Lavering. It was signed off, 'love, Tarka', which set the whole ward off and he had to explain what that was about.

"I didn't know how to address her in a letter," he said.

"Got a photo of her?"

"No."

"What does she look like naked?"

"Shut up."

"You could ask her for a photo."

"Fornicate elsewhere; I'll see her in the flesh next week so I don't need a photo."

"But we do."

"Bugger off."

The letter from Uncle Tom was likewise full of praise for his efforts in the community thus far and indicated, 'but it's a surprise so don't let on', that Mark's parents were both trying to make it to Lavering for the Christmas period, as well as 'one or two other house-guests'.

The chitchat of the ward focussed on how people reacted to Mark's horrible face in that community. Mark said that his uncle had forewarned his congregation from the pulpit, so the God-fearing amongst them were prepared for what they would see. That said, everyone had a good look when they met him and he had found that the children were quite accepting of the state of his face, once they had seen him and he'd explained his injuries. He just had to keep reminding them to be gentle with him and there were those amongst them who were testing the limits of his fitness.

The consensus was that people in East Grinstead were likewise getting used to them, since they were encouraged to use the pubs, library and churches, but that going elsewhere was difficult.

Mark said, "if you're travelling or visiting places you're not well known, I suppose that everyone you run into is looking at you for the first time. In Lavering, I see the same people every day, so I reckon that they've got familiar with my mug; I just hope they can see improvements when I get back there."

III

By the third of December, Mark's bandages had been removed so that the air could get to the repairs. He admired himself in the mirror: admired might be too strong a word, but he had a good look and the results were an improvement. There would be an important visitor today, who would be decorating Mark with the DFC, Barry with his DFC and John with the DSO.

"DSO third, after the two DFCs, Barry and then Mark. The ceremony will be in the main reception area."

Mark's mum arrived quite early, so they sat in the reception hall for her to get a good look at him, which gave him the time to take a good look at her: still the most beautiful woman he'd ever seen and nothing like any of the girls he'd taken a fancy to.

"What worries me is the hair loss," he said, "what didn't burn off fell out and it hasn't started growing again yet."

"That was the shock of it all," said Mum, "and your body has better things to do than generate new hair. It will come back once the main stages of healing are over, I am sure."

Mark wanted to know why his mum had written to him from Buckingham. "War work," she said, "keeps me busy; your father should be back to Britain in the new year, so we'll all get together somewhere."

Fellow patients and others had started to gather in the area, in anticipation of the important visitor. The doctors and senior administrators went outside to be ready to meet their guest. The reception hall gradually filled up with people and eventually the main doors opened and the senior administrator appeared, accompanied by some RAF brass.

"HER MAJESTY, QUEEN ELIZABETH, THE QUEEN CONSORT."

The announcement brought them to their feet and silence descended upon the gathering. Mark could see nothing now that everyone was standing up. He could hear a certain amount of shuffling about, as the party established themselves in the hall. The senior RAF officer present, whom Mark could not see from where he was standing, read out a script to the effect that Her Majesty was graciously pleased to acknowledge the heroism of certain officers of the Royal Air Force in the late battle. He then called them by name to receive their decorations. Mark knew that he was third in the pecking order and when his name was called, he eased himself through the throng in the direction of the commanding voice, his mother close behind him.

When he got to the front, there was a semi-circle of wheelchair cases forming a barrier to create a gap between the crowd and the dignitaries. John and Barry were standing to one side, edge on as it were, with the dignitaries on their left, the crowd on their right and their medals pinned on. Mark stepped into the open space and saluted the party in general. His mother curtsied. The Queen was a short woman, beautifully dressed and with a broad smile. She acknowledged his mother's curtsey, then beckoned Mark forwards.

He stepped up and she slipped the medal onto his tunic with the practised ease of someone who had decorated a lot of her people recently.

She asked him when he had been knocked out of the fight and he said thirty-first of August. She said that was the worst day, but she thought the battle had turned two weeks later, on the fifteenth of September. Speaking to the medal recipients, she said that one of their colleagues had headed off an attack on Buckingham Palace that day by ramming a German aircraft. After that, reports from the Air Ministry seemed to show a steady improvement, undoubtedly due, at least in part, to their contribution.

Mark took his place next to John and Barry, while his mother stayed in front of the Queen and they exchanged a few words. Then it was announced that the Queen would have tea and afterwards tour the hospital.

"Medal recipients and relatives please make for the refectory, everybody else please return to your duties or wards. Her Majesty will see you on her tour of the hospital."

In the refectory, Mark sat with John and Barry, neither of whom had any family present. The Queen was still talking to Mark's mother as they entered the room.

"Your Mum seems to know the Queen quite well," said Barry, "were they at school together or something?"

"We'll have to ask her," said Mark, "the subject hasn't come up before."

Mum split from the Queen Consort and joined them at the table. The Royal party went to a long table near the serving hatch and got their tea first.

"You know the Queen then," Mark asked as she sat down.

"Oh yes," said Mum.

"How, when, where, why? Do tell," said Barry.

"Careless talk costs lives," said John, "it might be better not to."

"I have met her several times before," said Mum, "but not since she became Queen Consort. We have shared interests, you know, such as horse racing and shopping, national security and the future welfare of our country. In the last war we both looked after casualties, so I know how to make you behave Barry," she continued, "Her Scottish estate was a convalescent home during the last war."

"Did you help out there or something?" John asked.

"Not at first, I was in France at a place called Etaples; got wounded there in a German air attack and I went to Glamis for convalescence myself; I stayed on to help."

Her face darkened as her mind dragged her back to that experience.

"It's different here," she said, "smells different; I hadn't thought about that before, but wounded soldiers smelled of earth, like potatoes. The mud on their uniforms, you see, but that could also carry traces of the poison gasses which evaporated into the air of the wards, mixing with all the other smells. Still, I hope that your nurses will not have to deal with gas gangrene."

"There's plenty of other gangrene around," said Mark, "I didn't know you had a nursing qualification."

"I don't, but my German is quite good and I was translating what German casualties wanted to say to French nursing staff.

I had a sort of knack with some difficult casualties, so I was useful in Scotland."

Tea and cakes reached them. The Royal party had finished theirs and were setting off on the tour. They all stood up as Her Majesty passed their table. The Queen Consort acknowledged them with a flashing smile;

"Lady Brabham, we must meet again soon." And with that she was off on her tour of the hospital.

"Lady Brabham?" said John.

"My husband's a baronet," she replied, "so Mark will inherit the knighthood, if he outlasts his father. I don't know which of them has the greater death wish."

"My first flight was sitting on my Granddad's lap in a Bristol in 1923," said Mark, "it's a family thing."

"How old were you then? It's hard to tell with you being all bald and wrinkly."

"I was four. My first solo flight I was eleven. By the time I joined the RAF I had quite a few hours logged."

"And he still couldn't keep out of trouble," said Mum.

John and Barry said their goodbyes to Lady 'call me Lillie' Brabham and headed for the ward in hope of seeing Her Majesty again. Mark lingered with his Mum until she said that she'd be off to catch the 12.30 to London. He had an emotional farewell in the front hall after which he doubled to the ward in time to see Her Majesty leaving it to continue her visit.

On the ward, the bedridden had enjoyed the bulk of Her Majesty's time, guided by Barry. Even the blind and usually silent Dying Brian in the corner had lit up and the post-visit conversation took place on his bed. Mark had to explain to Dying Brian how come his mother knew the Queen Consort and every moment of the morning was replayed for hours after.

It was tough trying to sleep after such a day, but Mark drifted off eventually, sleeping fitfully as he expected to be released to travel back to Lavering in the morning. The ward round was, as you'd expect on such an important day, late, but the doctor gave him the all clear to return to his convalescent leave, "but get back here for the twenty-ninth, no that's a Sunday, the thirtieth of December and we'll have a look at you then."

Mark took his leave of his chums. Dying Brian asked if he could come to Lavering for some convalescent leave when fit enough to; he could not go home as that was in South Africa. Mark guaranteed him a bed whenever he called for it. Then he set off for the uncertain journey back to Essex.

CHAPTER 11

In the event, the train made it to London Bridge without incident and although the station itself was a shambles the Underground was working so he telephoned to discuss the rest of the return trip. His uncle said that South Woodham Ferrers station was working normally, so take the Underground to Barking, switch to the Chelmsford line and he'd drive Mark's car to meet him at the station there, as the Eastminster line was closed again.

Despite being called the Underground, much of the journey was at ground level, some bits on embankments and a few sections in cuttings and Mark saw repeated evidence of the current conflict. Roofless houses and smoke rising on the horizon; a barrage balloon, deflating, had dragged its mooring cable along one urban street, catching and pulling along after it all the overhead wires for telephones, trams and trolley buses.

Uncle Tom was waiting at the station when Mark stepped out, kitbag on shoulder. He felt better than when he went into hospital and hoped that he looked better as well. Tom greeted him warmly and set off, a bit more sedately than the last journey Mark had endured with Tom as driver.

"I'm practising in case it falls to me to meet your Mum at the station," Tom said, "she thinks I'm a maniac at the wheel."

"And aren't you?"

"Of course not; I'm a slow and careful driver. Now your Dad, on the other hand, bit reckless. He's crashed four cars that I know about whilst I've only wrecked two."

"How about Granddad?"

"Six aeroplanes, but only one was a write off; two cars I think. You'll have to ask him. I wonder what happened to his motorcycle?"

Mark told him about receiving his medal and chatted a bit about other rumours, like the fifteenth of September being the turning point and Dying Brian's wish for convalescent leave in Lavering if he ever got well enough to leave hospital.

"That can be arranged, no problem, but what are his chances?"

"We call him Dying Brian for a reason, Uncle, although he seemed to get a new strength from the Queen's visit. I hope it lasts, for his sake."

"Well, you slept for the best part of two months in hospital and it seems to have done you some good. Meanwhile, we have had four casualties amongst evacuees' families in London whilst you've been in hospital. One of your cubs, Derrick Forder, has lost both parents; a bomb flattened their house and they were in it instead of being in their shelter. The boy working for Harry Roberts the butcher has lost his mother and one of the sea scouts has lost his older brother; he was serving on a merchant ship that sunk."

Mark had to face a close inspection by Aunt Hetty and Martha, both of whom seemed pleased with Doctor McIndoe's work. They were also impressed by the Queen Consort's endorsement of the good doctor's efforts. Mark had to relate the story of receiving his medal from her in some detail and at least twice.

II

This being a Wednesday, he could have the evening off, or he could go to the Home Guard parade and tell them about Her Majesty. Having the evening off won, but then it occurred to him that Elizabeth would be at the brownie meeting, so he decided to walk down to see her at the end of brownies and stay at the Home Guard parade long enough to pass on to them Her Majesty's compliments for the excellent work they were doing.

He accompanied Martha for the short walk, noting overhead aircraft noises and that the coastal searchlights were up. The shore batteries did not fire, but guns were sounding off in the greater distance to the south, somewhere along the river Thames shoreline. London was already glowing in the west, as it had night after night.

At the hall, Mark could hear the brownie meeting in progress, noisy as usual. He joined the gathering of grown-ups awaiting their charges and exchanged pleasantries with them, updating them on his medical progress.

The brownie meeting within wound up with the girls singing together to a piano accompaniment and then fell quiet for closing prayers, after which mayhem replaced decorum as the girls burst out of the hall. Mark wandered in to find Elizabeth, who was in the process of packing up books and training bits and pieces into the brownie chest.

She stopped to have a good look at him and then resumed her tidying, chatting all the while. The brownies thinned out and departed and after a few minutes Mark realised that the Home Guard were conspicuous by their absence.

"Are the Home Guard not parading?" he asked.

"I don't know," said Elizabeth, "we can check the signals book."

Mark followed Elizabeth up the spiral staircase, which boasted French doors that, if open, would provide a nice view of the village hall interior and opposite them a similar pair of doors opening onto a small balcony where a signaller should be standing to watch the church tower. No signaller was present, but the book was awaiting inspection.

"There you are," said Elizabeth, pointing to the last entry, "Southend bombed; Home Guard to report to police station South Street Rochford for rescue work in bombed area."

He had heard the bombs and the aircraft but had not connected the noises with a tragedy so close by.

"Should we go, see if we can assist?" he suggested.

Elizabeth looked at him, "No, you don't need dusk and grit getting to that open wound. Digging people out of collapsed houses is specialist work and the Home Guard have trained for it."

"Trained how?"

"They've been in London whilst you were away for a weekend, doing that sort of work with more experienced people."

During the winter of 1940, the Luftwaffe would bomb London nightly until early November and sporadically thereafter, as they divided their time between the capital and other cities to keep the defenders guessing.

When the bombs landed on Southend, it might have been an individual aircraft jettisoning his load on the way home after failing to identify his intended target, or it could have been somebody trying to hit the searchlights or coastal batteries, or a nervous crew dumping their bombs prematurely.

"What is the RAF doing about night raiders?" Elizabeth's question jerked Mark back into the village hall.

"We have some night fighters, Bristol Blenheims and Boulton Paul Defiants. They were just getting started when I was wounded so I don't know how they are getting on. The guns don't do much; most German losses were shot down by Fighter Command, but in the dark I suppose that the barrage balloons must help."

"You will find that the boys want to know more. Remember it's their homes and families under that bombing."

"I know. I heard about Derrick's parents. I can't tell them much, but what I do know is that the Germans have lost control of the daytime sky, which is why they are attacking at night and it is only a matter of time before they lose control of the night sky as well."

"How's that going to happen?"

"Ah-Ah, careless talk costs lives, you know, but if I were in charge, I'd be thinking about the fact that the Germans must land in the dark when they get back across the North Sea. I reckon that means landing lights or something on their airfields and I'd be bombing them as they land. See how they like it. Remember, that worked on the magpies."

They were now alone together in the hall, there being nobody on signal duty. Mark pulled the lamp out and signalled the church tower but got no reply. The Colonel's communication system of signallers had fallen apart, as everybody was in Southend.

Back downstairs, Elizabeth fumbled for the light switches on the basis that if the hall was not being used, the electric lights should be turned off. It took her a minute to sort it out, unaccustomed as she was to being the last person to leave the hall. Then she succeeded, plunging them into darkness. Mark turned on his tiny penlight to guide her, turning it off and opening the door as she got close enough.

She pushed the door back to and wrapped herself around him in the darkness, her lips searching for his.

"Gently, remember I'm a casualty."

Her lips found his and they kissed for almost as long as he could hold his breath before she pulled away slightly.

"You're quite good looking in the dark, you know," she said.

"Flatterer."

The action of her lips and tongue had stirred his loins into a hard erection; something he had not experienced, best as he could remember, since being shot down. He knew that she knew what had happened, as she was pressed against him; she must have felt it grow as he had. She was also pressed against his revolver, so he knew that she knew he had that as well, as she shifted her balance during the kiss to press more on the erection and less on the firearm. She lingered, pressing her hips against him for – not long enough – before allowing an air gap to develop between them.

Outside they studied the night sky. London was glowing again, showing up clearly in the southwest. The searchlights on the coast were up, as were those around Southend and Shoeburyness. The drone of aircraft engines could be heard, as could various pops and bangs. Mark saw a flame in the night sky to his south-southwest.

"Someone's in trouble, look!"

They followed the orange streak as it tracked south of them heading east.

"Probably German. He's got two engines so he's hoping to cross the sea on the good one, provided the bad one doesn't burn his wing off."

"Will he make it?"

"I can't say. He's lost a lot of height; they're too low to jump and he's got a long way to go."

They watched the orange streak heading east. Other people must have seen it too, because the searchlights started tracking it. Lavering was too far from the action for Mark to be able to see the 'plane in the searchlights, but he knew that they'd bracketed it when the orange streak was obliterated by the white light. Then the guns started up. Mark could hear them firing but could not see the shells bursting and had no idea if they'd found their range.

The noise of that desperate battle was drowned out by an aircraft passing low overhead; twin engines by the sound of it and not in trouble.

"He's circling," said Mark, "fetch me an Aldis lamp, would you please?"

Elizabeth slipped away into the hall. "Flare gun?" she shouted.

"No need."

Mark followed the engine noise. If it was an RAF machine, the pilot might be looking for a landmark, or possibly trying to signal a ground position. Night fighters had been known to ask for directions, or to order searchlights to shut down, or just signalled to indicate their presence to avoid being engaged by the batteries. If it was a German machine, he might be looking for somewhere to dump his bombs.

Elizabeth opened the lamp case and started setting it up while Mark kept watching. The aircraft turned his lights on briefly. Mark thought he was trying to communicate with the coastal batteries. He could not see whether the coast was acknowledging, but their searchlights went out.

"I think he's talking to the coastal batteries," he told Elizabeth, "we might as well pack this in."

She put the lamp away while Mark continued observing the night sky. The Southend guns had fallen silent and the unidentified night circler had set off heading northwest when he heard another low-flying aircraft. This one was heading east on a course that would put him over the River Crouch. His one engine was spluttering and coughing, sounded like fuel starvation and if the machine had two, the other was already silent.

Mark could see no fire, nor could he see anything of the machine in trouble. The engine continued to splutter and cough as it passed between his position and the Southend searchlights. In doing so it became a silhouette long enough for Mark to see it was a Junkers Ju88 going by. He did not hear the engine stall; he was straining to do so when yet another machine passed right overhead, higher up than the others. Mark thought he heard a machine gun popping, but in a moment the new aircraft developed a bright orange tail, which curved down through the night sky.

Something landed with a clang near where Mark was standing. He made a mental note to have a look, but that would be later as he was still following the spectacular events in the night sky above him. Elizabeth was back at his side, holding on tightly and that set his erection off again.

The stricken aircraft hit the ground with loud bang and the eastern sky between Lavering and the coastal searchlights briefly went orange and yellow; then black.

"I think that night-fighter got him," said Mark, "and something landed over here." He got his penlight out to have a look, but it was Elizabeth who found it with her foot.

"It's a cartridge case," she said, "still warm."

"Well, then, a souvenir of the night. I wonder if the crew got out?"

"If they did, they'll be … near Home Farm, over there, won't they?"

"Maybe. I'll walk you home, see if anyone over that way wants to surrender."

III

They set off for the thirty-minute walk to the farm, Mark now more confident of his fitness to walk that far, and back. The night continued to be a noisy one; distant aircraft droning, faraway bombs and ack-ack guns contributing to the din. They'd gone about a hundred yards before Mark addressed the fact that Elizabeth was gripping his hand firmly, almost uncomfortably.

"Remember I'm a casualty," he said, "that hand needs massaging, not crushing."

"Sorry, I'm scared, that's all."

It had not occurred to him to be scared until then. He had the Colt revolver in his pocket still, but had yet to try it out and he hoped that he would not be testing it tonight.

Mark assumed that a search party would set out from the coastal batteries, looking for where the machine had crashed, searching for survivors. The 'plane had nose-dived after passing the village and any parachutists would have left the 'plane before the impact, so the logical line was Lavering, the parachutists, then the crash site and the coastal batteries. Using that logic, Mark worked out that he and Elizabeth might encounter the parachutists before the army search party.

"Have you got a weapon?" he asked.

"I have a catapult," she said, "one of the Brownies lent me her spare, so that I should have something. And a knife."

A catapult; still, he had a revolver. He just did not know whether it would work and indeed whether he could fire it with his hands still being a bit gammy, although he had become used to gripping it in his pocket. He liked the feel of it and holding it stopped it banging on his leg. They walked on, closing the distance between them and the farm, stopping when they heard what sounded like shots. Mark drew the revolver and walked on, but now Elizabeth followed him at a discreet distance.

They turned into Home Farm's drive, the tall hedges hemming them in oppressively as they made for the farm itself. A few small gates into fields either side, then the orchard gate and then the farmyard, where a lantern shone.

"Blackout regulations!" shouted Mark, "Mister Murrell, you're showing a light."

"Flight Lieutenant Brabham," came the reply, "there's trouble here."

"What trouble?"

"Horse thief. He took shots at me."

Bob Murrell appeared in the glow of the lantern, with a long-barrelled revolver in hand; his leather belt holding his dressing gown shut.

"Where is he?" asked Mark.

Murrell led them across the yard; the lantern illuminated a figure sprawled on the ground. Luftwaffe flight suit; he'd discarded his parachute but kept his helmet on. Mark noted that he had one boot and one stockinged foot. He bent down and felt for a pulse, realising at the same moment that his hand had rested on the man's back, or more particularly, over a bleeding wound on the man's back. He turned the chap over and saw by the lantern light a similar wound on his chest. Shot right through, but front to back or back to front. He could not tell, so he asked.

"Shot front to back. He fired first."

Murrell holstered his revolver.

"Good looking young fellow, is he not? I wish he'd been more sociable and less hostile; he'd be drinking tea in the kitchen now and waiting for the police instead of stiffening there."

Mark felt for the man's firearm. He had a large leather flap holster on, which was empty.

"Where's his pistol?"

"It could have gone anywhere after I shot him. Dead men let go of their weapons."

They hunted around in the straw and dung in the corner of the yard and found the piece. It was different to the one Mark had from the fighter pilot. He could tell little in the dark so he put it in the man's holster, and stretched the corpse out, straightening his legs and arms. Elizabeth brought a horse blanket to cover him.

"I don't know what our beloved PC Fidgeon is going to make of this," said Murrell, "I have never liked his attitude you know."

"If you want it to have been me who shot him," said Mark, "I've got my revolver here."

"No; when I say I don't know what Fidgeon will make of it, I don't care what he says or does either. I beat that guy in a fair fight. He was using a firearm in a robbery and that's a hanging matter. I just got him with the gun instead of a rope."

"I'd better report this then, since I am headed back to Lavering. Can I use the horse?"

"Yes, of course; can he come back tomorrow?"

"Surely."

Murrell checked the saddle, since it was the German who put the tack on the animal, then handed the reins to Mark, who signalled goodbye to Elizabeth and set off, leaving the two of them with the dead German. He was passing the orchard gate on his right when a voice hissed;

"Kamerad, bitte?"

Mark pulled the horse up, dismounted to the left and drew his revolver.

"ROYAL AIR FORCE. ADVANCE AND BE RECOGNISED." He hoped that was loud enough to let Murrell know of more trouble.

The German speaker appeared at the gate. There was just enough light for Mark to see that he was bareheaded. Mark pointed his revolver in that direction and said, "PISTOLE BITTE."

The German undid his belt and held it up with the holster on it. Mark walked around the head of his horse, pocketed his revolver and took the belt from the flier.

They looked at each other in the faint light. The German a handsome fair-haired man, older than Mark, who took his hat off for his bald head and burn-scars to be seen.

"Mein Gott." There was a long pause before the German said in English, "Bad crash?"

"Yes."

The German jerked his thumb towards the farm, "Wolfgang dead?"

"Yes."

Tears pricked the German's eyes, "Good pilot, Gerhardt, bad man."

Mark fumbled for his handkerchief, which he handed over. He immediately regretted that act of kindness because he needed it himself; he felt tears coming for the German lying in the shit of Murrell's farmyard. Not much of a way for him to serve his country, he thought.

"Name please?"

"Quinkenstein, Dieter."

He told the German that they would go to the police station, but what of the others? As best as he could tell from the mixture of sign language, which did not work all that well in the dark, and bad English, this German had jumped first and the dead man second. That meant numbers three and four would be somewhere between Home Farm and the crash site; that is, not between Mark and the police station.

"On the horse?"

"On foot." He sent the horse back and it trotted off, relieved of night duties.

They walked together out of the farm drive and turned towards Lavering. Mark had a hot flush, which made him sweat and irritated his injuries. He wanted to stop.

"Wait a moment, momente bitte."

The German stopped. Mark sat down and took his hat off. The German sat down on the opposite grass verge and waited. They'd been there barely a minute before they heard a horse catching them up.

Mark shouted, "Mister Murrell,"

"It's me, boy; I thought I'd see you're OK after the horse came back."

"Yes, I met another German and I thought we should walk to the police station."

Murrell dismounted and took a look at Mark's captive.

"Any trouble?"

"No, he surrendered his pistol straight away. Best I can tell, there will be two more past your farm. Did you see where the 'plane crashed?"

"No. I was in bed until the bang got me up again."

"OK, somewhere between here and the coastal searchlights. I expect that they will have sent a search party out, so they'll locate the other two."

Mark felt ready to resume the walk to town. The German stood up and Murrell looked him up and down.

"You can't walk him to town, look at his leg."

Mark looked. He had not noticed before in the faint night light; the flying suit was ripped open from where his boot would have been had he been wearing it to where his belt would have been before he took it off.

"He's got no boots and a bad leg. Let him ride the horse and you lead it by the reins."

They assisted the German onto the horse, Murrell then turned back to his farm and Mark led the animal towards Lavering, where he arrived at the police station without further incident. The police station was unoccupied, but unlocked, so Mark tied the horse outside and led his German in. The gaslights were on, so they could take a good look at each other.

Mark tried the telephone; he did not know the doctor's number so he called the rectory and told a befuddled Uncle Tom where he was and what was happening. Tom arrived in minutes with Doctor Hardmann not far behind him. Neither had seen the policeman on their way down. The doctor accompanied his temporary patient to the cells and checked him over.

"His German's good," said Mark as the conversation from the cell drifted into the office.

"Yes," said Tom, "he was born there you know."

"I didn't know; so shouldn't he be interned, enemy alien and all that?"

"No," said Tom, "he's on a Dutch passport, been here five years. Jewish, you see, that's why he doesn't come to church. I like him a lot; I can talk to him about things that I can discuss with very few other people."

"Such as?"

"Now, now, we must be discreet. He flew in the German air force in the last war, you see, so he and I have a shared past of sorts. You'll understand in thirty years' time when young Quinkenstein back there comes to a remembrance service in this parish."

Doctor Hardmann returned to join them.

"He's got a nasty scratch all the way up his leg, but it's not deep and nothing's broken. It's clean; might have caught it on something on the 'plane jumping out, or maybe on a tree when landing. There's no point bandaging it except the deepest point where it's bled from. I've patched that. I haven't got anything for the pain, not that he's feeling it yet. That will hit him tomorrow."

Tom took the prisoner a glass of water and a blanket. The door had a small blackboard on it, so taking the chalk, he wrote 'POW', as the man's name was too long for the space available. He and Mark sat in the front area mulling things over. Tom reckoned that the police might have gone to Rochford along with the Home Guard and probably the signallers from the village hall and church tower had gone as well to act as runners. It was a bad night all over.

CHAPTER 12

PC FIDGEON RETURNED FROM Southend around 7am; it was still dark and he was a mess, having spent the night shifting rubble. The brick dust had got everywhere. It was in his hair, ears and nose; he could feel it in his boots and when he took his handkerchief out, more brick dust came with it and landed on the floor. His dark blue serge uniform looked reddish grey. He sat down at his desk and saw the handwritten notes awaiting his attention. One was from Tom Brabham to tell him that the prisoner enemy flier had been locked in the cell at 23.00 the night before. The second was a note from the doctor detailing the prisoner's condition and an account of the doctor's fees for attending him. Mark's note reported the dead airman at Home Farm, but no details as to what had happened, but it tacitly explained the presence of Murrell's horse outside.

The policeman walked through to the back and looked in the cell, where the airman was asleep, his injured leg outside the blanket. He returned to his desk and telephoned the police headquarters in Chelmsford to set in motion the chain of events that would relieve him of his prisoner. Then he set to the paperwork and while waiting for police support or some other assistance to arrive, he completed his application form for training as a Bomb Reconnaissance Officer.

II

Mark awoke late with a jolt, remembering first the horse and then the dead German in the farmyard. He dressed and slid into the dining room as Tom was finishing. Tom said that he'd planned on seeing if PC Fidgeon was back, returning Murrell's horse and seeing to the dead airman.

"If Mister Murrell is thinking straight, he'll deliver the poor chap to the doctor's for post-mortem and then the undertaker can have him from there."

"Won't the police have to investigate the shooting?" asked Mark.

"I don't know. If I was PC Fidgeon, I would like to know what Mister Murrell was doing getting in a gunfight with a German airman, but whether anyone's going to tell him that such a gunfight took place remains to be seen."

"The guy's been shot clean through."

"Yes, your night fighter would have fired bullets at the 'plane; that's what made it crash. Look, I don't want trouble for Mister Murrell, far from it, but neither do I want him going about shooting Germans."

"It was a fair fight."

"According to him. You weren't there. I'll see what's happening, you take a salt bath."

III

Tom walked down to the police station, outside which Robert Murrell's horse still stood patiently. Inside, PC Fidgeon was at his desk. Tom told him the bones of the night's events.

"So two men missing, possibly?" asked Fidgeon.

"Possibly. Your prisoner says he was first out and the dead man second."

"Right, I'll go and see the coastal battery people once this chap has been collected. Did he have a pistol?"

"Not that I saw."

"Did you search him?"

"No, but I reckon the doctor would have found his pistol if he had one and he didn't say anything. Mark didn't mention a pistol to me either. A lot of them don't carry hand weapons, you know."

Military police arrived by car as Tom unhitched Murrell's horse. Tom rode it back to Home Farm, where he found the farmer had loaded the deceased onto his haywain ready to take to the doctor's.

"I'll ride back on the wagon then," said Tom, "who's driving?"

"Oy, you."

Elizabeth came running.

"Drive the rector and the late German flier into town, then come back, soon as you can."

Elizabeth set the horses to the task of running them into town.

"How is Mark this morning?"

"Tried to rush out without a bath. I sent him back to treat his body properly."

"A bath; we're lucky to get one a week."

Otherwise, it was a silent trip into Lavering. Tom and the doctor had to manhandle the German out of the wagon and into the surgery, there being nobody about to help them. Those of the Home Guard who could do so had gone to bed, having been out all night; the butcher's shop was shut, the police station was empty. Elizabeth turned the rig round and set off for the farm as soon as they'd got the cadaver off: carthorses she could handle, dead bodies, she felt that she could not. Yet.

IV

Inside the surgery, the doctor formed the opinion that the chap had been shot and that the bullet was not to be found inside the cadaver. He also noticed that he was not wearing his parachute, which suggested that he'd been shot on the ground?

"Possibly," said Tom, "or maybe Murrell has kept the parachute silk as a souvenir."

"PC Fidgeon will want to know either way;" said the doctor, "he likes things to be accounted for. With this chap, we've got his pistol and that's a first, but we're lacking one boot, his parachute, life jacket; I'd say he landed, stripped off what he didn't need and got shot on the ground. Front to back, look at the chest wound."

Tom looked; the wound had closed to an oval shape, but the hole in the man's flying suit bore the distinct silver-grey halo of a lead bullet entering. Turning him over, the back wound was an exit; lung tissue and other internal debris that had been sucked through it was to be seen inside the chap's shirt.

The doctor turned to the pistol. "It's cocked." He fiddled with the butt catch until he got the magazine to slide out and then he pulled the action back throwing a cartridge across the room. Tom retrieved it while the doctor thumbed the rest out of the magazine.

"Six in all, counting that one off the floor," said the doctor, "the safety was off and the spare clip has eight in it, so I'd say this chap's been firing his weapon. Did Mark say anything?"

"Sort of; he said the chap was dead when he got there, thinks Mister Murrell shot him."

"Well that makes sense of the lead around the entry wound; Mister Murrell being the man of experience he is, he's still using lead bullets instead of bronze jacketed ones. That's got to have been one of the unluckiest places in Essex to land, you know; second only to Mallinson's lawn."

V

Out on the marshes, PC Fidgeon on his bicycle caught up with the army search party on foot. They had found one parachutist; he'd hit a tree and had a broken leg. They were still searching for the others, as their prisoner was sure that all four of them had jumped. Fidgeon told them that he'd got one in custody and that another was reportedly dead at Home Farm, which he'd check out next. That left one to find, so he let them get on with it.

At Home Farm, Robert Murrell was not about, but the land girls had two parachute sets; Peter Law and his brother had found one in the orchard when they got up for school and Hilda found the other behind the stable. They were repacking them into their bags when PC Fidgeon arrived. He told them that the RAF might come for the stuff, and if not they could have the silk. He enquired about weapons, of which there were none found and then he returned to Lavering. The doctor's report waiting on his desk said that the dead flier had sustained a single bullet wound to the chest and that the cause of death was 'act of war'.

PC Fidgeon went up to the doctor's surgery, where he asked if this flier had any weapons. The doctor showed him the deceased and his effects, which included a leather belt but no holster or pistol.

How come he wasn't wearing his parachute when you got him?"

"I suppose," said the doctor, "that it was easier to get him into the wagon without it."

"Would that wound have been immediately fatal?"

"Just about. He might have lasted twenty seconds or so; enough time to jump and pull the ripcord, or he might have been hit after leaving the 'plane."

Fidgeon wrote in his notebook and then took possession of the items that would not accompany the deceased into the ground for the RAF, if they came for them; the leather belt, some personal effects and a pay book. Back at the police station a note on his desk from the church tower signaller said that the army had found the fourth parachutist dead, probably drowned and that they would deliver his body to the doctor in Eastminster, along with their injured prisoner.

VI

Mark walked into the High Street just in time to see Elizabeth and the haywain disappearing at the other end of the street. That made him feel dejected; he let his head drop which meant looking at the ground, where he saw a lump of shrapnel, about the size of a square of chocolate but distinctive because it was slightly curved and part of the inside of the curve was screw threaded. He walked a little further down the street, studying the ground and picking up several more pieces and a cartridge casing like the one he'd found the night before.

Having no immediate plans for the day after concluding that the parish was littered with such debris, he started to head home when the postman hove into view.

"Busy night, then, young sir; I was in Southend with everybody else so we all missed the excitement with the fliers here. How did you get on?"

Mark told him of his arresting one flier and seeing another dead, then asked about Southend. The damage was, he was told, not too bad; some houses with roofs knocked off, two collapsed completely. Nine people dead that they knew about and the search continuing in daylight, but was being undertaken by the local volunteers, who had also been up all night.

"One 'plane came down in the estuary, heck of a bang; guns seem to have got another, so with the damaged one you saw and the crashed one up here I'd say Fritz should be sorry he came this way."

Mark showed the postman the bits he'd collected off the street.

"Yes, sir, it's why we advise people to at least stay indoors during air raids. We are within the range of guns north and south of us depending on which way they are firing, and as you know, what goes up must come down."

VII

Following supper, Uncle Tom accompanied Mark to the cub meeting. The bereaved Grey Brother Derrick was not on parade, so Tom led prayers for Derrick's dead parents before Kaa started the first game. The mood was subdued; Kaa looked exhausted, having been up now for thirty-six hours. Colonel Mallinson attended and he, Tom and Mark had a quick conference in the entrance hall.

"Excitement overcame discipline," said the Colonel, "so I finished up with the signallers from the hall and the tower with me in Southend. Young Frank Maynard was on the beach and he couldn't signal anyone so he stayed there keeping the logbook until I remembered him this morning."

The Colonel's feeling was that he did not have enough people, men and boys, to tackle a big job like Southend and keep all the positions he'd created in and around Lavering occupied during a crisis. Mark said that he could not think of a better way; use the local positions and network to instil teamwork and discipline until a crisis, then all hands to the pumps to deal with whatever came.

"That's what we did in the RAF," he said, "we flew standing patrols until the battle got going, then all our sorties were reactive to German incursions, like a fire brigade; no standing patrols."

"Yes, but we couldn't handle more than one crisis," said the Colonel, "German aviators parachuting into this parish and nobody to meet them."

"It wasn't the end of the world," said Tom, "they got dealt with. Two are dead and two in custody. You're just a bit sorry you weren't here to deal with them, I know, but they got dealt with. Mark and Mister Murrell…"

"Yes, Robert Murrell. 'English Bob' as he was known in New Mexico. I hope that was a fair fight he got in. I know something of his reputation."

The conversation did not continue in that direction because the man himself walked in.

"I haven't done a thing all day," he said, "just drifted about. I've been to see that boy in the chapel of rest; he looks peaceful."

"I saw him too," said the Colonel, "nice shot if I may say so."

"You may say so. I've been to see the police to confess," said Murrell, "and PC Fidgeon says the doctor's report put his death down to the air engagement; I didn't know what to say after that, so I didn't tell him anything."

"Least said," said Tom, "it's true though what Fidgeon has been told, isn't it; he got shot in the course of his military service?"

"Indeed," said Murrell, "and he got two shots off at me before I drew and fired. I didn't want to be in a gunfight after all this time, but he gave me no choice."

"His air gunner said he was a good pilot, bad man," said Mark, "he seemed to accept the outcome."

The point was settled. Tom took his leave and Colonel Mallinson went into the meeting to offer Kaa one of his yarns, leaving Mark and Robert Murrell in the entrance hall. Mark asked him about 'English Bob'.

"My mis-spent youth," said Murrell, "I told you about trekking round the territories, sometimes, taking sides; I tried to help bring the Tunstall killers to justice. Some people remember that, that's all and whilst I think of it, the girls collected up the parachutes, so you can have one of them for your collection. They can have the other for the silk."

Mark did not push the wild west point as he should have been in the cub meeting anyway. Murrell said he'd wait for the land girl to escort her home; that blew Mark's fantasies for what might happen after the meeting, so he went back into the fray, feeling frayed.

The best he got from Elizabeth was a little wave as she departed. He walked back with Laurie 'Kaa' Hilton, who filled him in a bit about the work they'd done in Southend. This had consisted of tunnelling through a collapsed house in search of people inside, whom they had found safe in the cellar. Digging through the rubble had not been difficult, according to Laurie and the reason for that was they'd inadvertently followed the track taken by an unexploded bomb. The house had collapsed because of the bomb hitting it, no explosion necessary. Once it was confirmed that the people were safe, they all cleared out, only to start again on another house. They were still working on that near dawn when the locals relieved them.

The night was quieter to walk home through, or so it seemed. London was aglow again but Mark assumed that the attacking aircraft had come in over Kent, as none of the local searchlights were in action and no aeroengines were to be heard.

Back indoors and port in hand, Mark asked about funerals. Tom said that the airman who died on Home Farm would be buried on Saturday. The one who'd drowned and been taken to Eastminster would be buried there as that was where he was. Mark started a letter to his ward at the hospital telling them about his adventures, but tired of writing and resolved to finish it in the morning.

CHAPTER 13

THE MORNING TURNED OUT to be a nice one, so he finished the letter and took it to the Post Office. Having been seen there and interrogated about his recent escapades, he went on down to see the butcher, Harry Roberts. He was out, but his Father was there.

"Harry's out doing the deliveries," said Harold Roberts, "anything I can help with?"

"Social call," said Mark, "is he out on the bicycle?"

"No, he's using the van. The bicycle is OK for the boy, but he's gone back to London for a funeral so Harry's taken the lot, morning and afternoon deliveries."

"Can I borrow the bicycle then?"

"Surely; what had you in mind?"

"Oh, I thought to ride out to where the 'plane crashed, see what there is to be seen."

Half an hour later, Mark was at the crash site, astride the butcher's bicycle. Two men from the searchlight battery were on duty there and they recognised him from his earlier visit to their positions.

"Not much to see, sir," said the sentry, "nose dived in over there; most of it's buried. The ground's soft and marshy under the grass and it went in like a nail."

The tail plane had ripped off and was lying on the grass about fifty yards from where the sentry indicated that the 'plane had dug in. The grass around the entry point had been burnt off. The site reminded Mark of a giant firework; the burned grass showing where the sparks had fallen. They talked a little of their respective experiences of the crew before Mark broached the subject of getting a souvenir of the 'plane.

They went to have a look at the tail plane. The Ulstermen wanted the swastika-painted tail panel for their collection, but with a little help from them and some effort Mark left the scene with the tail wheel in the huge basket on the front of the borrowed butcher's bicycle. He rode it back to the rectory, where he put his heavy souvenir in the garage and then returned the bicycle. Harry Roberts was back from his rounds, so Mark had a chat with him before heading home on foot.

II

He'd decided to turn out for the Home Guard parade as he now had, courtesy of his hospital stay and the Polish pilot who'd paddled ashore, a set of Royal Air Force kit; helmet, goggles, oxygen mask, Mae West and parachute to show the men. Also, courtesy of the doctor and the land girls, he had the German equivalents, all stashed in the small luggage boot of his car.

He drove down to the parade, picking Laurie up on the way to help him unload it and reported to the Colonel, who said that he could introduce the kit and explain the differences, as well as telling the men about the flier he'd arrested, after the main debrief into Wednesday night's activities in Southend.

After opening the meeting, Colonel Mallinson and the men sat down in a group and discussed how Wednesday had gone; what they'd done right, what had gone wrong and how things could be better handled next time. That led seamlessly onto Mark talking about the fliers who'd bailed out over their parish. Mark said that he saw nothing of the parachutes descending, but he'd thought that the men were bailing out because of the way the 'plane struggled to stay on an even keel and then suddenly went over, probably when the pilot abandoned the controls.

He said nothing of the dead man in Murrell's yard other than he'd seen him there and that the one who'd landed in the orchard had accosted him, not the other way around.

"I suppose it was pot-luck," he said, "if I'd been his pilot with a stolen horse he'd have hitched a ride; as I wasn't and I had a revolver, he surrendered without a fight. I've talked to the men guarding the crash site and looking at the map there's about two thousand yards between the first man in Murrell's orchard and the crash site. The second man seems to have landed behind Home Farm, that's about four hundred yards from the first man. I don't know where the other two were, but it's about three thousand yards from Home Farm to the crash site."

They had a look at the kit. Mark told them that the stockinged feet story seemed to be holding good, to the extent that the man he'd arrested had lost his boots and the dead man he'd seen had lost one boot. The gear was stowed in the Home Guard section of the hall for future training purposes.

There was quite a good turnout for the airman's funeral next morning. Mark wore his DSO and DFC medals together for the first time and discovered that he was the RAF's representative. Robert Murrell attended wearing his Great War decorations. His heavy watch-chain bore a large silver coin and a six-pointed star. Mark paraphrased Keith Park's eulogy when the time came, having no original thoughts to use and felt quite pleased afterwards with his public speaking effort.

III

With a fortnight to go until Christmas, Mark's thoughts turned to how the festival would be celebrated with a war on. Tom said that during the phoney war period last year, the convention had been to buy no presents other than for children; there was a collection at the pub to see that the evacuees got something each. Cards could be sent to relatives, but not to bother in his case, wink, wink.

"So what's happening for Christmas here?" He pressed the point, "I've to be back at hospital the Monday after."

"Remember this is still a secret; your dad is supposedly on his way back from Egypt and will be here for Christmas. Your mum will come down to be with him for a few days because there's nowhere for them to stay together where she's working at the moment. The Polish fighter pilot who came through here recently has invited himself for a few days..."

"Karol?"

"Yes, and I have spoken to the hospital about Dying Brian, but he's not well enough to travel, in their opinion. The land girls all have a week off from the farm and are going home. Miss Fforest's home is in Wales and she thinks it too far to go and come back in a week, so she will be staying here with us also. Your granddad is coming over and he'll be the first to arrive; he says it's too noisy in Brentwood just now. James can't get leave but hopes to pop in for a day."

The countdown to Christmas had begun; traditionally a feast, that meant saving what could be saved to make an event of it. Mark's contribution was to be shooting pheasant on Colonel Mallinson's land. The Colonel said that if he got a brace, he'd match them with a second brace for the rectory, so Mark borrowed Murrell's short Wells-Fargo shot gun and attended Colonel Mallinson for a day. It was easier than he expected; pheasants were less of a challenge than magpies. They walked along a hedge, spaniel ahead of them. The Colonel said that when the dog found a bird in cover her tail would go up; that gave you a second or two before the bird burst out into flight.

The Colonel got the first one, as Mark did not react to the dog's tail; he was waiting to see what happened and that made him too slow.

"Never mind, now you know what to expect."

And he did. The next time the dog's tail went up, so did two birds and Mark got them, a left and a right.

"Well done, we'll make a fighter pilot of you yet."

Colonel Mallinson got the fourth to make the promised set. As they walked back to the house a cock flew across Mallinson's path and he fired, dropping it.

"And one for luck."

IV

Mark was hanging his five pheasants in the garage when Annie and granddad arrived in his Rolls Royce, he complaining about the weather, the war, "and for the first time in your life I can't tell you to get a haircut, Mark; what is the world coming to?"

He looked like an older version of Mark's Dad; silver hair and moustache, slightly stooped at the shoulders, but otherwise quite trim and fit. He'd aged a bit more since they'd last flown together, but not by much; after all, he'd been old for as long as Mark could remember. He enquired as to whether Christmas dinner was going to be worth getting up for, since there was a war on. Tom said that the butcher had sent them some venison and Mark had managed some pheasants, "so we're living off the fat of the land, Uncle Herbert; venison and pheasant, salmon and eels."

"Is there a pudding?"

Once granddad was parked in the study with a large brandy, Mark thought of broaching the subject of the Bristol.

"Yes, still got it; don't fly it anymore, amateur licence holders were grounded for the duration last year and I gave the others to the RAF. I remember the last war. I bought a 'plane; they commandeered it. I bought another; they commandeered that. I taught a lot of them to fly, you know, at the aero club site in Sheerness. No problem about people like me flying in the last war. This time it's different; they don't like amateurs. Alex Henshaw applied to the RAF and got turned down; can you imagine? Anyway, when it was over they gave me three 'planes back. None was mine, they were all newer models; bastards had taken the guns off. I'd love to have tried the guns out on one, what's it like?"

Mark said he could hear the guns going off but could not feel them. The reflector gunsight enabled him to line his machine up with an enemy aircraft, but he'd had to learn to aim off, as with a shotgun, to score and that meant the gun camera was sometimes filming empty airspace. As he fired the vibration of the guns made the sight look fuzzy and it was difficult to judge distance, "I reckon most people miss underneath or behind when shooting," he said, "but once I got the hang of it the main trick is to get the shots into the enemy before one of his mates gets behind me."

They talked about Mark's injuries and his medals before the subject came back round to the Bristol, which, it turned out, was hangered in a farm near Brentwood.

"His back field is long enough to take off from, but I haven't done it for a while. We were all supposed to be grounded anyway, unless on RAF business."

Mark resolved to get a flight in the Bristol when the opportunity presented itself and the sooner the better; the 'A' licence grounding order did not restrict him, in his opinion, because he was a military pilot. Granddad wrote to the farmer where the 'plane was stored, advising him that Mark would be along to look it over and to test it if the weather permitted, after which the ball was in Mark's court. He decided to go over and see if it would start, clean it up and make it ready before Christmas for a flight afterwards, weather permitting.

In this mission he had Karol Dubiel as his accomplice, the Pole having turned up in a borrowed car with some petrol in cans. Mark said he wanted to fly the Bristol. Karol described it as ancient, but there was little to stop it flying except a bad pilot.

They took a run over to see it. The dust cover turned out to be a parachute and underneath the machine looked quite good; clean if a bit tired-looking, maybe ready for action, hopefully ready to start. Mark sat in the cockpit and had a play with the controls, of which there were few. He'd forgotten how few.

Karol turned the propeller over with the ignition off.

"I think it will go," he said, "you flying now?"

"No," said Mark, "not with today's weather; we'll come again after Christmas."

It was cloudy and blustery. Mark wanted a bright crisp day and an earlier start for his sortie. They covered the machine over and headed back to Lavering, plotting all the while Mark's return to the air.

V

The night of the twenty-second of December was a noisy one. German aircraft started intruding upon British airspace around 5pm. London seemed to be getting it as well as dock facilities along the south side of the Thames estuary and places further afield. The Home Guard assembled but found themselves impotent while the Luftwaffe droned high overhead, pricked at by the coastal batteries.

Mark and Karol stood to with the men; they heard one machine overhead turning around and losing height, but saw nothing and Karol's best guess was that the pilot got well out to sea before jettisoning his load. Some bombs were dropped along the north side of the river Thames mid evening; possibly near Canvey or maybe Barking, judging from the noise. There were also detonations to be heard to the west, so maybe Chelmsford was hit. Whatever action there was that night missed Lavering, so Colonel Mallinson stood the watch down around 10pm except for the signallers, who would call the men out again if needed. Mark returned home wearing the Brodie helmet that had been his headgear of choice since he found out about the amount of metal showering down on this rural community.

VI

The following morning his Mum arrived, delivered by an army car, before he'd had his bath. She offered to bathe him, which he resisted, as his age had crept up on him and with it the embarrassment that would have accompanied his mother seeing him naked. She desperately wanted to, however, and the compromise was that after he'd bathed, he would let her see all his injuries and how they were healing.

"Your left eye looks much better; the swelling's gone down and the new lid fits nicely," she said, "but I don't know about those thick scabs, they don't look right somehow; what did the doctor say?"

"It's to do with my early treatment," said Mark, "The scabs are a bloody nuisance and itch like hell, but where the smaller ones have come off there is new skin beneath."

"Mind your language and you think they are going to be alright?"

"The doctor is thinking about peeling off the natural membranes that grew under the scabs and replacing them with grafts. He thinks the repairs lack the subcutaneous layers that a graft would import. They might improve in time, or he might be able to accelerate the process using his grafting techniques. It's all in the balance for the new year."

Mark dressed and had just entered the room for breakfast when Uncle Tom took a telephone call, which seemed to drag on somewhat.

"The summary is that your father can't get through on public transport today, as far as he can tell. He spent last night on a camp bed in the Foreign Office and the nocturnal bombing has blown too many gaps in the railway network. He's trying to sort something out and he'll ring us when he has a plan."

"If he can get to Northolt or Croydon I could get him in the Bristol," said Mark.

"Or not," said Tom, "you'd have trouble flying the way things are and you don't want to get shot down again, surely."

Mark decided to await developments. Meanwhile, he had various souvenirs to show his mum.

"You're having a good time here," she said, "I hope you are putting some effort into getting better?"

"Lots; most of the activities I got into to help Uncle Tom and the parish are in the evenings, so in the daytime I go walking, or play the piano. I bathe in salty water daily and Martha's cooking has put ten pounds on me in five weeks, despite the rationing."

Mark needed to know what his parents were doing in the war; he wanted to know why he had no home to go to, why he was in Lavering with his uncle. He could not say that he felt abandoned.

"Secrecy is so important," said his Mum, "but just this once; I am in the middle of nowhere with boffins who find my language skills helpful. I can't tell you more than that, but after the war I'll write a book and give you a signed copy."

"Thanks."

"And you must do the same. I can't imagine what you've been through. I just smile blandly when my friends ask; I tell them about the DSO and the DFC and the burns and the hair falling out, but I don't know what any of that feels like, or how you live with it. Thousands of young men are going to burn in this war before it's over and your story will be an inspiration to them all, if you write it."

"There's not much to write," said Mark, "shot up a few Germans, got burned when my kite self-destructed, got rescued, got patched up."

"There's a lot more to it than that," his Mum taunted, "but you have to make the decision to write it the way it happened. Have you read 'All quiet on the Western Front'? What about the 'Patriot's Progress' or the 'Memoirs of an Infantry Officer'?"

"No," said Mark, "I read Wilfred Owen's poetry at school and Adolf Hitler's 'Mein Kamph', but not novels. I saw 'all quiet' at the cinema."

"Not just novels, Mark; the authors were there, although they were in the support trenches. Williamson and Sassoon on our side; Remarque and Hitler were in the German army. They wrote from experience."

"Well, the Home Guard here have experience and chests stiff with medals to prove it. Half the men were in the trenches during the last war. Colonel Mallinson and the postman were in the Boer War as well. One old boy at the Home Guard parade was in the Zulu war. There's plenty of people around here with stories to tell; old Mister Murrell was in the wild west..."

"Are you sure these people are a good influence, Mark, I mean, wild west? And the Boer War was a long time ago."

"They have experience, Mum; I respect that. They also respect my experiences. I don't know how to write about what happened to me when the local Colonel was pinned down at Spion Kop for a day and a night and the postman shook Baden-Powell's hand when he helped relieve Mafeking. Uncle Tom has the Victoria Cross. Farmer Murrell was on the same ship as Jack Cornwell when he died getting his VC. These men made history and cast long shadows, even in their twilight years they are still at it. Four men in Uncle Tom's congregation survived going over the top on the first of July in nineteen sixteen; Mister Hancock lost a leg. The parish lost twelve men in that war, six of them on that day. Their widows still parade each Sunday to remind us that their loss is shared by us all. Miss Fforest and four of my scouts took the boat over the Dunkirk to evacuate our army under fire. What have I done compared to them?"

"You're the man in this parish who helped win the 'Battle of Britain' honour for the RAF flag," she said, "and there will be other honours, other battles, other victories and losses. You talk it well; the trick is to write it. I was in the last war, nursing casualties. I was bombed in France. I hope to avoid that distinction in this war but I will do whatever has to be done to make victory possible and to bring peace upon us all. I prefer peace. I developed a taste for France and I love flying. I can't fly or drive, but I let people like you take me. I won't rest until there is peace and I can eat with your Father in our favourite restaurant in Paris, drop a few chips in the casino, watch a race of two, then on to Gibraltar, knowing it's British and that our money is welcome there. Nice view of Africa from Gibraltar."

"What's Dad been doing?"

"Working; he'll tell you himself, or as much as he can. I don't know what he does most of the time, I just spend the money, but now there's a war on and the people responsible for that must be brought to heel, as fast as we can and that means all of us working to that end. I want visit Paris again before I am too old to enjoy it."

Tom took another call and reported to them thereafter; "He can get to Hornchurch; can we pick him up from there?"

Karol was in the room by then, the proud custodian of a borrowed car. Granddad offered his car for the journey instead, being the largest vehicle cluttering the drive and full of fuel. Karol would drive, Mark and his Mum would accompany him and the journey from Lavering to Hornchurch should take about an hour.

"All set then."

In the car, Karol wanted to understand the family tree, while trying to master the huge car.

"The man we collect is your father?"

"Yes."

"And he is Sir Henry Brabham."

"Yes."

"So you will inherit the sir, one day, Sir Mark?"

"Yes."

"So why not Granddad or Uncle Tom?"

"Uncle Tom is Sir Henry's younger brother. Granddad is also younger brother to the Baronet of his generation."

"But he has the money for airplanes?"

"Yes, so did the Baronet, but it was Granddad who wanted to fly."

"I like him; he told me to get a haircut."

"You will like Sir Henry as well."

"That is good."

At Hornchurch airfield, it was Lady Brabham shrilly telling the military police that she was arriving to collect Sir Henry Brabham that got them through security. He had the looks Mark might have inherited but for his accident; well defined features, brown hair going grey at the temples and a neat moustache.

Sir Henry's achievements had been with the Arab Bureau. He spent much of his time in Egypt but now that General Wavell commanded the army there, a Christmas leave beckoned; a few weeks free of the burdens of Empire, a chance to see what the Battle of Britain had done to his son. His Westland Lysander had barely touched the ground before he saw his reception committee. A Rolls Royce, Lady Brabham, an RAF driver and the bald wreck must be Mark.

"DSO, DFC and well done, maybe overdone; must be Mark."

They hugged. Mark said, "If you told me you'd got a Lysander you could have flown to Lavering."

"There's no airfield in Lavering."

"That crate only needs a large field. Look, I'll fly you there now."

"No, no, no; we have a good car – your Granddad's by the look of it. Who's the driver?"

"Houseguest for Christmas; Karol Dubiel. Polish. Paddled ashore at Lavering a few weeks ago and surrendered to a brownie with a catapult."

"And a rifle," said Karol, saluting.

"Interesting; right, get back in the car whilst I greet Lady Brabham properly, no peeking; no interruptions."

Mark and Karol waited in the car until Sir Henry and Lady Brabham joined them.

"Good," said Sir Henry, "drive on."

CHAPTER 14

THE LAST TO ARRIVE for the Christmas holiday was Miss Fforest; so nervous of being a houseguest, she arrived at the kitchen door where Martha spotted her.

"Lord above, chile, the front door is where you knock to enter. The kitchen door is for people who just walk in."

"Well, I walked here," said Elizabeth, dumping her kitbag down and leaning her hoe against the wall, "Mister Murrell drove us all to the station, but I told him I'd walk the rest of the way."

"And so you did," said Martha, "but why?"

"I wanted to think," said Elizabeth, "I don't know how to fit in with this family for Christmas. I'd rather help you in the kitchen, or do a bit of gardening; I brought my hoe. Reverend Brabham is a good preacher but he's a rubbish gardener."

"Too many cooks," said Martha, "anyway, you won't have time to help; lots of people here want to talk to you."

Martha ushered Elizabeth through into the breakfast room, where Granddad was sitting. Elizabeth could see no family resemblance between him and Mark, but that was only to be expected as Herbert had not been burned in any of his crashes.

"So you're Elizabeth," he said, "pleased to meet you. I should say that I've heard nothing about you at all, but I have now put a new battery in my hearing aid so that I can hear it all from your own lips."

Elizabeth blushed. Granddad poured her tea.

"I'm Mark's Great Uncle Herbert," he said, but he calls me granddad because I'm the same generation as his real granddad, who was my older brother."

"You're the one with the aeroplanes?"

"Yes. Loved flying from the moment I found out about it. The French led Europe in building aircraft, you know, so I had been flying for some years before I could get a British-made one."

"How did you learn to fly?"

"Er, I let Tom and Henry try the 'plane – Henry is Mark's Dad – and once they'd figured it out they told me what to do. It's magic though. Have you been in an aeroplane?"

"No."

"I'm sure you'll love it when you do."

Tom arrived for breakfast.

"Good morning, can we call you Elizabeth and are you boring her with politics, uncle?"

She blushed again.

"Not at all," said granddad, "she finds me fascinating."

"Good; now then, have you had breakfast?"

"No; sort of – we had something at the farm."

"Well at the rectory, it's not a breakfast unless Martha cooks it. I'll see what she's got for you."

"I can do that, I should be helping her anyway."

"No, no; you're on holiday. I know how hard Mister Murrell works you. I'll sort breakfast out, Uncle Bert can carry on boring you."

"It wasn't boring."

"Good, 'cos there's lots more of it, you know. Mark is in the bath, I heard him, so he'll be down soon."

Elizabeth turned back to Herbert; "So, tell me more about flying."

"Well, years ago, I saw a red kite moving its tail to control itself in the air, but when I got my first machine there was no tail as such, so I dragged various aircraft people to see red kites flying and later aircraft got a separate tail for the pilot to control. I don't know if I can claim to have invented that, but I certainly got clever people thinking in that direction."

Mark came down wearing the bathrobe that dried him gradually, not realising that Elizabeth had arrived. It was his turn to blush.

"I usually dress after breakfast," he said, "I can't towel dry, so I wear this robe and the water sort of soaks into it."

"You're lucky to have a bath each morning," said Elizabeth.

Breakfast was difficult. Mark's Mum came in and Mark found himself the object of a discussion between Mum and Elizabeth; she unthinkingly trying to get Mark to show off his wounds at the breakfast table. She'd also lapsed into a Welsh accent when talking to Elizabeth; it sounded strange to Mark and hilarious to Herbert, while Elizabeth herself failed to notice, not having met her before.

Elizabeth liked Granddad – Herbert – but felt ill at ease as a houseguest. Mark slipped away to dress, leaving her at the mercy of Herbert's politics, his Mum's Welsh accent and Karol's poor attempt at chatting her up. Karol discovered, by chance, that Elizabeth spoke French. His French was better than his English, although not by much. He did English and French with a Polish accent. Elizabeth did English, like her dad, with a thick Welsh accent and when she spoke French she had her Mother's harsh Parisian dialect.

By lunchtime Elizabeth had met everybody and the conversation was being led by granddad talking to Karol, who was trying to explain the differences between Hurricanes and Spitfires to an old man who wanted to buy one of each. Tom had stayed to listen for a while, but had a sermon to write, so he drifted off to the study.

Mark joined the room for a while, but as everyone was now speaking French he retreated to the piano to exercise his fingers. Tom joined him with an English Hymnal, words and music.

"Try something seasonal; I like 'Hark The Herald Angel's Sing' or what about 'I Saw Three Ships' or something with Christmas in it."

Mark had a flick through the book and chose 'while shepherds watched their flocks by night'.

"Oh, the cubs have different words to that one," said Elizabeth, joining him and flicking back to English.

"And if they sing those different words in a Welsh accent, we'll know where they got them from," said Mark.

"Oy!"

It was ages since he had sight-read music, but knowing the carols from many a Christmas past, playing them was not difficult. His Mum joined them, she and Elizabeth singing the words, both leaning over him to read them from the hymnbook. It made him feel claustrophobic, so at a convenient moment, he said that he wanted to get things ready for a walk after lunch.

He was in his room when Elizabeth knocked on his door.

"This note just came for you, from the Colonel," she said, handing the piece of paper over, "brought by his butler chappie."

'Dear Mark,

It's traditional to have a pheasant shoot on Boxing Day, but as we've already done that, I thought it might be fun to have a pistol and revolver shoot instead. You may have one or two things to try out; I have plenty of ammunition and if that Polish airman has made it down for Christmas, I have his pistol to give back,

Kind regards,
Mallinson
RSVP'

Mark handed the note to Elizabeth, who read through it.

"Is it an open invite, or just for you and Karol?"

"He knows you're here, so I'd reckon that it's open to us all."

Back downstairs, Mark told Karol, who liked the idea. Granddad said it sounded like fun but it was probably too cold for him to be outside for long, but he might sit in the car and watch.

Mallinson's butler had not waited for the answer that Mark penned over lunch, so delivering it was his afternoon walk. Elizabeth joined him for the exercise; Karol would have, but granddad headed him off.

It was freezing outside; Mark had wrapped up well but was still unprepared for just how cold it had become.

"Snow for Christmas, do you think?"

"Maybe. There's something funny about your family and Christmas."

"What's that?"

"No tree, no decorations."

"Ah, that's because we put the decorations up on Christmas Eve; that's what usually happens anyway. Then they stay up until the twelfth night. If we put them up too soon, they get dusty and anyway, we're all grown up now and Christmas is really for children."

II

It took them half an hour to walk to the White House, where Mallinson's butler took the note and read it.

"Oh good, he'll be delighted. He's not here now, but if I could offer you tea?"

They went in and settled in the kitchen.

"I'm sorry, I don't know your name," said Mark

"Eric Love, sir. I've been with the Colonel quite a few years now; I was his batman in the last war."

"I saw you had the Great War medals," said Mark, "Colonel Mallinson only mentions bits about it in passing."

"That's his way, sir; the current war is important, whilst what we did in the last one isn't."

Eric sat down with his tea, having poured theirs.

"What is impressive is the way that you held them in the air," he said, "they didn't expect that, did they?"

"No," said Mark, "they didn't."

"So you boys have done in the air what the Belgians did last time; held them up, made them devote more to the campaign than they wanted in time, money and men and all that while we're regrouping, getting ready for them."

"Invasion, you think so?"

"No, I don't think they'll come. There was a moment when I suppose it was possible but the navy closed the English Channel and you boys closed the air."

Warmed by the tea, they headed home, which was a forty-five-minute walk, being uphill.

"I was wondering," said Mark, "I must go back into hospital on the thirtieth, so do you fancy a trip into London at the weekend?

"And where would we stay?"

"My Dad's club, maybe. We'll have to ask him why he slept in the Foreign Office instead of going there, but if they have rooms we could stay there. Separate rooms, of course."

"Of course. What would we do in London?"

"Have to see what's open; museums, zoo, cathedrals, theatres, bars, night clubs..."

"Unexploded bombs, demolished houses, crashed aircraft, the fresh graves of Grey Brother's parents?"

"I wasn't thinking of London like that," said Mark, "but it's true; Derrick hasn't come back since he went there to see about his parents. We could go and look for him."

"Maybe; so there are two Londons. The one the Germans bomb night after night and the one you're talking about."

"In some ways, yes, there are; most of the bombing has been concentrated on the London docks and the surrounding area. They haven't hit the West End so much, not yet anyway."

"When were you last there? I've only been in London to change trains and that was a nightmare."

Mark had only been in London to change trains too since his escapade with a parachute last August and that was before the blitz got started, so he cornered dad to ask. Sir Henry said that he'd stayed in the Foreign Office to see incoming signals from Egypt, as General Wavell had attacked the Italian tenth army."

"And how was it going?"

"Have to wait for the newspapers. The clubs are still serving as hotels, but you pay for a room and then sleep in the cellars; I don't think that's good value for money."

"How about places to visit? Museums and such?"

"The zoo is open; they closed it but the animals got stressed by not having visitors, so they opened it again. Some theatres and cinemas are working – the Windmill and some other West End places, some music halls, most pubs, but everything is dislocated. There are more than two thousand unexploded bombs, not to mention ack-ack shells that fall back to earth after failing to go off."

Mark said he'd been thinking of a trip into London with Elizabeth. "Christmas day is Wednesday," he said, "and Thursday we're at a shoot with Colonel Mallinson. That leaves Friday, weather permitting, to fly the Bristol, then down to London on Saturday, stay the night, see what there is to be seen Sunday, stay at the club again, then I go off to Sussex and Elizabeth comes back to Lavering Monday morning."

"Well if the party is moving to London, you should take me too," said mum, "we haven't been seen around town since the war started, you know."

"I know," said Sir Henry, "but there's always something to do. When are you due back at work?"

"I'm hanging it out until the thirtieth," said mum, "we'll all be back at work then."

Mark sat quietly as his plan evolved into a family plan. Karol was making faces at him. He might not be able to follow all the conversation, but he'd understood enough to know that Mark's plan for taking Elizabeth to London to stay for a couple of nights now included chaperones.

III

The Sunday service was the traditional Christmas nine lessons and carols and was one of the few that winter to be held after dark. The church windows were too large for blackout curtaining, which had meant services were limited to daylight until a slight relaxation of the regulations in time for Christmas 1939. Thereafter, Tom had stuck to daylight services, with exceptions for the carol service, midnight mass and early morning communion on high days.

Derrick 'Grey Brother' Forder had returned to the parish on the Saturday and was thus in the choir to lead the service off by singing the first verse of 'once in Royal David's City' as a solo from the gallery while the choir processed in silence through the candle-lit church past a congregation well aware of the need to extinguish the lights if an alarm sounded.

Towards the end of the service a dishevelled individual slipped in and took a pew near the back. The churchwarden took the stranger a carol sheet. Karol became aware that something out of the ordinary was happening. He slipped to the rear of the church, tapping Mark on the shoulder as he left his pew. Mark saw that something was up, so he followed and they joined the churchwarden and the stranger as Tom took the lectern to read the final lesson.

"Says he's Dutch," the churchwarden explained, "says he came ashore and walked up here following the noise. Says he was in a fishing boat, started taking in water, so he got into the rowing tender and has been at the mercy of the tide ever since."

"A refugee then," said Mark, "he is most welcome."

"Tide's wrong," said the churchwarden, "if he landed as he said and came straight here, he'd have been washed out of the Pool of London and not from up the coast as he says."

"OK," said Mark, "I will slip out and see if anyone is at the police station."

He returned with PC Fidgeon as Tom recited the benediction and grace. Karol was standing in the same pew as the stranger and saw them enter. The stranger also turned to see what had attracted Karol's attention and saw the policeman. He tried to push his way past Karol, who caught the stranger's lapel and rabbit-punched his kidney, bringing the man to a halt.

Fidgeon stepped round and took the man's arm, then he and Karol escorted him from the church, joined by Mark and Colonel Mallinson. The service ended and the congregation slid off into the night, so the church was just about empty when Karol and Mark returned, the latter being supported by his fitter companion.

"Interesting service," said Karol, "Colonel is still at police station."

"What's been happening, and what's up with Mark?" asked Tom.

"I wrenched that big scab on my back struggling with that fellow," said Mark, "I'm alright, but I felt quite faint for a moment or two. Hurts like hell now though. Is there a signaller on the tower?"

"I don't think so," said Tom, "I'll check."

There was not. The last log entry was shortly before the service had started, recording that the beach position was closing.

Colonel Mallinson returned.

"That chap seems to have clear marks of his parachute harness on his skin," he said, "so we think he landed nearby and then came into church with his story about being from the sea. We haven't got anybody on the beach now, but PC Fidgeon was in the High Street for a good hour and went into the police station, he thinks, about five minutes before Mark alerted him."

"So our man didn't come up from the beach," said Tom, "wouldn't have got past Fidgeon without them seeing each other."

"I'll get some people together in the morning for a search party," said the Colonel, "see if we can find anything he might have left nearby."

IV

Mark was grateful that the rectory was so close to the church. Once inside, Karol helped him peel his shirt off. The scab had torn loose on one side and got stuck to his vest. Martha produced a large pair of scissors and Karol cut the vest, then with Elizabeth's help, they peeled it away and studied the wound.

"Might be best to lift the whole scab," said Tom, "dress the wound as though it were a fresh injury."

Mark's mum thought that the scissors would cut the loose part of the scab away, so that the rest could be left in place. Mark was aware that his treatment was being decided by committee and that they were all behind him.

"It's not fair, he said, "I'm the only one who can't see what's going on."

"I can't see either," said Esther, "everybody's too tall and standing in front of me."

The consensus was to use the scissors to trim off what seemed to be the loose bit of scab and then see what sort of wound that left beneath. Mark could hear the snipping, but felt nothing apart from the general pain of the wound. Once they'd done with the scissors, it seemed that the room fell quiet for a bit.

"Well?" said Mark.

"Well," said Martha, "I think I should tie a ring bandage; that will hold the remaining scab down and keep your clothes off the open wound. I don't think we should treat the wound itself with anything other than fresh air and salty baths."

"I agree," said mum, "it's only a week 'till Mark goes back to the hospital and the most that the open area of the wound will do in a week is dry up a bit."

"No chance of an infection getting in?" asked Sir Henry.

"I don't think so," said mum, "not here. There would be in hospital, but that's because there are always bugs in such places looking for someone to live on."

Martha applied the dressing she had in mind, which meant that Mark could sit in a chair and lean back without pressing on the most sensitive part. Tom then sorted out port and brandy for his guests, while the ladies left them to it.

Mark, Karol, Sir Henry, Tom, granddad. Mark remembered his father and uncle retiring to the study with granddad after meals when he was a child on holiday and now he was with them, one of them, instead of playing Mah Jong with the ladies. There was much to talk about, but little to say.

V

Mark felt awful when he awoke. The bandaging and his pyjamas were stuck to the wound on his back, so he drew his bath and slipped into it with his pyjamas still on to soak the cloth off his wound. His Mum knocked on the door and then peeped around it.

"I don't know if the bandaging was a good idea or not," she said, "the wound looks no better to me; maybe letting the air get to it today would be the best idea."

Mark did not like the idea of wandering round a house full of people half naked and said so. Martha brought him breakfast in his room and an hour later Karol, who'd popped in to be nosy, said the wound looked dry. They tested it gingerly with the corner of the bed sheet and that did not seem to stick, so Mark dressed in a shirt without a vest beneath and joined the throng downstairs.

His Mum had been on the telephone to the hospital with a view to him being seen that day. Mark did not want to spend Christmas in Sussex so he put a call through to Doctor Hardmann and discussed how the wound had dried up after an hour or so of fresh air.

"Sounds promising," said the doctor, "so if you keep it clean, soak off anything that sticks to it and behave, it should not kill you before Monday. If it causes you any difficulty, let me know and I'll come right away."

Martha tried a different approach; she made up a thick pad and taped it to Mark's shoulder blade so that his shirt hung loose over the wound.

"Now, that might work as long as you don't lean on anything."

It seemed comfortable, but to go out for a walk, Mark borrowed Karol's greatcoat, he being broader and the garment looser. Karol borrowed a nice full-length leather motor coat from Herbert and, together with Elizabeth in her land army greatcoat, they set off into the weak sunshine.

"Are we going anywhere in particular?" said Elizabeth.

"I thought we might try looking in on Derrick Forder, see how he is," said Mark, "so we'll start at the church and see if he's rostered to be doing anything."

"He's not," said Laurie at the church, "he's got schoolwork to catch up on, so he should be in the village hall doing it."

The three walked down to the hall.

"He should be here this afternoon," said the teacher, "I can't have them all at once, there's not enough chairs."

"He's billeted in one of the alms houses," said Elizabeth, "there were problems when the evacuees arrived, because the reception committee were expecting all girls, so fitting forty boys in without notice was tricky."

Miss Evans, with whom Derrick was billeted, said that he'd gone off as though to morning school.

"He's a good boy, you know," she said, "If he's not at the church or the hall, I would think that he's on the beach."

A further half an hour got them to the coast. The pillbox crew when they got there were all girl guides. They had seen Derrick come down to the beach and they thought that he'd started walking north into the dunes.

Mark asked them to tell Derrick that he was looking for him if he returned via their position, and to signal the tower if that happened. Karol walked towards the sea from whence he came by dinghy to look along the beach to see if he could see the boy. Mark half followed him, since the guides had gone into a huddle with Elizabeth, their captain, and he was socially excluded.

Karol turned to see Mark following and then pointed out to sea. Mark hastened across the hard sand to see what Karol was excited about.

"I don't know the English," he said.

"Mine," said Mark, "It's a mine."

"It's yours?"

"No Karol, is A mine."

The tide was on the way in, bringing the sea mine with it. From what Mark could see it was still floating, but if it grounded there was always the chance of it going off if it settled on one of the detonating pins.

They walked back to the pillbox and pointed the new hazard out to the guides, who signalled the information to the tower and the coastal battery. There then followed a flurry of messages; the Colonel was at the village hall. Both he and the coastal battery knew how to deal with the mine by shooting a rifle at a detonating pin. There was not a rifle at the beach. The coastal battery did not want to come out to deal with it, let the Home Guard handle it; Home Guard had little ammunition, so, OK, if Mallinson deals with it the coastal battery will refund him the ammunition.

It took about an hour from when Karol spotted the device for these messages to be exchanged before Sergeant Pavitt attended the beach, carrying a rifle. He had a look at the mine through binoculars. "Still floating, it seems."

"And still coming in," said Mark, "it's moving left to right as well."

"Yes, that's what the tide does here," said Pavitt, "a lot of the water flows up the estuary to our right, then on the ebb it can't go straight out to sea because of the weight of dead water in the way, so it runs along the beach northwards."

"This makes sense," said Karol, who'd been on that tide in a rubber boat recently enough to remember the power of the water.

The mine was about four hundred yards out to sea when it changed attitude, quite distinctively. Instead of bobbing along showing about a foot above the waves, it was now showing more like eighteen inches and through the binoculars Pavitt could see it was rolling instead of floating.

"It's grounded," he said, handing the binoculars to Karol. After him they each took a look in turn, including the guides, so that they would all be able to recognise the difference, lest it happen again.

"What's the form now?" asked Mark.

"I'll try to hit one of the pins," said Pavitt, "to set it off. The water should cushion the explosion. Those things are designed to damage a ship by displacing the water, using the oggin as a battering ram to split the ship's plates. We should be safe here, shouldn't even get wet."

"We'll wait in the pillbox," said Elizabeth, "just in case."

She and the guides took cover. Pavitt lay down on top of the pillbox, resting the rifle on his haversack. The position was not right, so he relocated to the top of the signalling tower, then scrounged the greatcoat Mark was wearing to fold up on top of his bag. Karol took a position behind him with the binoculars.

"I haven't got a good view of any pin yet," said Pavitt, "and it's further out than I want to shoot. When we were briefed about these things, we were told that a hundred yards was the ideal sort of distance."

The mine could still be seen rolling, but now more than two feet proud of the water.

"Look now," said Karol.

"I don't suppose it'll come in any further," said Mark, "it looks stuck."

"I suppose so," said Pavitt, "I'll give it a shot."

Mark put his fingers in his ears. Pavitt adjusted the rear sight and settled down behind the rifle, taking careful aim. He cracked one off, which hit the mine, as they all heard the metallic ting of the impact.

Sergeant Pavitt worked the rifle bolt and aimed again. Mark saw the mine roll as he heard the crack and this time he saw a distinctive plume of water erupt just behind the mine to show where the bullet had gone over.

"Blast."

He jacked the action again, steadied himself and fired. This time any noise of the bullet's impact was drowned out by the explosion. The sea parted, water and sand thrown in all directions. Mark glimpsed this before ducking behind the pillbox. Pavitt slid down behind the haversack and greatcoat that the rifle was resting on, Karol folded himself down behind Pavitt and then the blast wave struck; a brief pulse of hot air.

As Pavitt had predicted, they stayed dry, although they had felt the blast.

"Signal," said Karol, pointing up the beach, "W.E.L.L. D.O.N.E."

The guides piled out of the pillbox to reply to the coastal battery and to exchange messages with the tower, which was a bit pointless in Mark's judgement, as he was quite sure the Colonel knew that the mine had exploded.

VI

The excitement over, Sergeant Pavitt packed up to head for the village, accompanied by Mark, Karol and Elizabeth. They went to the village hall to see the Colonel, who was suitably pleased and organised tea.

"I knew Sergeant Pavitt was the best man for the job; he was a sniper at Gallipoli you know."

"Any luck with the parachute search yet?" asked Mark.

"Not yet; I have eight men out on a sweep search, whilst Eric and Harry Roberts are trying their luck at tracking to see if they can find any signs as to where he came from."

Morning school had broken up and they were still drinking tea and talking of sniping in Gallipoli when Derrick Forder arrived for the afternoon session.

"I heard you were looking for me, Akela," he said.

"Yes, I heard you were on the beach."

Derrick showed them his sketchpad. He'd been drawing a device he'd found in the dunes when he heard the rifle fire. Then he saw the mine go off, so his second sketch was a vivid image of the explosion.

"I drew that whilst waiting for this shrapnel to cool down enough to be picked up," he said, proffering a piece of the mine's casing; about nine square inches of metal, with a ribbed hole through it where a pin had, until recently, protruded.

"Nice souvenir," said Mark, "how did you find it?"

"I saw it land," said Derrick, "about ten feet in front of me."

Mark had no idea how to ask the boy how he felt about losing his parents, nor whether asking such questions would do any good.

"It's a large piece," said Colonel Mallinson, gently taking it from the boy, "but what matters more is your sketch, Derrick; that's an anti-personnel mine."

"We've seen low-flying German 'planes sewing mines at sea," said Derrick, "so perhaps they are dropping stuff in the dunes as well."

"Possibly," said Mallinson, "you must show me where this one is and we'll see about dealing with it. Apart from that trip, we must make the dunes out of bounds until they are safe." He paused. "Derrick, we know your parents were killed in the London bombing, but none of us knows how to say sorry to you for your loss."

"I am sorry about it too," said Derrick, "I hadn't seen them for so long. They visited here last July; stayed in the inn for a few days, but that's more than six months ago. I remember them...what they looked like, but I can't remember what the house smelled like anymore. I fear forgetting them."

"I don't think we ever forget things like that," said Mark.

"We might," said the Colonel, "but that only happens as the pain fades. We all share in your pain, Derrick, even though the loss is not ours. Your loss hurts us all because we know you."

Elizabeth gave Derrick tea and they sat together, a silent group, while he drank it.

"I like it here," he said eventually, "I've been on the beach this morning; I like the fresh wind and the salty taste it has and I suppose that's just as well, as I have nowhere else to go."

He dissolved into tears and leaned onto Elizabeth's lap. She put her hands on his shoulders and supported his grief, but he pulled back after a moment.

"Sorry; being touched by other people makes remembering what my Mum felt like all the harder."

Mark got his handkerchief out, which had been washed since he lent it to the German flier and lent it to Derrick, who dabbed his face and composed himself.

"What happens when Miss Evans can't look after me?" he asked, "or if the war ends and we are supposed to go home? Mine's flattened. I couldn't find anything to remember the old house by. Just bricks. I'm not even sure if I was looking at my house or next door. They were all wrecked."

There was a long pause before Colonel Mallinson spoke; "we fitted you all in when you got here. We've juggled things a bit; have you always been with Miss Evans?"

"Yes."

"Well, some people had to move around. I've got six brownies and a teacher at the White House, because we were expecting girls when evacuation started and we'd planned on taking three. We doubled that to make room for boys elsewhere. Miss Evans has been helpful and I know from her how helpful you are, Derrick. In fact, I'd say you're really looking after her, which is a considerable burden for you at ten years old."

"It's not difficult. I just do the things she finds hard."

"And lots of them, make no mistake, Derrick; she has a better standard of living with you there chopping wood, lighting fires, washing clothes and cooking than she would have living alone. You may have been destined by fate to live in this parish, but whilst you are doing so you make life brighter for Miss Evans, you illuminate our church with your singing and you hold positions of responsibility in the cubs and in civil defence. This parish, in return, shall look after you."

"All my life?"

"As things are, you'll go and do national service when you're old enough. The war may still be on then or it may not, but you'll serve your country and then come home to Lavering. In fifty years, you'll be the old soldier with a string of medal ribbons and a brain full of war stories nobody wants to hear."

"But we like listening to your stories."

"Yes, but that's now. *'In fifty years, when peace outshines remembrance of the battle lines...'*"

Derrick picked up the thread;

> *"Adventurous lads will sigh and cast*
> *Proud looks upon the plundered past."*

"I was in Haig's last drive, you know," said the Colonel, "marvelling that any came alive."

"Poor granddad's day is done?" asked Derrick.

"Not this granddad," said the Colonel, "but also think *'Dulce et decorum est pro patria mori'*. It may be an honourable task serving our country, but it's also a grim one."

"I'd disagree with Wilfred Owen," said Mark, "Our duty to our country is clear."

"Well said, but the ancient Greeks had a maxim to the effect that you can always persuade men to fight for their country, but you can't convince old men it's going to be fun." The Colonel looked distant as he spoke, his mind wandering back to Flanders.

"I can't imagine it being fun," said Derrick, "but it's got to be done and that's that."

"Yes," said the Colonel, "I thought that last time. I stand by the war memorial every so often and read the names on it. I knew them all, you know. Would this village have been a better place had those twelve men lived? Would the world have been better or worse without their sacrifice? I don't know."

"We have each other," said Mark, "that's the basis of every unit isn't it; we're a village, a cub pack, a scout group, a Home Guard Unit, a church. We are banded together as are squadrons and regiments or ships' companies. We all share the battle honour of Lavering 1940 and always will."

"And 1941," said Elizabeth, "the end is not in sight."

Chapter 15

Grey Brother seemed at peace with himself, Mark concluded as they walked into the rectory drive. Now he wanted to get the heavy coat off and the dressings, just let the air get to his wound. That would be difficult with so many people staying; privacy was not possible; his Mum, or Elizabeth would want to keep him company.

Once indoors, his plans were overtaken by events. Martha was first to notice that his shirt was stuck to the wound, so she formed a posse of women to help him take it off.

"It's not too bad," she said, "maybe keep it bare for a while, and see if it dries up."

Lillie got an old shirt; Mark put on and then they cut out the area to expose the wound. That meant Mark looked dressed from the front and sitting on the piano stool, he looked in good form, while feeling a bit rough and cold, as the December chill crept in through the windows. Not to mention itching under his scabs. While they'd been out he'd been distracted from the non-stop irritation of his injuries, but indoors he felt imprisoned. He tried putting his forage cap on, and that made him feel warmer, so he added a scarf and was feeling much better when Tom returned.

"They've found that chap's stuff," he announced, "parachute, suitcase, radio set, everything."

"What happens now?" asked Mark.

"The police and security people will take care of things," said Tom, "In the last war, spies were shot or hanged."

The rest of the day passed slowly, so after dark and before dinner, Tom suggested that they break with convention and put the Christmas decorations up.

"I know we're supposed to do it Christmas Eve," he said, "but if we do it now we'll be free tomorrow to do whatever we like."

They got the boxes out and had a look at the paper decorations left over from previous years. They were uninspiring, but the tree had been sitting in the garage for a few days, so they brought that in and put the angel on it, then had a drink. Several drinks. Mark was feeling a bit light-headed when dinner was ready and didn't eat much.

After dinner, he excused himself and went to bed early. Karol went out for a walk, during which he checked with the church to see what air activity there was, only there was none.

"I think they're winding down for Christmas," said Derek Pilley at the church, "both sides. There has been little air activity all day. The action has been on the ground, that mine on the beach and then the parachutist's stuff being found."

He returned to the comfort of the rectory, where he spent the rest of the evening playing cards with Elizabeth, since that activity did not require him to struggle much with his English.

II

Christmas Eve dawned, late as it does 52 degrees north of the equator. The butcher's boy arrived with some sausages that Martha had ordered and a goose that she had not. This turned out to be a gift from the churchwardens and caused a rethink about what to eat when.

"There's a war on and we've got more meat for Christmas than we would normally get in a month of Sundays," said Martha, "it's a good job there's plenty of people here to eat it."

Upstairs, Mark had awoken, but stayed in bed. He slept on his front and felt comfortable; he also thought that getting up would make him feel worse, so he stayed put until his Mum came to check on him.

She had a look under the covers and said that his pyjamas did not look stuck to the wound, so he could get up and get a move on. Mark eased himself upright, while Mum prepared his bath. He favoured privacy that morning and she took the hint.

Downstairs, Hetty and Elizabeth were already out delivering a pheasant; Tom was out on a mission and Karol had gone with him. Mark was still eating in the company of his granddad when the telephone rang. Martha answered it; taking calls had become part of her job, which had caused some fun in the village, as while her Jamaican accent was not too strong in the flesh, telephones have the unfortunate knack of amplifying such things and a lot of people could not understand her on the telephone.

"Mark, take this call please," she shouted to him from the hall.

"It's James," said the receiver, "can you pick me up from Ongar station?"

"Yes," said Mark, "when?"

"What's good for you?"

"An hour?"

"Excellent. See you then."

"Anybody interesting?" enquired granddad.

"James, he'll be home today. I'm to pick him up from Ongar in an hour."

"My car, you drive; I'll come with you."

III

It was a nice day for a drive; bright and cold, but not frosty. Mark enjoyed driving his granddad's Rolls Royce, turning heads in each village they passed through. James was opposite the station when they arrived, in a group of air force uniforms, mixed trousers and skirts. The Rolls immediately commanded their attention.

"Ladies and gentlemen," said James, "may I present my cousin Flight Lieutenant Mark Brabham, DSO, DFC."

"And casualty," said Mark, taking a defensive position as James tried to bear-hug him, "Easy now, the bark's still loose or chipped in places."

Ongar's village hall had become the 'Ops' room for Eleven Group's North Weald aerodrome after Ops had been bombed there in July. A new subterranean facility was under construction, but in the interim the village hall served quite well and the ad hoc reception committee for Mark were people that should have been in it hard at work.

"Nothing's happening at the moment," said James, "so I've got a three-day pass; due back at North Weald on the twenty-eighth."

"Ah, I can drop you back," said Mark, "I'm going to Brentwood on the twenty-seventh to fly the Bristol, so twenty-eighth I'm free."

"Are you sure that's wise?" said James, "I mean, don't you know there's a war on?"

"Yes, and I've got to get back into it," said Mark.

"Haven't you done enough? Shouldn't you get a nice training job or a desk next?"

"No, I've got to fly."

"Well, Park has command of a training group now," said James, "and I'd bet he'd be delighted to have you as a flying instructor."

"I'm not so sure," said Mark, "my face suggests that I'm not necessarily the best person to learn from."

The reception committee had broken up, some returning to their positions, others standing back a bit, except for one willowy WAAF; fair hair and golden skin, she looked at Mark intently through huge brown eyes.

"Mark, this is Company Assistant Alma Burton; she wanted to meet you."

"I was on duty when...you had your accident," said Alma, "your microphone was open."

"Oh, I'm so sorry, did I scare you?"

"It was terrible; I could hear what was happening to you but I couldn't do anything. I am pleased to see you getting better. None of the others I heard like that survived, as far as I know."

Mark didn't know what to say. He looked at her soft brown eyes, which reminded him, quite inappropriately, of a spaniel staring at a biscuit.

"Could I see you again?" she asked, "You'll be up this way again soon? I'd like to see you."

"Yes, of course; I'll be bringing James back and...I don't know when I'll be fit, but I'm sure to be around soon. I'll keep in touch through James."

"Thank you." She saluted, turned and trotted off to the hall.

"Battle scars make you irresistible," said James, "I've been trying to pull her for over a month and it took you ten seconds.

Quite a catch if you can land it; her Dad's Air Commodore Burton."

"I'd have thought your handsome features a better bait than my overdone visage," said Mark.

"Not at all," said James, "WAAFs are stand-offish to people like me; untested in battle, you see, whereas you've been there and survived, so you'll get a desk job and promotions; makes you a safer bet to live happily ever after with."

"I'll be flying again as soon as I can," said Mark.

"Well, keep it to yourself; as long as they think you're grounded you're in with a chance. What a chance, what a field to play in..."

"If we don't get a move on," shouted Granddad from the car, "there won't be time for a pink gin before lunch and I deserve a large one."

Granddad shifted to the back seat so that the two young airmen could sit side by side to talk on the journey. James had joined a Spitfire Squadron at North Weald in mid-November, since which time he'd been on regular standing patrols in the short hours of daylight but had not yet fired his guns. He had applied for evaluation on night fighters; they had a hush-hush way of creeping up on German bombers in the dark and he wanted a crack at that.

"It's not all that dangerous; there have been losses, but they're accidents, crash-landings and the like."

"The trouble is, JB, that you have to land after each sortie," said Mark, "and get it right every time. I don't have a night rating, but I suppose that's the way the war is going for now."

"But not for long," said granddad from the back seat, "the Boche are flying by night just now because of the long hours of darkness; once the days draw out again, they'll have to change tactics, watch and see. Once the nights shorten, come May and June, they'll not be able to bomb at night."

"What do you think they'll do next?" asked James.

"In the last war, they put a lot of faith in their U-Boats strangling our imports," said granddad, "and this time they've got all the Channel Ports to launch them from, so I reckon you'll see the U-Boat war hot up. They couldn't beat you in the air in daylight, so they won't try that again; they'll consolidate in the spring and try to besiege us and we've got the largest navy and merchant marine in the world. They are already losing this war."

IV

By the time they got back to Lavering, the tree was decorated, live mistletoe and holly sprigs adorned various ornaments and paintings and the tired paper decorations had been put up in the dining room.

"Is Uncle Senry around?" asked James, using his baby-name for his favourite and only uncle.

"He went out to visit Colonel Mallinson in Mark's car," said Tom, "I think he also wanted something in Chelmsford. Lillie went with him. They said they'd be back for supper."

After lunch, Mark started trying to think. Elizabeth was, in his opinion, sweet on him. The indications were that he could take her on a proper date if he wanted, her working class background no issue. Uncle Tom had facilitated him seeing her to the extent that she was a houseguest for the week and she had elected to stay for Christmas instead of going home to Swansea.

She also had Karol's attention. James had ignored her almost completely since first meeting her just before lunch; she was not in the Royal Air Force, so she was ignorable. Meanwhile, the delightfully blond Alma Burton, whose father was definitely not working class, was keen on seeing him and was stationed a mere forty-five minutes, as the Rolls Royce purrs, up the road.

Mark interrupted Karol and Elizabeth to ask her to walk with him, just down through to the High Street. Karol would have joined them but James headed him off. They held hands as they walked.

"It's going to be a busy week," he said, "not like holidays in the old days."

"Busy doing what?"

"Well, we've got Midnight Mass in church tonight, then the Christmas service in the morning. Christmas dinner will take most of the rest of the day, then on Boxing Day we are invited to Colonel Mallinson's for a pistol shoot. The day after, Karol and I are going to try and get Granddad's old Bristol off the ground. I need to fly, Elizabeth; just briefly, I have got to make sure that I still can."

"So what will I be doing whilst you're pistol shooting with Colonel Mallinson and flying with Karol?"

"Holding my hand. You're welcome at the pistol shoot and you know that Colonel Mallinson will make you welcome. On Friday, come with us; I'll take you up."

"I don't know about flying," said Elizabeth, "God gave me no wings."

"Nor me; I got mine from Cranwell, but I'd been flying with granddad for years before that. The 'plane we're going up in on Friday – I think I was about four years old the first time I went in it. I am looking forward to sitting in it again."

PC Fidgeon came out of the Post Office as they approached it and they let go of each other's hands on sight of him.

"Did you hear that the Home Guard found that parachutist's kit?" he asked.

"Yes," said Mark, "radio and such is what I heard. A real spy then?"

"That's for a court to decide," said Fidgeon, "enemy alien, anyway, with a parachute, radio, codebook, money. Funny thing though, no weapon at all."

"What, no knife or anything?"

"No knife, no gun. Presumably he didn't intend doing anybody any harm. I bet he regretted that when your foreign pilot got started on him."

"Hmm. He could have surrendered without a fight."

"I suppose; you all set for Christmas?"

"Yes, thanks; and you?"

"I'm on a course for a few days," said Fidgeon, "unexploded bomb identification, it's for prioritising which ones to deal with."

"That's useful; have we many around here?"

"There's a few; all in fields so they will be low priority and might never be dealt with. London's got thousands, so once I'm trained I'll be able to take a turn there, helping out, gaining experience."

There being nothing else to say, they passed on, drifting towards the hall.

"How many of your girls have gone back to London for Christmas?" Mark asked.

"About half the evacuees," she said, "and some of the parents of the rest have come here."

Their conversation was interrupted by the sight of Mark's car coming up the street towards them. Sir Henry pulled up and hopped out.

"Just dropped Colonel Mallinson off," he said, "charming fellow; we've been to the police headquarters in Chelmsford to use their communications facilities. Jump in, tell you about it on the way back."

Lillie climbed out of the front and tipped the seat so that Mark and Elizabeth could squeeze into the back. It was quite cosy and Mark made a mental note to let Karol drive on Friday; or James, because he did not want either of them in the back cosying up to Elizabeth the way he had no choice about just now.

"I just had to know how things were going in Egypt," said Sir Henry, "when I left, General Wavell was gearing up for a push at the Italians in Libya. It looked promising and we had high hopes, but Wavell and his men have exceeded all expectations."

"Successful mission then?" asked Mark.

"Absolutely," said Sir Henry, "routed the Italian forces and he's taken over one hundred and thirty thousand prisoners. It's a significant victory. The Italians can only reinforce Libya by sea and that sea is controlled by the Royal Navy, particularly since the Italians got caught in harbour last month, like rats in a barrel."

That called for a drink, so by the time the evening meal was ready, the whole party were feeling the warming effects of alcohol.

"I'd better not have any more," said Tom, "I've got a sermon to give tonight."

The party sorted themselves out for the Midnight Mass service. Tom went on ahead; Aunt Hetty and James, Sir Henry and Lillie, Martha and Esther, Herbert and Annie, Mark, Elizabeth and Karol. The church was busy; a good turnout for communion in the dark. It was past 1am before the party reassembled in the rectory for sherry and mince pies.

CHAPTER 16

CHRISTMAS DAY, 1940. THERE was a war on, but they felt congenial and welcoming of their foreign visitors – Karol from Poland, Martha and Esther from Jamaica and Elizabeth from Wales. Standing in his pew for the Christmas morning service, Mark felt that no time had passed since he'd stood there the night before.

Another good attendance, he noted; a lot of whom had not ventured out in the dark last night. Once these two key acts of worship were complete, the feast of Christmas could begin with a large sherry before the dinner.

Christmas dinner started later than a normal lunch and ran on through the usual dinnertime. Elizabeth reckoned that they were at the table for over five hours altogether before the meal was over, enjoying cold meats, fish and then game courses. In Wales, they'd have pushed the furniture to the sides of the room and danced, but in this stiff English household, nobody had the energy so they had coffee and spirits to accompany their war talk. The ladies retired to play Mah Jong, the gentlemen considered their respective futures. They all felt it unlikely that they would be able to regroup in this way before next Christmas;

"But you should all come here if you can," said Tom, "it's important to have such things to look forwards to."

"Hear, hear."

II

Boxing Day dawned bright, although by the time it dawned most people were up and about. Granddad was sitting at breakfast when Mark walked in,

People drifted in for breakfast and by the time Mark had finished eating, only James was conspicuous by his absence. Karol went to look for him, while Mark joined his uncle in the study.

"These are the remaining cartridges for that Colt revolver," said Tom, "point four-five-five inch. British revolvers from the last war take the same cartridges. Here's my Colt automatic and I've got about two hundred rounds left for it, so take it easy."

Mark also had the fighter pilot's Luger and the Walther pistol from the chap who parachuted into Murrell's.

Karol had a pistol which he said took the same cartridges as the two German pistols Mark had. He showed Mark his gas mask case, in which he had quite a lot of ammunition, loose.

"We play cards for them at the airbase," he said, "I am a good card player."

James put in a sleepy-eyed appearance on his way to breakfast. He'd managed to come on leave wearing his revolver, for which he had three boxes of ammunition, each containing twelve rounds. He went off to eat. Tom said that he, his brother and Granddad Herbert would appear later.

Once James was ready, they put the kit in the Mark's car.

"You drive please James," said Mark, "I'll sit in the back with Elizabeth."

Bad idea. It was alright asking James to drive and letting Karol sit on the front seat, but the two of them kept such a close eye on Mark and Elizabeth that it was embarrassing for them to touch, even accidentally, and not touching was virtually impossible in the back of an Austin Seven.

"It's OK for you two to cuddle," said James, "I won't tell Alma Burton."

"Who's she?" asked Elizabeth; you could imagine her clearing her throat and spitting between the two words, although she did not quite do so in the car.

"Oh, just a WAAF officer at North Weald," said James, "she fancies Mark you know."

"I didn't know," said Elizabeth, making the limited gap between them on the back seat wider.

"I don't know her," said Karol, "yet; I hope to be friends with every WAAF in United Kingdom before I go home to Poland."

"I only met her once," protested Mark, "she was on duty the day I crashed and burned, that's all."

No other car used the street as they drove to Colonel Mallinson's, but several were parked around the White House when they arrived and their host was waiting to greet them.

"Thank you for coming, Merry Christmas," he said, "we should have an interesting morning, which starts with tea."

Mark recognised Sergeant Pavitt, the butcher Harry Roberts and his father as he entered the study; the other man sitting there was Doctor Hardmann, and the man serving tea Mark knew was Eric Love. Ron arrived shortly after, dressed in his Air Raid Patrol uniform. Colonel Mallinson handed Karol the pistol he'd surrendered to the Brownies when he came ashore. Karol handed it back;

"It's OK, I have another," which he produced, "same model. Please keep first one as souvenir."

"Thank you very much," said the Colonel, "we have several interesting pistols to try today."

Karol showed Mallinson his haversack of ammunition.

"That's good," said the Colonel, "nice mixture; I bought a nine-millimetre pistol a few years ago and I have some ammunition for it, which will also fit the German pistols."

"Oh good," said the doctor, "I was wondering whether we had any more; fourteen rounds don't go far in practice."

Next to arrive was Bob Murrell, carrying his revolver in a canvas shopping bag.

The tea ceremony complete, Colonel Mallinson led them outside to where he and Eric had set up some targets in the garden. The backstop was a grassy bank, which Eric said had the bomb shelter beneath it.

"Quite a bomb shelter," said the doctor, who had been in it, "more of a command centre, I'd say."

"I planned on being comfortable if I had to spend the war in it," said the Colonel, "and I am sure that Chancellor Hitler has made similar arrangements. He will certainly need them."

The shoot started with Elizabeth facing a target and half a dozen would-be teachers willing to tell her how to do it. Gradually, everyone had a turn at everything. There was a lull in the shooting when Granddad's Rolls Royce swept up the drive.

"There's a policeman standing on top of your wall trying to see what's going on," said Herbert, as slid out of the vehicle, "ought not to be allowed."

Eric Love went to get more tea, while Herbert had a play with Murrell's cowboy revolver and Tom showed off his lack of prowess with his pistol. Sir Henry kept to the rear, where he confided to the doctor that he preferred hand grenades because he did not have to aim them. He liked the look of a Walther police pistol though. Colonel Mallinson said that it had been found with the parachute and radio equipment of the fellow who arrived at church on Sunday, but there had not been any point handing it in, as it would have made no evidential difference to that chap's predicament. What was needed was more ammunition for it.

"We've hanged two German spies this month already," said the Colonel, "I mean us as a nation, not the local Home Guard. That chap may be for the drop, or not; but either way his thirty-two is more use to us than to a court."

Eric Love got the German machine gun out.

"Herbert, sir," said the Colonel, "if you please."

The weapon was on a crude tripod mount, the legs being secured to an old door, which lay flat on the ground so that the firer would be standing on it.

Granddad took his place on a stool behind the weapon with Messrs Love and Pavitt close behind him, one by each shoulder. He squeezed the trigger and five shots rang out. He repeated this, getting the burst down to three shots, repeated that a couple of times, then let a longer burst go.

"Nice piece," he said, relinquishing his position, "and that's what the Germans have on their aircraft?"

"Yes," said Mark, "above and one below the tail. Hurricanes attack them from over the wing from the side, bit of a blind spot there. If they want to break the formation up, they attack from the front."

"Flying straight at them sounds especially dangerous," said Herbert, "whose idea was that?"

"It's the way the battle developed," said James, "then there is no need to aim off and one Hurricane squadron attacking like that can scatter the bombers, making targets easier to pick off one at a time."

"And when we've seen the fighters off," said Mark, "we can take our pick. They try to get their formation back together to cover each other and to bomb together. If they can't, we do them more damage and they scatter munitions all over the place."

"You haven't tried anything yet, Sir Henry," said Mallinson, "bit of practice wouldn't hurt, would it?"

"Did my share with revolvers in the last war," said Sir Henry, "I used to put it on the table when eating in the trenches to keep the rats at bay."

By lunchtime, the brass cases were piling up on the lawn and ammunition was running out, but everyone was pleased with the practice.

"I don't know if I will ever have to shoot at a person," said Mark, "but if I do, I think I'll do OK with any of the pistols we've tried."

"Done it before, surely?" asked Murrell.

"Not exactly; in the air we shoot at the 'plane, because the pilot doesn't matter. If he gets out, like I did, he can't walk home because of the English Channel and if he doesn't get out, that's one less mouth to feed in the bag."

"Well, if it gets personal, remember; shoot as fast as you can shoot straight, look at the front sight; see the enemy though it."

"When you had the German to shoot at, was it like that?"

"Sort of; couldn't see the front sight, but I know where my gun is pointing. There's an old trick for shooting in the dark; the flash of the first shot gives you just enough light to line the front sight up for the second shot. I didn't know he was a German until after. He didn't introduce himself before he fired."

They convoyed along the High Street to get home for lunch, a policeman staring at them as they passed him near the village hall. Apart from he, nobody was on the street on this sunny bank holiday.

III

After lunch, Mark and his father got together in the study for a long chat; both of them aware that this did not happen often, that they should talk more often and that time was slipping by.

"Your wounds seem to be healing," said Dad, "but I wondered about your hair?"

"The quacks think it will start growing again when my body has time to worry about such things," said Mark, "most of it burned off anyway and at least without hair I don't have a dandruff problem."

"You still look poorly, but how do your wounds compare with other peoples?"

"The worst of it is on my back," said Mark, "which is why we are having problems with it, you know, the scab lifting. My face and head were not as badly damaged as some people, my left hand will never be up to concert pianist level, but the smaller burns on my left arm and my legs are healing. I hope to be operational again by Easter."

"That's a tight schedule," said Dad, "are you sure?"

"I want to fly," said Mark, "I can't bear standing in the High Street here watching other people overhead. I should be up there with them."

"I know what that's like," said Dad, "but I also know about our frailties and limitations. I'm the one who pulled Uncle Herbert out of the Bleriot before it caught fire. I've been at the front; I wouldn't have missed it for anything; Flanders,

Gallipoli, Jerusalem and Damascus, but you've done your bit, surely?"

"No; not yet. There's more to do. Granddad said that the Germans changed tactics as the nights drew in. I think he's right and that means they'll change tactics again in the spring, when the days draw out and I want to be ready for them then."

"Yes, I agree with his assessment. The night bombing is risky for them and their casualties are mounting. They are taking off and landing in the dark, which is dangerous; over our cities the guns are having some successes, even the barrage balloons get them. Their morale is quite low and some aircraft are being sent over here without their gunners. Our spirits seem quite high. When the days lengthen, the pattern of war will change. We will have to support our garrison in Egypt and that means strengthening Gibraltar, Malta and Crete; our Mediterranean axis."

"What about the home front; will they try to invade us next year?"

"My guess is no; they can't cross La Manche in force without air supremacy and you wouldn't let them have that this year, nor will your mates let them have it in the spring. The RAF is building up daily and weekly; while our cities are taking a battering this winter, the RAF is able to gain strength. When Uncle Tom went to France in 1914, do you know how many aircraft we had to support our land forces?"

"No, but it was a tiny number wasn't it?"

"Yes, about four squadrons, maybe sixty machines, but by the end of the war, we had more than twenty-two thousand of all types."

"No wonder they could give granddad three."

"Yes, but it took time to get there and it's the same now; the Germans aren't shooting us down in any numbers and every week new aircraft roll off production lines and new pilots graduate. When your granddad Herbert got his Royal Aero Club certificate in 1910 less than one hundred other Englishmen had one; in 1914, sixty British fliers crossed the Channel to engage the Germans and by 1918 thousands more of our airmen had made that journey."

"I thought you and Uncle Tom got into flying before granddad?"

"We did, well, Tom did. He was in the first hundred flying certificates issued as well. I did mine later; after the war in fact. Never saw the point in the early days – preferred Bisley to Sheppey and I paid for that, I suppose; spent that war in trenches and deserts, but the point I'm making is that there are twice as many RAF fighter pilots now as there were on the day you crashed. By this time next year, the RAF will be bigger than it was in 1918. That's a lot of young men to do the job; you don't need to go back into front line service. Keith Park would be delighted to have you in his training wing, preparing the next generation of fighter pilots."

"It's not what I want though; granddad asked me what it was like to fly the fastest aircraft in the world with eight guns to fire at the enemy all at once. It's like nothing else; Colonel Mallinson is jealous of me – he'd love to have had a chance to do that and I must have another."

"Are you sure that's what you want?"

"Yes, more than anything. No; not quite. I'm looking forwards to a few more repairs to reduce the itching; this damn scab on my back reminds me I'm mortal whenever I move."

"Mind your language; you're back to the hospital next week?"

"Yes, Monday. So that's enough about me, what are you doing?"

"Busy as usual; compass has been a great success and that's why I think the war will develop in the Mediterranean next. Mussolini was overstretched in Greece before he lost his fleet last month and half his Libyan army last week so he's going to have to ask for German troops to support him. The way to North Africa from Italy is by sea in between our positions on Malta and Crete and anything destined for Libya has to go in between them."

"So, you think Hitler will divert his forces from attacking England to supporting the Italians in Greece and Africa?"

"If he doesn't, we'll clean the Italians out of Africa and then use Libya as our springboard to invade Italy. He hasn't got a choice. The war is wider than just Germany attacking Britain from occupied Europe. The Italians saw to that, but they can't win; they're bogged down in the Balkans, losing in Libya and we've got them surrounded in East Africa; the campaign there should see them mopped up in the new year, you'll see. There's also the Vichy to sort out. Their fleet's destroyed, but they have land forces in North Africa and the Lebanon. I can't say too much more, but the planning was near enough completed before I came home. We will be on the offensive in January and that will draw German forces away from the French coast."

"So what's mum doing?"

"She's looking for a good niche in which to use her language skills. I don't know what she does in the war effort, but I am sure it's useful; it's not enough, you know. She wants to do more."

"So it will be the war's end before we're a family again?"

"We've always been a family, Mark, but time moves along and so do our lives and careers. When you were at school we always got together in the summer holidays and at Christmas. Now you're a grown up and here we all are at Christmas. We couldn't get together last summer because you were busy and there was a German army in between us and all the places we like in France. The first summer after they've gone will be quite a party."

"Was it like that last time? I mean, you and Uncle Tom were away for the war, what were the holidays like before that? What did you do?"

"We always got together when we could. We bumped around the social season; our dad always went to Bisley for the imperial meeting. I met your mum at Wimbledon; she competed in the ladies' singles, you know, so we always had plenty to do, but those happy periods were separated by school and work; then the war came."

"And how was it, in the war?"

"Well, we didn't all get together again until after the war."

"So it will be the same this time; get together when we can?"

"Yes, that's it. I need to get back to Egypt; Tom will be here, you and James will be in the air. I haven't mentioned it before, but the army want the old family estate, don't know what for but it's quite secluded, so I suppose - and we'll seek Tom's blessing for this - it will be here that we meet up whenever we can. Make it a party."

"Party, uncle Senry?" James had wandered in.

"Yes, when the Brabhams get together it's a party. We don't all meet up often, James, so holidays when we're together should be memorable."

"I'll drink to that."

"Are you old enough to?"

"I'm old enough to fly,"

"That doesn't mean much in this family; when did you complete your training?"

"Four months ago, just after Mark broke his Spitfire."

"Well, let's drink to that."

It was a bit early but James spotted a sherry bottle, small one each. They were feeling quite mellow when granddad Herbert ambled in.

"I don't know what's the matter with young people today," he said, "I was thinking of taking a stiff walk, make room for dinner."

"Thinking is what gets you in trouble," said Sir Henry, "but if it pleases you, we'll take a walk."

"Dad was telling me about you crashing the Bleriot," said Mark.

"Accident, pure and simple," said Granddad, "could have happened to anyone; just my bad luck that the clubhouse didn't get out of the way quick enough and as for that idiot who parked his car in front of it...I paid for the damage and that was that."

Mark excused himself, claiming he was due for a bath. James could not think of anything and went for the walk. In private, Mark mulled over his girlfriend options; apart from Alma Burton at Ongar, he had frequent telephone calls from Carol Davies and his doctor had said that there were more problems with burn victims getting girls pregnant than there were with treating the wounds? Thinking of doctors, some of the nurses at the burns unit were attractive and there was one in particular – Gertrude Hough - whose hands seemed to linger on him more than was necessary. Was that a relationship he should explore? He did not know and he felt magnificently unprepared for such experimentation. What he could not work out was whether he wanted to experiment or not.

The Boxing Day dinner was the finale of the Christmas break. Traditionally an evening meal, following a day's game shooting or fox hunting, this year it was a glorified buffet of leftovers after a morning of pistol shooting.

The evening meant a division of the sexes again. Martha went to clean up the kitchen, wash the pots and pans, so Lillie, Esther and Elizabeth went and joined in, while Annie kept by the fire in the main sitting room and the men stayed close to the port and brandy.

IV

The next day was when Mark planned on taking his little flight and he found Karol at breakfast when he came downstairs.

"Flying today?"

"Yes."

"That is good. Where to?"

"Circuits and bumps, I think, then maybe try flying over here and waving to the church tower."

Elizabeth bounded in for breakfast, keen to see the aeroplane as well. When they left in Mark's car, the house was still quiet. Martha was up, but they saw nobody else. Mark's guess was that they'd overdone it with the port last night.

At the farm, they slid the barn doors open and then used Mark's car to pull the old Bristol out into the sunlight. It looked good and felt sound. They knew it would start, but they delayed that moment for a while, poring over the machine, checking the set-up and then studying a map. They reminded Elizabeth of boys with a train set, working out what to do with it.

Mark had a leather helmet and goggles; he also had good motorcycle gauntlets and silk lining gloves and a heavy coat to wear over his RAF tunic. Dressed up, he sat in the cockpit and set the contacts while Karol spun the propeller. It fired on the second attempt. Mark let the engine warm for a few minutes before taxiing to the edge of the field. Elizabeth raised a semaphore flag as high as she could to show Mark the direction of the light breeze and then he went for it.

The 'plane bounced along the short grass, the tail lifted and…off the ground it came, Mark climbed rapidly and banked to his left to keep the field in sight. The rudder felt heavy, stiff. He needed to find ground markers with which to relocate his landing strip. The church tower, the river Roding, complete the circuit, ease down, slow down, bounce on the grass and up again, wider circuit this time.

He was free for the moment, carefree, off the ground. The sun was shining weakly, his nose felt cold; he adjusted his scarf to protect his face better. He felt good; he felt in control. On the fourth circuit he landed and taxied to his waiting audience, now swollen by the arrival of the farmer.

"Karol's turn," he said, climbing out, "see if you like flying something this slow. The rudder seems stiff."

"Bit of oil maybe?" said the farmer.

Karol sat in the cockpit and juggled the rudder bar with his feet. The farmer took a look at the tail and then wandered off, returning a few moments later with an oil can. He put a bit on the hinges, Karol kicked it about a bit and said it was OK.

"Slow, is it?" said the farmer, "looked fast to me."

"Spitfires go faster," said Mark, "but they also need more space to take off in. If granddad buys one, he won't be able to land it here without a few more trees being taken down first."

Karol played in the air for what seemed like ages before returning to the field.

"Now I'll take you up," Mark said to Elizabeth, "sit in the back seat; used to be the gunners position."

They settled in and Mark ran it along the grass and kicked it into the air. He could feel the additional weight of his passenger and the rudder felt better, but still a bit heavy. He headed east, intending to take a spin over the village, which, even on Great War flying times was only twenty minutes away. He climbed to a thousand feet; high enough to see all the landmarks at once, but below the usual cruising altitude of military aircraft. He picked out the village easily enough and descended to treetop level, running past the church and along the High Street.

Then he climbed and banked to the left, passing Mallinson's house on his right, over the Murrell Farm and towards the coastal batteries. He could see all the places he'd walked and cycled, but now set in the context of seeing them all at once from the air. He took the machine into a barrel roll, the better to see the ground and was half way through the manoeuvre when he realised that he could hear Elizabeth screaming over the noise of the wind and the engine, so he hastened to get the machine upright. He decided against over-flying the batteries and turned west, heading for Brentwood, but at that moment another aircraft flashed across his bow.

Mark scanned the sky around him and saw a Hawker Hurricane behind him, swinging side to side to compensate for the newer machine's much greater speed. The first one that had darted across him came up in front and the one behind him came alongside. The pilot had his cockpit cover open and was giving him hand signals, which meant that he was to follow the machine in front. In effect, they'd been arrested.

Both Hurricanes had problems flying as slowly as the Bristol, which meant that they kept changing places, looping or making wide turns; all the while the direction was a bit west of north. Mark assumed that these 'planes were from Twelve Group and had been flying a standing patrol covering Eleven Group airfields. He'd flown within sight of Rochford, so perhaps that's why they'd been alerted to his presence.

Alternatively, they might just have seen him as the Bristol was painted training yellow.

Then he saw Duxford in the distance; Twelve Group's southern-most sector airfield. They guided him onto the landing flightpath, then peeled off while he put it on the grass. As the Bristol came to a halt, Mark was aware of the interceptor Hurricanes landing and quite a crowd of pedestrians ambling towards him. He shut the engine down and climbed out, at that moment feeling quite stiff from the cold of flying for nearly an hour in an open cockpit that December morning.

"Good morning sir," said a military policeman, "name and unit please."

"Brabham, Mark, Flight Lieutenant, Royal Air Force." Mark removed his scarf and unbuttoned his coat as he spoke so that his uniform tunic could be seen.

"Where are you stationed?"

"Royal Victoria Hospital, East Grinstead."

"I see."

"What do you see?" The speaker limped up, his squadron leader insignia marking him out from the crowd. "You see a pilot who should be on sick leave instead of jaunting about in a machine that's older than he is."

"Flies it well, sir," said a pilot from one of the interceptor Hurricanes.

"So why are you out flying that string bag this sunny morning?" enquired the squadron leader.

"Because I could," said Mark, "I haven't been in the air since last August. This machine belongs to my granddad, so I thought I should make sure that I haven't lost my touch."

"Indeed," said the squadron leader, "I was grounded for years after my accident and you think you should fly again after, what, a few months?"

"Yes sir, but there's a war on; you might have heard about it up here."

"Less of your cheek, Brabham; we have been heavily engaged. I suppose you were in Eleven Group?"

"Yes, sir, at Croydon."

"And you have been recognised, I see from your tunic, as someone who did his bit? DSO and DFC."

"I like to think so sir, and there's more I can and will do."

"That's the spirit. I can match you; got the DSO in September and the DFC caught up with me on Christmas Day. Who is your passenger?"

"Elizabeth Fforest, sir, Land Army."

"Well," said the squadron leader, "If you mean to return to flying duties, I suppose we'd better make sure you're up to it. Tommy – lend him your parachute and your kite. You, Brabham, see if you can fly Tommy's Hurricane. I'll fly with you."

Mark took the long greatcoat off. Tommy, who'd been one of the interceptor pilots, gave Mark his flying jacket and parachute harness, helping him into it.

"I'll take your machine, since it's warm," he said to the other interceptor pilot, "where did you find him?"

"North of Rochford."

"What were you doing there, Brabham?"

"I was overflying Lavering; that's where I've been staying. My uncle is the rector there."

"So, to Lavering we will go; you lead."

Tommy accompanied Mark to the 'plane. "Have you flown a Hurricane before?"

"Once; I was a Spitfire pilot in the battle. Where are you from?"

"Canada. We all are. No problem switching to a Hurricane; I'll run over the controls quickly and you'll be fine. How's that Bristol?"

"Nice, but slow. The rudder's heavy, don't know why. What's the squadron leader's name?"

"Bader; he was grounded for about six years after his crash."

"What happened?"

"Lost both legs; hit the ground during a low-level prank."

"No legs? He's walking OK; you're kidding me?"

"Not; he's got no legs. You watch when he gets into that 'plane."

Mark watched as Bader lifted his leg impossibly high and folded it into the cockpit. Then he got stuck into listening to Tommy explaining things to him while settling into the seat. Bader's voice came through his earpiece.

"We haven't got all day; there's a war on. Taxi to the start point."

Mark shook Tommy's hand and then closed the cockpit. He felt warm, out of the wind and at home. He fired the engine and spun the tail wheel to turn the machine round, then taxied it to where he assumed the start point would be. Bader came alongside him.

"Take off together, then you lead, south-southeast."

The Hurricane roared along the grass, the speed pushing Mark back into the seat, the way the Bristol never would. The tail lifted, he changed pitch and kicked it off.

"Hurricanes have a retractable undercarriage," a voice snapped in his ear. He changed hands on the stick to reach the control for raising the wheels and then concentrated on climbing and adjusting his course to the compass, south-southeast. The Hurricane flew about three and half times the

speed of a Bristol, so in less than eight minutes he started his descent towards Lavering's High Street.

"Is that it?"

"Yes."

"Well, get lower; nobody can see you way up here."

Mark let the Hurricane down to less than one hundred feet. He saw that the church tower was manned as it flashed by but could not see by whom. Seconds later they were over the beach; he turned north over the batteries, then back round to fly by the church again. On this pass there seemed to be quite a lot of people in the street. He allowed himself a little wing-waggle as he went by, then vectored towards Brentwood where he easily spotted the field on which he hoped to land the Bristol again. He saw his car and Karol before turning north towards Duxford.

The airfield came into view and Bader complimented his navigation as they came into land. Flaps down, throttle back, too much speed; shit, landing gear! Mark had not let the wheels down and thus lacked their natural drag on his speed. He changed hands and got to the control; he saw a figure emerge from the hut at the start of the landing strip, but he'd got the undercarriage down just in time to be spared the ignominy of a flare warning him that he must go round again. Coming in too fast is the classic beginner's mistake.

He stayed up a bit longer than he should have to let the speed down before his wheels contacted the ground; bit of a bounce, yawed to the right, corrected it, bounced again, got it under control, tail wheel down, slowing down, slide the cockpit cover back, look for the ground crew signal, follow that man, park it there. No sign of the Bristol.

"Not bad," said Bader, once they were both on the ground, "bit of a bounce, but the Hurricane lets you do that; Spitty might have dragged a wing at that moment."

"Sir."

"Anyway, let me know when you're fit. I don't know what the attitude will be, but I'd be happy to have you in my squadron. They are all foreigners you know; it's nice to hear an English accent."

Tommy appeared to retrieve his kit.

"Bit rough on landing."

"Forgot to put the wheels down, sorry. Bristol's have fixed undercarriages, speaking of which…"

"It's over there, by the hanger."

They walked over to where the Bristol had been pushed to one side. Three mechanics were meddling with it, while Elizabeth stood to one side like a stranded motorist watching the Automobile Association at work.

"Fixed the rudder sir, it's sweet now. Filled it up and we're just checking a few bits and pieces."

Mark did not know what to say. Bader said it for him. "Thank you, gentlemen; a good service and it'll last another twenty years. How long do you need?"

"Half an hour would do it, sir; haven't worked on one of these for a while."

"Indeed, well, we'll be in the mess; come along Brabham: Miss Fforest can wait with the machine. Can't have a civilian girl wearing trousers in an officers' mess, after all."

Seated in the warm with some tea, Mark sensed that Bader had something to say, and so it turned out.

"Brabham, there's some animosity between Eleven and Twelve Groups over battle tactics, is that fair?"

"Yes, sir; it is common knowledge that Air Vice Marshal Park's tactics were criticised by Air Vice Marshal Leigh-Mallory. Different men, different tactics."

"Yes; when you were up you were always outnumbered, like a bunch of gnats trying to bite an elephant."

"Some gnats, sir; some elephant."

"Indeed, but what we did was to assemble as many aircraft as we could, hit them hard, all at once, outnumber them, put them on the back foot. The big wing; fifty or a hundred aircraft falling on their bomber formations."

"Yes, sir and it worked in mid-September; Her Majesty the Queen Consort said as much. The trouble was, as I understand it, that the Germans only got in range of you when they started bombing London and that only went on for about three weeks in daylight before the winter set in and they took to bombing at night."

"That's fair, but it's not the whole picture. Park wanted us to cover his airfields whilst you were up after the Germans, but as we got organised to do that, the Germans switched to London from airfield attacks, so Park was expecting us to be in the wrong airspace, covering southern England whilst the Nazis were over London."

"I can't speak for Air Vice Marshal Park, sir, but he led us from the front; he's a gallant and brave officer and he was my uncle's squadron leader in the last war."

"Brabham...yes; I've met him then, Tom; Tom Brabham, and he's vicar at Lavering now?"

"Rector, sir."

"Well, give him my best regards. As far as the war goes, you're right that the German night offensive put my big wing on hold but come the spring we'll go looking for them. I hope you'll be with us."

When Mark returned to his Bristol he found that Elizabeth was not perturbed by the invite to the mess not stretching to include her. She said that the Land Army were routinely treated badly by the armed services and anyway, the mechanics had brought her tea and three biscuits.

Squadron Leader Bader instructed the two interceptors to escort the Bristol back to the Brentwood area and then went about his business. The flight back was uneventful, but after the Hurricane, flying the Bristol was like swimming in glue. On the ground, Karol wanted the whole story, as he'd seen Mark in the Hurricane.

"Are you grounded?" he asked, "Did Bader say no more Bristol flights?"

"No, he didn't," said Mark, "and the ground crew have fixed the rudder and given us fuel, so maybe we can fly again soon."

"You can, I'm back to Hurricanes on Monday."

IV

The reception in the village was interesting. The church tower had logged the Bristol flypast and being buzzed by Hurricanes.

"That policeman was up here," said Frank Ball, "to see if we'd logged the letter codes. There's a no low flying rule according to him and people who don't obey it will get a letter from the chief constable."

"And he sends them to Goering by air mail I suppose," said Mark, "did you see the codes?"

"No," said Frank, "I was too busy looking at the pilot. It was you, wasn't it, skipper?"

"Yes but keep it quiet."

"Everyone knows it was you," said Frank, "except the policeman, as far as I know."

Granddad Herbert was a bit miffed. He'd seen the Bristol fly over and then the Hurricanes; "you managed to borrow a

Hurricane and didn't find a way to let me have a go, that's not fair. I lent you the Bristol."

"Nowhere to land it, granddad; and I was escorted by a squadron leader with no legs."

"Bader," said Uncle Tom, "I've met him."

"He said; sends you his compliments."

"He's arrogant, that one," said Tom, "be careful about him, Mark, he'll stick his neck out too far, just you wait and see."

"The beach," said Karol, "maybe good place to park a Hurricane."

CHAPTER 17

SATURDAY MORNING'S PLAN WAS that Mark and Elizabeth, Sir Henry and Lillie would travel to London. James had to get back to North Weald, so Granddad Herbert would drive them all in the Rolls Royce to Ongar, where they could find out if the London trains were running. If they were, James would get off at North Weald.

Granddad Herbert and Annie planned on seeing in the new year in Lavering, since their housekeeper was away until the beginning of January. Karol would return to his duties, leaving on Sunday after the morning service. Sir Henry had booked rooms at his club; the porter had assured him of comfortable nights, as the Germans had not over-flown London since the twenty-third. Mark and Elizabeth would have separate rooms, Sir Henry and Lillie would share. On Monday morning they would all go their individual ways. The car thus packed, they all said their farewells and set out for the weekend's adventure.

Ongar station was a hive of inactivity, but the train sitting at the platform, they were promised, would shortly depart for London; so they settled into the carriage and Sir Henry got his pipe out.

"I've asked for tickets to the cinema for this evening," he said, "new Charlie Chaplin film at the Prince of Wales, called the 'Great Dictator'. Should be funny."

The train chuffed away, the second stop being North Weald, where James would alight.

"See you all soon, I hope," he said, grabbing his kitbag, "Mark, I hope we'll fly together."

"You never know," said Mark, "at the present rate, we'll probably both be promoted to desks in a year."

The door slammed and James was gone. Mark caught a glimpse of him striding along the station, kitbag on shoulder. He'd be flying in the next day or two, thought Mark, and I won't.

After that, he settled down to the train's stop-start routine and dozed until prompted by his Dad's pipe stem to wake up. Fenchurch Street station was quite busy with lots of uniforms milling about; young servicemen trying to make sense of travelling through London. Sir Henry steered the party through the station and across to the Tower Hill Underground line platform with practised ease. It confuses a lot of London visitors that Fenchurch Street mainline station is seemingly not on the Underground network.

Their train purred and whined its way through the tunnels, with the added novelty of the automatic doors at each stop until they got to Embankment Station, where they changed lines for two stops to Piccadilly Circus.

At the club, Sir Henry was greeted as a long-lost patron should be. Mark's room was small, but comfortable enough and while there was only one bathroom on the second floor, it was a huge communal affair. A row of washbasins faced a wall-sized mirror opposite the water closets that were in individual cubicles, as were the four slipper baths. There was no sign on the door to suggest that it was a male preserve, leading Mark to think about what facilities Elizabeth might or might not have.

Beer and sandwiches were served for lunch in a ground floor dining room. Sir Henry said that the tickets arranged for the cinema meant being there at ten past five, so he and Lillie would be visiting the West End shops in the meantime. Mark said he'd take Elizabeth sightseeing and they arranged to regroup in Piccadilly Circus just before five.

On the street and technically alone together for the first time in days, Mark was thinking about where they should go, while Elizabeth had quite different matters on her mind.

"I can't open my mouth in there except to put food in it," she said, "everyone's so plummy, even the boy who carried my kitbag up to the room."

"That's OK," said Mark, "just look pretty, be seen and not heard. Ow, gently, I'm a wounded man you know," he added after she punched him.

They walked up Piccadilly, crossed the Circus and wandered down Haymarket; Mark's geography was hazy, but he knew that a left turn at the bottom should lead them into Trafalgar Square, which it did.

"Where are we going?" enquired Elizabeth.

"Don't know, really, just sightseeing."

"Old buildings, some of them still standing."

"Don't you like it? London's a great place to be; Big Ben, St Paul's Cathedral, Buckingham Palace..."

"How about a Lyon's corner shop? Tea and cake?"

It was a deal. They walked back up the Mall, across Trafalgar Square and into the Strand. Taking a seat in the shop, a nippy was at hand to take their order before Mark had even looked at the menu.

"Tea pots for two, please; two Bakewell tarts and two sultana tea cakes as well," said Elizabeth.

Mark sat down.

"Been here before?" said Mark.

"Same menu in all the shops," said Elizabeth, "and at least I can talk here."

"I should have ordered," said Mark, "you didn't give me a chance. Everybody heard that; now they're watching to see what happens next."

"Mister Murrell taught me," said Elizabeth, "get in first, shoot straight."

The teapots arrived, followed by the crockery and lastly the cakes. It was not long after lunch, but Mark enjoyed the sweetness of the cake and was refreshed by the tea.

"What's next?" He wondered.

"Do you want that Bakewell?" Elizabeth was reaching for it as she spoke. Mark held his hands clear in submission.

"I was thinking of a bath before the cinema," he said.

"Should be easy at the club. Do you have salt?"

"No; I didn't think of that."

"Well, I'll scrounge some here. They must have it in the kitchen. What's your bathroom like at the club?"

Mark told her about the huge second floor facility.

"Well, I have one to myself," she said, "the only door to it is from my room, so you could use that one if you like, after me maybe. It's such a luxury, a bath; there's a tub on the farm, but heating enough water is a slow business."

Mark felt quite naughty slipping from his second-floor bedroom to Elizabeth's third floor one, carrying his clean clothes and towel. Her room was small, comfortable and as she said, had a door to a bathroom to which nobody else had access. The warm water was in it ready when he got there, so he started undressing and she watched until he needed help with his shirt and vest, which were stuck to his wound. Once freed, he continued undressing and stepped into the salted water, realising as he sat down that he was naked and she was still in the room.

"Oh," she said, "all your hair fell out."

She set to bathing his wound, using a flannel to clean the sticky excretions from around the scab. He sat in the water, conscious that without soap and bubbles he was still obviously naked. As she worked on his back and upper arm, he used his damaged left hand to massage the smaller wounds on his legs. He took the flannel and cleaned the undamaged skin with a little soap, then asked for his towel.

"I can't dry myself properly yet," he said, but I can wear it until the water soaks into it."

Thus, undressed but feeling a bit more decent, he sat on the edge of her bed, letting the towel do its job.

"So what's this flick your Dad wants us to see?"

"Charlie Chaplin, should be funny."

"I've seen him; the little tramp."

"Yes, but this is a talkie, so we'll hear what he sounds like."

"Last time I went to a cinema it was to see Paul Robeson; he came to Wales to make a movie, you know, but didn't sing in Welsh. Such a voice: what a waste."

The film, when they got to it, was not what any of them had expected, but it was nevertheless a good evening's entertainment; funny in places, thought provoking and at times quite intimidating.

"I don't think Mister Chaplin was on Herr Hitler's Christmas card list this year," said dad as they walked into the cold night, "he might be on a to-do-in list though."

II

Sunday twenty-ninth December dawned, dull and average. Sir Henry and Lillie had plans; people to meet, which meant that Mark and Elizabeth had the day to fill in as they chose and what Elizabeth wanted was to visit the parts of London from whence the cubs and brownies had been evacuated. On paper, this was a simple enough exercise on trains and buses, but on the Sunday after Christmas and during the war, it was also clear that anything which could go wrong probably would.

They walked to Marble Arch carrying their gas masks and tin helmets, as was de rigueur and descended to the platform, taking an eastbound train to Liverpool Street. Each time the automatic doors opened, they noticed the distinct smell of unwashed bodies and stale urine emanating from the people who used the platforms as air raid shelters.

At Liverpool Street they sought a train bound for Chingford, which trundled out of the station through a tunnel and then onto a series of viaducts passing through Bethnal Green and Stoke Newington before crossing the wide marsh of the river Lea valley and on into Walthamstow. Evidence of war was all about, ranging from damaged buildings and barrage balloons to gun and searchlight emplacements. They saw a crash-landed Me110 on the marshes, and a Blenheim, upside down. Alighting at St James Street station, they walked up the deserted High Street and into Hoe Street, pausing at Lyons for tea, then on through the village via St Mary Road and Church Path, then down the hill to Wood Street station.

"I've seen enough," said Elizabeth, "mixture of little houses and nice houses, like Llansamlet; big church, small alms houses, fields and ruins."

It was getting dark when their train returned them to Liverpool Street station, from which Mark thought that a walk through the city would be all right.

"We're sure to spot a Lyons, get a proper meal."

"Yes, meat pie and chips," said Elizabeth, "maybe some spinach and parsnips."

The city was a muddle of roads closed due to unexploded bombs, piles of rubble, pedestrians walking with varying urgency, blacked-out buildings, not to mention the odd bus, tram and taxi passing by. St Paul's cathedral came into view in the gathering gloom and they passed along Cathedral Close and down to Ludgate Circus, where the Lyon's shop was open.

"All day and all night," said the nippy, "to serve the print trade along Fleet Street."

Elizabeth ordered the meal that she'd been planning for all day. Mark ordered the same, which saved checking the menu. It was strange, sitting in the lighted shop with heavy blackout drapes across the door. Despite the curtains there was a steady stream of people coming in to eat or to buy cakes to take with them.

After the main course and a ginger pudding with custard, Elizabeth was reviewing the menu for a cake to go with her tea when the air raid sirens started to sound. The nippy gestured defiance with a hand signal directed at the ceiling and then took Elizabeth's order. By the time the cake arrived ack-ack guns could be heard in the distance.

"You can come down to the cellar," said the nippy, "that's what we do when it gets too rough up here."

"I think we might make a dash for it," said Mark, "along the Embankment."

"Take care," said the nippy as Mark settled the bill, "you can always double back if you need to. We never lock the door, 'cos there's no lock on it, so you can always get in and come downstairs."

Bombs started cracking and booming in the distance; Mark judged them to be falling on the docks again, east of the City. That suited him, since they wanted to go west to their beds, even if they did have to sleep in the wine cellar.

Elizabeth helped Mark with his greatcoat and then slipped hers on. The moment they stepped through the blackout curtain onto the street, Mark pressed Elizabeth back. He could hear the bombs whistling, which meant they were coming down close by, too close for comfort. The ground shook as they landed; multiple impacts, as though two or more aircraft had dumped their loads.

The street was no longer dark; the ambient light came from searchlights reflecting off the clouds, bursts of flak above and the fires that the bombing had started. Another cluster of weapons whistled down, striking somewhere up Farringdon Street, maybe the market or around the Old Bailey. From the doorway, Mark could see fires developing the other side of the Cathedral from where he stood.

There seemed to be a bit of a lull; explosions in the distance, fire engine bells closer by.

"We can go now," he said, "helmets on."

They stepped out into the street. Mark glanced up the hill towards the Cathedral and stopped in awe. The whole dome was illuminated by the fires about it.

"It's huge," said Elizabeth.

"This may be your only chance to see it," said Mark, "it's on fire."

At that moment more whistles started and a further cluster of bombs landed north of them. They scuttled across Ludgate Circus and down New Bridge Street towards the river. More bombs whistled and crumped; one so close that

Mark hit the ground, pulling Elizabeth down as the blast went over them, showering bits of masonry, wood and lots of dust across the street.

"Over here you idiot," shouted a voice, "come and take shelter."

Up and running again, Mark led towards the voice that belonged to a tall City policeman.

"Down there, follow the steps, you can shelter under Blackfriars Bridge."

They went down the steps to find some twenty people already below. They could see along the river, the water of which now glowing bright orange as it reflected the fires raging on both sides.

"Welcome to the new great fire of London," said a voice, "shouldn't you be up there doing something about this lot?"

"I'm on sick leave," said Mark, slipping his helmet off, "but maybe next week."

"If there is a next week; this is the worst I've ever seen it."

More bombs whistled and then landed south of them, straddling the power station, Blackfriars Bridge Road and the river itself, which reared up in huge columns of boiling water.

"They want the bridge," said a voice.

"They want bloody London," said another, "all of it."

There seemed to be a slight respite again. People in the group took the opportunity of the lull to continue their journeys.

"I'm going to cross the bridge," said one, "if they want the docks and the city, that's the way to safety. You coming?"

Several people seemed to like the idea and got ready to make a run for it. Mark did not, as his destination was west rather than south.

"It's quiet for the moment," shouted the policeman, "can't say how long for; there's no 'all clear' signal yet."

The crowd thinned. The policeman came down and said he was heading towards Snow Hill and some people got ready to join him. Mark said he'd wait a while, then cut along the Embankment towards the Temple. He and Elizabeth were left alone, briefly. Time for a smoochy kiss? Maybe; not that she seemed interested at the moment. Running feet, noisy laughter. Kids. They came clattering down into the area below the bridge.

"Down 'ere, under cover. Look!"

The first boy had spotted Mark and Elizabeth.

"Lover's corner then. You sharing her?"

"No." Mark looked at the youths and they looked at him, all illuminated in shades of orange from the fires reflecting off the water. Four of them, carrying various bits and pieces: looters, feral hobbledehoys running wild in a city that no longer had the time or the infrastructure to control their behaviour.

"You should be up there fighting, not down 'ere hiding like a rat." The nearest boy gave Mark a shove. Mark's helmet jerked forwards over his face as a result so he slipped it off, revealing his bald and mutilated head.

"It's Frankenstein!" shouted one, making a grab for the helmet. Mark pulled the helmet away, at the same time pulling his revolver out of the greatcoat pocket.

"Look out, 'e's got a gun." The youth made a grab for the revolver, so Mark hit him with the helmet in his other hand. Several things happened at once. One of the lads made a violent grab for Elizabeth, who started fending him off. The other three dropped their loot and all made for Mark, who pocketed the revolver and started thrashing at them using his helmet as both sword and shield.

"Get 'im. Freak."

One got half behind Mark and was trying for the revolver pocket. Mark got him a good jab with his elbow and smacked another quite hard with the helmet, conscious that he could not last long in a fight like this and that Elizabeth was his responsibility and was also in trouble. The lads closed on him again, three of them getting their hands on his greatcoat. Mark spun hard clockwise, sweeping them with the helmet as he did so. Breaking free, he ran a few steps, then drew the revolver and turned.

The nearest one pulled out a knife, the blade of which flashed in the infernal light of the surrounding fires. The other two seemed a bit more distant, as more bombs started their whistling descent and Mark could see them in peripheral vision, while concentrating on the knife. The furthest one seemed to glance upwards as the bombs came down, then folded up and lay down on the floor, Elizabeth behind him. The second one turned away from Mark and then also fell to the ground. The knife wielder ran at Mark, who held the revolver out at arm's length and then fired when the youth ran into the muzzle. He crumpled to the floor, letting the knife go.

Elizabeth stood over the other two, holding the half-brick that she had used as a weapon of convenience to interrupt their involvement in the attack.

"Is he dead?"

"I don't know."

Bombs blasted around them, forcing them both to the ground. The bridge shook and the area in which they lay filled with dust.

Elizabeth was up first.

"Let's get him into the river."

"What if he's not dead?"

"If he wakes up he'll remember who shot him."

"So will his mates."

Another huge blast nearby was followed almost immediately by a bomb hitting the river. The water and mud thrown up by it exploding hit the underside of the bridge and thundered down onto the dust and rubble on the ground where this fight had taken place. Mark picked himself up.

"Let's go; that way, along the Embankment."

They left the prostrate youths and their loot in the mess of rubble and water and ran out onto the Victoria Embankment. Bombs were still whistling down, but it was as though they had been dropped in a stick south to north, so each explosion was further away. A few hundred yards along, Mark dragged Elizabeth through the open gate into Middle Temple Lane. He thought that the garden there might be a safe place to hide for a while, but a few doors up he spotted one that was ajar.

"In here," he said, leading her up the steps and into the vestibule.

It was a different world; seemingly quiet, separated from the horrors outside and calm. It was also deserted. Mark called out but got no answer. Walking through, they found stairs and followed them to the basement level, thinking that they would find people there.

Nobody. It was quiet and calm, not to mention empty. Mark illuminated it with his penlight to see a desk and some chairs, a table under and around which books had been stacked to make an improvised shelter, empty bookcases and some candles on the mantelpiece. There were blackout curtains in place, so he lit some candles and then had another look around. The room did not seem to have been used recently.

"I was thinking," said Elizabeth, "Laurie Hilton asked me out last May. Five days and four nights on that scout boat, hardly any sleep; bombed, machine-gunned, starved and ogled at by hundreds of men who should have been too tired to notice me. Then you ask me out to London and we get bombed, attacked by thugs and now we're hiding in someone's house without their permission. You scouts certainly know how to give a girl an interesting time. Anyway, how are you?"

"Quite good," said Mark, "But how are you?"

"Fair to middling," she said, "that thug tore my shirt and I think I have a black eye coming up."

"How did you get away from him?"

"Oh, well; he grabbed at my bosom, so I got him low down with my knee, and then whilst he was doubled over he sort of tripped and went over the railings into the river. Then that bomb landed in the water, so I don't think he'll be in any state to complain to the police about us."

"Hmm, and the one I shot may not be able to talk either; what about the other two?"

"Maybe talkative, maybe not. They've got their loot to explain."

Mark had no idea what to do next. He could look for that policeman and tell him he'd shot one lad... no, that wouldn't do. He wanted to rest, so he undid his greatcoat.

"I want to lie down for a bit," he said, "get some rest, then we'll head for the club. I think that those lads brought whatever misfortune they've suffered on themselves."

"They might remember the bald RAF man."

"I know."

He slid under the table and Elizabeth slid in next to him. He felt relaxed, surprisingly relaxed, having just shot and possibly killed someone, albeit a knife-wielding someone who might have killed him if given the chance.

Elizabeth was on an adrenalin high; fired up by the fight and fidgety. She lay down next to Mark and started teasing him gently, rubbing the front of his trousers with her knuckles. When he took her hand to stop her, she leaned over and kissed him passionately, so he let go of the hand and let her play. He could feel his body reacting to her playfulness and her hand fiddling with the buttons of his fly. He could not stop her as she was lying on his right hand and his left was the damaged one. He felt the buttons popping, one at a time. Then she started on his tunic buttons and lastly his waistband, sliding her hand into and beneath his underwear.

His erection rose to meet her hand and she played with it, rhythmically, slowly at first, getting faster. The background noise seemed to support her rhythm, rising in intensity as her hand action sped up; bombs whistling and landing and she worked him up and then the shock of ejaculation. He felt sticky and dirty, all at once. He looked at Elizabeth in the faint light of the candles. She was wide-eyed and playful.

"Your nose is dirty," was all he could think of saying at that moment.

"You should see your face," she said, "like a chimney sweep."

"Let's head for the club," said Mark, "we have proper beds there."

"And loads of other people."

"True."

Mark made no immediate attempt to get up and as she was no longer pinning his right hand to the ground, he slid his fingers up her shirt towards her bosom.

"Gently," she said, "I may have a bruise or two there, you know."

"I know."

Mark fiddled with the bulges in her shirt for a few minutes, but he felt unable to undo the buttons one-handed and she neither helped nor encouraged him, so he pulled her down on him and groped around her waistband. He had no luck there either, so he stopped trying.

"I think there's another lull in the bombing."

"Seems like."

Elizabeth slid off him; he thought reluctantly, but as she seemed disinclined to go any further in this deserted barrister's bolthole, it was best to make for the club and see what would happen there. They adjusted their clothing, put the candles out and used Mark's penlight to find the outdoors again. The Temple was in deep shadows, while all around the sky glowed orange. They walked up through the Temple and out into Fleet Street, across the Aldwych and along the Strand into Trafalgar Square. They seemed to be walking away from the bombing, although there were also explosions to the north and further away to the west and southwest, maybe around Victoria or Kennington. There were other people about who'd been to restaurants, cinemas and theatres and lots of them in uniform.

"Brabham!"

Mark turned; three RAF types were heading for him, with some navy personnel in tow.

"God, it is you, Mark, you been in a war or something?"

"Same war as you, Fred," said Mark.

"Nah, you've been in one tonight, what a mess; you need a drink."

Mark told Elizabeth that he knew Fred from the burns unit and Fred in turn introduced his party; two Dutch navy officers and two Canadians from Duxford.

"And you're Tarka," said Fred, "Mark wouldn't get us any pictures of you; he's difficult like that."

"We're headed for the Aero Club," said Mark, "will you join us there for drinks?"

"Sure. I'm staying at the RAF Club myself, just a few doors down."

Fred's RAF companions were both Canadians, with a short leave in London to enjoy. They knew about his visit to

Duxford in the Bristol, which Fred thought was a wonderful story that he would use, repeatedly, back at the hospital.

"When are you due back?" he asked.

"Tomorrow," said Mark, "which is why we're having tonight in London, what's left of it."

"Me too, we can travel together."

The Royal Aero Club staff were delighted to serve drinks to Mark's friends on Sir Henry's account and they were still in the bar chatting to the background distraction of explosions and the windows rattling when Sir Henry escorted Lillie in.

"Rough out there tonight; good God, Mark, what have you been doing?"

"We had supper in a place near St Pauls," said Mark, "got bombed and barely got out with our lives."

Having been introduced to everyone who was drinking on his mess bill, Sir Henry settled down with a cigar to interrogate the Dutchmen. He was still enjoying the information exchange an hour later when Mark said it was time he fell down.

"What's the form tonight; are we using the bedrooms or the cellars?"

"I think it's dying off," said Sir Henry, "so I think the bedrooms, but we'll check with the staff."

The feeling was that upstairs would be safe enough, so Mark, Elizabeth and Lillie excused themselves. Mark thought that his Mum might be chaperoning, but no, she breezed straight to her room saying goodnight as she went. Elizabeth followed Mark into his room and lit the night-lights while he peeled off his greatcoat. He felt dirty, but in no mood to bath. His shirt came off easily, which surprised him given the exertions of the night. His vest was a bit stuck, but Elizabeth soon freed it. He kicked his shoes off and then stood up, taking Elizabeth by the shoulders for a kiss.

She kissed him and let his hands wander around for a bit.

"Are you going to stay with me tonight?"

"No, I have a nice room and a private bath."

"If you're going to bath, I could come and watch; you've seen me bathing, after all."

"No, I think you've had enough excitement for one night; more than you should get on the first date."

Her hand crept to his fly as he continued to hold her in his arms. She flicked the buttons undone, then the buttons of his waistband.

"There you go, ready for bed."

"Ready for something."

"Goodnight, Mark."

She picked up her coat and slipped out of the door, the cheekiest grin on her face as she did so. Mark cleaned up at the washstand and put his pyjamas on. In bed, he could not sleep as his mind was still replaying the night's events. Had he really shot someone? How close had they come to making love? Would they to being arrested for murder? Who would be the architect of the third St Paul's Cathedral?

III

He was still mulling these things over, half awake and half asleep when there was the most appalling crashing explosion. His bedroom windows were blown in, the blackout curtains catching most of the glass, but they were blasted across the room in the process, still clinging to their pole. The noise outside was amazing, as though the club were the epicentre of a bomb attack.

Dammit, that's what this is, Mark realised with a jolt. He rolled out of bed and then slid under it as the building shook. There was a terrific crash as part of the ceiling collapsed, the falling plaster smashing the nightstand. Another blast seemed to come in through the shattered window making his ears pop. He crawled across the room, grabbing his greatcoat and shoes, then made for the stairs and the comparative safety of the basement.

In the wine cellar, Sir Henry was still holding court with the guests Mark had brought in.

"Good Lord, you have been in another war," said Fred as Mark walked in covered in plaster dust, "what a mess."

Mark took some brandy to clear his throat. The war above seemed to have abated, at which point Mark said that as neither his Mum nor Elizabeth had come down, he should check on them.

"Yes, good idea," said Sir Henry, "you go; you're already a mess."

Lillie was in the lower ground floor scullery with the staff. Mark made his way upstairs to the third floor and knocked on Elizabeth's door.

"It's stuck," she said through the wood, "it's not locked but I can't open it from this side."

Mark wanted something heavy to batter it with and returned a few moments later with a fire extinguisher. He whacked the door a few times experimentally and decided that it was stuck against the floor. He could not see why, but a couple more hearty blows and it opened enough for him to squeeze in. Elizabeth was wearing her coat over a nightdress.

"What kept you?"

"Didn't know you were in trouble."

"I thought you might have come up anyway."

"You'd said goodnight."

"And you think I meant it?"

"Yes."

Another series of blasts shook the building. Mark took her hand and led her down to the wine cellar where the party eventually deteriorated into fitful sleep while the Nazi bombs continued falling, as the third wave overflew the city.

IV

Elizabeth was the first to stir. She could hear an all-clear siren in the distance, but could not tell if that meant London was clear or just the bit where the siren was. It was still dark, but there was plenty of ambient light filtering its way through the shattered windows and shredded blackout curtains into the club. She ascended to the third floor, but from her bedroom window all she could see was fire and smoke. There was no water to the taps in the bathroom, but there was some in the nightstand jug and she used that to get cleaned up. Then she packed ready for her return to Lavering, to the farm, to be a midwife to two hundred sheep.

She moved her kit down to Mark's room, which was quite a mess. All the glass gone from the windows, the curtains were in a heap against the wall and about half the ceiling had come down. She put his stuff together, brushed the plaster off as best she could and then went to get him from the cellar. He washed in what water was left in her nightstand, his having been destroyed during the night.

Fred had gone to the RAF Club for his things and returned to say that they had fared better and hot breakfasts were available. They trooped over to be Fred's guests, after which the party broke up. While packing, Mark asked Elizabeth to take the revolver in her kitbag, as he did not want anyone taking a close look at it. They had a kiss and cuddle and then they left with Fred to find out what trains were running. The

Underground seemed to be working, so they said goodbye to Elizabeth, or Tarka as Fred kept calling her loudly, as she went down the stairs to return to her duties.

Fred and Mark found a taxi to take them to their station. Mark saw that St Paul's dome was still apparently standing, but wreathed in smoke. At the station, police were at the entrance, checking passengers.

"Carrying revolvers, gentlemen?' enquired the officer.

"No," said Fred, "they don't let burn victims have them in case we shoot ourselves."

Mark said nothing, but pulled his greatcoat open to show that he had no belt over his tunic, while feeling aware of the possible significance of the question to his actions the previous night.

"Wonder what that was about," said Fred as they got into the train, "they don't usually care."

The journey was bitty and difficult, but eventually they reached East Grinstead, where there was no RAF car and no taxi.

"Oh well," said Mark, "we know the way."

He felt quite fit, having walked at least six miles the day before. Fred also seemed in good form, despite his artificial leg not being quite the right length, but in half an hour they were at the hospital, where the news was not good. Barry had stayed in over the festive period due to a post-operative infection afflicting his ear and Dying Brian had died Christmas morning.

"And you're demoted," said Barry, "we've had a VC in here since your last visit."

"Wow; what did he do?"

"He was halfway out of his burning 'plane when a German got in front of him so he got back in to use up his ammo and then bailed."

Morale seemed low, the hospital quiet. A lot of people were still absent, both nursing staff and patients and they all knew the sort of punishment London had taken from the air over the weekend. Many people associated with the hospital were Londoners or, like Mark, would have travelled through the metropolis on their way to or from the hospital. Some might be casualties. It would take time for the unit to pick up after the Christmas lull and meanwhile, the fires of London were making new burn victims of people on the ground: civilians and firemen, police officers and servicemen, children and babies.

Mark and Fred both needed to clean up and Mark found that his favourite nurse Gertie Hough was on hand to help him.

"Looking at you, I'd say that you're healing up quite well," said Gertie, "the wound on your back looks manageable now, so maybe a decent graft and you'll be on your way back to a medical board."

V

Elizabeth had reached Essex; there were no trains to Lavering, so she got a bus to Chelmsford from which there were no connections to the coast She telephoned the rectory for advice, there being no telephone on the farm.

"Should be no problem getting you from there," said Tom, "I'll ask granddad Herbert."

He was quite amenable to driving his Rolls Royce to Chelmsford to pick up the stray land girl, who was really thrilled when his car pulled up to meet her less than an hour later.

"You can sit next to me in the front," said Herbert, "otherwise I'll look like your chauffeur."

It might have been a silent journey back, but Elizabeth decided to ask questions.

"How is it that you've had money for aeroplanes?"

Granddad Herbert trundled out his life story; timber magnate, soldier when necessary, two grown up sons currently in India managing timber extraction from the jungles using elephants.

What about you? Land girl in this war, then what's next?"

"I don't know; I picked up skills in farming. I'd hate to go back to Swansea, maybe I could be a farmer's wife."

"You have other skills, I hear. Navigated that scout boat to Dunkirk; you're running the girls' units."

"Hmm. Maybe I should start collecting the testimonials."

Herbert drove straight to the farm, where his car looked odd in the muddy yard. Elizabeth grabbed her kit, thanked him profusely and then prepared herself for the work ahead. Murrell was pleased to see her back, but there was little time to be sociable as lambing had started. Elizabeth went straight into the thick of it and it was the following morning before she was able to speak to Mister Murrell about Mark's revolver. She told Mister Murrell the bones of what had happened and handed him the gun. He took a look at it.

"One shot, just?"

"Yes."

"And the empty case is still in the chamber, good."

VI

By the time Mark was enduring his skin graft in the hospital, his revolver was in Colonel Mallinson's desk drawer and a similar one from Mallinson's collection was in his bedroom at the rectory, clean and loaded.

The police had conducted discreet enquiries at the hospital, where they were told the hospital policy that patients should not have revolvers. They further enquired about bald burn casualty air force personnel and were given a list of twenty-seven names and addresses; the list included Dying Brian and the police were somewhat disconcerted to find, on arriving at the address the hospital gave them, that it was an undertaker's chapel of rest and that Brian was there but could not be interviewed.

Another week went by before a detective from Scotland Yard in London, accompanied by the ubiquitous PC Fidgeon, called upon the Reverend Tom Brabham to enquire after Mark's health and whereabouts. Tom referred them to the hospital in Sussex, so the detective asked whether it was possible that Mark's service revolver was in the rectory. Tom asked Martha, who went and retrieved it from Mark's bedroom. The detective explained that it would be helpful if he could borrow the piece for a test shot. Tom said that it was possible for them to do so, but not during his lifetime.

A compromise was reached; PC Fidgeon obtained a suitable piece of pine log from the woodpile and the detective fired the revolver into the soft wood. Satisfied that the billet had captured the bullet, he went on his way with the sample, leaving Tom to clean the revolver and put it away. Tom eventually received a letter from Scotland Yard which said that the revolver Mark had was not the one they were looking for, so sorry for the inconvenience

In hospital, Mark knew nothing of any of this while he experienced his most uncomfortable and painful period for some months as the hard scab on his back was replaced by a series of skin grafts harvested from the inner sides of his upper arms. By the time they'd done with him he felt worse, but his favourite nurse Hough assured him that he was much better.

At the farm, Elizabeth knew nothing of the police enquiries either. Her days and nights went on the care of the sheep, as each of the two hundred or so in the flock had up to three lambs. The girls took the third lambs away from the ewes for hand rearing, as it was thought that three was too much of a strain for the sheep to handle. She heard news of Swansea being bombed but heard nothing other than the BBC reports. By the end of January, the three girls had nearly fifty baby lambs to hand feed, night and day.

Swansea had been bombed again by then; a blitz that lasted for three consecutive nights in which her home in Teilo Crescent was destroyed. She did not hear that detail from the BBC, nor anything from her parents, as they did not survive the attack.

CHAPTER 18

BEING SO BUSY ON the farm, Elizabeth did not find out about her bereavement or Herbert's great adventure until later. Granddad Herbert was an easy person to get along with; Elizabeth had enjoyed his company and his straight way of telling things as they are. Herbert was a man who was comfortable in any company, so talking to a working-class land girl from Swansea was no different to talking to the Prime Minister. Karol had also found Herbert delightful and exciting and he had plotted a way for the old man to experience a Hawker Hurricane.

Karol had told his squadron about his Christmas in Lavering. Most of the men he flew with had managed some leave, but that had meant a few days in London for most of them. One or two had gone home with English pilots and thus had the sort of domestic experience Karol had enjoyed, but none of them had flown a Bristol or driven a Rolls Royce.

To the plan. The squadron would buzz Lavering at low level on a standing patrol on their way to the North Sea. The rest of them would not notice if Karol dropped off the patrol and caught up later. The squadron-strength buzz would be Herbert's signal to make for the beach, on which Karol reckoned he could land at low tide, the sand being firm. And that's what happened.

Karol set down and taxied to where Herbert was waiting, dressed in his Sidcot suit and Mark's parachute harness and helmet. Karol helped him into the machine and explained the controls. While Herbert played the duffer admirably at family functions, no aircraft kept secrets from him. He had flown in air races in the 1920s, funded development and enjoyed watching such events in the 1930s, so after being walked through the controls, he felt able to fly the machine.

"Ten minutes only; I must not be missed," said Karol.

"Ten minutes it is," said Herbert, "thank you very much."

Herbert spun the machine into the wind, taxied down the beach pushing the throttle and lifted off. Experienced though he was in a wide variety of machines, the Hurricane had more speed than anything he'd flown since a sneaky run-out in Supermarine's Schneider Trophy seaplane a few years before. The power thrust him back in the seat as he climbed into the weak morning sunshine; terrific feeling, flying over the sea. Then an orange blob passed in front of his nose followed by another.

"WHAT THE BLUE BLAZES?"

Herbert rolled the machine on its side so that he could look at the sea from whence came the orange blobs; a surfaced submarine with machine guns firing in his direction. Without thinking about it, Herbert pulled the stick round to put the machine less than a hundred feet from the sea, then he turned and prepared his guns. The submarine was in front of him so he fired, the bullets immediately kicking up spray short of the boat.

By holding the nose in the same position, he walked the bullet strikes onto the submarine and got a good burst off before breaking left. He flew round in a wide circle and when he next got it in his sights he was approaching from astern, which meant that the big gun on the ship's deck forwards of the conning tower could not be brought to bear on him. He pressed the fire button again and saw yellow flashes of impacts on the boat and surrounding splashes until he released it and pulled up.

This time he peeled to the right and took another wide turn, which brought him around to a broadside view. The crew were trying to rotate the deck gun in his direction and he could see one machine gun firing from the conning tower. He could also see casualties on the deck and smoke, so he thought he'd done some damage. This time he got the vessel to fill his sights before firing; another good burst, yellow flashes of impact and then he was over the boat and heading for the shore. He knew the Hurricane had been hit.

On the beach Karol heard nothing of the engagement twenty miles out to sea, but as his Hurricane approached he heard that distinctive and somewhat mournful whistling noise the wind makes against the leading edge of the wings after the machine guns have been fired through the protective tape. Herbert landed and spun it round head to wind as Karol ran over.

"Surfaced U Boat, bearing ninety-two magnetic, four minutes out. Got three bursts into it; go get him Karol."

Karol scrambled into the cockpit; Herbert closed the hatch, pushed the canopy shut and then slid off the wing as Karol started taxiing. He saw that the linen fuselage cover had rips and tears in it in between the cockpit and the tail, so some shots fired must have come quite close to him. He sank to the ground as the aftershock of the pressures that tight turns in a fast aeroplane put on the human frame caught up with him. He watched Karol getting airborne despite the ragged fabric peeling off the fuselage with some slight irritation about his own frailty and maybe just a touch of jealousy for the younger man's role in this war.

As soon as he got off the beach Karol radioed the submarine's position and then headed for the reported location himself. A Lockheed Hudson of Coastal Command responded and asked Karol if he still had visual; Karol had not at that moment, but thirty seconds later he said he could see smoke and the Hudson closed on his position, as did Karol's squadron.

The Hudson attacked the submarine with bombs, huge columns of water blasting into the air. Karol went in for a low level attack, but when he pressed the button he got a one-second burst of tracer and then nothing. Herbert must have used most of it up, he thought, while reporting that he was out of ammunition to his squadron leader who ordered him to Rochford to re-arm. It took Karol more than half an hour before he was airborne again, as Rochford did some running repairs to stop any more linen tearing off the weakened airframe, by which time the patrol had landed at Bradwell for fuel.

Karol reported the attack as described to him by Herbert at daily debrief and thought no more of it until the end of the week when the Adjutant congratulated him on his shooting.

"I've got the gun camera film back, you've finally learned to get in close and shoot straight; nice job, Dubiel."

The film did not offer interpreters a clear identification of the submarine. It was not a German U Boat, as initially assumed, but possibly an Italian submarine. It was still on the surface and clearly in trouble when the Hudson broke off from the engagement but was not located when Motor Torpedo Boats from Sheppey reached the area.

II

Mark awoke after a difficult night feeling sore all over but buoyed up by the expectation of being discharged to Lavering for a further period of convalescent leave after nearly a month in hospital. That meant a round of cubs, scouts, Home Guard, Elizabeth, church services, Martha's cooking, chats with Colonel Mallinson and he was looking forward to all of it.

Letters had been sporadic and bland. One brief note from Elizabeth about the number of lambs she had to look after and a thoughtful letter from Uncle Tom expressing surprise that the police had wanted to check his revolver and it being no surprise at all that it was not the one they wanted. James had written three times without saying anything interesting. Alma was playing hard to get and the other WAAFs all seemed too busy to date airmen. Another note from Elizabeth to say that Swansea had been attacked, her parents were dead and that a Spitfire had crashed on the farm, so all the cubs and scouts had played with it.

Granddad Herbert had written from Brentwood to see if Mark wanted to meet him on his way back to Lavering and Mark had replied in the affirmative. Both Mark's parents had returned to work and there was no word from either of them. Mark wrote to Elizabeth the vague sort of commiserations about Swansea and her family that a bored officer would write in ignorance of the subject at hand.

His plan on discharge was that he'd travel into London and then out to Brentwood, where Granddad Herbert would meet him and take him on to Lavering.

Released he was, for a month; with a suitable supply of medication and the usual advice about keeping clean and out of trouble, a car took him to the railway station. Fred came for the ride although it would be another two or three weeks before he could leave the hospital.

"Remember the trip down?" said Fred, "Police looking for revolvers."

"Yes."

"Have you got one?"

"No."

"Do you want one?"

"Not really. In these days of closed cockpit canopies we can't go blatting at each other like in the last war."

"Pity, I scrounged this one for you. It was Dying Brian's; got it off a nurse."

Fred handed the piece over, in its smart leather holster on a Sam Browne belt. Mark pulled at the stud and had a look; it had Colt's logo on the grip.

"Takes the usual three-eight-zero ammunition," said Fred, "don't know where he got it, but there's a lot of foreign pieces around made for British cartridges."

"Yes, I think the last war was the same," said Mark. He strapped the belt on over his tunic and under his greatcoat, shook hands with Fred and slipped out into the late January rain. There were few people travelling that day and he found that he had the compartment to himself. That gave him the chance to have a better look at the revolver, which felt a bit slight in his hand when he compared it mentally with his New Service model, but perhaps Elizabeth would like the smaller hand grip: but should land girls have guns?

III

Granddad Herbert met him at Romford station for the short drive to Brentwood. It was market day, so the animal pens had sheep in them; it was busy and the streets were clogged with wagons and a few motor vehicles.

"Being a taxi is habit-forming; I picked your Elizabeth up from Ongar, you know and took her back to the farm."

"My Elizabeth; did she say much?"

"Little bit about her adventures in London with you; I'm not sure you have any idea how to show a girl a good time. We are going to have to talk, you know. She said you had dinner in a Lyons at Ludgate Circus. Five minutes along Fleet Street and into the Strand and you'd have been at Simpsons. Better wine list for a start."

"I suppose you know more than me, granddad, but would they let her in? Wearing breeches and all. Even NAAFI canteens won't serve her since she's a civilian. Anyway, how do you get the fuel to run this car?"

"Three rations, Mark. My boys are both in India so they don't need their fuel coupons. I don't think that's cheating; I make a considerable contribution to the war effort one way and another. Have you spoken to Karol recently?"

"No."

"I'll have to tell you myself then, dying to tell someone. Karol managed to get me a flight in a Hurricane."

"Wow, how did he manage that?"

"He landed it on the beach at Lavering and I took it for a quick spin. Got in trouble though."

"I'm not surprised, what trouble did you get in?"

"I got shot at by a surfaced submarine; fired back, did it some damage, then I beetled back to the beach and gave Karol his 'plane. There's some nice pictures of the attack on Karol's gun camera and, and this is the best bit, he's been recommended for a bar to his DFC."

"For 'his' attack on a submarine?"

"Yes. I got three bursts into it and he got the fourth."

"Granddad, it's dangerous in this war, look at me; no don't, look at the road, but you know what I mean."

"I know, but I was desperate to have a go, just once. Eight machine guns: I ripped that submarine heartily I can tell you. Nearly killed me though; the pressure when I turned. What an experience, wouldn't have missed it for anything and they only slightly damaged Karol's 'plane."

"With you in it. Has James used his guns yet?"

"No, and he doesn't know about my submarine either. Need to keep it a secret for Karol's sake. He's trying to get me a still picture from the footage that I can frame for my mantelpiece."

"On a different note, I haven't heard from Mum or Dad," said Mark, "so have they kept in touch with you?"

"Your Uncle Tom is the family co-ordinator," said Herbert, "your Dad has gone back to Egypt. Your Mum is looking for a different way of using her talents, so last heard of she was in London. You had a rough last night in London, didn't you?"

"Yes, the club was damaged; my windows were blown in and the next morning there was no water and no breakfast."

"Elizabeth said. She also mentioned the night before. The streets just aren't safe anymore. I'll write to her about her family. Changing the subject, I've also been over to London Colney to see de Havilland. He's got a flying prototype twin engine aircraft."

"What's it going to be for?"

"The Ministry haven't decided, mainly because they don't know about it yet; heavy fighter, light bomber maybe, but it's plywood and has two Merlin engines; speed wise I think it at least matches the Hurricane, so it could be interesting. I'm hoping for a ride in it later this year."

"The Germans have a twin-engine fighter and it's a death trap; too slow for daylight operations. All it's got going for it is a good range."

"This new de Havilland will have the range, I'm sure. Speed too. I'm supplying some of the timber and I have almost got a contract for one of my factories to make up the airframes if the Ministry adopt it. We'll see where the project goes. I'd like all my factories to be turning out aircraft rather than utility furniture."

Annie had tea and cakes ready for them in granddad Herbert's house. The mantelpiece in the study bore a photograph of the Brabhams at war; Sir Archibald with his sons Henry and Tom, Herbert with his sons Neville and Archie all staring at the camera from the past.

"Christmas 1916, or just after from memory," said Herbert, "I think that's the last time we got together before my brother was killed."

"Where was it taken?"

"Photographer's studio in Calais; that's why our ladies are not in it. There's one in the drawing room of us all in 1912. Sad occasion, we'd got together for my dad Sir Neville's funeral and it seemed a good idea to take a picture."

"I hadn't thought about it before, but there aren't many family group pictures," said Mark.

"That's because it meant going to a studio in the old days; now you can carry a camera and take the film to the chemist afterwards, but those pictures, big camera, glass plate negative...anyway, we'll head for Lavering straight after this," said Herbert, pouring his tea, "I'd like to be back here before dark."

"Is the war catching you much?" asked Mark.

"From time to time; we've got an Anderson shelter in the garden, but it's full of water so we don't use it. It'll make a nice pond when it's safe to get rid of the corrugated iron roof. There have been a few stray bombs; Chelmsford's been a target, as has Dagenham and we're in the middle. Mostly, it's noisy and the windows rattle. I can see London burning in the distance."

IV

Lavering in January was a cold place. The wind swept in off the North Sea, bringing the chill with it. Both Tom and Hetty were out when they reached the rectory, so granddad bad him farewell and Mark walked to the church to see the logbooks.

"More of the same," said Andrew Taylor, who was on tower watch, "German planes some nights; fireworks over London, sometimes Southend and Chelmsford. Guns and searchlights up along the river. The end of December was the really heavy time for Londoners. We could see the fires glowing here in daylight." For a ten-year-old, Andrew sounded quite mature. The war had obliged him to grow up.

"Any more crash landings or parachutists?"

"There was the Spitfire, you heard about that?"

"Yes."

"He made a forced landing in the field next to Murrell's orchard. Great fun; I sat in it. I saw Tarka...you know her parents were killed like Derrick's?"

"Yes."

"She hasn't been to any meetings since; busy on the farm, she says. None of us know how to say sorry to her for her loss, even Grey Brother doesn't know what to do. We tried when we went to play in the Spitfire."

"So did everybody else I suppose."

"Yes it was a fortnight before it was collected. We tried to be a comfort to Tarka, but I think we just got in the way."

"Anything more recent?"

"A possible two nights ago. Heck of a bang overhead and some debris. Colonel Mallinson thinks that one of our night fighters collided with a German bomber, but so far the Home Guard haven't located a wreck-site, just a few bits and pieces."

"What sort of bits?"

"All I saw was a flying boot with a foot in it; that's at the doctors. The brownies found what they think is part of a propeller and that's at the hall. There are a few other small bits of wreckage, but only the one body part so far."

Mark walked down to the surgery to see the boot, which was British. Next he went to the hall, where, just for a change, the Colonel was not in the reception area with his pipe. The cubs on logbook duty said that he was out with the search party looking for wreckage. They showed him the brownies' propeller fragment, which looked as though it had been lying around for longer than a couple of days.

He considered walking down to Home Farm, but this being a Monday, he figured that Elizabeth might be along to guides, so he'd try to see her after the meeting, maybe walk her home. He'd written to let her know when he'd be back in Lavering. Martha said that dinner would be at six, so he changed and played the piano for a while until Aunt Hetty returned.

"You're looking tired," she said, "how was the food at hospital?"

"Not as good as here," said Mark, "but they've done a lot of work on me; that big scab on my back is gone, replaced with skin grafts. It's delicate, but it feels better."

Hetty seemed to be studying him intently; then she got a magnifying glass from Tom's desk and advanced with it.

"I think your hair has started to grow again," she said, studying his scalp, "come over to the window, and get some light on it. Yes, some hair there."

"Oh good," said Mark, "they gave me a wig at the hospital, you know, but I didn't want to wear it, so it's in my bag."

"I must see that," said Hetty, "do put it on for dinner; if your hair is growing it will be the only time we get to see you in it."

While it looked quite good on, his hat would not fit over it; he'd tried it under his helmet and that had worked, but the wig came off with the helmet and he thought that was more alarming for anybody watching than just seeing him bald in the first place. Nevertheless, he wore it to please Aunt Hetty at dinner and then discarded it in favour of a bald pate and helmet for the walk down to the Guide meeting.

V

Elizabeth was a no-show and the patrol leaders were managing the meeting. She had not been to any hall events since Christmas; such was the pressure of looking after sheep during lambing. Quite a few of the guides had been down to help, but the novelty of feeding lambs was wearing off and they hoped that the wretched woollies would start eating grass so that their captain could resume running meetings. They told Mark of her bereavement, that her parents were casualties of the blitz on Swansea.

They also said that Carol Davies, the WAAF from Rochford, had been over twice to help them, but it was a bicycle journey of more than twenty miles each way for her. They pressed Mark for a yarn or two, so he re-told them the story of his capturing the German flier in Murrell's orchard and then described Karol's attack on the submarine.

Colonel Mallinson had arrived while he was lecturing and waited at the back. Mark handed the meeting back to the patrol leaders and joined the colonel, who told him that the search had found nothing yet. They had a look at the map and Mallinson outlined the areas that had been patrolled.

"The hours of daylight are so short, though," he said, "we can't do anything much in the dark."

The guides' meeting ended and the girls left the hall. Once they were alone, Mallinson asked Mark about the revolver.

"You don't need to tell me if you don't want to," he said, "but Tarka was quite worried about it, so after Murrell cleaned it I sent a similar model from my collection to the rectory."

Mark told him about the incident with the yobs under Blackfriars Bridge.

"I think the police know something," he said, "because they have taken an interest in bald RAF men."

"Still," said the Colonel, "they've tested that revolver and eliminated you from their enquiries, so I suppose the matter will rest there; except for our charmless PC Fidgeon, who, I am sure, will continue to think the worst of you."

Mark resolved to visit Elizabeth the next day; it was also a chance to try starting his car and to drive it if it would start. Since it did, he set off for Home Farm. Halfway down the High Street and just past the Post Office he noticed PC Fidgeon on foot patrol; he could not resist stopping to pass the time of day with the police officer.

"Heard you were round checking my revolver while I was in hospital."

"Yes sir, Mister Brabham; report from London of a shooting incident. The suspect was believed to be in RAF uniform, but fire-damaged and without hair, so you naturally came to mind."

"Naturally; shooting incident?"

"Yes sir, the alleged burned RAF man shot one victim dead, beat two others about the head with something jagged and threw one into the River Thames; except the tide was out so he fell thirty feet and sustained a broken neck."

"Quite a rampage then; four victims and one attacker, wouldn't you say?"

"Indeed sir, but we've established that you had nothing to do with it. That said, if any of your burned and bald colleagues seems a likely suspect for this massacre, I'm sure you'll let me know who."

"Massacre?"

Two dead, sir: one shot and one killed by his fall. The two that were battered remain alive, but one is still in hospital and may never be as well as he was before the incident."

"Interesting; good morning."

It had been a momentary shock that the yob he'd shot was dead; he had expected the one Elizabeth dumped over the parapet had not survived and the other two had, hence the police suspecting someone who looked like him. At Home Farm, Elizabeth was in a shed full of young lambs, all of which were clamouring for her attention. She looked exhausted. Robert Murrell was working with her and he, too, was shattered.

"Never had so many sheep before," he said, "I'm a cattleman at heart; didn't know how much work there was in getting lambs to market. Never will I do it again."

"Makes two of us," said Elizabeth, "I've told him that I can't do this. I have applied for the WAAF."

"Oh," said Mark, "and what will you do in the WAAF?"

"Meet a nice airman, perhaps," she said, "and learn a trade. All I've learned here is how to drive a tractor, a haywain and a trap; look after carthorses and ponies, harnessing and ploughing, seed drilling, care and maintenance of the reaper-binder, planting, hoeing, dibbing, weeding, calving, lambing, cross-cut saw, pit-saw, baking, milling, pistol shooting, shotgun cartridge reloading, aircraft recovery, knitting, laundry, milking, butter-making, creaming, cheese-making, darning socks; I've laid out a dead German, repacked parachutes, marked unexploded bombs - oh, and I can thatch a hay-rick, measure a field, fell a tree and hang a gate."

"So now you want to learn a trade?"

"Yes."

"What about farming? You could learn to look after carthorses..."

She hit him with the milk bottle she was holding.

"Gently, I'm a wounded man you know."

Murrell knew that farming was getting too much for his land girls.

"The farm is too productive for the few of us there are. I could have had twice as many sheep. I thought the girls might manage; we had land girls here in the last war, you know, but I was away and Mrs Murrell ran the place. This time, I thought with me here we'd make a good showing of ourselves, keep the Ministry from thoughts of throwing us out, but maybe I bit off too much at once."

"You've done a great deal for the war effort," said Mark, "the girls..."

"Girls have done well," said Murrell, "so well I can't get any more; word got around and all the farmers want them now. So many of them coming into the area they've got a hostel to live in; we need more, we also need men."

"I suppose the war should find a way of putting men back on the land," said Mark, "We captured thousands of Italians just before Christmas, I wonder if they can be made to work."

"Not much call for picking olives and trampling grapes on this farm," said Murrell, "but I suppose they can be trained; after all, the girls have managed to learn a few tricks between them."

Murrell left Mark and Elizabeth alone, having other things to do. Elizabeth looked ready to cry but said nothing.

"I had your letters," said Mark, "the blitz on Swansea…"

"Yes," she said, "My sisters are with a farm out near Carmarthen, but Mum and Dad are gone. I've applied for WAAF intake and I hope to be in there by Easter. I'll miss the people here, the guides and my brownies; you are all so kind, but I must move on."

"I don't know what to say," said Mark, "I suppose that when I came to Lavering I thought of everyone as always having been here doing what they're doing, but that's not so; you weren't here a year ago; evacuees come and go, other people will too. I'll be gone, not by Easter, but possibly May or June. How are we going to see each other?"

"I don't know."

"We'll find a way," said Mark, "and meanwhile I got you this revolver."

He gave her the belt and holster.

"I don't know," she said, "after all, my hoe is my sword; I read the rhyme in the magazine – *but when the war is over and peace at last restored, I shall always remember the land girl, who made her hoe her sword.*"

"I won't have to remember you," said Mark, "all I'll have to do is look across the fireplace to where you're sitting."

"You think?"

VI

Nobody knew anything of recent wreckage on the farm and Mark left not knowing when he would see Elizabeth again. The Christmas holiday had been great, but with all the work she had to do meeting was going to be difficult, despite them both being in the same parish. He drove away down the lane and on the spur of the moment turned towards the beach.

There was debris near the pillbox to remind him of the war; in a matter of minutes he had spotted an anti-personnel mine, two different cartridge cases and some bits of shrapnel, a spent bullet and a piece of metal he thought must be from an aircraft. The area could not be searched properly on the ground, he decided, so he placed a telephone call to the duty officer at RAF Rochford.

"I don't want to be unhelpful to your Home Guard boys, so could you manage the recon in a Lysander?"

"Yes, of course," said Mark.

"Excellent; we have three here, so give me the reference for the Lavering beach and I will send one to meet you there tomorrow. What time would suit you?"

"Can we say 09.30?"

"Indeed we can. Our pilot will look after you and you can observe. There would just be room for another observer if you can rustle one up."

Mark telephoned the colonel and left a message with Eric. Mallinson had not flown before so tomorrow would be his chance.

Colonel Mallinson attended the scout meeting that evening to see what the form would be for the morning.

"Comfortable clothing, wrap up well. Binoculars would help. I'll pick you up in the morning." Mark had decided to use his car again. His recent skin grafts and other treatments had made him feel quite a bit more able.

VII

The morning was bright and a bit frosty when Mark and the colonel met the Lysander on the beach. The pilot was a cheerful Scotsman who said he's been in the duty officer's room when the call came in. Mark decided against going on the sortie to give the colonel the seat. Mallinson suggested up the beach to the searchlights and back as the first sweep to look at the dunes, then up and down again to cover the salt marshes and creeks behind the beach area.

"Fifteen hundred feet," said the pilot when they reached that height, "I can always get you lower, but I think this gives you the best overview to start with."

"Yes indeed," said the colonel, taking a general look at the layout of the ground below, before applying his binoculars to the search. He concentrated on the beach and marshland, while the pilot kept an eye on the sea.

They reached the southern edge of the searchlight battery encampment and made a wide left hand turn south to overfly the salt marshes. These were honeycombed with creeks as the sea sought ways of venturing inland and freshwater from the higher ground sought egress to the sea.

They were about halfway along this leg of the flight when Mallinson spotted something and the pilot descended to give him a better view.

"That's part of a German machine," said the pilot. "a Dornier," front fuselage and one wing anyway."

"I can see the tail," said Mallinson, "over behind the Eastminster road."

"What now?" enquired the pilot.

"Can you signal the church tower?"

"Yes, with the lamp on the undercarriage; if I point the nose at the tower, they'll see it."

The pilot aimed at the tower and keyed in the colonel's message.

"Tower's acknowledged," said the pilot, "I'll loop right and overfly the wreck again, then we'll pick up the scent. What else do you expect to see?"

"British night fighter," said Mallinson, "the only human remain found was an RAF boot with a foot in it. We're looking for the owner."

Once on track again, they spotted the major parts of a shattered Bristol Blenheim scattered about the marshes. The pilot expressed surprise that, with so much rubbish lying about, nobody had tripped over the wreck site as yet.

"It's quite different at ground level," said the Colonel, "when I first moved here I went out with the wildfowling club each winter. Great fun, but you can't see much ground, which doesn't matter when you're looking up for geese and ducks all the time, but to find that wreck site we'd have to literally crawl up every creek."

"Are we done then?" asked the pilot.

"Yes," said the Colonel, "could we go over my house on the way back to the beach?"

"Surely."

The pilot flew down the High Street low enough to wave to the scouts on the church tower, then climbed and banked to give Mallinson a good view of his house and gardens before descending to the beach.

"Excellent," said the Colonel, climbing down from the cockpit, "exciting and efficient. I didn't get the chance in the last war, you know. I'd love to have seen the German trench systems from the air, but division always sent junior lieutenants up."

Mark exchanged addresses with the pilot and then drove Mallinson up to the village hall where he sketched what he'd seen on the blackboard. The Home Guard concentrated on the Blenheim site, while men from the searchlight battery went to the German wreck.

RAF units arrived later in the day and while good progress was made it would be three days before the site was regarded as cleared. Even then, recovery was incomplete: the Dornier site yielded enough body parts to account for a crew of three. Night bombers did not always carry a full crew, but there was no way of knowing.

The Blenheim was similarly a problem; the RAF had been keen to recover the wreckage due to 'secret equipment' and for reasons of national security would not say how many men had been in the crew. Mallinson took that as reason enough to stop looking.

The scouts looked at Mark's diagram of the pieces and added the location of the recovered flying boot to the jigsaw. That spurred them to check the wooded area again and on that final sweep they found a flying jacket arm with a limb in it and some smaller pieces of flesh. The body parts were interred in Lavering and eventually marked as 'an airman of the Second World War – known unto God'.

CHAPTER 19

MARK DID NOT KNOW how to talk to Elizabeth about the loss of her parents; Colonel Mallinson's chat with Grey Brother after his bereavement was the only guidance he'd had, so he took his lead from Uncle Tom.

"Bereavement is a process," said Tom, "a lot of people can't talk about it at first. The mood changes after about six weeks, but the pain gets worse until about three months have gone by, then it starts easing."

"How long does it take to ease?"

"Forever. My Dad was killed in the last war and none of us ever got over that. I think of him most days and whenever I take a funeral he seems to be standing near the back of the crowd."

"You can see him?"

"No, I just think I can. It's as though he has never left me; but to answer the question, there are corners that are turned in the process. The first is the funeral, then people feel different about six weeks later and I reckon it takes a year before they get over the worst of it."

Mark continued teaching his cubs and scouts. They felt the intensive nature of his training; the urgency with which he pressed them to take in new information, to train and practice. Time was moving on for them all and at the end of February, both Grey Brother Derrick Forder and red sixer Andrew Taylor had turned eleven, so their transition to the scouts had to be organised.

Carol Davies got a three-day pass, so she was able to help at guides on the Monday night, stick around and help at brownies on the Wednesday. Mark did not dare invite her to the rectory, but she was able to billet at the old 'Coaching Inn', which now served as a land army hostel. Mark accompanied her around the village on the Tuesday, turning a few heads. She hoped to make the three-day visit a monthly one, which Mark thought would be helpful to the youth groups, particularly after Elizabeth had gone. Whether he could, should or would take any advantage of her – or her of him - remained to be seen.

II

The week before his appointment was a quiet one for London, the German's venom being directed at regional cities. At hospital, his doctor was pleased with the repairs, but kept him a week to make a few more. After that, he told Mark, it's a matter of time.

"How much time?"

"Give it two months, see me again at the end of April. That will give the repairs time to settle down; I notice your hair is growing again, and that's a good sign."

It felt more like fur than hair, but it was a head covering and it was brown like his old hair, so he was pleased about it. It was only growing on the right; the side of his head over the remains of his left ear remained stubbornly bald. In Lavering,

Elizabeth finally had time for Brownies and Guides again and a little time for him. Saturday the eighth of March, to be precise; they went for a walk. She had taken to wearing the holstered revolver on her belt and nobody had mentioned it.

"The Swansea I knew seems to be all gone," she said, "and most of the people I knew with it. I don't think I want to go back to see what's left; not ever."

"What about your sisters?"

"They are still on the farm in Carmarthen. They know more about sheep than I do. My auntie is going to look after them, but she works in London and only visits Wales occasionally, so I don't really know what will happen."

"I don't have an experience like that," said Mark, "we're sort of sheltered here. We saw London burning, but that will be rebuilt. Swansea, I don't know. I'm sure they'll rebuild it, but not like it was."

She took his hand.

"Thirty-first of March I go into the WAAF," she said, "I've told Mister Murrell and the land army headquarters. I'll tell the girls and boys at meetings over the next week or so. I'll be trained over the spring and summer and then I'll be posted, so I'll let you know where."

"I'll be reviewed at the end of April," said Mark, "and if I pass fit to fly I will then find out whether I get back to my old squadron or a new posting."

"What do you hope for?"

"I want to be in a front-line unit. I need to be in action."

"Will you want to see me?"

"Yes."

They walked back towards the village in the last hour of daylight.

III

Across the North Sea, German fliers were preparing for the night attacks on Britain. Their bombers were armed with a mixture of high explosive and incendiary weapons. Targets included London's docks, the weapons factory at Enfield and some coastal sites; Southend and Maldon, Chelmsford and Romford.

As Mark walked Elizabeth along Lavering's High Street, the German machines started to taxi to their take-off points, timing the sortie so that they could take off in daylight and arrive over Britain in darkness.

The rectory was dark and silent as they approached it. The back door was unlocked, but nobody was home. Martha was out with Esther at a birthday party for one of Esther's friends, for which she had baked the cake, so they were at the far end of the village in a cul-de-sac of small cottages built, many years ago, for agricultural workers to live in.

Tom and Hetty were out on a rare trip together to London, where they might well stay the night.

"I don't think I've ever had the rectory to myself before," said Mark.

"You haven't got it to yourself now," said Elizabeth, "I'm here too, don't forget."

"How could I forget?" Mark turned and put his arms around her. She felt tense for a moment and then relaxed, as though she were melting.

"Shall we go upstairs?" she asked him before he got the chance to ask her.

Mark led her to his room, silently grateful that, courtesy of his RAF training and Martha's constant reminders, his room was tidy and the bed made. They walked in holding hands, Elizabeth pushing the door shut behind them. Facing each other in the dark and standing next to the bed, they started fumbling with each other's clothing.

They separated and sat on the bed to get their footwear off and then the struggle started again, as Elizabeth undid his buttons and he did the same for her. Her skin felt smooth when he got to it and she smelled earthy, like a freshly dug flower bed. Her hand crept into his underwear;

"Your hair is growing again."

Mark found that funny and could not stop giggling. Elizabeth used his being distracted to kneel up and discard some of her clothes before returning her attention to Mark's. Having undone his shirt buttons, she pulled him up into a sitting position so that she could pull his shirt and vest off over his head. The garments came easily. She'd had a hand in undressing him several times before and this was the first time that his clothing had not stuck to a wound. She rolled him over, still giggling, onto his front. She could not see his back properly, so she climbed off him and went to the door to turn the light on.

Mark watched her as she walked across to the bed, dressed in just her bra and panties. She got on top of him, kneeling astride him, holding his face down while her fingers ran over his back, which was healing up nicely.

She turned him over and lifted his legs onto her shoulders so that she could strip his trousers off him. Casting them to one side, she settled down on top of him to kiss again. Mark fiddled with her bra strap. She let him fumble for a while, before kneeling up and undoing it herself, letting it slide off her arms.

Mark stared at her breasts.

"What do you think?"

"You expect me to think at a moment like this?"

He pulled her down and played with her body, slipping the elastic waistband of her knickers over her buttocks so that he could push them down later. She let him explore between her legs with his fingers until she was sufficiently excited and needed him inside and used her hand to guide him. He felt stuck for a moment, like it was too big; then it shot in and she squawked, so he froze. She started moving her hips and he started thrusting to her rhythm. She knelt upright and he watched her breasts bouncing as she moved progressively faster.

Although he was excited, he became aware that he was rubbing the skin grafts on his back against the candlewick bedspread and that felt like lying on a cheese-grater. He pulled her down to kiss her; felt her straighten her legs so he was then able to roll over, getting her underneath him. Now the thrusting was his job; he continued until he became aware of the climaxing sensation.

He pushed harder and faster, three more times, three more, and three and then he felt it go in a gush. Elizabeth must have felt it too, as her muscle contractions seemed to slow down. He also slowed and then stopped, bringing his weight down on his elbows. She straightened her legs and with a little struggle he repositioned his legs outside hers, while remaining inside her.

"We did it with the light on," he said.

"Yes."

"Uncle Tom told me that grown-ups do it with the lights out."

"Maybe grown-ups do. What do you prefer?"

"I haven't done it before. I like it with the light on. I could watch your tits bouncing."

"Tits?"

"Yes. Every button in a Spitfire cockpit is called a tit; now I know why."

"So why are they called tits?"

"I don't know. I'll have to ask granddad."

"Do you like mine?"

"Yes."

"Are they better than Alma Burton's?"

"I haven't seen hers."

"And if you haven't done it before, how did you know what to do?"

"It was natural; anyway, you led the way."

"I haven't done it before, not all the way like that."

"So how did you know what to do?"

"I work on a farm; seen animals. My aunty told me a bit. She does it for a living you know."

Mark did not know and now was not the time to ask. He slid out of her so that they could get comfortable. The air was cold on his skin, so he pulled the cover up and over. They lay quietly for a while.

"Do you love me?" She asked.

"Yes."

"And?"

"And what?"

"I haven't got anyone else."

"You've got me."

"For always?"

"Yes."

Mark had been attracted to Elizabeth from the first time they met and he'd assumed, as had the older members of his family, that he would develop a relationship with her. He had not thought it through though; he'd kept in touch with Alma Burton, letters and telephone calls, but he'd not attempted to see her. He'd also kept in touch with Carol Davies at Rochford, same sort of deal. He was sure that both those WAAFs were interested in him, but he did not know how far that would go.

Elizabeth was the first one to take him all the way, but she was vulnerable, having recently lost her parents and being in the difficult and insecure position of leaving the land army in favour of the WAAFs; moving from a hard and tiring job to an unknown one. She clung to him; she wanted security. He knew that if he did not provide that security she'd probably look elsewhere. She'd eyed James up, Mark thought; and Karol had spent a lot of time with her, so if he had not been the one, there were others in the queue.

Had he just promised to marry her? Maybe he had. If so, he would not regret it. Alma was more his class; looked different, willowy, blond and honey-coloured where she'd caught the sun. What would she look like naked? He could not imagine. Would she go all the way? He did not know. What would her father think?

Carol was dark haired, freckled face and working class like Elizabeth. She seemed to have more figure, bigger bust, bigger hips, real hourglass shape in her uniform, but what would she look like naked; what would she feel and taste like? What would any of them be like in thirty years time? He was in the process of choosing the next Lady Brabham; the one to succeed his mother, but how? Mum was so beautiful and always had been, always would be.

He sat up so that he could look down on Elizabeth lying on her back. She looked up at him, reached up with her arms and pulled him down for a kiss. And what a kiss; many more to come, he hoped, over many years.

CHAPTER 20

AT THE POLICE STATION, PC Fidgeon was preparing himself for the night shift by reading the logbook of signals from the police headquarters and notes made by officers who'd been on the day shift. Next he would walk down to the village hall and consult the logbooks there. It had become a standard drill. The movement logs collated information gleaned by the observers at the beach and on the church tower and that information helped build up a picture in their minds as to what the night might bring.

He had developed an instinct about when trouble was brewing and thus what sort of night the village would have and he was usually right. He somehow knew which nights would be quiet and he expected tonight to be a busy one. German aircraft had flown along the coast several times during the day probing; looking for a compass bearing that might get them around active ack-ack and searchlight positions.

The coastal batteries were shifted from time to time. The scouts had built some dummy guns that were easy to move, being made of wood. They also had one dummy searchlight made from an oil drum. These quakers could be positioned in gaps in the defences and periodically the real weapons were moved. Nobody had any idea whether this ruse-de-guerre was effective or not, but the fly-bys suggested that the Germans were kept busy checking. They'd also scattered small anti-personnel weapons about the dunes, which made deploying the wooden guns that much more dangerous.

There had not been a large-scale raid up the Thames estuary for five nights, so PC Fidgeon thought that it was about time there was one. The last one had kept south, closer to the Kent coast, so tonight it would be the Essex side. He shared this thought with the ARP and Home Guard, who agreed with him.

After qualifying as a Bomb Reconnaissance Officer in January, PC Fidgeon had returned to the village with a hand-operated tripod-mounted air raid warning siren. There was nowhere to put it at the police station so they fitted it to the observation balcony on the village hall. A notice in the Post Office explained that if the alarm sounded it meant enemy aircraft overhead and that the guns might engage them, so it was a warning that people should take cover. What was not mentioned on the notice at the Post Office was that the siren would also be the signal for the village to go to action stations.

That meant the Home Guard deploying with their rifles. Scouts and guides would go to signal stations, firewatchers to their vantage points. All the various organisations and individuals with a duty or a responsibility would be on the alert. They had rehearsed a few times, but as there were so many real alarms the procedure had bedded down quite well. They were prepared for the worst, or so they hoped.

II

Over the North Sea, the Heinkel triple one bombers climbing out of Holland had reached nineteen thousand feet. They had to overfly Britain's coastal defences and head for targets in South Wales and the industrial Midlands. Ten thousand feet below them, bombers from Belgium had targets in Essex, London and Hertfordshire to attack.

The developing bomber streams started to appear on radar screens in the Chain Home stations, so operators on the coast sent messages to warn night fighters and gun crews. In addition to the regular Blenheim squadrons, there was a plan to try using the day squadrons, so on the alert that evening, James Brabham was sitting in his Spitfire, one of twenty-seven on stand-by at North Weald.

The plan was that they would scramble to intercept the bomber stream over the North Sea with the setting sun behind them. They'd have one chance to do some damage, then they'd break off and be guided into airfields that were not thought to be on the target list for the night. It meant landing in the dark, but if there was no enemy activity the runways could be lit briefly with flares and searchlights. After that, the bombers would still have to run the gauntlet of anti-aircraft gunnery, barrage balloons and night fighters.

III

James was dozing when he got the order to scramble. He went through the drill and took position ready to take off. The Spitfires formed up in threes and took off line abreast, climbing into the darkening sky. The old form of flying in tight V formations had given way to a looser way of getting into action. The German fighters flew in fours and that seemed effective, so the RAF tried loose threes and liked it better than tight formations, especially in low light.

Ordered to head east, eighty-five magnetic, angels two-zero, James climbed steadily, keeping his leader in sight. He flew as left wingman to a pilot who'd been in last summer's battle. The right wingman was in the same position as James; joined too late to take part in that engagement and itching for action.

"Bandits steering two-six-five, angels one niner. Vector zero-niner-one. Bandits should be in sight."

James was sure that was Alma's voice; he could picture her firm lips intoning the words, her white teeth flashing as she spoke. He imagined her breasts heaving with anticipation as the adrenaline kicked in. Imagine it was all he could do; she was interested in Mark, who had been stringing her along with phone calls and letters. She'd cornered James once, but that was only to see if he was going to Lavering for a three-day, in which case she'd try to get one too and tag along.

"Tally Ho!"

The squadron leader in front had spotted the bombers. In the control room Alma changed the board to 'enemy sighted' and waited.

James' flight was the third in the first squadron. He saw the black bombers, silhouetted against the dull clouds below them as the squadron leader shouted the battle cry.

"Blue section left, red section up, cover us, tally ho!"

James eased to the left as his flight leader got closer; in doing so he saw where they were going; loosely formed squadron of Heinkel and Dornier machines; his would be the one on the extreme left of his sight picture. He flicked the cover off the gun button and focussed on his target. The machine he chose was lower than him and heading right to left through his reflector sight. He adjusted his position slightly, waited until the machine filled the sight and fired.

Inside the Heinkel, nobody had seen the Spitfires closing with them and the first the crew knew about James' attack was bullets smashing into the cockpit. He had left the burst a bit late. The guns in his left wing put bullets into the cockpit and starboard wing, while those fired from his right wing went over the Heinkel and off into the gathering gloom.

Nevertheless, he'd hit it. One bullet hit the pilot just above his left collarbone. The rear high gunner was killed instantly and the starboard engine stuttered and started smoking.

James pulled around and got aligned with another bomber, coming toward it over its starboard wing. He fired, but too soon, his bullets dropping below the machine. He was still closing so he fired again and saw bright yellow impact flashes on the cockpit and the fuselage before the 'plane dropped out of his sight. A few seconds later a hefty explosion rocked James' machine; he thought the one he'd hit must have blown up somewhere below him. He was aware of other machines and people shouting through their radios in his ears. He pulled up and turned east, but could not see any more targets, so he came around to two-seven-zero magnetic and nineteen hundred feet to have a good look round.

The first 'plane he'd hit was by then about eight miles west of him, losing height. The pilot was in agony and bleeding profusely, so the nose gunner was trying to treat him while he tried to keep the machine steady. The damaged engine was not doing them any favours; he wanted to feather it, see if that would prevent a fire. They could not maintain height with a full bomb load and one engine and he said so.

The pilot wanted a hospital bed and no more excitement for a while, so he authorised jettisoning the bombs, turn for home. The bombs hit the sea five miles from the English coast. Some exploded and the rest sank. The scouts on pillbox observation heard the crumping noise as it rolled in off the sea. They signalled the church tower to report offshore explosions.

James had hit two enemy machines out of more than seven hundred attacking Britain that night. The high stream had over one hundred and fifty bombers in it, so picking on them with twenty-seven Spitfires was a gamble, but one that paid off. Squadrons from other airfields had also been directed onto the bomber stream and the pilots engaged would claim more than forty enemy aircraft damaged or destroyed in that first engagement, without loss.

Radar had meanwhile realised that there were two bomber streams at different heights so the second wave of fighters, fifty-one Hurricanes from Duxford, were directed at the lower formation. In the last of the light, these men spotted and engaged the bombers. Pilots would claim over thirty machines damaged, but such claims could not be confirmed, as the casualties would crash in the sea or struggle back to the low countries.

The Duxford wing were ordered back to base, while the North Weald, Rochford and Hornchurch machines were directed to Biggin Hill, since that seemed clear of the direction of the bombers.

As the fighter squadrons made for their respective destinations, it was the turn of coastal batteries to have a go. In the air, damaged machines, some with casualties on board, were trying to decide what to do. In the high formation, a Heinkel that had been bracketed by machine gun fire was nevertheless maintaining course and speed. That was until they noticed the fuel gauges dropping.

"Are we over land or sea?" the pilot enquired.

"Sea for three more minutes, then land."

"We drop the load on land and then turn to sea. Open the bomb doors."

The moment the crew thought they had crossed the British coast, they released their load. Three and a half miles below, the bombs landed in a line across the marshes, so close to the boathouse that it collapsed. The last one blew a hole in a field some seven feet deep and nearly twenty feet across next to the Eastminster road. The bomb went in behind the hedge, which was blown out of the ground for thirty feet of its length, torn at the point nearest the blast and dumped across the road like the frayed ends of an old rope.

Other aircraft commanders were assessing their chances. Being hit hard like that over the sea was a new experience and although British claims were exaggerated as to how many machines they'd successfully attacked, plenty of German aircraft had been damaged and individual crews now had to make decisions pertinent to their survival.

Dumping bombs and heading for home was favourite, so every few seconds the scouts in the pillbox logged new blasts in the sea and signalled the tower. In the village, the tower signaller relayed these messages to the village hall where PC Fidgeon authorised the use of the siren. It was still wailing when the first stick fell in the marshes.

IV

Most people were ready for that signal; like PC Fidgeon, the Home Guard had a sense of when trouble was coming and the wisdom of experienced men had fed down to the children, so when the siren sounded, everyone got weaving. Mark heard it just before a series of explosions.

"Air attack, let's go."

"Go where?"

"The church first; see what's happening."

They started struggling into clothes that had not been taken off with any thought about them being put back on quickly.

On the coast, the searchlights had lit up and the guns had started on the first target, a Ju88 in the lower stream, flying at ten thousand feet. Inside the machine, which was already damaged by machine gun fire, the crew struggled to get rid of their bomb load. A nearby blast shattered part of the cockpit and mortally wounded the pilot. He could not turn out to sea; he thought the rudder was jammed, although what was jamming it was his own foot stuck under the rudder bar and he was trying to press on the bar with the stump of his severed leg, not realising why he could not control the 'plane, nor appreciating that the light-headed feeling he now experienced was due to his falling blood pressure.

"Bombs gone."

"I can't steer," was the last thing he said.

The crew struggled in the dark. An ack-ack shell exploded in front of them. In the briefest of illumination it gave, the men saw their pilot was dead.

"Rous, rous."

With the bomb doors already open the men dropped into the night sky, leaving their dead pilot at the controls. The machine lost height and without anyone in control it would gradually flip over onto its back and then crash into the river Thames thirty miles away.

Dangling under his parachute, Heinrich Reif tried calculating how long it would take him to reach the ground. He enjoyed navigating and he liked mental arithmetic; his hate list included being in the Luftwaffe, getting shot at and parachuting into enemy territory.

He heard a dull whistle, then another. He could not make sense of the noise for a moment and then he realised; an aircraft above him had jettisoned its load and they were dropping past him in the dark. He looked down to see an explosion below, then another and another. He got a brief image of the ground below when the bombs landed, but only enough to gauge that his parachute ride was far from over.

The whizzing that he'd heard turned out to be incendiaries; as he drifted down the fires started below helped him work out how high he was and as the flames developed he could see the church and space between that and the burning woodland. Otto Botling could also see the ground in the light of the incendiary fires and he started trying to steer his parachute to keep away from the conflagration.

Somewhat detached from the other members of his crew, Franz Weite drifted downwards, unable to see the ground below him. He too could see the fires, but he seemed to be clear of them.

Ten thousand feet above them, Friedrich Zywek knew that his Heinkel was doomed. The Spitfire attack had damaged the machine, although he had been able to maintain height and speed until he crossed the coast. Oil pressure was dropping in the starboard engine and the controls felt sluggish. A blinding flash and a shrill noise persuaded him to abandon ship.

"Schnell, rous."

The gunners scrambled for the hatch; the rear gunner, having no pistol, detached his machine gun and took it with him. Friedrich realised that the shrill noise was his co-pilot screaming. The oxygen bottle had burst and Ernst's face and hands were burning. He struggled desperately to get Ernst out of his seat and to do something about the flames. He could not drag him to the rear escape hatch, so he opened the bomb doors, released the load, then pulled Ernst through the hatch into the empty bomb bay and they dropped into the darkness together.

V

On the ground, the war had come to Lavering. The first bombs had hit the marshes and cut the Eastminster road, although nobody in the village knew that as yet. The next stick of bombs whistled in closer. One landed in the woods, the next one in the churchyard and the third one behind the rectory, each exploding on contact. On the church tower, Frank Maynard threw himself flat, Vic Jessup doing likewise. The trees absorbed much of the blast from the woods. Two dozen of the mixed oak and hornbeams were knocked over like dominoes and a crater formed in the soft ground that would eventually become known as the lost pond, but that was the limit of the damage.

The blast from one landing in the graveyard hit the church tower blowing all the battlements off the south side. Most of the rubble landed on the roof, lumps of it striking the boys where they lay huddled against the east side, wearing helmets that were a bit too big for them. The large corner piece of the battlements went off into the darkness below.

"That was close," said Frank picking himself up.

"And again," said Vic, so they went prone.

"That went over the allotments."

Vic looked over the remaining battlements, "the allotments are over that side."

They had a look down into the churchyard but the darkness cloaked it. The bomb had landed towards the southeast corner and neither of them could picture what had been there in daylight.

Mark was ascending the spiral stairs to the top of the tower when the bombs landed. He braced himself and he felt the impact that damaged the battlements before sprinting up the last two dozen stairs and out onto the roof, just as Vic said, "and again."

Mark ducked down in the doorway. He heard the whizz of another bomb and the crump of its impact, then silence. He stood up and had a look over the parapet but could see nothing of where the bomb went. Another whizz.

"It's an incendiary, it's gone through the south aisle roof."

He shouted down to Elizabeth to deal with it. The incendiaries were quite small, about twice the diameter of a rolled umbrella and half as long, but the phosphorus in them would start a fire that, unless smothered, would burn for up to an hour and anything they lit might burn for days.

Looking over the parapet he could see another blaze in the churchyard, and more in the woods beyond. They were starting to illuminate the church. He picked up the Aldis and pointed it at the village hall.

I.N.C.E.N.D.B.O.M.B.C.H.U.R.C.H.

No answer. Another bomb whistled its way down, landing with a terrific bang at the far end of the street somewhere.

"You two must take cover," said Mark, "get down to the …"

Another blast.

"Here is as good as anywhere else for now," said Frank, "what's happening anyway?"

At that moment, Mark was looking up and that's when he saw the first parachute.

"Must be damaged machines, or it's an invasion. Get on the Aldis, signal parachute sighted; make that parachutes, I can see another."

The incendiary bombs in the woods were now making quite a bit of light, as was the one in the churchyard. Smoke was also billowing out of the hole in the south aisle roof, so Mark figured that Elizabeth had more than just the bomb to deal with.

"The church is on fire," he said, "signal that to the hall, then get down from here. If you don't get a reply, go there as runners, tell them I've got parachutes coming down and the church is burning, but don't stay up here. If the fire spreads there'll be no way down."

The Home Guard had mustered as the first explosions were heard. Then there was a massive blast from the lower end of the village, which turned out to be behind the cottages where Martha and Esther had gone for a birthday party. Four cottages had collapsed and Colonel Mallinson sent White Section to deal with it. He saw a clump of incendiaries land somewhere between the village and the beach. He could not judge quite where they were in the dark, but not too near to his house.

"Red section, take a look at those incendiaries, see if they need dealing with. Then relieve the signallers on the beach; they should take shelter."

"SIGNAL FROM THE TOWER," shouted Derrick Forder.

Mallinson looked along the street; he could see the tower back-lit by the incendiaries in the woods.

"The church is on fire," he said, "Blue Section..."

"TOWER SAYS PARACHUTES." Derrick made himself heard over the general din.

"Bother. Right; red section, rifles, with me. Blue section, rifles and sand, regroup at the church. Grey Brother, to me."

Derrick padded over.

"Go as a runner to find White Section; tell them parachutes sighted over the village. Then go on to the pillbox on the beach, tell them to take cover. If the church is on fire, the signallers on the tower will have to abandon that post, so the beach won't be able to signal. You and they must run with messages, understood?"

"Yes colonel," Derrick saluted and sprinted off into the night, carrying his War Office rifle at the trail. Andrew Taylor picked up his rifle and deployed with the Home Guard, heading for the church.

The seven men of blue section were halfway up the High Street when another bomb landed somewhere behind the Post Office. The blast came across the street, catching three of the men, while those lagging behind were showered by the tiles blown off the Post Office roof. The taped windows on the front of the building remained intact, the blast having been deflected upwards by the back wall of the building. The roof stayed on, but seemed to have jumped off the building and then landed back on top of the walls, but after rotating about forty-five degrees. Colonel Mallinson and his red section were about fifty yards behind, thus seeing the blast and its effect. Hurrying forwards, they spread out to see to their casualties. One broken leg, one concussion; the rest picking themselves up.

"Two men form a first aid party here; everyone else with me."

The Home Guard continued up the street towards the burning church, middle-aged men running as best they could. Andrew ran on ahead, spotting one parachute as he entered the churchyard. It seemed to be dropping behind the church somewhere.

Inside, Elizabeth had climbed the stairs into the south gallery. She could see the hole made by the incendiary bomb, which was still stuck in the rafters, despite having punched the plaster out below it. She decided that she needed something long to dislodge it and headed down the stairs to look for a suitable pole when the bomb that landed in the southeast corner of the churchyard struck. She did not know where it landed, but the blast blew the trefoil window at the east end of the south gallery in, showering the gallery and main aisle with glass and masonry. The main east window was also destroyed, but due to the angle the bomb-blast hit it at, the glass was sucked out rather than being blown in.

She was sheltered from the main blast and shower of glass, being in the stairwell at the time, but emerged into the church to a scene of devastation, illuminated by the developing fire in the woods beyond. The long-poled cross that the choir paraded behind stood in its mount on the end of the choir stalls, glinting at her as it reflected the light of the fire in the south aisle roof. She ran down the main aisle to get it and sprinted back, not realising that the blast had bent the tubular metal pole.

In the gallery, the bomb had either been dislodged by the blast, or had burned its way in; it was now lying on a pew in the gallery setting the ancient oak alight. Water will put the phosphorus out briefly. A small amount will spread the fire but sand will smother it. Laurie Hilton arrived at that moment with a bucket.

"I'll get it; what have you done to the cross?"

"Nothing, yet."

"It's bent."

"Never mind, get to that fire."

Due to the way that Colonel Mallinson rotated the youth organisations, the children on duty when the excitement started were Frank Maynard and Vic Jessup in the tower, Derrick Forder and Andrew Taylor at the village hall and Peter Law with George Ibbett at the pillbox on the beach.

Explosions and the siren got the rest moving, scrambling into uniforms, grabbing rifles and heading to rendezvous. Those under fourteen were not expected to turn out and any under-fourteens on signal duty were supposed to be relieved so that they could go home and take cover, but everybody got moving – cubs and brownies, scouts and guides; grabbing rifles or first aid kits, catapults, sand bags, water bottles, knives, helmets and heading into the fray to support the Home Guard, Police, Air Raid Patrol, first aid parties and firewatchers, who were already being supported by those residents who were able and willing to help.

Frank Ball arrived at the police station with his rifle, a small first aid kit and his incendiary bomb kit, consisting of a rucksack full of sand from the beach and a large trowel. PC Fidgeon had started directing volunteers, his first priorities being rescue work where the cottages had collapsed and any casualties from the bomb behind the Post Office. When he saw that Frank was equipped for incendiary bombs he sent him to the church, knowing that there was at least one there to deal with. He could see that there were others in the general direction of the beach, but judged that they were in open countryside and some in the woods beyond the church, which were also a low priority.

His next priority was the Post Office. Miss Everett and her sister were unaccounted for and a lot of debris from the stables had landed on their Anderson shelter. If they were in it, they'd need digging out. If. There was also the risk of looters. Although most evacuees and villagers were law-abiding and God fearing, some were not and damaged buildings were always attractive to night prowlers.

Derek Pilley ran to the beach pillbox with his kit, as he lived the closest to it and he knew that Peter Law would be there.

"What's happening?"

Peter briefed him; "Luftwaffe overhead, seem to have started dropping their bombs in the sea, some on land in the marshes and in the village. The searchlights are up and the ack-ack have been busy. I think one 'plane ditched on the beach. I've seen several burning overhead."

"Invasion?"

"Seems to be a bombing raid with us as the target. Last signal from the tower said the church had copped an incendiary bomb."

"Anything out to sea?"

"Nothing visible."

Derrick Forder arrived, puffed out. He sat down to get his wind back before reciting the Colonel's message.

"Home Guard are standing to with their rifles, parachutes sighted over the village. There's nobody on the tower because the church is on fire, so we have to run any messages."

"Well it's quiet here," said Peter, "and if there's an invasion fleet out there the tide's wrong; it's going out and they'd need it coming in."

"Or land at low tide," said Derek Pilley, "let's look at the tide table."

"04.30 low tide," said Peter, "that's no good for them; three mile walk to the dunes across flat sand. They'd be mown down if we had a mower and they could not outrun the flow tide anyway. High tide at 10.00; that would work, daylight and a short beach."

"OK, so nothing's likely to happen here for now."

They fell silent to think. Derrick and Derek had just run to the beach and needed a breather. Nothing was happening on the shore and their logic was that nothing would before it got light.

"Right," said Peter, "George and I will go to the village, you two stay here and keep look out. I'll see if I can find some brownies to relieve you. Look out up the coast towards the searchlights. I think a 'plane might have landed on the beach there. If nothing happens in an hour, come back to the hall."

He and George grabbed their rifles and ran for the village.

CHAPTER 21

LAURIE HILTON HAD BEEN first to the church and others soon arrived. His sand was insufficient to deal with the incendiary, but Frank Ball added his to the heap, which seemed to do the trick. Once the thing had cooled, it could be moved outside.

The roof was still on fire, though, so the next problem was to get some water onto that blaze; with the two from the tower, they were five and others were arriving. There was one tap in the vestry, but the vestry was locked. The next nearest tap was in the churchyard on the north wall, intended for the convenience of people putting flowers on graves.

There were two fire buckets containing water and two of sand in church, so with Laurie's bucket they had five to hand, but the fire was fifteen feet above the gallery floor and that was too far to throw water upwards.

"Need the stirrup pump from the hall," said Laurie.

"Or a rope," said Frank, "might be able to climb down onto that roof from the tower and then haul buckets up."

"Bell ropes," said Laurie, "let's go."

He and Frank ascended the tower to the bell room, where Frank cut the rope off the nearest bell and pulled it up. On the roof, Frank tied it around his waist and then climbed over the side. Laurie, Frank Maynard and Vic lowered him the twenty feet onto the roof, letting the rope go when he got there. Elizabeth was by this time at the bottom of the tower with Mark, two brownies and buckets of water.

Frank threw the end of the bell rope down to them, noticing as he did so the first parachutist landing to the east of the church.

"PARACHUTE."

Mark looked up to see where Frank pointed and then headed in that direction. Laurie picked up his rifle and waited. Frank hauled the first bucket up and threw it on the fire. He lowered the rope.

"Send a brownie up, I need to cover the skipper."

Frank tied a bowline in the rope and lowered it for the smallest girl to slip into. He pulled her up, undid the knot and dropped the rope for the next bucket.

"Throw the water at the sides of the hole, not all at once," he told her, "I'm going to the other end of the roof with my rifle, so you will be able to see me all the time."

He ran along the roof to the east end, dropping flat to crawl the last few feet. At the edge, he loaded his rifle with a cartridge from his woggle.

The fire had started melting the lead roof, so the hole was getting bigger. Thelma Burchett half dragged, half carried the bucket to the fire, then tipped it over so that the water ran into the hole. That seemed to work, so she hastened back to get another bucket; trouble was, pulling the bucket up on the rope was difficult.

On the tower, Laurie could see Frank on the far end of the south aisle roof, but nothing beyond that.

"I'll go and back the skipper up."

"Get me down onto the roof first," said Vic, "I'll help with the fire. Let's get another bell rope."

Doing that took time, but leaving one small brownie to fight the fire would have been the wrong thing to do.

Heinrich Reif landed first. His parachute caught on the side of one of the horse chestnut trees along the edge of the churchyard, so he stopped with a jerk and hung for a moment before the thin branches of the tree bent gracefully to let his journey continue. He hit the ground hard, his parachute remaining in the tree, stuck to the sticky buds that would release the new leaves in time for Easter that year.

Climbing out of his harness, Heinrich had a quick look round. The woodland was burning behind him, illuminating the church in front of him that was also alight. A dark area to his left looked inviting, so he started hobbling towards it.

People were shouting; he did not think they were shouting at him but understanding no English he could not be sure. He went behind a gravestone, comfortingly tall, and hid for a moment. Peeping over the top he could see movement on the church roof, so that fire was being dealt with. There were also people in the churchyard, but they were concerned with the fire. One person coming his way; he drew his pistol and immediately felt somewhat ridiculous.

He was in enemy territory. These people had just been bombed and would hold him responsible. He could not surrender to anybody, nor did he want to. Evading capture was his priority, at least until things calmed down.

II

Otto Botling landed barely two hundred yards from Heinrich beyond the trees on the north side of the churchyard in an allotment. It was quite dark there, so when he stood up all he could see was the vague shape of the church silhouetted by flames beyond it. He started pulling his parachute together but it was stuck on something, so he left it where it was and made his way to towards where he'd last seen Heinrich.

Voices sounded distantly. He tried to listen; more bomb blasts in the distance, then getting closer. He squatted down; more whizzing noises and a cluster of incendiary bombs landed somewhere to his right.

Mark had walked along the south side of the church until he was below the shattered trefoil window. He could see the parachute hanging on the tree, but not its owner. All he could be sure of was that the man had reached the ground, so he started walking towards the parachute, picking his way between the gravestones.

On the roof above, Frank could see the parachute and the skipper making his way towards it. He scanned the area watching for any movement.

Heinrich could also see the figure crossing the churchyard in the general direction of his parachute. He looked around. The light generated by the incendiary fires was getting brighter and the dark area behind him seemed to be a hole; a bomb crater. Slipping into it seemed a good idea, as it would hide him for now, but the advancing helmeted figure was annoying. Heinrich still had his pistol out and was covering the advancing figure when he felt a really sharp punch on his jaw. He felt light-headed and then he passed out.

On the roof, Frank had seen Heinrich's movement behind the gravestone and fired his .22 rifle. After the shot, he could see nothing at all, except the skipper still walking towards the parachute. Maybe he'd imagined the movement. He opened the bolt to reload the chamber and waited.

Laurie Hilton was descending the spiral stairs from the tower roof when Frank fired, so he did not hear the shot. On the tower, Frank Maynard did not hear it either. He could see

Frank Ball in position at the far end of the roof and Thelma Burchett, now assisted by Vic, drawing buckets up to the fire. He stayed in position, conscious that there were three people on the burning roof, who might have to climb up ropes to the tower and then down the stairs. They would need his help if that turned out to be their escape route.

Mark reached the parachute; he could see that the harness was undone, so whoever landed had survived the experience and fled. He had a look around, but saw nothing. His head felt itchy under the helmet so he took it off to scratch. Two hundred yards away, Otto could just see the parachute and a figure next to it, so he moved forwards into the churchyard, there being no railings to identify that boundary anymore.

He approached Mark from the north, just as Laurie Hilton was doing the same by following the path Mark had taken, walking east along the south side. Otto was thirty yards from Mark when Laurie appeared around the end of the church, wearing his helmet and carrying his rifle. Otto took him to be an enemy and Mark a friend. He had his pistol in hand, so he shouted "Achtung" and fired at Laurie.

The nine millimetre pistol made a lot more noise than Frank Ball's rifle, so the shot got everyone's attention. It missed Laurie, who ducked back behind the church cycling the bolt on his rifle. From the roof, Frank Ball saw Otto and fired at him. Mark had his Colt revolver in hand and also fired. That alerted Otto to the man by the parachute being an enemy, so he took a return shot at Mark.

Frank's bullet missed Otto, but hit a gravestone behind him, which made Otto think that he was surrounded. Laurie came around the end of the church, rifle shouldered;

"HANDS UP."

Otto turned towards Laurie who fired as soon as he could see that the man's hands were not going up. The Home Guard rifle made a lot more noise than Otto's pistol and the shock of the bullet just missing his neck but ripping through the collar of his flying suit was enough to put Otto out of the fight. He put his hands up as high as he could and just in time to stop anyone firing again. Home Guardsmen started arriving. They assumed that the parachute in the tree was Otto's and thus that the action in the churchyard was over.

Andrew Taylor, looking up at the burning roof after Otto was escorted away saw the next parachute descending and raised the alarm. Frank Ball rolled onto his back to look up. The three crewmen from Friedrich Zywek's Heinkel were floating down onto the village. The Home Guard started sorting themselves out to be in position for the men landing, so Mark resumed worrying about the church. Elizabeth and her crew had sent two dozen buckets of water up and above them Vic and Thelma thought that the fire was out.

"We'll have a look inside," said Mark, "see what it looks like. Keep adding water meanwhile."

The interior of the church was still illuminated by the incendiary fire in the woods, so Mark could see quite clearly when water poured through the hole in the ceiling. The fire was definitely out, he decided. The trouble was that he formed that opinion from the ground floor. If he'd gone up into the gallery for a closer look he might have noticed that the water pouring through the roof had washed the sand off the incendiary device lying in the pew beneath that hole.

III

Back outside, the air armada seemed to have finished passing overhead. There were distant explosions to be heard and closer to home the searchlights had been switched off;

Lavering was illuminated by incendiary fires and the sky was brightening in the distance as other targets were bombed.

Colonel Mallinson's immediate concern was the three parachutes descending, although he gave no orders to his men as they were already deploying themselves to deal with the problem. This proved quite simple, as they'd had plenty of time to get ready. Stanislaus Marcinkowski, who'd jumped with his machine gun, lost it in the sudden jerk when his parachute opened. He landed near the village hall and surrendered to white section after trying to hide in a ditch. His machine gun was never found and presumably remains wherever it landed.

Adolf Adler landed behind the Post Office, near the crater left by the bomb that wrecked the building. He slipped out of his parachute and drew his pistol. Somebody shouted at him to surrender, but he did not want to so he ran across the street towards the Post Office building. A fusillade of bullets followed him, fired by scouts. The bullets zipped and cracked about him, bouncing off the stonework. He decided surrendering was a better option after all and did so, but not quickly enough. A Home Guard bullet ripped through his chest and he collapsed to die in the street.

Gerhard Manteuffel drifted away from the village into the marshes. He had a bad landing that was both hard and wet. It was quiet when he struggled out of the boggy creek. Looking around, he saw what he thought was the roof of a building, so he made his way over to it; difficult though that was due to flooded bomb craters. When he got there, he saw that the building had partly fallen down. The roof looked not too bad, so he crawled in to find that it was a boathouse. The largest boat within had a small cabin on it and although the boat was held down by the roof, he thought it safe enough to hide in and rest for a while.

IV

Colonel Mallinson knew that there were more parachutists in the vicinity than were accounted for. They had seen two groups of three descending; one of the first three and two of the second trio were accounted for, but that meant three more potentially hostile enemy aliens were somewhere and German bombers did not have crews of three; up to four or five so there might be four more in the area without even thinking about how many more might be scattered around the county.

The village was a shambles; four cottages destroyed at the lower end and all the others in the Crescent were damaged. The Post Office was badly damaged, as were the shops next to it and those opposite, as well as the old stables and smithy behind. The railway station had been damaged by one blast and then set alight by the incendiaries. The church was damaged and various incendiary bombs were still burning themselves out in woods and fields and, dammit, the church is on fire again.

Mallinson rounded up the available personnel and made for the church, assuming that the incendiary in there had not been properly put out. He organised a chain to get water onto the pews, damping them down and gradually moving closer to the seat of the fire. The smoke was horrendous, but in a large building with huge windows that lacked glass in them, it was possible to get close to the fire and deal with it. The fire got closer to them when the gallery collapsed.

Other people came in as they realised what was happening; Mark found himself in a chain of bucket passers in between Frank Ball and Thelma Burchett and it seemed to him that he must have handled fifty buckets before the fire was finally dealt with. The roof and tower had been evacuated, so once the church was safe, Mark and Elizabeth found each other in the churchyard and gathered to them the fifteen or so lads and lasses who had worked hard that night.

"Stick here for a bit, I'll find the colonel and see what's next." Mark set off for the High Street, certain of finding Colonel Mallinson somewhere. The first people he met, though, were PC Fidgeon and the two boys who'd just returned from the beach. They told Mark what Peter had said; that there was nothing likely to happen on the beach before daylight.

"He said there might be a 'plane on the beach, but all we saw was one parachute, only a glimpse. He might be near the boathouse."

"We can look for him at first light," said Fidgeon, "I doubt if there's enough water up that creek to float a boat whilst the tide's out, so he's unlikely to steal one and row home. So that's one. We've seen six parachutes between us and we've got three airmen in custody. If one is near the boathouse that still leaves two to think about."

"And while we saw two lots of three," said Mark, "there may be one or two more from each 'plane that we didn't see."

"The Home Guard are spread out and patrolling," said Fidgeon, "and your other two from the beach and some others are with them. How many have you got at the church?"

"About fifteen," said Mark, "of all ages."

"I don't think there's a lot we can do before daylight," said Fidgeon, "and the fire brigade can't get to us as the road is blocked. When the sun comes up, we can be looking for parachutes on the ground and such, but in the dark it's dangerous. There were shots fired in two of the three arrests and we don't know what's lying about, UXBs and enemy fliers with guns."

"Alright," said Mark, "I'll send all the youngsters home; see if they can sleep. We'll get volunteers together for, what, half past seven and then start patrolling."

Mark released the boys and went back to the church to send the rest home. It was nearly midnight and they all needed some rest. He told them to reassemble at the village hall in the morning, ready to look for the missing airmen.

A problem arose; some of them did not have homes to go to due to the bomb damage, so Elizabeth formed them up crocodile style and led them to the rectory. Mark had hoped that Elizabeth would stay the night, but he had not anticipated so many chaperones. They were in the kitchen with Elizabeth trying to sort out hot drinks before it occurred to him that Martha was missing. Remembering that she had taken Esther to a party in the cottages, he asked the group if any of them had been at the party; none had.

"I'd better find out what's happening," he said, "so fit this lot in with blankets and make them comfortable and I'll see about Esther."

The High Street was dark and seemed deserted as he walked down it. There was a slight breeze bearing the smells of the night; smoke, hints of the explosives and that strange mustiness where fabrics have got wet. He looked in the police station; PC Fidgeon was out; it was occupied by a special constable whom Mark did not know and the postman.

"Postie, what happened at the cottages? Martha and Esther haven't come home."

"Bad blast there, Flight Lieutenant Brabham, the Home Guard are still working on the site and they've got help now from the batteries. Some people are casualties and ... well, it's not good."

"Is Colonel Mallinson there?"

"I think so. I came here to use the telephone, so if you're thinking of going down there I'll walk with you."

They plodded along the street together, just like the first time they met and that seemed a long time ago. When they reached the Crescent, Mark realised there was nothing much he could do. The explosion had caused four of the cottages to collapse and had ripped most of the thatch off the others. A fire had started in one of the less damaged buildings and spread along the terrace. The party was thought to have been in one of the collapsed buildings and the rescuers worked on the basis that there might be survivors in the cellar.

Colonel Mallinson had gone home, so Mark decided to do the same, the better prepared he'd be for the morning.

V

The scouts Mark had dismissed the night before started assembling at the church in the hour before dawn. Mark and Elizabeth joined them just after seven o'clock, having left the younger children sleeping.

"Our first job is to look for signs of the parachutists from last night. We know one landed in the churchyard and there will be others. We are looking for their equipment and anything else relating to last night's bombing; UXBs, incendiary fins, aircraft bits."

"Body parts like last time?" asked Thelma, "I'll get the wheelbarrow."

"Yes; anything to do with last night."

"We'll get that parachute out of the tree then," said Andrew Taylor. He set off followed by several of the smaller children.

Next to the bomb crater, Heinrich Reif stirred. The sky above him was grey rather than black. He was terribly cold and stiff. His jaw felt stuck. He slipped his glove off and explored his face gingerly with his fingers. He could feel blood or mud stuck to his face. Inside his mouth he could taste blood and he was certain that his jaw was broken. He tried to stand up and managed it with difficulty. He could hear voices, so he got his pistol ready.

Andrew got to the parachute and shouldered his rifle to help drag it off the tree. It was a struggle, but with four of them pulling, they got it down.

"Look at that," said Laurie, pointing to the crater.

Laurie and Andrew set off towards the damage, leaving the others folding the parachute. Andrew was in front when Heinrich, now in the crater, saw him; what he saw was the rifle muzzle against the greying sky and the shape of the helmet. That was enough; Heinrich fired his pistol twice and the helmeted figure disappeared.

The first bullet missed, but the second caught Andrew in the face, just to the right of his nose. The bullet ploughed through his brain at an upward angle and blew a hole the size of a penny in the back of his skull as it exited. Striking the inside of the helmet, the bullet could not penetrate the metal, but in trying to do so it jerked the helmet backwards and Andrew with it; he was dead before he hit the ground.

Laurie fell flat and shouted an alarm, cycling his rifle bolt as he did so. Heinrich climbed up the side of the crater until he could see over the edge. Laurie had turned away to shout at the youngsters recovering the parachute to take cover. Mark had started running through the churchyard with Elizabeth behind him. As Heinrich tried to climb out of the crater, he fired his pistol again at nothing in particular. Mark saw him and drew his revolver.

Laurie eased himself up to look; Heinrich saw him and took aim. Mark did the same, shouting at the German to surrender. Heinrich turned his pistol towards Mark, who fired immediately. Elizabeth, now beside Mark with Dying Brian's revolver also fired. Laurie got up onto his knees and aimed. Heinrich seemed to have paused, as though uncertain of what to do next. Mark watched as Heinrich's pistol gradually turned toward him, ever so slowly. He and Elizabeth both fired again and Heinrich seemed to lose his balance, tumbling back down into the crater.

"Andrew's hit," called Laurie, advancing on the crater, rifle at the ready.

"Where?"

"There."

Elizabeth crossed to where Andrew lay. He looked surprised, staring at the lightening sky, rifle at the high port; surprised at being dead. Then she walked towards the crater and without breaking her step went straight in. Heinrich lay on his back near the bottom of the hole. Elizabeth fired her revolver into his face, duplicating the fatal wound Andrew had received. Without a word, she picked up his pistol and climbed out of the crater.

"Now what do we do?"

She was thinking of what should be done at once, while Mark was already thinking much further ahead. Until now, letting the cubs and scouts run around with rifles trying to be useful had been fun, kept them busy and focussed. Now one of them was dead, as predicted by PC Fidgeon and that death would have all sorts of consequences. For a start there could be umpteen more Germans around and they'd got kids scattered all over the place with rifles; all vulnerable to getting shot.

"What do we do now?" She repeated.

"We've got to get Andrew to the doctor; get the rest of the kids out of harm's way. There's a war on." Mark was in shock and not thinking clearly.

"The war got here last night," said Elizabeth," and they all know it. Andrew's dead, so he doesn't need a doctor. He's not the only one. Esther's missing, might be dead; half the brownies were at that party, we don't know about any of them, but they didn't have a chance. Those that are with us this morning carrying weapons do have a chance to make a difference. We must let them."

Laurie called on the cubs with the parachute to use it to cover Andrew, but before they did he straightened the ten-year-old's limbs and put his own handkerchief over the boy's face. Next he lifted the rifle and removed the ammunition from Andrew's woggle, handing the weapon and cartridges to the nearest cub.

"We're done here," he said, "I'll send boys for stretchers. We'll finish checking the churchyard, then move onto the allotments. We can't stop now."

Fifteen minutes later, cubs searching the allotments found Otto's parachute fouled up on beanpoles. That made sense of last night; two parachutists close together.

PC Fidgeon and Colonel Mallinson came in response to messages about shots fired and casualties in the churchyard. Fidgeon had a quick look at both bodies before they were stretchered away to the temporary mortuary that the village hall had become. He met Mark by the tower door and was going to say something when he noticed the hole in the ground next to the tower.

"I'd better check that," he said, "could you keep people away for a few minutes?"

He climbed down into the hole, which was big enough for a policeman twice his size. He had a feel about with his feet, then with his hands.

"I can feel the shape of a bomb and the jagged edge of its fins." He said when he climbed out of the hole, "So I'll get some tape and a UXB warning sign. Post boys at each end of the churchyard to keep people clear."

The grey sky brightened to a lighter dull grey and help started to arrive. Military policemen and RAF recovery from Rochford came by road and a Lysander aircraft overflew the area looking for downed Luftwaffe machines: police and four ambulances arrived from Chelmsford, soldiers from the coastal batteries and a fire engine from South Woodham Ferrers. Rescue work continued in the Crescent, search parties fanned out looking for anything. The damage to the village started to be assessed; the injured were treated, the dead laid out in the village hall for identification and post-mortem work.

Scouts and guides on the signals rota took their positions at the beach pillbox, the village hall and the church tower. Gaps in the rota were filled ad hoc. It did not occur to the boys as they climbed the spiral steps of the damaged building that the 'UXB' signs below were meant to keep them from their appointed post eighty feet above the suspected device.

CHAPTER 22

TOM BRABHAM HAD SPENT the night at his Uncle Herbert's house in Brentwood. He had driven there the day before and then took the train the rest of the way into London. He figured it was Herbert's turn to get some decent bottles out and, with their wives, they'd had a pleasant evening despite distant bombing in all directions.

It was just starting to get light when he and Hetty left and bright enough to see the road without the aid of the blinkered headlamps. By the time he was past South Woodham Ferrers, it was quite light. He'd seen little from last night's action; a fallen tree, some rubble in the road and now, a man in his way signalling him to stop.

Friedrich Zywek had discarded his parachute, but made no attempt to disguise the fact that he was a Luftwaffe officer. He did not care who was in the car, but it was the first one to pass him in daylight. There had been some traffic on the road in the dark, including a fire engine, but they all drove as people in a hurry. This car sounded safe and he was pleasantly surprised to see the driver's dog collar, the mark of a clergyman.

"Pater, Ernst ist tote."

Tom got out of the car and followed the airman as he walked away. In the nearby field, Ernst Gregor was propped up against a fallen tree, wrapped in parachute silk. Tom bent down to check for signs of life. The man's face was gone, burned black; hands too, when Tom searched for a wrist and a pulse, but no rigor. He felt for a heartbeat and there was one, but ever so weak.

"Still alive, let's get him to my car."

They picked up the crippled Ernst in the parachute and manhandled him to the gate. Hetty opened it and then the car door. It was easiest to put Ernst in front, so Hetty rode in the back with Friedrich. Arriving in the village the first thing Tom saw that told him of the air raid was the church tower. The damage was obvious in daylight, battlements missing and the flagpole at a strange angle. Next he saw the 'UXB' warning sign, so he took the south road to get into the village.

A military policeman stopped him just before the pub. Tom said he had the casualty for the doctor. The policeman said the doctor was inundated. He ordered Zywek out of the vehicle and searched him. Another policeman searched Ernst where he sat.

"Nothing; he's gone."

"He had a heartbeat when I picked him up," said Tom.

"OK, take him to the village hall. We'll keep this one."

Hetty decided to walk while Tom disposed of the body. The police asked her about where and when they'd picked the Luftwaffe people up before letting her go on her way.

Tom drove slowly, taking in the damage to his village as he did so. He had not seen how badly hit the church was, but he saw the wrecked Post Office. The village hall was intact and busy. RAF men lifted Ernst out of Tom's car and took him in. The doctor assessed him as still alive, but beyond help.

"He's far worse than Mark was, Tom," he said, "he's not just burned he's cooked in places and that's fatal. His hands are completely gone, his eyes. He can hardly breath."

"Tracheotomy?" asked Tom, "Help him breath, make him comfortable, something for the pain. If he's going to die, let it be in peace."

"Take a look around, Tom; count the bodies. The way it's going they'll be more people in here waiting for cardboard coffins by nightfall than you get in church on a Sunday. See how many dead children there are under those blankets then come back and tell me again about making this killer comfortable."

"He's no different to us," said Tom, "what did you get the Blue Max for? And me the VC?"

He turned away from the doctor and walked into the main hall where the first person he encountered was Sergeant Pavitt.

"Bad night padre," he said, "bombs dropped on the Crescent; we've got eight dead from there, four of them are children. Search and rescue are still in there. One of the cubs is dead, got shot by a downed flier and the flier's dead too. Another airman was shot outside the Post Office."

"I saw the Post Office and stables were hit."

"No casualties there, apart from that airman; same with the church. It's been damaged but nobody hurt."

Tom left the hall without saying anything to the doctor. The doctor injected the flier with morphine and tracheotomized him without saying anything to the rector. Then he asked the RAF people to shift the injured flier to the cottage hospital.

Tom left his car outside the village hall and walked into the street intending to see all the damage for himself. He also wanted to find Colonel Mallinson and that wish was immediately granted as the Colonel was heading toward the hall.

There was nothing to say. Tom knew it had been a bad night and did not need telling. Colonel Mallinson knew how bad but was not ready to summarize it. They stood silently together for several minutes before an army lorry pulled up.

"Colonel Mallinson, Lavering Home Guard?" asked the driver.

"Yes," said the Colonel.

"Oh good, got two Bren Gun kits for you sir and some ammunition. I am ordered to deliver them and give you or your men a brief introduction to the equipment."

"It's a bit difficult at the moment," said Mallinson.

"I can see you're busy, Colonel. I'm sorry, but I've got weapons for other units and I need to hand yours over and get on to Eastminster, Bradwell and Maldon."

"Yes, of course; Tom, give me a hand here if you would."

The driver passed down two wooden crates with rope handles containing the weapons; four metal boxes containing the spare magazines and four chests of ammunition. They lugged the kit into one of the side cloakrooms.

The driver opened the wooden case and pulled the gun out. He set the weapon on its bipod and showed the Colonel the salient operating points, handed him the manual, made his excuses, and left.

Mallinson returned to the Centre of the entrance hall and lugged his pipe out.

"There's eight dead from the Crescent cottages. It could have been worse, but for the fact that your housekeeper relocated the birthday party to my house, so when I got home last night I had two dozen extra guests. Did you go home last night?"

"No, I just got here this morning; picked up two fliers on the way in, one mortally wounded and the other in shock."

"Well when you do get home, I think you'll find that you had a load of houseguests as well; so many of the children – evacuees and locals – had nowhere else to sleep last night. We'd better get started on sorting out who needs billeting. The Crescent's residents need somewhere; the Post Office and six other buildings around it can't be used."

"How's the church?"

"Incendiary bomb through the south aisle roof; the gallery's collapsed. Bomb in the churchyard took the east windows out and there's a suspected UXB right next to the tower."

"MESSAGE FROM THE TOWER," hailed a voice from the hall's balcony, "READS, PLANE ON BEACH. TIDE COMING IN."

"What the hell?"

It was only at this moment that Mallinson realized that the tower signallers were stationed above the suspected UXB.

"SIGNAL THE TOWER TO ABANDON THAT POST AND REPORT HERE AFTER THEY HAVE SIGNALLED THE BEACH THAT HELP IS ON ITS WAY."

"Tom, I'll go and see to the beach, can you start thinking about where everyone will sleep tonight?"

"Sure."

Colonel Mallinson gathered up some people including the hall's signallers and headed for the beach. Tom was still surveying the street when the army lorry returned.

"Sorry sir, but the Eastminster road is blocked. Is there another way around?"

II

PC Fidgeon, accompanied by Harold Roberts, two scouts, Derrick Forder and a brownie had started to search the area towards the boathouse, as a parachute was thought to have drifted that way. The boathouse was a Victorian structure, built by the people who owned the White House before Colonel Mallinson to garage their steam yacht in. When Mallinson acquired the property in 1911, he had no use for the boathouse itself, so he leased it to the butcher Harold Roberts. Roberts had used it to keep his punt gun and canoe in; there was also space for him to hang game, dress birds and he had built a smokehouse next to it in which he'd prepared a variety of delicacies over the years.

When the sea scouts were formed in the village shortly after the Great War, Mallinson asked Roberts to make room for them, which he did without asking for a reduction of the rent. Mallinson realized what he'd done a few months later and stopped collecting the rent, so Roberts had kept his punt there for the last twenty years rent free and the scouts had gradually acquired boats that were also stored under cover.

The prize scout boat was their old lifeboat. It was over thirty feet long and had a small cabin, sails, oars and an engine. All three propulsion systems had been used when it went out on the Dunkirk evacuation, during which it had been damaged by machine gun fire. The crew nursed it back to the boathouse, from which it had not moved since. It seemed unlikely that it would ever move again, as the building had collapsed on top of it and, when Manteuffel awoke, the tide was coming in; the boat could not float due to being held down by the roof and the small cabin in which he had been sleeping was filling up with water.

He struggled to his feet, knee deep in North Sea. The early light was making its presence known, so he could see his way onto the jetty and then out of the door. The weak sun climbed out of the sea to the southeast and Manteuffel looked around at the salt marshes. He could see the track by which anyone approaching the boathouse would travel, but he could not determine where that track might lead. He could also see the roof of a large house someway to his right, so he started off to reach it and in so doing came to the opinion that the old track leading there had seen little use in recent times.

While he walked along the old track to Colonel Mallinson's house, PC Fidgeon and his party were walking towards the boathouse along the main track from the coast road. Coming that way, they found some of Manteuffel's kit, but when they got to the boathouse they were distracted by the damage and it was several minutes before PC Fidgeon, looking into the submerging lifeboat's small cabin, saw that a parachute had been used in it as bedding.

"When were you last here, Mister Roberts?"

"Before Christmas; I had that morning out with young Hilton to get the ducks for the festivities and I haven't been down since."

"That's three months ago."

"Yeah, well the duck season ends with January, so I wouldn't go out after that. January was too cold for me and the birds weren't here in any numbers so I didn't bother."

"I see; this damage is recent, I reckon. Bomb over there and the footings on one side of the hut have kicked out, letting the roof drop."

"Nothing to be done now," said Roberts, "we've got the village houses as our priority."

Casting around, Derrick Forder noticed where Manteuffel had bent blackberry runners back to use the track to the White House.

"Sir, look; somebody's been that way."

Fidgeon decided to use his bicycle to ride round to the Colonel's, telling the others to walk that route, but carefully.

"If you see him, don't catch him up; he may be armed."

Riding hard, he got around to the Colonel's gate and parked his bike in the bushes just inside. He walked in, trying to orientate himself as to where in the grounds the track from the boathouse might be found.

III

Three hundred yards away, Manteuffel already knew the answer to that one, as he'd followed the track to the back of Colonel Mallinson's garage. He stood by the wood pile contemplating the axe sticking out of a large log, when something hard and travelling fast struck his cheekbone.

"BASTARD!"

Esther reloaded her catapult and fired again, this time hitting his leg. The brownies had watched a scout rifle practice in the dunes last summer and had afterwards riddled the spent bullets out of the sand to use as ammunition for their catapults, so she had just shot Manteuffel twice with pre-used bullets.

Martha heard Esther shouting and ran to see what was up, grabbing a butcher's cleaver from the kitchen table as she went. Eric Love also heard the commotion. He was in the Colonel's study, so he took up a rifle and piled out of the French doors to see PC Fidgeon running across the lawn. He decided that Esther wasn't shouting at the policeman and when he heard her again he knew that the fuss was around by the kitchen door so he turned in that direction.

Manteuffel did not like being shot with the catapult, so he turned and ran back along the track the way he'd come. Fifty yards later he saw the people following his trail from the boathouse; more particularly, he saw Derrick Forder aim his rifle and fire and he heard the bullet zing past him. The black girl with a catapult was, after all, less of a threat than the kid with a rifle, so he turned and ran back towards Esther.

As he rounded the garage PC Fidgeon brought him down with a rugby tackle. He struggled until he saw Eric Love pointing his rifle and the police uniform of his assailant.

IV

At the top end of the village, Tom reached the UXB warning sign where Mark started telling him of the night's events. They walked home together, Tom by now wanting some tea and a chance to get a large-scale plan of the village from his study.

"We can survey the village area and mark the damage on it," he said, "and then decide what to do next. We all have to sleep somewhere tonight."

"Those who survived last night," said Mark, "and we don't know how many casualties are still in the damaged buildings."

In the study, Tom settled at his desk and pulled the village plan out, Mark leaning over his shoulder to start pointing out what he knew was damaged. Hetty brought tea for the three of them and when Tom glanced up to say thank you his eyes rested on the cherry tree across the lawn. It was wearing a parachute.

"I say!" Tom fumbled in his desk for his Colt pistol and strode outside, Mark at heel with his revolver. Franz Weite had hit the tree and then tumbled through it, getting tangled in his parachute lines as he did so. Struggling to free himself, he'd made matters worse and had asphyxiated when the cords tightened around his neck. He had one leg on the ground and the other tangled up behind him. He might have survived for a while, balancing on one foot, but he was quite dead when Tom checked him for a pulse.

"Stiffening up as well," said Tom, "better get me a knife and we'll get him flat on the ground, then I'll let the military police know he's here."

"Why not just tell them anyway?" said Mark, "let them get him down."

"I'd rather do it," said Tom, "the military police might be none to careful about my tree."

In the event, the redcaps arrived before they did anything, Hetty having gone to fetch them. They told Tom that Colonel Mallinson had found five more dead in a crashed aircraft on the beach.

V

It was three days before a bomb disposal team arrived to make the church safe for the funerals that were queuing up to use it. The young officer slid into the hole next to the tower without preamble, armed with a small tool kit and an electric torch, while his team kept at a respectful distance.

Two minutes later he climbed out of the hole and re-joined his men.

"No bomb down there; there's a lead coffin and it's been damaged by the rubble. I suppose that lump of the tower punched through the roof of the vault and what the policeman could feel in the dark was the damaged coffin. Got anything else around here to deal with?"

Nothing had been identified, although there would undoubtedly be unexploded devices in the fields round and about. The bomb disposal crew headed off to deal with the next one on their list. PC Fidgeon collected up his warning signs and tape, thus opening the church for use. Volunteers cleared up inside as best they could ready for the funerals, while the gravedigger got busy outside.

Thirteen local people were interred during the following week and three evacuee children who'd died were returned to London by train. Andrew Taylor's family could not be contacted, so he was buried in the war graves section on the north side of the church, next to the grave containing the body parts of a British airman. The dead Germans were taken elsewhere for burial or cremation and the captured ones went into the bag for interrogation.

Only Ernst Gregor remained in the village at the cottage hospital, overlooked in the excitement. Mark visited him the following week; he was badly burned, worse than Dying Brian. The nursing staff could not tell if he was awake or asleep, conscious or comatose. He did not appear to hear anything and could not speak. The doctor kept him as sedated as he thought wise and was grateful when his patient died a couple of weeks later. They buried him next to Andrew Taylor.

CHAPTER 23

THE VILLAGE WAS NOT the same after that night in March 1941. Parents of evacuees felt that nowhere was safe and a lot of those children who'd been sent to the village in 1939's Operation Pied Piper went home to London where schools started reopening to deal with the returnees.

Mark and Elizabeth found themselves presiding over falling attendances at their meetings. The units also had to cope with Elizabeth's departure for the Royal Air Force that spring, Laurie Hilton's call-up and Mark's medical, which pronounced him fit for light duties. Mark had felt Elizabeth becoming more distant as her departure date approached. They had no further chance to make love and Elizabeth did not go out of her way to create an opportunity, despite Mark's best efforts. On the day, he collected her in his car from the farm and drove her to the station. He was rewarded with a very smoochy goodbye kiss and a vague promise that she'd write.

Those who were left rallied around to keep things going; Derek Pilley taking Laurie's place as Troop Leader and Mrs. Harvey again stepping in to lead the girls, now assisted on occasions by Carol Davies from RAF Rochford. Alma Burton, following a promotion to section officer and her transfer to Bradwell, also put in appearances, helping as often as she could with the brownies and guides.

In the church, temporary windows were installed in the east end and the remains of the south gallery were used to make good the roof and various other properties that had suffered in the bombing. The four cottages destroyed in the Crescent were never rebuilt, but all the others were repaired and re-thatched.

The bomb crater in the churchyard was tided up and eventually became a sunken rose garden in memorial to all the casualties of the village. Tom Brabham felt out of place after Mark returned to duties and he struggled with his conscience for a month before going to see his Bishop to obtain a period of leave for contemplation and reflection.

Mark's tour of duty on the home front in Lavering ended with his posting to Biggin Hill. He left looking forward to getting his career back on track. His respite in a rural community on the home front had been a great experience and he came out of it feeling more mature, more experienced. The crucible of Lavering also served many scouts and guides well in their preparation for military service during the war, or national service after the end of hostilities.

The trouble with the RAF was that it was so much like school; lots of young men running a bit wild and the more mature officers trying to make them behave. In Lavering, he'd had to become the mature one, guiding and setting boundaries for those younger than he. That had made him think about his own future and how he would behave upon re-joining the ranks of those defending Britain's skies and that maturity got him noticed on his return and marked him for a future leadership role.

Biggin Hill gave him a Lysander and lots of free time, which he used to make visits to other airfields. It was not cavalier enough, though, turning up in a Lysander, so he bent a few ears and got the use of a new Spitfire for visiting military airfields, while keeping the Lysander for clandestine work. He had to be introduced to the Spitfire though, as the burning one he'd bailed out of the previous year was a mark one and the new machines arriving at Biggin Hill that spring were mark fives; such was progress.

Flying to North Weald to see his brother or Alma and her friends at Bradwell was a Spitfire job. Dropping in on Lavering beach, or the farm near Brentwood to take Granddad Herbert for a spin was a Lysander job. Rochford to see Carol Davies and all her friends, Spitfire, as was Duxford to see Wing Commander Bader, but he was out. Uncle Tom had a go in the Lysander the last week he was in Lavering before his sabbatical started.

Of Elizabeth there was neither word nor sightings: no letters, no telephone call or a visit to anyone in Lavering. She made no attempt to contact Mark, as far as he knew. He asked around, but security concerns meant that nobody was willing to talk about such things as where new WAAF girls might be training.

In between joyrides, Mark had some work to do; ferrying other pilots about in the Lysander, but sometimes running errands in the Spitfire. He knew from granddad Herbert that de Havilland had a twin-engine project on the go, but on the very day that the prototype flew at Hatfield he was at Cranwell watching Britain's first jet aircraft take its maiden flight.

In the summer, he had a three-day pass to London, which he spent at the club entertaining Alma Burton. Being with her was quite different to being with Elizabeth and there was no easy way of comparing them because they were so different:

Carol Davies was different again and represented the middle ground. Her Dad was civil servant, while Alma's was the eldest son of a Marquis and a senior officer in the RAF; Elizabeth's had been a dockworker before being killed in an air raid. Carol was proud of being seen with Mark, walking in Southend. She liked meeting his family; Mark had taken her to Brentwood to see granddad Herbert, but he was not there, so they took the Bristol for a spin and she enjoyed that.

She was easy to please; Alma was sophisticated in her tastes and thus comparatively expensive, while Elizabeth had been more interested in the quantity and quality of food than its price. He worked out, without needing to test the water, that Alma would not be seen dead in a Lyon's shop: Carol might, but he had yet to test that hypothesis. The passage of time blurred his recollection of Elizabeth. If he had promised to marry her, how come she made no attempt to keep in touch?

II

On Mark's third night in London with Alma, they'd spent the afternoon in bed and afterwards dressed in their uniforms for a night on the town. On coming out of the club into the street, Mark found a middle-aged man in a shabby mac blocking his way.

"Flight Lieutenant Mark Brabham?"

"Yes?"

"I'm Detective Superintendent Miller from Scotland Yard. I would like you to accompany me to the police station at Snow Hill where I have some questions to put to you."

"I see."

Miller advised Alma to wait in the club and she was still in reception trying to get a call through to her father when two military policemen walked in to ask for Flight Lieutenant Mark Brabham. Alma's dad answered at that moment, so she handed the telephone to the policeman who stiffened up slightly when talking to the Air Commodore.

"My orders are from the Minister for Defence sir; I am to find Flight Lieutenant Brabham and take him to the Ministry for a briefing."

Alma said that Mark had already been picked up by Miller of the Yard and taken to Snow Hill.

"So, to Snow Hill we will go," said the policeman.

At the City of London police station, Miller was just getting comfortable.

"Flight Lieutenant Brabham, on the night of twenty-ninth December last, a young man was murdered under Blackfriars Bridge, shot with a point four-fifty-five bullet at point blank range. Can you tell me where you were on that night between, say, eight in the evening and midnight?"

"I don't have my diary with me," said Mark.

"Of course not, sir, but I can assist you to this extent. You were a registered guest at the club where I met you earlier this evening and according to their records you spent the night in question there and the previous night also. The question is what did you do with the hours between those two nights you spent sleeping at the club? The evening hours in particular."

The interview room door opened.

"Sorry sir, the military police are here for Flight Lieutenant Brabham."

The uniformed officer entering to explain this was elbowed to one side by the military police entering.

"Flight Lieutenant Brabham, your presence is required at the Ministry of Defence, to which we will take you right now."

"Look here," said Miller, "I am interviewing this officer about a serious matter..."

"I'm looking," said the redcap, "but I see nothing that matters."

Mark accompanied them to their car for the silent drive to Whitehall, where they stopped near the Trafalgar Square end of the street.

"The meeting is down here sir, follow me."

Mark followed, wondering if this was out of the frying pan or what. The policeman led him into what seemed to be a waiting room, which was already crowded with people he knew. Granddad Herbert, his dad Sir Henry and cousin James. They all looked at each other. The policeman filled the door through which Mark had entered the room and at the other end stood a Wing Commander, who turned and opened the door behind him.

"Flight Lieutenant Mark Brabham is here now sir."

"Wheel them in," snapped a voice from the office beyond.

They filed in to find themselves opposite a desk behind which sat Prime Minister Winston Churchill.

"I had expected five Brabhams," said the PM, "but in the circumstances I suppose that four will do."

"The Reverend Tom Brabham is on a train between Prestwick and Liverpool," said the Wing Commander. "He was early at Prestwick and got on the train before the police caught up with him."

"You may remain standing, gentlemen," said Churchill, "this meeting will be brief, and, I trust, to the point."

Mark glanced around and noted that sitting was not an option, as there were no chairs for them.

"Gentlemen, your loyalty to our country and your courage is beyond question; however, the way in which you are each trying to serve our island nation does merit a few words from me. Sir Herbert..."

"Herbert, Prime Minister, my late brother was the baronet."

"Don't interrupt me, Sir Herbert; His Majesty's equerry has written to you and if you'd visit your wife – tonight would be good – you will find the letter waiting for you. Sir Herbert, your services to the aviation industry are very much respected and admired. I have never forgotten your patient guidance when I took an interest in flying before the last war. Your knowledge and opinions then have stood me in good stead ever since and as for your plywood products and the work you have done developing lightweight materials for de Havilland towards his twin engine project – you have been most helpful. Getting the furniture industry making wooden aircraft and glider parts – masterful piece of lateral thinking, but to balance that, your attempts to pinch the de Havilland prototype and fly it for a joyride are just the opposite. You're seventy-two, sir; a decade older than me and you should not be pinching aircraft."

"Prime Minister..."

"There are rumours that you are a serial offender, Sir Herbert; something about a Hurricane, and while I think of it, weren't you the idiot who flew under Tower Bridge during the general strike? Anyway, let me just say that you are close enough to your wings already sir; your sterling contribution to this war effort is to be made at ground level in future; am I clear?"

"Yes, Prime Minister."

"Now then, Sir Henry; excellent work in Egypt, got General Wavell moving, finally and the Italians on the back foot – a great victory when we badly needed one - and then you resigned."

"Matter of honour, Prime Minister, I didn't foresee the Germans invading Crete."

"It wasn't your job to, Sir Henry; your job was the Italians. Crete was an excuse, wasn't it, and what are you doing now? Flying for Ferry Command."

"Ferry Command?" said Mark, not meaning to interrupt.

"Ferry Command," said the Prime Minister, "flying new machines from Montreal to Britain. Essential work, undoubtedly, but you have talents that would be much better spent elsewhere. You gave up a promising career in the Arab Bureau to fly aeroplanes."

"There were good people to take over from me, Prime Minister."

"Which is why I can't send you straight back there tonight. As you say, good people; they have to be given their chance. I can't send you back to Egypt, but what I am going to do is send you somewhere else. We have started a little department called the Political Warfare Executive and that's where your talents will be directed with effect from tonight. Crete. Bloody sideshow; albeit a costly one. A month later they invaded the Soviet Union and that's the real war."

"It's taken the pressure off us here;" continued Churchill, "many of the squadrons that attacked us during the winter have been moved to the new eastern front; gives us space and time. We have to use that to best advantage and not spend our time joy riding about the skies. The Reverend Tom Brabham is not here because he's also working in Ferry Command. Whose idea was that I wonder?"

Nobody moved.

"His Bishop is most distressed; he thought the sabbatical was for contemplation and reflection, not for flying aeroplanes about. When I see him tomorrow, I will tell him what I think and, as you may have worked out for yourselves, what I think matters."

"He's not ready to go back to Lavering," said Mark, "the bombing, the casualties; he was like a caged bird the last month I was there."

"Maybe so," said Churchill, "but I'm not having a Victoria Cross flying the Atlantic week in, week out. We can hire Americans to do that; it's dangerous, lot of machines being lost in the bad weather. We cannot spare your talents, Sir Henry, nor your brothers in that way. You all must be more useful. Listen; after the war, you can all get together and start an airline if you want. They'll be plenty of aeroplanes to be had and you can fly about Europe or wherever you like. But right now, there's a war on and you must all focus on doing your best for our country. Am I clear so far?"

They all nodded in assent.

"Right then, moving on a generation; Mark – recently recovered from burn injuries and passed fit for light duties?"

"Yes, Prime Minister."

"And what have you been doing? Trying to get into Bader's flying circus; well, don't bother – he is reportedly missing – didn't come back from a sweep over France yesterday. I know you are keen to fight, keen to die maybe, I don't know, but what I do know is that you have been a powerful influence on your family and that's why they're all flying – some of them in stolen machines - instead of being useful. You must do your best too and that means doing what your country requires of you, not what you think you should be doing. I know you didn't go to the de Havilland prototype test flight. I also know where you were that day, at the Gloster jet thunderbolt prototype's maiden flight and I suppose that I should be grateful you didn't try pinching that. Well then, the Wing Commander will talk to you later about your posting and you will nod your head up and down and say, 'yes sir' and then get on with it; am I making myself clear?"

"Yes, Prime Minister."

"Good; James, same goes for you. You are a young pilot with experience of single-engine monoplane fighters?"

"Yes, Prime Minister."

"With no business accompanying Sir Herbert to the maiden flight of de Havilland's and absolutely no business trying to pinch the prototype with Sir Herbert afterwards."

Silence.

"That's what I thought. The Wing Commander will talk to you as well and you will give his advice your undivided attention. Good. Two more points and then you can leave me in peace. One: Mark, how did you get on with Superintendent Miller?"

"None too well; but the military police interrupted, so I have that conversation to finish."

"Indeed; what you don't know is that Superintendent Miller arrested Miss Elizabeth Fforest for murder and she has exonerated you, so Miller will give you a hard time, but he can't charge you with anything. The police don't like us going around shooting people and you have been a bit handy with your gun, haven't you?"

"Self-defence…"

"Self-defence under Blackfriars Bridge and in Lavering; shot a downed Nazi flier I heard. Exercise your judgment wisely before each gunfight, but always quickly. I have shot a few people, never regretted any of them. How about you?"

"If Miss Fforest is in trouble…"

"Not your concern."

"It is my concern."

"It is not and that's final."

"If she needs help?"

"She doesn't. She joined the WAAF; she had aptitude for a specialist role and her training was interrupted by the police investigation. She gave a full and clear account of the incident under Blackfriars Bridge in which three young people died. She has been charged with murder. There will not be a trial as she intends pleading guilty."

"But that's an outrage; those ruffians…"

"We can't interfere with the course of justice, not much anyway. It's a capital crime, murder with a firearm, as is multiple murder, so think yourself lucky that Miller can't charge you with it; according to Miss Fforest you were unconscious throughout the incident. If you tell him a different story, he might feel inclined to charge you both and let a jury decide, but I prefer my solution."

"What, let her hang?"

"I never told you what I have in mind, and it would be impudent of you to ask. Anyway, we don't hang pregnant women – not until after the birth. You have a job to do in the air, or the ground, so see you get on with it, exonerated from the inconvenience of that incident last December. You said goodbye to Miss Fforest in April; neither of you has written to the other since, so kindly get on with choosing between Alma Burton and Carol Davies. If you can't decide, widen your net."

"You said two things, Prime Minister." Herbert looked ashen, trying to compose his thoughts.

"Yes, while I've got you and James together, what use is this new de Havilland machine going to be?"

"It's a bomber that flies faster than German intercept fighters," said Sir Herbert.

"Long range fighter," said James, "day or night."

"Fighter-bomber," said Mark.

"If I'd had one in Egypt," said Sir Henry, "I could have flown home for weekends."

III

The Brabhams got no chance to take advantage of the family reunion after attending Winston Churchill, as the military police separated them as soon as they came out of the meeting. The Wing Commander told Mark to meet him at the War Office in the morning and, after a hushed agreement to meet at the club the next night, Mark was driven to Snow Hill where Superintendent Miller awaited him. Sir Herbert was driven straight home to Brentwood, James to RAF North Weald and Sir Henry to Bush House in the Aldwych.

Miller picked up the conversation where he left off, as though the interruption had not taken place. Miller thought he had all the cards, so Mark took it steadily although his mind was racing and desperately confused. He confirmed that he'd stayed two nights at the club and that Miss Fforest had been a guest also with a room to herself. He confirmed that they'd been out together during the day, travelled into the east end and beyond, done some sightseeing and eaten out several times, got caught in the bombing, made their way back to the club and got bombed there as well. Met Fred and the Dutch officers, dad was at the club. What else is there to say?

Miller pressed him about the Blackfriars Bridge incident, at which point Mark told him about being directed to shelter there by a police officer, who had left after the next wave of bombs. Then there were more bombs after which he proceeded along the Embankment and into the Temple Inn of Court to seek shelter. He described the empty building, entering the property and hiding in the barrister's bolt hole for a while before returning to the club.

"Was Miss Fforest with you throughout?"

"I think so. I don't remember a time when she wasn't there."

"Under the bridge, do you remember being accosted by four young men, after the policeman left?"

"I remember one hell of a bang – bomb in the river - and I remember picking myself up soaked through and needing shelter, but the men who were there – I thought that those who didn't leave with the policeman set out to cross the bridge in hope of better safety on the south side."

The policeman looked at Mark, waiting to see if he would add anything. Mark looked at the policeman and then at his watch.

"Is there anything else, Superintendent? I have an appointment with Air Commodore Burton that I am in danger of being late for."

"Just one more thing, Mister Brabham, when did you last see Miss Fforest?"

"April; I saw her off when she left the farm to join the WAAF. I drove her to the railway station."

"Have you heard from her since?"

"That's two things; no, I haven't. She has not written and I have no address to write to her at. She left Lavering at the beginning of April and I at the end of the month. If she's written to me there, any such letter has yet to catch up with me."

Outwardly composed, or so he hoped, Mark was inwardly filleted; he could have exonerated Elizabeth, although the whole truth would only have helped her in part since she'd told him about bricking two of the attackers and one of them had died. She'd also killed the one who fetched up in the river by putting him there, so the whole truth would put him in a noose for murder with a firearm and Elizabeth for two murders: that is, unless self-defence prevailed as an argument. Would it prevail? Had she been legally advised?

Superintendent Miller made no move and kept looking at Mark, who looked at his watch again.

"Am I under arrest, Superintendent?"

"No sir, merely helping me with my enquiries."

"Well, I'm done doing that, so please call me a cab."

Miller could not keep the meeting going without giving away information that he did not yet want to discuss with his suspect, so he asked the desk sergeant to procure a cab and then guided Mark through to the front door.

"Carrying a revolver, sir?"

"No."

That was true. Given the potential difficulties of being associated with the Colt, Colonel Mallinson had persuaded him to switch to a pistol that he'd acquired from a German pilot. It was almost the same as his own Browning GP35A but made after the Belgian factory had fallen under Nazi control. Mark had carried it ever since, having learned to love it.

"Thank you, sir and goodnight; oh, it may be that I will need to speak to you again, so do please let the City of London Commissioner know your whereabouts."

Mark asked the cab driver for the Royal Aero Club and then tried to think, but no thoughts came. At the club, Alma was in the bar perched on a stool and her father stood close by chatting to the barman. Alma made the introductions and they adjourned with a bottle of wine to the comparative privacy of a booth in which Mark had to explain both civilian and military policemen picking him up.

Mark realized as he sat down opposite Air Commodore Burton that Alma must have inherited her looks from her mother. What he wanted to know was what to do with the information now that he had it. Burton said that forewarned was forearmed; if something happened, he was the better prepared for it. If the Ministry had wanted him to do something, he'd have been given orders.

Upstairs and after the Air Commodore had left, Mark could not concentrate on Alma's charms; even after she'd peeled her uniform off and undressed down to sexy camisole and knickers. She was sweet, and sweet on him; but she was also sweet on James and James on her. Mark's problem was that she seemed not to know how to choose between the good-looking Spitfire pilot Brabham and the disfigured future-baronet hopeful Spitfire pilot Brabham.

He suspected that his two arrests that night and her father knowing about them might complicate matters. His other problem was that the Prime Minister knew exactly what he was doing, probably at that moment. It was like having Winston Churchill in the room, peeking from behind the curtains and that was very off-putting.

IV

Mark's War Office meeting was brief. The Wing Commander checked that an active-duty post, flying, was what Mark sought.

"Yes."

"Egypt then. For strange bureaucratic reasons, you're not fit for active duty here, but you will pass as fit when you get to Egypt. You'll go to Gibraltar first and then onwards. I will draft orders and deliver them to the club. Be prepared to depart by the end of the week."

"Can you tell me any more about Elizabeth Fforest sir?"

"No."

"Can you tell me any more about Egypt, sir?"

"Your commanding officer will be Park, same as last time you were in action."

Sir Herbert arrived at the club late in the afternoon, panting for a large gin and tonic.

"I've been busy," he said, "firstly, I have the letter, so my knighthood is real; just didn't expect one. Next, I've been to see my lawyer about Miss Fforest. He's trying to find out what's happening and if there is anything to be done, he'll get on with it."

"What can he do and does he need any money?"

"Money, no; he couldn't lift what I left him in gold so he's in funds and he will do whatever he can as those are my instructions. I have been to the newspaper archive and there's nothing published at all. I know a few hacks and I've got them asking, but it seems quiet. I hope to see Beaverbrook tomorrow."

"What do you make of that, granddad Sir Herbert and how do you know Lord Beaverbrook?"

"I don't know what to make of it. If she'd been arrested and charged with three murders, you'd think that at least the reporters who follow the assizes would know something, but they don't. I've known Beaverbrook for several decades; I took my ideas for wooden aircraft to him, you know, and that's why the furniture industry now make gliders and Mosquitoes. You last saw her in April?"

"Yes. Mosquitoes?"

"That's what de Havilland's twin engine machine is called. Well, the Central Criminal Court didn't break until the first week of August, so if she was charged before that there should have been some mention and there hasn't been, so that suggests recent charges and nothing will happen until the Court resumes sitting in mid-September."

"Is she in prison or something?"

"She's not in Holloway, the women's prison, I checked. She might have been bailed to her unit, since she's in the WAAF, but

Churchill said she's pregnant and if that were true the WAAF would have demobilized her. Is she pregnant, do you think?"

Mark blushed. If she were pregnant it would have been the night Lavering was bombed; it was exciting and he'd been none too careful.

"This is not the time to be embarrassed," said Herbert, "if she is and you're the dad, she'd have to be about five months into it; it would notice by now, she's too skinny to hide it and if she is for the drop such a pregnancy will protect her until about Christmas and that gives us time."

Herbert drained his glass and waved it at the barman for a refill.

"I'm grounded. Henry too. What about you?"

"Egypt."

"You'll love it; going home, you were born there you know."

"I want to throw my medals in the river and then kill myself."

"Hmm. I know how you feel, but, killing yourself; bad idea. You can't help anybody like that. Killing Germans will take your mind off your troubles."

"I could write a confession first."

"Wouldn't be admissible. No. I'll take care of Elizabeth and you go about your flying, since you can. We'll take Churchill at his word. He has a plan and maybe we should trust him. He also said that we can start an airline after the war and I'm looking forward to that already."

Tom Brabham walked in, looking thin and grey.

"I feel like a naughty schoolboy, what a lecture!"

"You should feel like a large gin, I'll get it."

Herbert went to the bar while Tom embraced his nephew.

"Lots going on then."

"Yes, granddad's grounded for trying to steal the de Havilland prototype and James is in trouble for helping him. You and dad are in trouble for helping the war effort by flying; I'm ordered to Egypt – I suppose to replace dad so there's a Brabham out there - and Elizabeth is … we don't know."

"Sacrificing herself to save your career as I heard it; argued with the Prime Minister and got nowhere."

"I wish I knew what he was up to."

"He's a politician Mark, so he won't tell us yet. The fact that he told us anything at all means that he wants us to know that he's got something up his sleeve."

"Five aces and a good watch," said Herbert, returning with the drinks, "so how's Ferry Command treated you?"

"It's been great," said Tom, "I brought a Boeing B17 over to Prestwick; four engines and it's not the first big machine I've flown. I had a Short Sunderland seaplane. It's a variation of the old Empire flying boat."

"I know that machine," said Herbert, "been in one to the Riviera. Pilot wouldn't let me have a go. What else?"

"Lockheed Hudson; twin engines. I've brought two of them over so far. But all good things have to come to an end. I told the PM that I can't face Lavering just yet, so I'm attached to the War Office as a chaplain for now, but the good news is that I may get to fly VIPs around; good practice for starting an airline."

The barman brought a message from James to the effect that he wasn't allowed off base, so the three went to dinner at Simpsons where Sir Henry managed to join them about halfway through the meal.

"Grounded; still, the new job is definitely going to be interesting, so let's drink to doing what our Prime Minister wants us doing instead of what we were doing."

"How's Mum? Has she contacted you?"

"She's busy, work's a secret. A full colonel visited me this morning in my new office and passed me a message from her. She hopes to get a break at Christmas."

"So where will we spend Christmas?" asked Mark, "the family plan was Lavering, but if Uncle Tom won't go there…"

"I didn't say that," said Tom, "but just not yet. I was shaken by the damage and the casualties. I wanted to take a step back and then Henry got me into flying and whilst I'm treading the clouds I don't have to think. Now I must make my peace with God and my congregation and get things organized. It's hard for the youth groups without you and Elizabeth, but you built some remarkably firm foundations upon which those boys and girls will surely develop. There's other help – Carol Davies comes over when she can and Karol Dubiel has been back helping at scouts."

Mark started giggling, "Sorry, can't help it; but if Sir Henry is 'Uncle Senry' to James, that knighthood makes you 'Granddad Sherbert' and that's funny."

"I don't think so."

CHAPTER 24

THE COURSE OF THE war was such that they did not all get together for Christmas 1941 and Mark did not get the chance to visit Lavering again until 1943. He managed to time this with Carol Davies getting a few days leave and he did invite her to stay at the rectory; separate rooms, of course.

Tom had returned to the parish and made a great effort to get things back to normal. The village had been patched up, although the scars were visible to anybody who knew what had happened there. They went to the morning service and Mark was struck by the number of new faces in the congregation, and the other changes. A new organist; Derrick Forder, now a scout and Esther, now a guide; the children were growing up. Many of the evacuees were long gone and new faces belonged to children whose parents were based in Rochford, Bradwell or other military facilities round the area.

There were also new grown-up faces; more land girls and more young men and women in uniforms and not all of them British. Americans serving in the Eighth Air Force and some army units had started to arrive and getting off base to worship in ancient British churches was on many a 'to-do' list. This proved to be Mark's first encounter with coloured

Americans. Four of them came to church, bemused and somewhat enchanted by the absence of a colour bar. The sight of Esther marching with white girl guides was a thrill that they appreciated and which Mark did not understand. Chatting outside with Martha, they said that America was divided on such matters and coloured soldiers served in segregated units, as they had since the civil war.

Colonel Mallinson was absent, so Mark and Carol went to see him at home, where Mallinson was comfy on a large sofa with his foot bandaged. After the pleasantries, Mark got to the point.

"What happened to your foot?"

"Would you believe frostbite?"

"In August?"

"Yes, in August. It gets cold at twenty thousand feet; you don't need me to tell you that."

"You've been flying again? Where and how?"

"The Americans; couldn't resist it. When they got here, all serious and quite scared, I visited them and they felt that they were here to fight our war for us and I just said that they'd brought the tools and if they wanted us to do the fighting, we'd do it. Well, to cut a long story short, I went up with them in a B17, a 'flying fortress'. I had the machine gun on the starboard side of the waist and I'm not the only one. Eric Love has been up and Bob Murrell."

"Bob Murrell is over fucking eighty; what are you doing letting him up in a 'plane?"

"No need for profanity; he wanted to go and he gave a good account of himself; got one of those twin engine Germans – a 110 and a fighter. Had a great time, but I fear the cold and the low oxygen got to him. After four trips he packed it in."

"So what happened to your foot?"

"Nothing serious. A German got behind us and did some damage – turns out he shot the sole off my boot, so I was resting my bare foot on bare metal and froze it – I think I got him though; the doctor says I'll be alright in a few weeks, but he's grounded me."

"So I should think. Doesn't my face remind you how dangerous it all is?"

"I know, Mark; but it was worth it. We showed the Yanks that we are not afraid to fight and we've made a lot of friends. Murrell has had American visitors telling him all the things he wanted to know about places he used to live in. Anyway, I've seen action before and I know the risks."

<h1 style="text-align:center">II</h1>

They went on to see Bob Murrell, who was not in the best of health.

"Old and tired, Mark, that's all. Should've listened to my son when he wanted me to join him in Australia; left it too late. The parish has changed; I've got German and Italian prisoners working the farm now, so we have the men we need. When you were here it was just the girls and they did a good job, but I always pushed them that bit too far. Now, the men; I can push them."

"Heard you've been flying?"

"Yes, had to try it, just once; but I didn't get a shot first time, so I went again and on the last run I got two 'planes, so now I've done my bit. I can look that land girl in the eye if she comes back. I can't do what she's doing, but I've done all I can and that's more than most."

"Land girl? Elizabeth?"

"Yeah, the one that helped you with the cubs and such."

"What's she doing? I haven't heard anything since she left the village last year."

"Got her letter somewhere; I'll find it for you and get someone to drop it in to you."

Mark would cheerfully have torn the place apart looking for it, but the need for dignity prevailed.

"I've had Americans over to see me," said Murrell, "country boys from the mid-west; it's changed in some ways, but not others. I've enjoyed their stories and, guess what? Some of them have heard of me!"

"Is that good?"

"Yes and no; it was all a long time ago – Lincoln County and the Regulators, Tombstone and the Clantons. I was a part of it, you know, and there are those who remember that."

"With affection, or animosity?"

"Bit of jealousy, I'd say; I was a suspect for the murder of Morgan Earp, you know, because he was shot gunned and I had that Wells Fargo gun. Anyway, those days are long gone."

"Did you shoot him?"

"He was back-shot, not my style. Anyway, Wyatt got someone else for the crime, so nobody worries about what I might have been doing that night anymore."

Mark could empathize with him; nobody apart from Superintendent Miller cared any longer about what he'd been doing on the night of the twenty-ninth of December 1940. Murrell kept his word and sent Elizabeth's letter on to the rectory. In it she said that she was busy with war work and that she enjoyed being in the forces; best wishes to all and to give her love to Mark, wherever he might be. The letter itself was undated, but the postmark on the envelope was in September 1941; about two weeks after the Brabham meeting with the Prime Minister and the letter had no return address.

"You still carrying a flame for her?" enquired Carol.

"Sort of; I don't know how to put it though. We went through a lot together – working with the youth groups and the bombing here – I thought she'd keep in touch with me, although he hasn't, so I suppose she's history now."

"A girl needs to know these things," said Carol, "after all, sharing you would be difficult; there's not much of you to go round."

III

Brabham reunions happened but rarely as the war went on; James did not make any of them after meeting the Prime Minister, as he managed to get shot down near Split in Yugoslavia later that year and spent months with the partisans before the chance of evacuation to Egypt presented itself in the form of a Dakota aircraft delivering weapons to the insurgents landing to make the delivery. Mark was in Egypt for Christmas 1941 and when he got back to the UK in mid-1943 he stayed those few days in Lavering and saw his dad, briefly, in London.

Family news was hard to come by, as the government's 'careless talk costs lives' campaign had sunk into even the thickest skulls and it had become the convention simply not to discuss one's work, or to chat about what other people were doing or where they were. Mark had occasional sightings of old friends; Karol had kept in touch with people in Lavering and took leave there when he could. As a source of gossip, however, he was quite useless.

Carol Davies was a bit less discreet;

"That land girl you fancied, went in the WAAF didn't she?"

"Yes, and that's the last I heard of her."

"Well, that may be because she's on overseas service."

"How do you mean?" Mark was all ears at once.

"Careless talk costs lives, you know, but quite a few WAAFs and FANYs are working in occupied France right now."

"That would make sense; she speaks French fluently." He kept 'the last I heard she was incarcerated for murder and due to hang after her baby was born' to himself.

"It might just be coincidence then, but our Lysander squadron deliver stuff to undercover operators in France and I heard mention of a delivery going to Tarka."

"Why tell me? careless talk costs lives and all that."

"Yes, but we'll never make any progress together whilst she's on your tiny mind. Unless she's dead, or still alive and rejects you..."

"I suppose. I Just don't know, Carol. I was attracted to you from the first moment we met, but...I made a commitment to Elizabeth and I can't take it back without seeing her again."

"Well, I would rather you sorted that out. We're still friends, of course and I will continue visiting Lavering when I get the chance, but I don't think we should be lovers before you decide who you want to propose to."

Mark also felt Alma distancing herself from him. Literally, with a posting in the United States. He knew that to see her he was competing with James, who had been trying hard to make her his from the first day he met her. The fact that James spent most of the war overseas did not seem to bother her; there were letters and she also spent time at the rectory on short leaves until she was posted abroad.

Granddad Sir Herbert's enquiries after the whereabouts of Elizabeth ran into a brick wall, which if nothing else assured him that she must be alive, well and useful.

"Nobody can tell me anything, Mark and that means she's up to something. If she'd been convicted of murder and hanged, there'd be no point in keeping it a secret, would there?"

"I suppose not; it's maddening not knowing, though."

"True, but that's the same for everyone we love. Apart from Tom being in Lavering, we know your Dad is in London – most of the time – but we don't know where Lillie is, or James; even my boys don't tell me much. They are in India and that's as much as I know. We are all on one front or another."

EPILOGUE

By 1944, Mark had been promoted and posted back to England in preparation for the Allied invasion of Europe. His wounds had healed as much as they ever would without more help and although he kept meaning to go back to hospital for some other tidying up, the war kept him busy and even the allure of certain nurses at the burns unit had not made him find the time. Not that he wanted a romance; nice girls were shy of a commitment in these uncertain times, if only to spare themselves the pain that Miss Everett lived with, or the widowhood Mrs. Harvey endured. He thought of Elizabeth often, but that was as far as he could take romance in the run up to the great invasion.

Enjoying a few days leave in London, he was walking from the club in Piccadilly to meet his father at the Aldwych, when he noticed two women ahead of him. Everybody else had spotted them as well; smart suits and fancy hats decorated with bright feathers. Women stared in disgust at such opulence during the hardship and shortages of the war. Mark noticed the clothing afterwards, though. The woman nearest the kerb was his Mum; at three hundred yards, that was the way she walked, no mistake. He ran to catch up.

"Mum!"

The women stopped and turned. Lillie's face broke into a smile as he lumbered up.

"Mark, it's supposed to be a surprise. Your dad has lunch arranged and we wanted to sneak up on you."

"Bore da, Wing Commander."

Elizabeth looked stunning. In the three years since he'd seen her she'd grown more beautiful, more poised and shapely. The smart Parisian fashion she was wearing made her seem quite different to the earthy land girl he remembered. Words failed him, as they had the first time they met.

"Cat got your tongue?"

"Yes."

They walked together along to Sir Henry's office where the military policeman asked them to identify themselves. Mark handed over his form 1250 and noticed that Mum and Elizabeth had similar identity cards. While the MP went to show Sir Henry the cards, Mark needed Elizabeth to tell him about the missing three years.

"Working hard, Mark. Careless talk costs lives, you know."

"Working for me," said Lillie, "and that's difficult, but she's very good at what we do and we can talk about it more when the war is over."

"Did you get my letter?" asked Elizabeth, "I wrote to you via Mister Murrell."

"Yes, but all it said was that you were having a good time and you posted it two weeks after I'd been told that you were pregnant and had confessed to three murders."

"Ah, no, there was another letter after that. Glad you haven't seen it really; I got things sorted out..."

"I got things sorted out," said Lillie, "the hardest part of which was dodging uncle Sir Herbert's lawyers and private detectives. I had to tell him in the end."

"Tell him what?"

"That Elizabeth was safe and working for me. It's hard, secrecy; we went to a wedding yesterday of two people I know from…somewhere I used to work. I know they both work there in different sections, but they haven't told each other; that's how sensitive everybody is about their war work."

"I appreciate that," said Mark, "and I don't need to know about yours; granddad said you were safe, but that's all. I wondered about us. Three years. I think of you all the time."

"Not chosen between Alma Burton and Carol Davies then?" Elizabeth seemed to know what the Prime Minister had said to him.

"Alma's sweeter on James, probably saving herself for him. Carol knows she can't get anywhere with me until you turn me down and she's got that Polish Karol after her as well."

"And do you think I will turn you down?"

"I don't know, but I wanted to marry you and said so the night Lavering was bombed. You didn't say no; I hope I'm still in with a chance."

"Yes."

"Yes what? You'll marry me?"

"Yes, you're in with a chance. I'll put your name in the hat with the others."

"Others?"

"Don't tease him," snapped Lillie, "she's done nothing but ask me whether you're still interested in her all the way here, Mark, and it's been a three-day journey."

Sir Henry emerged at that moment and took Lillie to one side for their customary greeting for which he always wanted as much privacy as he could get.

"Never stopped thinking about you," said Elizabeth, "but, posh family and little rich girls like Alma chasing you; I didn't know if you were still free."

"I didn't know if you were free either," said Mark, "literally; what happened? That's got nothing to do with the war, has it?"

"Yes and no. I joined the WAAF and realized I was pregnant; kept it a secret, tried to get rid of it, but near the end of my course a notice went up asking for French speakers. I went for an interview and was accepted for special training. Then Superintendent Miller came and arrested me, so I told him about the people who attacked us under the bridge and that got me charged with murder. I told the prison staff I was pregnant and they sent me to hospital for a check up and the doctor classified me as 'feeble minded' and had me moved to a mental hospital. Then Poles came; don't know who they were, British uniforms with black webbing. They took me out of the hospital despite staff protests and to a big country house, special place for pregnant land girls."

"So, what happened to the baby?"

"Born on Christmas Day 1941. I called him Alan and he's been adopted by some nice people. I was angry with you at first; the pregnancy and the shooting incident, but it all worked out in the end. I stayed in the hostel until the adoption and then those Poles came again and took me to your mum, who got my training started."

"So I'm a dad; another new identity. What about Miller and the charges?"

"That's where it got interesting," said Lillie, joining them; "the attorney general told Miller that he had insufficient evidence to proceed, since the one surviving witness was in a mental hospital and the confession was from a feeble-minded person. He was still trying to find a way to proceed when the file was destroyed in an air raid. Nothing much he can do; the only eye witness escaped from the asylum and his whereabouts are unknown."

Elizabeth punched her playfully for calling her feeble minded.

Mark thought back to the last time he'd seen Miller; a man irritated, if not desperate, who'd got an inch from his face and told him that there was no time limit on murder charges.

"So that's why; the evidence, such as he had was gone in the bombing."

They walked arm in arm to lunch.

"Been a dad and didn't know it. I'm sorry for getting you in the family way like that – I suppose I was careless and selfish." Mark now felt regret, at several levels all at once, for what he'd put Elizabeth through.

"Maybe, but it takes two and anyway, being pregnant is what saved me from the gallows, I think; gave your Mum time to sort things out. I've seen a hanging; German police tipped everyone out of the cafés and shops, made us watch it in the town square." She shuddered, "I'm glad I didn't go that way. I said too much."

Lunch was a slightly uncomfortable affair; Mark wanted Elizabeth to himself, but his parents were there and a couple of Sir Henry's colleagues joined them. It was mid-afternoon before they could go for a walk and have some privacy.

"We came round here before," she said, "and the cathedral is still there."

"So's the bridge," said Mark, "I have been tempted to visit the scene, but also scared to."

"String of medals and a wing commander is scared of a bridge he's not attacking with bombs and rockets?"

"Funny that; yes. It's in the past but seems to keep catching me up."

"I don't worry about it; they got what they deserved, same as that airman in the churchyard. I've been in action since, been shot at, shot back. I worry about the next fight, not the old ones."

"There's still more to do," said Mark, "the invasion; that will be the biggest military operation since Xerxes crossed the Hellespont and I'll be a part of it."

"We all will," said Elizabeth, "I'm going back to work on Saturday."

"Taking my love with you, I hope."

"Yes."

"What I don't get," said Mark, "is how we became lovers and then you dropped out of my life for so long."

"Hard to explain briefly," said Elizabeth, "but Mister Murrell told me that a good man could not be hurried, so I thought you to be a good man but then you were – in Murrell's words 'too slow to catch a cold dinner', whatever that means. So I tried speeding you up, gave you something to remember me by, something to think about. Got more than I bargained for though, something to remember you by, but never mind. I couldn't tell you that in a letter and I knew we both had the war to fight so I thought that maybe it was best just to get through that first."

"So what do we do?"

"Your Mum said if we wanted to get married we could do it after the war, or sooner. Some people rush in, others wait."

"And do we want to get married sooner or later?"

"Speaking for myself," said Elizabeth, "sooner; if you want me. I regret leaving it this long. We are both at risk in this war, so if we don't tie the knot now we might never get another chance. I know the risks, but I'd rather be like Mrs. Harvey than Miss Everett, if you know what I mean. But, a girl likes to be proposed to properly and so far all you've done is made vague suggestions that you think will keep me on the hook."

"Will you marry me, now?"

"No...not now; we need a special licence and I need time to sort out a dress and you'll need to get the ring. I hope you'll get me a ring. Tomorrow's Tuesday, so I could be ready for Thursday, if you can wait that long. I'll ask your granddad Sir Herbert to give me away."

Mark asked his dad that evening about the special licence.

"The Bishop of London can issue them and here's one I acquired earlier. I've booked you two a slot at All Souls Langham Place for Thursday. I married your Mum there in the last war, you know."

Wide grins from Lillie and Elizabeth.

"I don't know what to say," said Mark, "you arranged it all before asking me."

"I didn't ask you," said Elizabeth, "you had to do things properly by asking me."

"Indeed," said Sir Henry, "we just got things ready in case you did. Congratulations to you both. The war has been very harsh to each of you, but you've both aged and strengthened enormously and it's a wedding I will be proud to attend. I'm sorry that the war separated you for so long, Mark, but..."

"But it's going to be alright now," said Mark.

A happy ending means picking a moment in time; lives go on and always end sadly, but a few people gathered in the church for the joyful occasion of a hasty wedding on Thursday the first of June 1944. The only old chum Mark had managed to tell was Frank Ball, by then in the RAF. He managed to get a pass so that he could attend as best man. That was difficult, as most units were confined to camp by then in anticipation of the next big push. Uncle Tom and Colonel Mallinson attended, with apologies that there wasn't time to arrange a scout guard of honour.

The bride wore a white wedding dress, borrowed from Barbara Cartland. Her something old was Dying Brian's Colt revolver, tastefully concealed in a clutch-bag, having had its barrel shortened by an SOE armourer. To complete the ensemble, she had new shoes, recently bought in Paris. Her 'something blue' was her land army greatcoat; girls who left the LA were permitted to keep the garment, provided they dyed it blue.

Mark wore his uniform and decorations. The pistol was in his greatcoat pocket as usual and made a frightful clunk on the pew when he put the coat down. Parading up the aisle with his new bride on one arm and his coat slung over the other after the brief service, he noticed Superintendent Miller had joined the small congregation. They made eye contact, so Miller knew that Mark knew he was there, but neither betrayed any emotion about seeing the other. Mark was enjoying his new identity as a husband. Miller's presence reminded him of that less welcome identity of 'suspect'.

Elizabeth did not notice Miller; she walked up the aisle with Mark but listening intently to Colonel Mallinson's bad French. He had ideas about everyone posing in Lavering with all the gang sometime soon to make for a better wedding photograph.

A brief reception at the club, where they stayed the night, was all the honeymoon the war could afford them. Great events were about to unfold after years of preparation and months of detailed planning and each of them had a role to play in Operation Overlord - that great enterprise to establish a second front in Eurpoe. Each family member entered June, 1944, facing death or glory and the hope of a family reunion, be it in this world or the next.

Sir Herbert would sneak to Normandy shortly after the invasion to examine gliders in situ on the landing fields to see what improvements could be made in case another glider assault became necessary. He persuaded James to take him there in a captured German Storch machine and they'd have got away with it but for the fact that they picked the same day as Winston Churchill to visit the landing zone near what is now called Pegasus Bridge. Suitably admonished and grounded, yet again, he was in London to see his nephew Sir Henry later that summer when a most dreadful sense of foreboding overtook him.

He could not have known, but perhaps nevertheless felt, Mark's anguish in France as he tried desperately to kick his way out of a burning Mosquito aircraft. Mark had been afflicted by similar feelings of foreboding, one of which probably coincided with the moment Elizabeth lay in a Paris street, bleeding onto the cobblestones and watching a German officer with a machine pistol marching toward her intent on delivering the coup de grace; but that all happened after the happy ending their wedding provides and is, as you'd expect, another story.

For which this was just the prequel.